The
Martian Ambassador

A BLACKWOOD & HARRINGTON MYSTERY

ALAN K. BAKER

snowbooks

Proudly Published by Snowbooks in 2011

Snowbooks Ltd.
Kirtlington Business Centre
Oxfordshire
OX5 3JA
Tel: 0207 837 6482
email: info@snowbooks.com
www.snowbooks.com

British Library Cataloguing in Publication Data
A catalogue record for this book is available from the
British Library.

Hardcover 978-1-907777-10-3
Paperback 978-1-907777-08-0

To Mum and Dad,
for all their love and support

Speculation has been singularly fruitful as to what these markings on our next to nearest neighbor in space may mean. Each astronomer holds a different pet theory on the subject and pooh-poohs those of all the others. Nevertheless, the most self-evident explanation from the markings themselves is probably the true one; namely, that in them we are looking upon the result of the work of some sort of intelligent beings.

– Percival Lowell

From The Times,
23rd October, 1899

MARTIAN AMBASSADOR DIES

Seized by a strange malaise, say witnesses.

His Excellency Lunan R'ondd, Martian Ambassador to the Court of Saint James's, died last night at a banquet held in his honour at Buckingham Palace.

Witnesses to the event stated that the Ambassador appeared in good health when he arrived with his entourage. The banquet had been intended to celebrate the new free trade agreement between Earth and Mars, which Ambassador R'ondd had been instrumental in securing; however, the evening turned to one of horror and consternation when he collapsed after complaining of nausea and biliousness.

Although doctors were quickly called, they could do nothing to aid the Ambassador, who expired shortly thereafter. The cause of death is unknown, although an unnamed Whitehall source has stated that foul play cannot, at this stage, be ruled out.

Lunan R'ondd was eighty-nine Earth years of age and leaves behind three wives and fifty-two children.

PART ONE

In Which Mr Thomas Blackwood Investigates a Strange Death

CHAPTER ONE:
The Frustrations of Modern Technology

Thomas Blackwood was having problems with his cogitator.

He had purchased the device only a few hours earlier, the sales clerk at Cottingley's Cogitators Limited having assured him that this was the very finest machine on the market and that he would experience not a moment's regret in purchasing it. Unfortunately, his regrets began almost as soon as he had set up the infernal contraption on the desk in his study.

It certainly *looked* fine enough. The craftsmanship was quite evident in the polished teak of the cogitator itself, not to mention the mahogany keyboard inlaid with intricate seraglios of flawless ivory. The keys themselves were capped with mother-of-pearl, while the oval scrying glass looked most impressive on its stand of filigreed steel.

At first, Blackwood was eminently satisfied with it – until he threw the large brass switch on the side of the box to turn on the gadget and was rewarded with... absolutely nothing. The cogitator simply stood there, completely inert, about as useful as an empty ale barrel.

Blackwood gazed into the scrying glass, which remained intractably dark, and muttered under his breath, 'Bugger it.'

Blackwood was the first to admit that technology was

not his strong point: like most people, he knew how to use it (most of the time), but he didn't give a fig for how it actually worked, preferring to leave that to the fellows who designed and produced it. It was the same with cogitators: their usefulness notwithstanding, he didn't like them, didn't trust them, didn't understand them, and when they went wrong (as they all too frequently did), he invariably found himself in a fog.

In Blackwood's opinion, a cogitator was no substitute for a well-ordered and astute human brain.

Heaving a frustrated sigh, he filled his pipe with his favourite cherry tobacco from the large jar on his desk, pulled up a chair, sat down and glared accusingly at the contraption which stood before him in blissful inactivity.

'Why won't you work, you infernal, bloody thing?'

His eye drifted across the keyboard and fell on one particular key, which was marked HELP. Laying his pipe aside, Blackwood stroked his chin contemplatively for a moment.

Tentatively, he pressed the key.

A small panel on top of the teak box whirred open on a delicate and complex hinge mechanism, and a tiny man, no more than an inch tall, with iridescent dragonfly wings, fluttered out. Peering at him intently, Blackwood could just make out, through the pale lilac glow that enveloped the man, that he was dressed in clothes that had been fashionable perhaps a century ago. He had short, untidy hair of a dark, sandy hue, and his tiny, jewel-like eyes curved gracefully up towards his temples in a manner which reminded Blackwood of the people of the Orient.

'Good afternoon, sir,' said the little man in a lilting Irish brogue. 'I am the Helper. How may I be of assistance?'

'Ah... good afternoon,' Blackwood replied. 'I purchased this contrivance from Cottingley's Cogitators not long ago, and I can't seem to get it to work. I was wondering if there's anything wrong with it.'

The tiny man flew backwards a few inches on his shimmering wings, giving Blackwood the impression that he was affronted. 'Indeed *not*, sir! This machine is the finest on the market. Allow me to assure you that you have made a most judicious acquisition.'

'I'm gratified to hear it,' said Blackwood in the politest tone he could muster. 'And yet, the fact remains that it isn't working...'

'Excuse me, sir, but would I be correct in assuming that your knowledge of cogitators is – how to put this delicately and in a manner unlikely to cause offence – less than absolute?'

Blackwood sighed. 'Yes, I suppose that would be a correct assumption.'

A broad and sympathetic smile spread across the Helper's face as he replied, 'I see. Well, in that case, allow me to put your cares to rest. Lean forward, if you will, and look inside the cogitator.'

When Blackwood hesitated, the man fluttered to one side and held out an arm, indicating the opening from which he had emerged. 'Come, sir!' he exclaimed in a humorous tone. 'Are you afraid? I can assure you it isn't in the least dangerous, and I'll wager you'll find it a gratifying and educative experience.'

'No doubt,' Blackwood muttered as he slowly leaned forward towards the opening. In fact, he was rather intrigued: he had never looked inside a cogitator before – had never seen the point of such an exercise – but now that the invitation had been extended, he found himself possessed of a newfound curiosity as to how the contraption worked.

He peered into the opening while the Helper took up a new position next to his left ear, the fluttering of his dragonfly wings sounding pleasantly like the rapid turning of a book's pages. As he looked inside the machine, Blackwood felt a sudden wave of nausea assail him; however, the sensation was mercifully brief, like the fleeting feeling one experiences when standing up too quickly, and as the giddiness abated, he found himself looking into a tiny compartment which, in spite of its diminutive size, nevertheless gave the impression of extreme capaciousness.

Blackwood frowned at the paradox. Noting his expression, the little man chuckled and said, 'Don't be alarmed, sir. You are merely looking at the cogitator's central processing chamber. This is where the work is done, as you can see from the frenetic activity occurring in there as we speak.'

Peering more closely, Blackwood realised that this was indeed true. He suddenly became aware of numerous diminutive individuals rushing here and there amongst a veritable forest of hair-thin pipes and tubes, which were apparently made of a faintly-glowing metallic substance akin to brass. The people inside the machine were similar in size and appearance to the man hovering beside Blackwood's left ear.

'What are they doing?'

'My colleagues are preparing the cogitator for operation. This is not a process that can be hurried with a brand new machine, sir. There are complex procedures to be followed, otherwise things will not go as they were intended.'

'What kind of procedures?'

The little man shrugged apologetically. 'Begging your pardon, sir, but given your lack of knowledge concerning the science of artificial cogitation, I very much doubt that a comprehensive explanation would provide much in the way of enlightenment. Suffice it to say that my colleagues are at present engaged in the delicate process of connecting the machine to the great repository of knowledge which surrounds the Earth, and which defines the border between our world and the Luminiferous Æther beyond.'

'You are speaking of the Akashic Records,' said Blackwood, without taking his eyes from the machine.

'Indeed I am, sir! Are you familiar with the nature of the Records?'

'Somewhat,' Blackwood replied. In spite of himself, he felt glad that he seemed to have impressed the little man. 'The Akashic Records have been known about in the East for centuries, if not millennia, but only in recent years has their existence been accepted by men of science in Europe and America.'

'Absolutely correct, sir. Do go on.'

'Well... as we here understand it, the Akashic Records constitute a kind of energetic field, a semi-material, plastic substance which retains an impression of every thought, action and event that has ever occurred on Earth – and retains it for all time.'

'Bravo! A most impressive and concise summing up, if I may say so, sir.'

'Thank you.'

'And it is the Akashic Records which have allowed the development of artificial cogitation,' continued the Helper enthusiastically. 'It is from the Records that cogitators retrieve their information. Look, sir,' he added, pointing into the opening. 'This is how it's achieved. Do you see those tiny pinpoints of æthereal light issuing from the ends of the tubules? They are echoes of the information contained within the Records. My colleagues are transferring them to the inner mechanism of the cogitator; these are the means by which the machine is being prepared for its operation.'

Blackwood continued to gaze at the frenetic activity. The tiny people gathered the atoms of information as they emerged from the ends of the metallic tubes and flitted like tiny shards of lightning across the processing chamber to deposit them in other pipes and tubes that emerged from the floor. So quickly did they work that Blackwood could hardly follow their progress.

Periodically, one of the people would stop, give a little whistle to attract the attention of his fellows, and hold up one of the pinpoints for them to see. These atoms looked different from the others: dimmer and of an unhealthy, livid colour. On these occasions, the little people would shake their heads vigorously, and the person who had gathered the offending atom would toss it into a small hole in the floor of the chamber before continuing with his work.

'What are those?' asked Blackwood.

'The Akashic Records occupy but one æthereal plane amongst many, sir,' replied the Helper. 'And some of them are not the most salubrious of places – far from it, in fact. Some of them would drive a human being such as your good self quite insane at a single glance. Occasionally, during the operation of a cogitator, atoms of information from these dark planes of existence come through to our world, and it does the machine no good at all when that happens, I can assure you. It is therefore one of our top priorities to guard against such infections and to minimise the likelihood of their occurrence.'

'So, the rumours of some people being driven mad by their cogitators are true,' said Blackwood. 'I've heard tell of horrible things being glimpsed in scrying glasses – horrible enough to drive people to insanity or suicide.'

'Oh, I wouldn't go *that* far, sir,' chuckled the Helper.

'Really? Some of my associates at New Scotland Temple are investigating just such a rumour as we speak.'

The Helper glanced at him, and Blackwood could have sworn he saw a look of profound apprehension flash across the man's tiny features. 'Oh, well, I don't really feel qualified to comment any further on that score, sir... except to say that no such infestation has *ever* occurred in a Cottingley Cogitator. As to our *competitors'* products... well, let's just say that one gets what one pays for.'

'Yes,' said Blackwood with a faint smile. 'Let's just say that.'

There followed a rather awkward silence, during which the Helper gazed into the processing chamber with elaborate concentration, and which was presently broken by a loud knock at the door of Blackwood's apartment.

'Excuse me,' he said to the Helper, who still seemed somewhat out of sorts at the turn their conversation had taken.

'Oh, of course, sir. Of course.'

Blackwood walked from his study, through his living room, to the apartment's entrance hall, and opened the door.

A young man was standing in the corridor. He was dressed in a conservative suit of grey pinstripe and carried a bowler hat in one hand, a sealed envelope in the other. 'Mr Thomas Blackwood?' he said.

'Yes.'

'My name is Peter Meddings. I have a message for you, sir. It's imperative that you accompany me at once.'

Blackwood took the proffered envelope, glanced at the wax seal on the reverse, and told the young man to wait a few moments. He then hurried back to his study to find the Helper still hovering above the cogitator on his desk. 'I have to go out on business,' he said. 'Will you chaps have that thing working by the time I get back – say, in an hour or so?'

'Oh, indubitably, sir, indubitably!'

And with that, the tiny man dived back into the machine, and the door slammed shut behind him.

'Hmm,' muttered Blackwood. He returned to the hall, gathered up his coat, hat and gloves, and stepped out to join the young messenger who had brought his summons.

CHAPTER TWO:
Her Majesty's Bureau of Clandestine Affairs

The late afternoon air was dank and chilly; a light yet cloying fog swathed the streets of the capital, and Blackwood raised his collar against it as he and Meddings descended the steps from his Chelsea apartment building. A hansom awaited them at the roadside, the driver hunched forward in a dark, bulky overcoat, his whip held still before him, giving him the appearance of a fisherman sitting on a bleak, silent riverbank.

Along the far side of the road stretched one of the new omnibus lanes, a shallow trench of grey concrete three feet wide and a foot deep, which ran parallel to the kerb. As Blackwood reached the street, the air began to tremble with a dull vibration, an intermittent *whump* which startled the birds from the nearby trees and sent them fleeing into the fading, watery light of the foggy sky. Blackwood looked up and saw the faint outline of an intercity omnibus making its way across central London to parts unknown. The omnibus consisted of a lozenge-shaped hull suspended between three multiple-jointed, insect-like legs which carried it high above the ground. Numerous windows, glowing with interior lights, dotted its gunmetal-coloured flanks, casting an eerie luminescence into the surrounding fog.

Blackwood gave a slight shudder as he watched the thing's progress above the streets. Although the tripods were welcomed by most as a sign of the healthy economic relationship between Earth and Mars, and were already beginning to supersede the train and canal barge as the favoured method for the long-distance transportation of passengers and goods, Blackwood couldn't get used to them. There was something uncanny and unsettling in their measured gait as they strode purposefully across the countryside between towns and cities, in the incessant *whump, whump* of their rubber-shod feet upon field and moor and the concrete omnibus lanes that threaded through London and the larger towns and cities. The machines' components were manufactured on Mars and ferried to Earth by interplanetary cylinder, where they were assembled in a large factory in Wapping by Martian-trained engineers and craftsmen.

Progress, thought Blackwood as he climbed into the cab. *I suppose one must accept the inevitable.*

Meddings climbed in behind him and called up their destination to the driver, who roused himself from his melancholy pose and gave the horse's hide a flick from his whip.

Blackwood opened the envelope the messenger had handed to him and read the contents.

To Thomas Blackwood, Special Investigator for Her Majesty's Bureau of Clandestine Affairs:

You are to proceed without delay to Bureau Headquarters, to be briefed on the death of Lunan R'ondd, Martian Ambassador to the Court of Saint James's.

You are to consider this case Top Priority, and are to place all other cases on which you are working in Pending Status.

Grandfather.

He smiled as he folded the piece of paper and returned it to the envelope. Short and to the point: a typical communication from Grandfather. Blackwood had read of the tragedy in *The Times* that morning and had wondered at the identity of the Whitehall source who had suggested that the cause of death might not be natural. He would, he supposed, find out soon enough.

It was a risky strategy, he mused as he watched streets made dreary by the fog drift by. On the one hand, such talk could upset the Martians, who might consider it both crass and alarmist if the Ambassador's death proved merely to be from natural causes; yet, on the other hand, if he had been assassinated, it would do no harm for Her Majesty's Government to be seen to have been ahead of the game, as it were, in their readiness to accept the possibility of such an unpalatable alternative.

Blackwood found his mind drifting from the tightrope walk of diplomacy to the motives an assassin might have for killing R'ondd. Was it because he was the Ambassador... or was it because he was a Martian? The alternatives were equally unpalatable; each presented its own problems and pointed towards divergent lines of enquiry, but the latter possibility made Blackwood feel far more uncomfortable.

The vast majority of people went through their lives without ever seeing a denizen of the Red Planet in the flesh: the difference in atmospheric conditions on the two worlds made it impossible for Martians simply to stroll around on Earth without elaborate and cumbersome breathing apparatus (and, of course, the same was true of human beings on Mars). As a result, most of the people of Earth gleaned their information on Mars and Martians from newspaper articles and popular magazines, and, regrettably, from the lurid pages of the penny dreadfuls. In those dire publications, supernatural ne'er-do-wells such as Spring-Heeled Jack and

Varney the Vampire competed with Maléficus the Martian for the public's attention; to Blackwood, at least, there were times when Maléficus's nefarious exploits came perilously close to anti-Martian propaganda.

During the first few minutes of the drive to the Bureau's headquarters in Whitehall, Blackwood and Meddings exchanged a few trivialities concerning the weather but said little more to each other. Blackwood was not in the mood for conversation, and his young companion was astute enough to notice the fact. However, as they turned into Parliament Street, they passed a newspaper boy on the corner, who was shouting at the top of his lungs, *'Read all abart it! Spring-Heeled Jack strikes again! Anovver attack in the East End! Read all abart it!'*

Blackwood chuckled to himself, and Meddings turned to him. 'Do you not place any credence in those reports, sir?'

'Most certainly not! Although I'll admit that the business is somewhat interesting from a socio-anthropological point of view.'

'I'm not sure I follow.'

'Do you know anything of folklore, Mr Meddings?'

'Not a great deal, Mr Blackwood, I'm bound to say.'

'Most people, if they consider the subject at all, believe folklore to be little more than a collection of quaint beliefs from the past, with precious little relevance to the modern world. But that is not so: folklore – by which I mean the traditional tales and beliefs of a people, widely-accepted yet spurious – is in a constant state of development and modification. It is happening all around us, if we would but pause to take note of it. This business about Spring-heeled Jack is a case in point.'

'How so, if I may ask?'

Blackwood turned to his companion. 'Have you ever seen Jack?'

'No, sir.'

'Do you know anyone who has?'

Meddings shook his head. 'However,' he added, 'a friend of the fiancée of my sister's best friend's cousin claims to have caught sight of him about a month ago, in Spittalfields, so I understand.'

Blackwood chuckled again. 'My dear chap, you make my point for me! Spring-Heeled Jack is no more than a creature of modern folklore, with no independent existence of his own. He is the subject of tales told by those wishing to add spice to their otherwise mundane and dreary lives. No offence to the friend of the fiancée of your sister's best friend's cousin, I hasten to add.'

'None taken, sir, I assure you.'

'Thank you. I merely wished to impress upon you the point that creatures such as Spring-Heeled Jack may cavort through the pages of the penny dreadfuls, but they most certainly do not cavort through the streets of London.'

'Creatures like Spring-Heeled Jack and Varney the Vampire.'

'Precisely,' Blackwood smiled.

'And... Maléficus the Martian?'

'Ah! I see your line of reasoning: Maléficus the Martian and Spring-Heeled Jack are both written about in the penny dreadfuls, and since Martians exist, Jack must exist also.'

'Not the sturdiest of arguments, I suppose,' said Meddings a little ruefully.

'Indeed not,' Blackwood replied, although his smile had faded at the mention of Maléficus.

Fortunately, he was spared any further unsavoury contemplations by their arrival at the Foreign Office. He stepped down from the cab while Meddings paid the driver, who tugged at his cap before spurring the horse away into the fog, and together they walked through the great arched doorway into the building.

Almost as soon as they had entered, Meddings made to take his leave of Blackwood, who asked, 'Will you not be joining us, Mr Meddings?'

'Ah, no sir: I was instructed merely to deliver the message to you.'

'Very well. Then I'll bid you good day.'

'And to you, sir,' replied the young man with a slight bow, before hurrying off to attend to his other duties, whatever they might be.

Blackwood's footsteps echoed in counterpoint to the murmur of voices as he made his way across the vast, richly-decorated entrance hall. The designer of the Foreign Office, George Gilbert Scott, had described the building as 'a kind of national palace or drawing room for the nation', and Blackwood, who admired the ancient, the traditional and the permanent, never failed to appreciate the timeless elegance of the building's classical design, even on a day like today, when he was here on urgent business. He now moved swiftly amongst the clerks and other functionaries who seemed to inhabit the place constantly, some carrying sheaves of papers between departments, others congregated in groups of varying sizes, discussing the issues of the moment.

The Special Investigator went straight to a nondescript door in a far corner of the room and unlocked it with a key selected from a small bunch that he withdrew from an inner pocket of his overcoat. He went quickly through the door and closed it behind him, then descended the ancient stone staircase that wound deep into the ground.

The bottom of the staircase gave onto a short corridor, also constructed of ancient and pitted stone and lit by flickering gas lamps, at the end of which was another door. A black-uniformed guard stood stiffly to attention at the door, and he watched Blackwood's approach with unblinking eyes. He remained perfectly still, but the Special Investigator knew that he would fly instantly to violent action should the credentials Blackwood now displayed prove to be anything but perfectly in order.

The guard examined the leather wallet which Blackwood held open for him, then nodded once and stepped aside. Blackwood opened the door and stepped into an outer office whose walls were lined with heavy oak filing cabinets, and at the centre of which stood a large desk. An impeccably-dressed woman in her middle years looked up from the scrying glass of the cogitator which dominated the desktop.

'Ah, Special Investigator Blackwood,' she said in a quietly mellifluous voice.

'Good morning, Miss Ripley,' he replied, taking off his hat and overcoat and hanging them on the stand by the door.

'He's waiting for you. Please go straight in.'

'Thank you.' Blackwood crossed the room to the heavy oak door behind Miss Ripley's desk, knocked once and entered the inner office.

The head of Her Majesty's Bureau of Clandestine Affairs, who was known only by his codename of 'Grandfather', was pacing back and forth on his steam-powered artificial legs, clearly in a state of great distraction. As he stopped, turned and paced back the way he had come, tiny white clouds emerged from the knees of his black pinstripe trousers, accompanied by the faint but unmistakeable sounds of whispering pistons and gurgling water. Grandfather had lost his legs twenty years earlier during the Second Afghan War while serving with the Kabul Field Force under the command of Major General Sir Frederick Roberts. Although the British victory over the Afghan Army at Char Asiab had cost him dear, Grandfather looked back with great fondness on those days, and a portrait of Sir Frederick hung alongside one of the Queen on the wall behind his desk.

'Blackwood!' he said, turning with a faint hiss and clank. 'Good of you to get here so promptly.'

'Not at all, sir.'

'Have a seat.' Grandfather indicated one of the two burgundy leather chairs facing the desk.

'Thank you,' Blackwood replied, carefully refraining from looking at Grandfather's legs. It was a shame, he reflected, how the pipes and miniature boilers in the thighs ruined the line of the man's otherwise elegantly-cut trousers. *For Queen and Country*, he thought, philosophically.

Grandfather sat down heavily in his own chair and pressed a button on his desk. 'Darjeeling?' he asked.

'Yes, please.'

The door opened, and Miss Ripley poked her head into the office.

'Would you be kind enough to bring us a pot of tea, Miss Ripley?'

'Certainly, sir,' she replied, and closed the door again.

'Although I dare say you'd prefer *coffee*, eh, Blackwood?' Grandfather pronounced the word 'coffee' as if it were a particularly fulsome oath. Blackwood merely smiled. It was true that he had grown accustomed to the beverage during his previous assignment to America to investigate the case of the Wyoming Mummy. When Grandfather had overheard him confiding to a colleague upon his return that he was not absolutely sure that he didn't prefer it to tea, he had informed Blackwood that he would have been only slightly more dismayed had his operative proclaimed allegiance to President McKinley over Her Majesty.

'No, sir,' Blackwood replied. 'Darjeeling would be capital.'

Grandfather eyed him suspiciously. 'Hmm...' He turned his attention to a buff-coloured folder on his desk, which he opened slowly, almost tentatively, as if he half expected something profoundly unpleasant to jump out of it into his lap. 'A dreadful business, this.'

Blackwood assumed he was referring to the death of the Ambassador rather than his taste in beverages. 'Indeed, sir.'

'The press has got the jump on us, which is never a good thing.'

'It's difficult to imagine otherwise, in view of the seriousness of the event. Someone attending the function obviously notified them at the first opportunity. Do we know yet how Ambassador R'ondd died?'

Grandfather rested an index finger on the contents of the folder. 'I have here the report on the preliminary post-mortem, which was conducted by Dr Felix Cutter, a forensic pathologist attached to the Foreign Office. It does not make for comfortable reading.'

'How so?'

At that moment, there was a discreet knock at the door, and Miss Ripley entered bearing a silver tea tray. The two men lapsed into silence while she set the tray down on Grandfather's desk and retreated.

'Thank you, Miss Ripley.'

'You're most welcome, sir.'

When the door had closed once again, Grandfather handed the top sheet of paper to Blackwood. 'Read this.'

While Grandfather turned his attention to the tea things, Blackwood read the report, his eyes skimming along the lines quickly, taking everything in. 'Good grief,' he said quietly when he had finished. 'I'm no expert on Martian physiology, but this doesn't look like a natural death, even for our singular cousins across the Æther.'

'Quite so,' replied Grandfather, placing a cup before Blackwood.

'These things that were discovered in the Ambassador's oesophageal tract...'

'Tracts,' Grandfather corrected. 'All four of them.'

'The pathologist likens them to larvae of some kind.'

'Of a kind not seen on Earth... or Mars.'

Blackwood glanced at his superior. 'But they must have come from Mars. The Martians are incapable of breathing our atmosphere: it's too rich for them. Their Embassy is hermetically sealed and contains its own atmosphere with the correct proportion and density of gases; in addition, they always carry their own breathing apparatus whilst abroad on Earth. There's simply no conceivable way in which such organisms could have been introduced into Ambassador R'ondd's apparatus.'

'Isn't there? At any rate, that's what you'll have to find out, Blackwood,' said Grandfather, his face clouded with a pensive frown. 'As I said, this is a dreadful business, and it could very quickly become even worse. No Martian has ever died in such suspicious circumstances whilst on Earth – and no human on Mars. We must move quickly to ascertain exactly what has happened.'

'What do the Martians say? Do you think they might perceive this as an act of aggression on the part of Humanity?'

'They haven't commented, as yet. The Martians are essentially a peace-loving people, as you know.' Grandfather took a contemplative sip of tea, and continued, 'Nevertheless, their technology is somewhat in advance of ours. If they perceived us as aggressors, I think it's reasonable to say that we wouldn't do very well.'

Blackwood sighed. 'Indeed not.'

'Her Majesty is at present preparing an official letter of condolence for the Martian government, which will be carried aboard the next interplanetary cylinder to Mars – as will the Ambassador's body.'

'When is the cylinder scheduled to depart?'

'In five days' time. Her Majesty would be most gratified if she were able to assure them in her letter that no human

26

being was to blame for their Ambassador's untimely death
... and it would be even better if she were able to offer a
true and accurate explanation of exactly what happened at
the banquet, and why.'

Blackwood was silent for several moments. Then he
said decisively, 'I think it will serve us best to go on the
assumption that the Ambassador was the victim of foul play.'

'Intuition?'

'Quite.'

'Then our instincts are in accordance, Blackwood. Begin
your investigation immediately; use whatever resources you
see fit, and do please bring me an answer before that cylinder
leaves for Mars in five days' time!'

CHAPTER THREE:
The Monster

The cottage stood near the village of Old Ford, to the east of London, and visitors or even passers-by were few and far between, especially in the evening. It was a quarter to nine, and the Alsop family were gathered around the fire in their sitting room. Outside, the air hung cold and still upon the land, like a breath held in expectation. There were the beginnings of a light frost on the curtained windows, and the crystal stillness of the night pressed in upon the little house sitting alone beneath the stars.

Mr James Alsop was sitting in his armchair, reading to his family from a book of Longfellow's poems, while his wife, Elizabeth, sewed, and their three daughters, Mary, Jane and Sarah listened attentively. The fire crackled in the hearth, and the clock on the mantelpiece measured the passage of the quiet evening with a barely audible tick... tick.

The evening might have proceeded thus for the next hour or two; it might have concluded with Mr Alsop closing the book and discussing the poetry with his family in a relaxed and amiable way, before they retired to their beds. It might have been merely one more pleasant evening in the uneventful lives of an ordinary family... had not the bell at the garden gate rung.

Mr Alsop stopped reading and glanced at the clock on the mantelpiece. 'Who can that be at this hour?' he wondered, sighing in mild irritation.

The bell rang again, louder this time, and for longer.

Mrs Alsop looked up from her sewing and said, 'Jane, be a good girl and see who is there.'

'Of course, Mother.'

Jane Alsop, eighteen years old, slim and pretty with long auburn hair and a quick smile, stood up and walked to the sitting room door. Her mother watched her go, her own smile of affection briefly turning her lips. Jane was a bright, friendly girl, whose gracefulness was not studied, as with so many her age, but natural and effortless; Mrs Alsop had little doubt that she would one day make a fine wife for some as yet-unknown young man.

Jane hurried along the short corridor leading to the tiny hallway and opened the front door, shivering suddenly as the cold night air enveloped her. The small garden glittered faintly with its light dusting of frost, and beyond the low wall surrounding the cottage, the night was silent, the land and sky asleep.

Peering into the darkness, Jane saw a figure standing at the gate leading to Bearbinder Lane. She couldn't quite make out the details of his appearance, for her eyes had not yet grown accustomed to the night, but he appeared to be quite tall, and he wore a cloak... and something on his head which Jane took to be a helmet.

She stepped out towards the figure. 'Who are you?' she called. 'What is the matter?'

The figure answered immediately in a loud, urgent voice, 'I am a policeman. For God's sake, bring me a light, for we have caught Spring-Heeled Jack here in the lane!'

Jane gasped and took an involuntary step backwards. Spring-Heeled Jack... a vicious criminal according to some, a ghost or demon according to others, he had been terrorising London for nearly a year. No one had been able to apprehend him, for he was, so they said, possessed of supernatural strength and was able to leap over buildings, but many had been frightened half to death by his horrific appearance and the cruel and motiveless assaults to which he had subjected them.

Without a word, Jane hurried back into the house and fetched a candle, which she carried to the garden gate and the man who was still standing there, waiting silently. Without a word, he took the candle from her...

But then, instead of hurrying away to secure his quarry, he threw off his cloak and held the candle to his chest, so that its flame illuminated his face.

Jane screamed at the apparition that was thus revealed to her; she screamed at the eyes burning like red-hot coals in a grimacing, tight-skinned, mask-like face; at the strange metal helmet she had at first taken to be that of a policeman; at the tight-fitting white suit that shimmered like oilskin in the fitful candlelight; at the device that resembled a lamp that was strapped to his chest...

Jane barely had time to register these details – barely had time to realise that this was no policeman but Spring-Heeled Jack himself – before the apparition lunged at her. He opened his lipless mouth and vomited a seething ball of blue fire into her face. Jane screamed again as he grabbed her by the back of her neck and thrust her head under one of his arms, holding her there in an iron-fast grip while, with his other hand, he began to tear at her dress. In the chaos of her terror, Jane realised that her attacker did not have hands, but long, razor-sharp metal talons. She felt them biting into the skin on her back and arms, felt the warm blood begin to dampen her clothing.

She screamed again, louder and more desperately and, with an immense effort given yet greater force by her instinct for self-preservation, managed to wrench herself free of the horror. Without a backward glance, she dashed headlong up the garden path towards the house, and safety.

But the monster would not be denied his prey. He leaped over the gate and caught Jane just as she reached the front door, tearing at her neck and arms with his claws and ripping clumps of hair from her head.

'Oh God!' Jane screamed. *'Oh please, God help me!'*

At that moment, the front door of the cottage was flung wide open to reveal James Alsop. 'Great God in Heaven!' he cried and threw himself without a moment's hesitation upon the apparition which held his daughter in its loathsome embrace. Jane's older sister, Sarah, also appeared in the doorway and gasped when she saw the nightmarish spectacle; as their father struggled with the monster, Sarah grabbed hold of Jane's wildly flailing arms and pulled with all her might in a desperate effort to drag her away from the creature.

For some moments the violent and macabre dance continued, until Jane felt that she would lose consciousness through fear and loss of blood and be carried away into the night towards some unimaginable fate, in spite of the efforts of her father and sister.

Presently, though, James Alsop, driven to unsuspected heights of physical strength by his outrage and instinctive desire to protect his daughters from this eldritch maniac, managed to place a well-judged kick at the attacker's legs, momentarily knocking him off balance. For an instant, his vicelike grip on Jane loosened, and it was long enough for Alsop to wrench her free.

'Back, Sarah!' he cried. 'Back into the house!'

His eldest daughter obeyed immediately, allowing Alsop to retreat behind her. Hauling the weeping Jane across the threshold, he took hold of the door with his free hand and slammed it hard, just as the apparition regained its balance and lunged towards them once more.

'Oh, good Lord, whatever has *happened?*' cried Elizabeth Alsop, who had emerged from the sitting room into the corridor leading to the entrance hall. Beside her stood Mary, who was holding onto her mother, her face a pale mask of uncomprehending terror as she regarded the ghastly tableau with wide, unblinking eyes.

Alsop was about to answer, but was interrupted by a thunderous banging upon the front door. 'Great God,' he shouted desperately, 'that fiend will not be denied!'

His wife's hand flew to her mouth, and tears of consternation welled up in her eyes. 'James, what is happening?'

Shouting above the infernal banging, Alsop replied, 'We are being attacked, Elizabeth! Take Mary and Sarah, and go upstairs immediately!'

The three women rushed along the corridor and up the stairs, while Alsop gathered Jane in his arms and followed them. At the foot of the stairs, he glanced down at her bloodied face and the unruly mass of her beautiful auburn hair, now damp and matted with more of her blood. She appeared to have fainted, for which Alsop was grateful. Whatever happened next, he reflected, she would be unaware of it.

With a final glance over his shoulder at the front door, which was shaking in its frame under the ceaseless onslaught of the fiend outside, James Alsop carried his unconscious daughter up the stairs to his and his wife's bedroom, where the others had already gathered.

Laying Jane upon the bed, Alsop went to the window that overlooked the front garden. Beyond the low stone wall, Bearbinder Lane lay in darkness. Away in the distance, he could see the scattered lights of Old Ford. The banging below continued, and Alsop realised that it was only a matter of time before the creature managed to break the door down.

'James,' said Elizabeth, 'what are we going to do?' She was kneeling beside the prone form of her injured daughter. 'We must get Jane to a doctor without delay!' Mary and Sarah were kneeling next to her, and the three women gazed up at him, their eyes full of pleas that he do something – anything – to save them from the nightmare that was still hurling itself against the door downstairs.

James Alsop realised that there was only one option open to him. He turned from his family, flung open the window and, leaning out, began to scream for help at the top of his lungs in the direction of Old Ford.

CHAPTER FOUR:
Curious Specimens

'Thank you for agreeing to see me at such a late hour, Doctor,' said Thomas Blackwood.

Dr Felix Cutter smiled at his visitor from the other side of his desk. Both men knew that he had little choice, since Blackwood was here on business of the Crown, but he appreciated the man's courtesy nevertheless. 'Not at all, Mr Blackwood. I was working late anyway, and I am more than happy to render to you any assistance you may require.'

'I take it you have now had a chance to perform a more detailed examination of the body?'

'Indeed: that was, in fact, the reason for my being here still.'

Dr Cutter was a small man whose face was almost invariably impassive, save for his quick, darting blue eyes whose constant movements were amplified by the lenses of his thick spectacles. Blackwood had to admit that he found this trait rather unnerving; this, combined with the man's profession and curiously appropriate name, made him wish to conclude his business here as quickly as possible and be on his way.

His mood was not helped by the general mien of Dr Cutter's office. The walls were painted a particularly unattractive shade of green, and were decorated (disagreeably, if appropriately) with unsettlingly accurate renderings of the human body and its various components in diverse stages of dismemberment. The fire burning fitfully in the small hearth did little to lighten the atmosphere of the place, nor did it produce sufficient heat to banish entirely the chill that hung insistently upon the air.

'And what are your conclusions?' asked Blackwood.

Dr Cutter leaned forward, placing his white-coated elbows on the blotter of his desk. 'My conclusions, Mr Blackwood, are perplexing, to say the least. Ambassador R'ondd was killed by the presence of a large number of mites which had infested all four of his oesophageal tracts...'

Blackwood held up a hand. 'Pardon me for interrupting, Doctor... *mites?*'

'Yes. As far as I have been able to ascertain, these mites absorbed the gases from the Ambassador's breathing apparatus before they could reach his lungs. Simply put, he died of hypoxia.'

'He suffocated.'

'Precisely.'

'Have you ever encountered such a phenomenon before?'

Dr Cutter shook his head. 'You must understand that my experience of conducting post-mortems on Martians is by no means extensive; however, I am well-versed in the physiology of the species, and I'm quite sure that this was not a natural occurrence.'

'May I see the body?' asked Blackwood.

Cutter rose from his desk. 'Of course. We are storing it in the morgue until its return to Mars.'

*

Their footsteps echoed dully on the stone floor of the corridor as they walked towards the morgue. The gas lamps along the walls had been turned down for the night, and their anaemic glow lent a sepulchral aspect to their surroundings. Blackwood hated this place – or rather, he hated what it represented: it was the penultimate resting place of those who had died in mysterious (and usually violent) circumstances; a cold, impersonal way station on their journey to the grave. As much as he respected Dr Cutter and his colleagues, Blackwood felt a profound sadness that they were the only companions to the recently departed, that their only concern was to ascertain the manner of death with scalpel and bone-saw and microscope. It was a place where unpleasant questions were asked and horrible answers discovered amid the death-flower scent of formaldehyde.

'These mites you discovered, Doctor,' said Blackwood as they approached the door to the morgue. 'Were you able to ascertain their type?'

Dr Cutter sighed. 'That, too, is perplexing. As close as I can judge, they bear a resemblance to *Acarus siro*...'

'*Acarus siro?*'

'Flour mites.'

'I see. But a resemblance only, by which I take it that you mean they are not *actually* flour mites.'

'Indeed not: they behave in a way which is quite impossible for ordinary mites, regardless of phylum, class or order. No ordinary mite can do what *these* fellows appear to have done...'

'Which is to feed directly on the gases of their environment.'

Dr Cutter nodded. 'Directly... and ravenously. Here we are.' He opened the door for Blackwood, who thanked him and stepped through into the morgue.

The air in here was even chillier, and Blackwood shivered involuntarily as his companion crossed the room to the row of stout metal doors which dominated the far wall.

While Dr Cutter unlocked one of the doors and pulled it open, Blackwood glanced around the room, at the examination table sheathed in white porcelain, the workbenches with their sinks, microscopes and neat rows of chemical reagent bottles, the closed drawers which he knew contained the glinting tools of Cutter's profession... and shivered again. As a Special Investigator for Her Majesty's Bureau of Clandestine Affairs, he was well-acquainted with death in many of its forms, but he never got used to its presence and had long ago vowed to himself that he never would.

There was a sound like distant thunder as Cutter pulled out the tray on its well-oiled rollers. Blackwood turned and looked at the white sheet draped over the tray, took a deep breath and nodded to Cutter.

The pathologist pulled back the sheet to reveal the corpse of His Excellency Lunan R'ondd, Martian Ambassador to the Court of Saint James's. Blackwood stepped forward and looked down at the body. It was a little over seven feet tall and skeletally thin; the muscles of its arms and legs, which looked like slender, ribbed pipes, clung to the underlying bones beneath the skin, which was a pale duck-egg-blue in colour. The metal leg and back braces which Martians habitually wore while on Earth to protect them from the gravity, which was significantly greater than that of their home world, had been removed prior to the post-mortem examination.

There was a Y-shaped incision across the Martian's great barrel of a chest, where Cutter had performed the second stage of the post-mortem, following the external examination. Although the incision had now been stitched closed, its edges glinted with a pale-yellow mucilaginous substance, which had leaked out during the procedure. The chest cavity contained the Martian's heart and the four pulmonary sacs, analogous to human lungs, but larger and more efficient: an evolutionary necessity, since Mars's atmosphere was much thinner than Earth's. His neck had also been opened to reveal the four oesophageal tracts connecting the pulmonary sacs to the gill-like openings beneath the narrow, protruding jaw.

Strangely, in the midst of this death, in the archetypal horror of an intelligent, living being's reduction to the status of carrion, the thing which Blackwood found most disturbing was the eyes. Even in life, a Martian's eyes were unsettling to look upon. Since Mars was so much farther away from the Sun than the Earth, and daylight therefore so much dimmer, the logical response of the forces of evolution had been to maximise the amount of light falling onto the Martian retina. A Martian's eyes were therefore large, typically three inches across, with enormous black pupils. To look into such eyes was like looking into the depths of Space itself, and it was a sensation which many human beings, including Blackwood, found uncomfortable. It was ironic, he reflected, that one could read so much in a fellow human's eyes, but so little in a Martian's...

Lunan R'ondd's eyes were half closed, and the thick, blue-veined nictitating membranes, which in life had kept them clean of the ubiquitous dust of his world, were drawn partway across the empty blackness of the pupils. The strangeness of his face had been transformed by death into hideousness, and Blackwood felt a great sadness closing upon his heart. This was a man from another world, of another order of being... but he was still a man, and quite apart from his obligation to the Crown, Blackwood felt an obligation that was perhaps greater still: to discover the reason why this being had died before his time.

Dr Cutter drew Blackwood's attention away from the body and towards a workbench beside which he was standing. 'Look here, Mr Blackwood,' he said. 'This is what we found in the Ambassador's oesophageal tracts.' He was holding a glass slide, which he proceeded to place carefully onto the stage of a compound microscope. After making several adjustments to the focus, he stepped aside and indicated the instrument. 'See for yourself.'

Blackwood leaned over and peered through the brass eyepiece. What he saw made his skin crawl. There were perhaps a dozen mites on the slide, with bulbous, pearl-hued bodies, each with eight stubby legs bristling obscenely with long, thin hairs.

Dr Cutter noted the grimace which quickly spread across Blackwood's face and chuckled quietly. Blackwood looked up, a trifle embarrassed, gave a wan smile and said, 'I don't like insects.'

'They're not insects, Mr Blackwood. Mites are of the class *Arachnida*: the same class as spiders.'

Blackwood sighed. 'I like spiders even less, Dr Cutter.'

'Really? But they're fascinating creatures; quite magnificent, in their way...'

'I'm sure they are, but I still find them repulsive. Now, to return to the matter at hand...'

'Of course. Forgive me.'

'You said that these creatures are akin to *Acarus siro*, but that they are not *actually* of that type.'

'That's correct. These fellows are of a type I've never seen before, and I'll wager no one else has, either. In addition to our examination of the Ambassador, we also examined his breathing apparatus and discovered a large number of these creatures' eggs inside the air tanks, the compressors and the connective piping. As far as we can determine, the eggs must have been intentionally introduced at some point and allowed to hatch.'

'What makes you think that?'

'The Martians' methods of decontaminating their breathing apparatus prior to operation in the Earth's atmosphere are quite rigorous. This infestation simply couldn't have occurred by accident.'

'I see. How long does it take for ordinary mites to hatch?'

'It depends on the temperature and humidity of the environment. In optimal conditions, say at around eighty degrees Fahrenheit, with adequate humidity, they can reach the adult stage in about three weeks. The humidity must be at least sixty-five percent, however, otherwise the animals will desiccate and die.'

Blackwood indicated the microscope. 'You said earlier that this particular type is not known on Earth *or* Mars. Are you quite sure of that?'

'Oh yes, quite sure.'

'How?'

'I took some of the adult specimens and attempted to ascertain their resilience to different liquid and gaseous environments.' Dr Cutter paused before continuing, 'I quickly discovered that these creatures are virtually indestructible.'

Blackwood glanced at him sharply. 'What do you mean by that?'

'Precisely what I say. It seems that they can withstand almost any conditions, but they appear to be most comfortable in concentrated solutions of copper nitrate, copper sulphate and zinc sulphate. Quite astonishing, really. I then decided to apply an electrical current, to see if they were susceptible to that; however, instead of killing the specimens, I only succeeded in creating more...'

'*More?*' cried Blackwood. 'What the devil are you talking about, man?'

Cutter reached across the workbench to a test tube stand and retrieved one of the glass tubes, which was sealed with a cork stopper. He held it up for Blackwood to see. Blackwood peered closely, and could just make out a tiny, pale yellow smudge on the inside of the glass.

'These are more of the creatures – or at least their larvae,' Cutter said. 'But they are ones which *I* created, quite inadvertently, through the application of an electric current through a solution of zinc sulphate.'

'That's impossible,' Blackwood whispered as he took the test tube from Cutter and held it up to the light. 'Life cannot be spontaneously created that way.'

Dr Cutter shrugged. 'Until a few hours ago, I would have agreed with you, Mr Blackwood, as would any man of science. Nevertheless, you hold the evidence in your hands.' He took the test tube from Blackwood and returned it to the stand. 'And my conclusions are supported by some additional research I conducted on the Æther, just before you arrived.'

'Hmm,' Blackwood muttered, recalling the frustration he had experienced earlier that day with his own cogitator.

'If you would care to return to my office, I can show you,' suggested Cutter.

'What? Oh... very well, Doctor. Lead the way.'

*

Back in Dr Cutter's office, Blackwood took a seat while the pathologist fired up the cogitator on his desk. There was a faint whirring from inside the unpolished hardwood casing, and after a few moments, a pale, milky mist began to form in the scrying glass. Cutter turned it on its pedestal so that Blackwood could see it. It might have been an inferior model to his own, the Special Investigator reflected, but at least the damned thing worked.

'Where did you get this from?' Blackwood asked.

'The cogitator? Cottingley's of Mayfair. We have a contract with them. Why do you ask?'

Blackwood shrugged. 'Just curious.'

Dr Cutter flexed his fingers and began to tap commands into the keyboard. 'Do you have a cogitator, Mr Blackwood?' he asked as he worked.

'Yes. In fact, I bought one earlier today... from Cottingley's, as it happens.'

'Which model?'

'A Tara III.'

Cutter glanced at him. 'Really? Must have set you back a pretty penny.'

'It did.'

'It uses the new De Danann control system, doesn't it?'

'So I believe,' Blackwood replied, wishing he hadn't started this conversation.

Cutter smiled wistfully. 'I'd love one of those, but our budget won't stretch to it, I'm afraid.'

You're not missing much, Blackwood thought.

'Ah! Here we are,' said Cutter, indicating the scrying glass. 'As I mentioned, I retrieved this information from the Æther not long ago.'

Within the oval glass, black characters were forming against the pale background, gradually resolving themselves into words.

'What is this?' Blackwood asked, leaning forward.

'It's the text of a paper delivered to the Royal Society a couple of years ago, by a gentleman named Andrew Crosse.'

Blackwood read the title aloud. '"The Creation of Life from Lifelessness".' His eyes moved rapidly back and forth as he scanned the text. 'Good grief, this seems to be describing precisely the method by which you accidentally created the *Acarus* mites!'

'Quite so,' Cutter nodded. 'Mr Crosse even provides his own binomial classification for the little blighters: he calls them *Acarus galvanicus*.'

'Who is Andrew Crosse? I've never heard of him.'

'There are few who have – at least outside the Quantock Hills, where he has his home.'

'Somerset?'

'Yes. He's something of a recluse, I believe.'

'But he isn't a professional scientist.'

'Oh dear me, no!' Cutter laughed. 'He's an amateur – an enthusiastic one, but an amateur nevertheless. That's why his paper was dismissed in such short time by the Royal Society: the consensus was that he had inadvertently allowed his experimental apparatus to become contaminated by dust- or cheese-mites. No one took his results seriously, and he was sent home with his tale between his legs.'

'Poor chap,' said Blackwood. 'That must have been terribly humiliating for him.'

'Humiliating? Well, yes... I suppose so. Although it's difficult to imagine what other conclusion the Society could have come to. After all, his claims were quite outrageous...'

'Not *that* outrageous, Dr Cutter,' said Blackwood pointedly.

'Well, no... in light of what I've discovered today, I suppose I would have to say that they have more than a passing acquaintance with fact.'

'And so instead of attempting to replicate Crosse's experiments in their own laboratories, they simply dismissed him as a buffoon and a charlatan.' Blackwood shook his head in disgust. 'How very broadminded of them!'

Dr Cutter regarded his guest in silence for a few moments, then said, 'Do you think that Mr Crosse may be a suspect in this case?'

'It does sound rather outrageous, doesn't it? But it's the only lead I have to go on so far – although it is, of course, early days. Even if he didn't place the *Acarus* larvae in the Ambassador's breathing apparatus himself – and the security arrangements in the Martian Embassy make it a virtual certainty that he didn't – he may have supplied the creatures to whoever did.'

Cutter sat back. 'You know, Mr Blackwood, even though the evidence points towards foul play, it's difficult to believe. What is the reason behind it? Why would anyone wish to assassinate the Martian Ambassador? And why choose such a bizarre method?'

Blackwood gave him a grim smile. 'That, sir, is what I must endeavour to find out.'

CHAPTER FIVE:
A Harrowing Interview

The driver brought his vehicle to a halt and called down, 'This is the place, your Ladyship. The Alsop residence.'

'Thank you, John.'

Lady Sophia Harrington opened the door and climbed down from the carriage. She looked around briefly, taking in the small, neat house with its well-tended garden, the surrounding fields and the sleepy village of Old Ford which lay a little way off in the distance at the far end of Bearbinder Lane. The morning sun was struggling to penetrate the overcast sky, its feeble rays lending an air of melancholy to the scene. From a nearby stand of trees, a lone meadow pipit sang, a little forlornly, Sophia thought. She reflected that on a warmer, brighter day, the Alsop house would have presented a charming picture of bucolic peace and tranquillity.

But not today.

She sighed, drew the collar of her black woollen coat tighter around her neck to ward off the chill that promised to linger for the rest of the day, and glanced up at the driver. 'Would you please wait here for me, John? I shouldn't be much more than half an hour or so.'

'Of course, your Ladyship,' he replied, tugging at the brim of his cap.

She smiled her thanks, walked across the shallow ruts of the lane to the garden gate and rang the bell. At first, there was no answer, and Sophia wondered if the family were out. She knew that she should have sent a message requesting an interview before she came here, but in cases such as this, time was of the utmost importance, and the longer one delayed in gathering testimony, the less likely it was that people's recollections would remain accurate.

She rang the bell again, noting the pale yellow glow in one of the downstairs windows, which suggested that there was indeed someone at home.

Presently, the front door opened a little way, and a man peered out.

'Mr Alsop?' Sophia called. 'Mr James Alsop?'

The man hesitated for a moment, then stepped out onto his porch. 'I'm James Alsop. How may I assist you, madam?'

Sophia rested a gloved hand on the gate. 'May I?'

Alsop nodded stiffly, and Sophia opened the gate and walked up the garden path towards him. As she approached, she took in his appearance. He was slightly below average height and stocky in build. He was unshaven, and the collar of his shirt was unbuttoned, giving him an unkempt look which contrasted sharply with the neatness and order of his house. Sophia reflected that this was quite understandable in view of what the man and his family had experienced just a few hours ago.

'Allow me to introduce myself,' she said. 'I am Lady Sophia Harrington, Secretary of the Society for Psychical Research.' She offered him her hand, which, after another hesitation, he shook reluctantly.

'James Alsop,' he muttered. 'A pleasure.'

In a soft tone, Sophia said, 'Please forgive me for calling on you unannounced, Mr Alsop, but I would greatly appreciate a few minutes of your time.'

'May I ask for what purpose, Lady Sophia?'

She took a deep breath and replied, 'We at the SPR are aware that something frightful happened here last night. I would be most grateful if you would allow me the opportunity to discuss it with you.'

Alsop frowned at her. 'How can that be? We have told no one except the police...'

'And that is how we came to hear of it,' she replied.

'I don't understand.'

'We have an arrangement with New Scotland Temple, whereby information pertaining to the Society's interests is routinely shared with us. In cases such as this, the Temple acknowledges our greater experience and resources and engages us as consultant investigators. We were notified as soon as you spoke to the police early this morning.'

Alsop's frown remained as he continued to meet Sophia's gaze. He was clearly debating with himself whether to admit her to his home or respectfully ask her to be on her way. After a few moments, his eyes dropped, and his hand went to his open collar. He briefly touched his unshaven chin, clearly embarrassed at his appearance, and Sophia felt a surge of sympathy rising in her breast. She had the sudden desire to reach out and give his shoulder a reassuring squeeze but refrained, understanding the impropriety of such a gesture.

Instead, she offered him a smile and, clutching the collar of her coat, said, 'If nothing else, I would appreciate the chance to warm myself a little.'

This caused Alsop's good manners to reassert themselves. Evidently, he realised how remiss of him it was to keep a young lady of clearly impeccable upbringing standing on his doorstep in the cold, for he said, 'Forgive me,' and moved aside to allow her to enter.

'Thank you, Mr Alsop.'

As she passed him, Sophia noted the state of the front door, which appeared to have been violently gouged: the dark maroon paint was split in numerous long swathes, revealing the pale hardwood beneath. It was as if some wild beast, such as a lion or bear, had raked its claws along the surface.

Alsop led her into the sitting room, which Sophia noted was simply yet tastefully furnished. She also noted the two young women sitting on the Chesterfield across from the fireplace, whom Alsop introduced as his daughters, Sarah and Mary. Sophia guessed Sarah to be in her mid-twenties and Mary in her late teens, and she smiled warmly at them as she shook their hands. Of Alsop's wife and remaining daughter there was no sign. Sophia knew the reason.

'How is Jane?' she asked, as Alsop indicated his own armchair and invited her to sit.

'Her condition is stable, so the doctors say. We took her to St Thomas's Hospital last night, after... after it happened. My wife, Elizabeth, is at her bedside as we speak.'

'I see,' Sophia nodded. 'Although of course she doesn't know me, I would be most grateful if you would pass on to Mrs Alsop my sincere wishes for Jane's speedy recovery.'

'Thank you,' said Alsop, his voice catching slightly.

Sarah glanced at her father and then turned to Sophia. 'May I bring you some tea, your Ladyship?'

'I would like that very much, Sarah. And please, I would much rather you called me Sophia.'

The two girls glanced at each other in surprise at this, and Sophia smiled. 'I'm afraid I've never much cared for titles, my own included, and in any event, I believe that such formalities are of little consequence here.'

When Sarah had left the room, Sophia turned to Alsop. 'May I enquire as to your profession, sir?'

'I work for the legal firm of Horton, Giles and Winston,' Alsop replied, taking a seat opposite her. 'I sent word to them this morning, explaining what has happened. Mr Horton paid us a visit not an hour ago, to express his concern and assure me that I should not think of returning to work until Jane has recovered enough to come home.'

'That was kind of him.'

'Indeed. He is a good man.'

'May I ask how long have you lived here?'

'A little over three years.'

'You have a very charming home.'

'Thank you. We've been very happy here.'

'I've no doubt. Now... I know how difficult this must be for you, but could you describe to me the events of last night?'

Alsop sighed. 'I really don't see what good it will do. I've already reported the incident to the police – they have my statement, which I'm sure they've given to you. Forgive me, but what more do you require?'

'I understand your reluctance, Mr Alsop, but over the course of many years, during which the Society has investigated an extremely wide range of paranormal phenomena, we have found that it is most important to gather testimony from witnesses directly, in face-to-face interviews. In this way, we are able to observe nuances and details that may have been missed from earlier testaments to others. It also provides us with the opportunity to examine the scene of the event...'

'This wasn't an "event",' whispered Alsop. 'It was a *crime*, a hideous, motiveless crime!' And with that, James Alsop buried his head in his hands and began to weep.

'Oh, father!' said Mary, and rushed to his side, putting her arms around him.

Alsop hugged his daughter and turned haunted eyes to Sophia. 'You cannot know what it means... for a man to be unable to protect his family.'

Sophia looked at him in silence for several seconds, struggling to prevent the tears from welling up in her own eyes. *Yes, Mr Alsop*, she thought. *I know exactly what that means.*

At that moment, Sarah returned to the sitting room, bearing a tray. While she poured tea for them all, Alsop took hold of himself and said, 'Until last night, I'd considered Spring-Heeled Jack to be nothing more than some perverse fairy tale, a creation of the yellow press, with no basis in fact whatsoever. I had considered those who claim to have seen him to be nothing more than deluded fools or outright liars. Now I know better: he exists, and he is not human. In fact, he is very far from human.'

'What makes you say that?' asked Sophia, accepting a cup from Sarah.

'The way he looked... the way he acted.' Alsop went on to describe the events of the previous evening. Sophia maintained a neutral expression, although she felt her heart lurch at Alsop's description of the outrage perpetrated upon his daughter by the creature. 'We sought refuge in my wife's and my bedroom,' he concluded, 'and I was reduced to opening the window and screaming for help in the direction of Old Ford.'

'Did anyone come to your aid?'

Alsop shook his head. 'I don't think my voice carried that far; nevertheless, it must have deterred the fiend, for he abandoned his attempts to gain entry and made off across the fields. Good God, the way he *moved!* It was like an animal... a great jumping insect! No man could have made those leaps and bounds.'

Sophia's gaze drifted towards the fire. 'Almost as if he was used to a denser atmosphere,' she said, more to herself than to her host.

'Pardon me?'

Her eyes found his again. 'Nothing, Mr Alsop. Merely a speculation; pay it no mind. I wonder if you would allow me to examine your doorstep and the damage to your front door.'

Alsop sighed. 'I see no reason why not. Do you intend to search for physical evidence?'

'I do indeed. The creature may have left something behind – some residue, perhaps. At any rate, it's worth looking.'

'In that case, I have no objection,' said Alsop.

*

Sophia stood before the open front door and examined the marks. They were numerous and criss-crossed each other, as if someone had assaulted the wood with arms flailing in a windmill motion. She recalled Alsop's description of the creature's hands – or rather, lack of hands. He had described metal talons instead of fingers, long and razor-sharp, a description that was amply attested to by the state of the door.

Taking a small magnifying glass from her purse, Sophia slowly passed it back and forth across the damaged areas, starting at the top and working her way down. She had no idea what she was looking for but supposed that she would know it if she found it. She knew that her chances of finding anything useful were slim, since one of the most mystifying aspects of the Spring-Heeled Jack phenomenon was that he never left any evidence behind after an attack – other than the lingering terror of his victims, of course. It was as if he *were* a ghost, just as some of the lower-quality periodicals claimed. However, Sophia had seen her fair share of ghosts in the five years since she had joined the SPR, and she was quite certain that Jack's origin lay elsewhere...

She was about to give up on the door and turn her attention to the front doorstep when something glinted beneath the magnifying glass. Her breath caught in her chest, and she moved the glass slightly to bring the object into sharper focus.

Good grief! she thought, and, reaching into her purse, withdrew a pair of eyebrow tweezers, which she used to pluck the object from the furrow of splintered wood.

Alsop appeared in the doorway beside her. 'Have you found something?' he asked, his voice barely more than a whisper.

'I have indeed, Mr Alsop... I have indeed!' She held the object up to the light with the tweezers, turning the magnifying glass so that they both could see.

It was a fragment of metal, a tiny shard no more than an eighth of an inch in length. It glinted as Sophia turned it behind the glass, and as the light caught it, she and Alsop could detect tiny scintillations of a greenish-purple hue flickering across its narrow surface, almost in the manner of a film of oil on water.

'What is it?' asked Alsop.

'I suspect it's from one of the creature's talons. Will you hold this, please?' She handed him the magnifying glass, and then withdrew a small waxed paper envelope from a pocket of her coat, into which she placed the tiny metal shard. 'This is a considerable breakthrough, Mr Alsop; it's the first time anyone has ever secured a piece of Spring-Heeled Jack.'

'Perhaps so... but what good will it do? What can such a tiny fragment tell us?'

'That, of course, remains to be seen, but I suspect that a careful physical analysis may well yield useful information.'

'Such as?'

She gave him a broad smile. 'Such as where this creature came from.'

Alsop regarded her in silence for a moment. 'Where do *you* think it came from, Lady Sophia?'

'I have my suspicions.'

'Do you think it's from another world? From Mars?'

Sophia hesitated and then held out her hand, saying, 'I owe you a sincere debt of thanks, Mr Alsop. Now I must be on my way. Will you say good-bye to Sarah and Mary for me?'

'Of course,' he replied, shaking her hand. 'If there's anything else I can do, please do not hesitate to call again.'

Sophia's smile grew broader as she replied, 'When I call on you again, it will be to meet your daughter Jane and to give you a full and accurate explanation of the origin of Spring-Heeled Jack!'

And with that, she turned and walked away towards her waiting carriage.

As she closed the door and settled herself into her seat, the driver called down to her, 'Where to now, your Ladyship?'

'To Whitehall please, John,' she replied, and added to herself, *To Her Majesty's Bureau of Clandestine Affairs.*

CHAPTER SIX:
The Queen and the Martian

Thomas Blackwood had returned to his rooms the previous evening to find that an envelope had been slipped beneath his door, and he had felt a slight trepidation upon opening it and seeing that it was a summons to Buckingham Palace. The Queen wished to discuss Lunan R'ondd's death and to receive a progress report on Blackwood's investigation. That she wished to do so after less than a day was testament to the seriousness with which she viewed the situation, and Blackwood was immensely relieved that he had something to tell her – even if he was still unsure as to its ultimate meaning. Nevertheless, he had made a mental note to present a gift to Dr Cutter of a particularly fine Scotch at the earliest opportunity.

As he rose, washed and shaved, however, Blackwood could not shake himself free of the apprehension which he invariably felt on those rare occasions when his presence before the Queen was requested. There was something deeply unnerving about Victoria, an otherworldliness which, he supposed, was a combination of her own powerful personality and the Martian rejuvenation drugs with which she had been treated over the last few years, and which had gradually returned her from extreme age and infirmity to vibrant youth again.

It was perhaps unsurprising that Victoria had agreed to undergo the treatment, since she had always embraced the new scientific developments of her own race. She had enthusiastically sat for photographs when that technology was in its infancy; she had greeted the invention of the telegraph and, later, the telephone with undisguised glee, making extensive use of both instruments; she had even allowed chloroform to be administered to her during the birth of Prince Leopold in 1853, scorning the belief that it was a woman's lot to suffer the pain of childbirth. The concept of life extension had immediately intrigued her, and had conjured seductive images in her mind of the simultaneous continuation of the era to which she had given her name.

The treatment produced a transformation which the masses had greeted with jubilation, and which had prompted the Prime Minister, Lord Salisbury, to declare that 'the sun would set neither on the British Empire, nor the reign of Queen Victoria'. Blackwood had no idea what Salisbury thought in private, however (although there was a rumour at court that he considered anything which delayed the accession of that buffoon Bertie to be most welcome). Nevertheless, Blackwood sometimes wondered whether the Prime Minister felt as he did: that there was an unnatural light in Victoria's eyes, the smouldering light of a red, alien world, containing all the strange secrets of that world and the technological geniuses who inhabited it.

Blackwood tried to push all such thoughts from his mind as he quickly breakfasted on the sausages, bacon and toast which had been prepared for him by his housekeeper, Mrs Butters, who knew better than to place any eggs on his plate. (Blackwood had developed a pathological fear of eggs following his involvement with the case of the Cosmic Spheres three years previously, and the very sight of them brought him out in a cold sweat.) He drank two large cups of the excellent Jamaican Blue Mountain coffee which he procured from a small and exclusive establishment in Knightsbridge and, thus fortified, left his apartment and took the carriage which had been sent from the Palace to collect him.

The mist and fog of the last few days had finally lifted, for which Blackwood was grateful, and he felt his mood lightening somewhat as the carriage passed through busy streets awash with bright sunlight. The cloying dampness of the air had also been banished, leaving a cool crispness which cleared his mind and lifted his spirits still further.

Away in the distance, high above the surrounding rooftops, he could see several intercity omnibuses, their metal hulls gleaming in the sunlight, the great pillars of their legs moving with a strange, languid elegance. He found himself staring at them, unable to look away, fascinated in spite of himself. They looked like small airships perched atop living, moving scaffolds. Each of their hulls was dotted with numerous portholes, while at the front, the single large, circular observation blister of the bridge gazed blankly across the cityscape, towards the horizon. And yet, as Blackwood continued to watch their progress, it seemed to him that they were not really like airships at all: they were more like colossal insect Cyclopses surveying a world which was not theirs.

Although only in his mid-thirties, Blackwood was old enough to remember a time when life on Mars was nothing more than an intriguing speculation. Then, in 1877, Giovanni Schiaparelli made his monumental discovery (later confirmed by Percival Lowell) of the global canal system which extended like a vast cobweb across the surface of the Red Planet, signifying the presence of a great civilisation. The scientific community was sceptical at first, of course, with many claiming that the 'canals' were no more than optical illusions caused by the human eye's tendency to connect isolated and ill-defined features. They had assumed the matter to be settled, until the great inventor and engineer Nikola Tesla decided to use his giant Magnifying Transmitter in Colorado Springs to send a radio signal towards Mars on the 1st of April 1893, and was gratified to receive the honour of a reply just a few days later.

A few weeks after that initial tentative exchange, the first exploratory cylinders arrived, landing in all the capitals of the civilised world (the cylinder bound for London had evidently miscalculated its trajectory slightly and landed on Horsell Common near Woking instead, causing no small measure of alarm among the local inhabitants). After they had learned English and a few other European languages (a feat performed in an astoundingly brief time) the Martians stated that they had been observing the Earth through their telescopes for many years and had been waiting for Mankind to display a sufficient level of technological advancement to allow contact. Tesla's radio transmission had proved to them that human civilisation was mature enough to receive visitors from another world.

The good people of Woking were not the only ones to express concern over these astonishing events, of course: all over the world, voices of fear and consternation were raised in response to the arrival of these strange beings from across the Æther. There were many who claimed that the Martians were conquerors who had come under the guise of friendship, and that Mankind should make ready to do battle for its very survival.

Thankfully (and unusually), however, reason prevailed: scientific institutions throughout Europe and the United States of America considered the situation, and quickly came to the conclusion that the Martians could have no conceivable reason for wanting to conquer the Earth. For one thing, they could not survive in the atmosphere without elaborate and cumbersome equipment; for another, the chemical constituents of Earthly food offered no nourishment to their alien metabolisms; for yet another, it was quite possible that there were certain germs and bacteria in the Earth's atmosphere that would prove lethal to organisms which had evolved on another world, and which therefore had no natural defence against them.

And in any event, the scientists concluded, if the Martians had wanted to attack Mankind, they would surely have done so already, without first alerting Earth to their existence.

In the six years since first contact, it had become apparent that the scientific community was quite correct. It seemed that the Red Planet, so long associated in the human mind with violence and war, in fact wanted nothing but friendship and peaceful cooperation with the people of Earth. (It had amused many to learn that the Martian name for Earth, *Azquahar*, translated as 'Blue Planet'.) Plans for an economic relationship between the two civilisations were carefully laid, whereby the Martians would purchase certain useful raw materials in which their own world was growing deficient, in exchange for granting Mankind access to some of their technologies.

Cultural bonds were likewise quickly established, with scholars from each world being invited to the other to learn of its history and to sample the vast range of its artistic endeavours. The results of these commercial and cultural exchanges could now be seen in the streets, drawing rooms and art galleries of many a city and town, in Great Britain and across the world.

And yet, in spite of the apparent cordiality of relations between Earth and Mars, there were many who still mistrusted their planetary neighbours, believing them to harbour secret designs upon Earth and to be waiting patiently for an excuse to bring to bear the full force of their technology against Mankind.

As his carriage made its clattering way along the Mall towards Buckingham Palace, Blackwood found himself wondering whether those people were justified in their suspicions. At the very least, their concerns were understandable: it was not easy to go blithely about one's business, knowing that across eighty-million miles of space there was another inhabited world whose denizens possessed technology far superior to one's own; it was not easy to have to rely for one's continued existence on the benevolence of a superior civilisation.

For some, the very idea that there *was* a civilisation superior to that of the British Empire was difficult to accept, and it was for this reason, as much as any other, that the Martians were so heartily disliked and mistrusted by so many.

Blackwood tried to put these thoughts from his mind as the carriage entered the East Front of the palace, passing beneath the great portico and continuing on into the vast quadrangle beyond. Designed by Edward Blore and built by Thomas Cubitt in 1847, the East Front had been intended to provide more space for the court activities and growing family of Victoria and Albert, and yet, although the edifice possessed a certain monumental grandeur, Blackwood still considered it to be rather austere and foreboding, a vast and immovable barrier which prevented the people from appreciating the beauty of what he thought of as the palace proper.

As the carriage came to a halt, an immaculately liveried footman stepped forward and opened the door. 'Good morning, sir,' he said, as Blackwood stepped down into the crisp air.

'Good morning. I believe Her Majesty is waiting for me.'

'Indeed, sir. If you would be so kind as to follow me...'

The footman led Blackwood into the palace, up the Grand Staircase and along several long and opulently decorated corridors, finally coming to a halt before the door to the Queen's Breakfast Room. He gently knocked three times.

A voice from within said, 'Enter.'

The footman opened the door for Blackwood, who took a deep breath and stepped across the threshold. The room was richly appointed, the warm burgundy of the carpet echoed in the heavy drapes flanking the three tall sash windows. The ceiling was dominated by a single large crystal chandelier that hung eight feet above the floor, while the wallpaper displayed an elegant riot of gold seraglios in the Martian style.

These details were all but lost on Blackwood, however, as he surveyed the strange tableau at the far end of the room. Queen Victoria was seated at her breakfast table in front of the marble fireplace, while at her side stood a Martian, seven feet tall and skeletally thin, his bizarre head enclosed within the pipe-festooned glass bubble of his breathing apparatus, his narrow shoulders enveloped in an iridescent cloak of purple glowspider silk.

'Mr Blackwood,' said Victoria.

Blackwood bowed as the footman silently closed the door behind him.

'Please join us.' The Queen indicated the vacant chair at her breakfast table.

'Thank you, Your Majesty.' Blackwood walked the length of the room, forcing himself to take confident strides while trying to ignore the vague feeling of unease which was gradually increasing in his mind like the burgeoning glow of an alien sunrise.

Victoria was dressed in black, as she had been ever since the death of her beloved Albert in 1861, and Blackwood reflected sadly that her overpowering grief was the one thing that the powerful Martian rejuvenation drugs had been unable to ameliorate. As he approached her, he noted the smooth, white skin of her oval face, the bright petal-like fullness of her small lips, the youthful limpidity of her heavy-lidded eyes, the dark lustre of her hair, undiminished by the severity of the tight bun which she still favoured – and was astonished anew by the potency of the strange chemicals coursing through her veins.

Victoria indicated the Martian, who was still standing perfectly still beside the fireplace. 'Allow me to introduce Petrox Voronezh, Assistant to His Excellency Lunan R'ondd.'

Blackwood bowed, noting the shapes of the metal braces beneath Voronezh's clothing, which enabled him to withstand the higher gravity of Earth. 'An honour, sir,' he said. 'May I offer you my sincerest condolences on the loss of Ambassador R'ondd?'

'You may,' replied Voronezh. 'And they are gratefully received.'

Not for the first time, Blackwood was taken aback by the singular sound produced by the Martian vocal chords. It was a sort of lilting, high-pitched chirrup, not at all in keeping with the being's imposing appearance and bearing. And yet, when one considered the fact that the dominant life form on Mars had evolved from flightless birds, similar in appearance to egrets, one was bound to admit that the sound possessed a certain logical aptness.

'Please be seated, Mr Blackwood,' said Victoria. 'Would you care for some breakfast?'

Blackwood had already glanced at the table and was relieved to see that it contained only toast, butter and marmalade, along with a large silver teapot and two cups and saucers. 'No, thank you, Ma'am. I have already breakfasted.'

'I see. In that case, you will at least join us in a cup of tea.'

Blackwood could see that this was, in fact, a command, and replied, 'I would be most grateful, Your Majesty.'

As she poured the tea, Victoria said, 'I hope you will forgive us for requesting a progress report at such an early stage in your investigation, Mr Blackwood, but as I am sure you will understand, the present circumstances are as delicate as they are tragic.'

'I can assure you, Ma'am, that I am distinctly aware of that unfortunate fact,' replied Blackwood, accepting the cup.

'Excellent. Well, then. Please tell us what, if anything, you have discovered so far.'

Blackwood felt Petrox Voronezh's huge, dark eyes upon him as he described his meeting with Dr Cutter and the pathologist's bizarre conclusions as to the cause of the Ambassador's death.

'Then he *was* assassinated,' said Voronezh when the Special Investigator had finished.

'I'm afraid that is the likeliest explanation for his tragic demise.'

Victoria glanced from Blackwood to Voronezh. 'We hope that you are now pursuing at least one line of enquiry,' she said in a quiet yet stern voice.

Blackwood returned her gaze and gave a very small shudder. There it was, that quality in her eyes, that light which was not a light, as if something strange and rarefied were moving subtly there. He forced himself to concentrate on the business at hand. 'Indeed I am, Ma'am. It seems that the microscopic creatures which proved so lethal to the Ambassador are related in some way to the experiments of a certain Mr Andrew Crosse, an amateur scientist who lives in Somerset...'

'You are saying that a human was responsible for the Ambassador's death,' interrupted Voronezh, leaning over Blackwood.

'No sir, I am not. I feel that it would be premature at this stage to arrive at such a conclusion. I am merely saying that it *appears* that the cause of death is an organism native to the Earth.'

'Who is this Mr Crosse?' demanded Victoria. 'We have never heard of him.'

'It seems there are few who have, Ma'am, for the man is evidently a recluse, an idiosyncrasy made worse by his spurning by the Royal Society some time ago, when he tried to present the results of his experiments in the creation of artificial life to them.'

'*Artificial life?*' echoed Victoria, aghast.

Blackwood nodded. 'It seems that Mr Crosse managed somehow to develop a means of creating microscopic living creatures from inanimate matter, through some electro-chemical process. Dr Cutter discovered very similar organisms in Ambassador R'ondd's breathing apparatus and oesophageal tracts, which absorbed the air before it could reach his pulmonary sacs.'

The Queen quickly recomposed herself, and added, 'Leaving aside the outrageousness of such experiments, why would anyone contrive such a bizarre method of committing murder? It is utterly outlandish!'

Blackwood was about to agree, but before he could do so, Voronezh spoke up again. 'Psychological warfare,' he said.

'I beg your pardon, sir?' said Blackwood.

Voronezh began to pace back and forth across the carpet, his thin arms clasped behind his back, his long legs moving in a strangely elegant way which reminded Blackwood of the motion of the Martian tripods. 'Allow me to explain,' he said. 'There are certain things of which we Martians are profoundly afraid; I suppose that you might call them phobias, pathological terrors which afflict all of us, haunting our racial memory at a deep, primordial level. We have tried to rid ourselves of these fears through various means – psychological and chemical – but they are tenacious, drawing on the strength of accumulated ages, and they will not leave us. One of those fears is that of parasitic infestation...'

Voronezh hesitated, as if he were finding it difficult to speak of this. 'Do please go on,' said Blackwood, fascinated. This was a side of Martians he had never seen before; they seemed so coolly and calmly logical in their thoughts and actions that the thought of their being subject to an irrational fear of any kind was shocking.

'Our scientific research has caused us to conclude that every inhabited world undergoes periods of natural upheaval, during which great extinctions occur. On your own Earth, this has happened several times – to the great saurians which once roamed its primeval forests, for example. Similar extinctions have occurred on our world also, one of which nearly destroyed our entire race.'

'When did this happen?' Blackwood asked.

'A long time ago: many hundreds of thousands of your years. But the memory of those dreadful times is with us still, dwelling like some horrible canker in the depths of our psyches. It was a plague, caused by microscopic larvae which descended upon the surface of our world from the depths of the Æther, and which, once inhaled, grew to maturity within our bodies. I will not describe the symptoms of that affliction, or the manner of the death which was the inescapable outcome of infection. I will say only that our race was all but decimated: our archaeologists estimate that upwards of ninety-five percent of our people perished.'

'Good grief,' said Victoria, casting an uneasy glance at Blackwood. 'Did you ever discover the origin of this horrible scourge?'

'Our astronomers and archaeologists have concluded that it was caused by our world's passage through the tail of a comet in the distant past. We have long speculated on the possibility of comets being bearers of primitive life, or at least the building-blocks of life. We discovered that Mars's proximity to this comet coincided with the period of the great catastrophe, the near-extinction of our race.'

'How *did* your people survive?' Blackwood asked, his voice tinged with appalled sympathy.

'The immune systems of some proved capable of defeating the infestation, and once our planet had passed out of the comet's tail, the rain of death ceased.'

'And I take it the comet has never returned,' said Blackwood, thinking of the horrific consequences of such an event befalling the Earth.

'No, it has not. We assume that its period is long... perhaps it has left our Solar System entirely, never to return. We hope so.'

'And the memory of that dire event has remained with your people, down all the long millennia since it occurred,' said Victoria in wonderment.

'The concept is not nearly so strange as you might believe, Your Majesty,' replied Voronezh. 'Your Mr Darwin explained the true history of your species fifty years ago, and there are memories of your earliest times that exist still in the dimmest recesses of your minds: memories of the caves in which you dwelt, memories of the dangers lurking perpetually beyond your ill-defended thresholds, memories of your own trials and disasters which have given rise to the myths and legends on which your civilisation has been built. And would you deny that there are yet other memories unaccountable in their strangeness, the origin of which has long slipped from the consciousness of your species? I am reminded of words written by your fine essayist, Charles Lamb: "Gorgons, and Hydras, and Chimeras – dire stories of Celaeno and the Harpies may reproduce themselves in the brain of superstition – but they were there before. They are transcripts, types – the archetypes are in us, and eternal." The great catastrophe which befell my race all those hundreds of thousands of years ago has become just such an archetype in the collective consciousness of all Martians. It has been strengthened by the passage of time, and will, I fear, never leave us.'

Blackwood considered this in silence for a long moment. Presently, he looked up at Voronezh. 'So what you are saying is that this was more than a "mere" assassination, if you will forgive the expression. In fact, it was an act of terror, calculated to cause maximum fear and distress among your people.'

'It is the only explanation I can think of to account for such a bizarre method of committing murder, to use Her Majesty's phrase.'

'Be that as it may,' said Victoria, 'the question remains: why? Why commit this act of psychological warfare? Who is behind it, and what are their ultimate intentions?'

Blackwood sighed. 'I regret to say, Ma'am, that I have yet to discover the answer to those questions.'

'Apologies are quite unnecessary, Mr Blackwood,' replied Victoria decisively. 'I am sure Mr Voronezh will join us in thanking you for your work thus far, with which we are quite satisfied.'

Victoria glanced up at Voronezh, and Blackwood couldn't resist doing so as well. The Martian regarded them in silence with his huge, inscrutable eyes.

'Is that not the case, Mr Voronezh?' she persisted.

After a moment's hesitation, he bowed slightly and replied, 'Quite so, Your Majesty... although I would repeat my earlier request to you to allow our own investigators to handle this affair.'

'And we repeat to you our earlier response,' said the Queen forcefully. 'We believe that the answers we seek will be discovered much more quickly by operatives who can blend in with their surroundings, which would, with all due respect, be quite impossible were your own people to become directly involved.'

Voronezh seemed to bridle somewhat at this. He blinked rapidly several times, and his head gave a spasmodic twitch.

'This crime,' continued Victoria, driving her point home, 'was committed on British soil, and it will be investigated – and solved – by the British authorities. Make no mistake, Mr Voronezh, we are quite adamant in this!'

Blackwood waited with more than a little trepidation for the Martian to respond. Presently, Voronezh bowed again, and replied, 'As you wish, Your Majesty. But I have been instructed by my government to inform you that we *do* require a satisfactory conclusion to this lamentable affair. As you yourself have noted, this crime – the first of its kind: the murder of a Martian – took place on British soil, and if the British government cannot solve it and bring the perpetrator to justice, I can assure you that the Martian government will.'

And with that, Petrox Voronezh turned and stalked from the room.

When the door had closed behind him, Victoria looked at her Special Investigator and said, 'Mr Blackwood, we are presented with the greatest crisis in six years of relations between Earth and Mars. For the love of God, sir, get to the bottom of this, and quickly!'

CHAPTER SEVEN:
The Ætherial Virus

It was mid-morning when Blackwood returned to his rooms in Chelsea. His meeting with the Queen and Petrox Voronezh had deeply disturbed him, particularly Voronezh's outburst. He had not expected the Martian to be so forthright in delivering what was in fact a thinly-veiled threat of direct intervention in the affairs of Her Majesty's Government. Victoria had been visibly shocked, and Blackwood sympathised entirely: such was the Martian level of technological development that, were they to decide to make good on their threat, there would be precious little to be done about it.

For his part, Blackwood felt that the ultimatum had been presented a little too quickly: it had been only three days since the Ambassador's death, and already it looked like the Martians were beginning to draw plans against the British Empire. While human relations with the Red Planet were, of course, still in their infancy, the Martians had until now shown themselves to be a very calm and level-headed people, and while the loss of Ambassador R'ondd was a tragedy of the first order, it was most worrying that they had reacted in this way.

And yet, he mused, according to Voronezh, the manner of the Ambassador's death had been intended to create the maximum level of fear and revulsion in the Martian mind, to rekindle the ancient terror the species felt for the notion of parasitical invasion. Voronezh was quite correct: this *was* an act of psychological warfare. Was it any wonder, then, that the Martians should react with such anger, that they should be prepared to act in such a peremptory fashion?

In addition, Blackwood supposed, the intricacies of Martian politics and governance were ill-understood by Humanity, and one could easily imagine the existence of movements and factions which would demand strong and decisive action in response to this crisis. He found himself wondering how long it would be before the Human Ambassador to Mars, Lord Ashbourne, was expelled and diplomatic relations between the two worlds broke down completely.

Heaving a dejected sigh, Blackwood went to his study and sat down at his desk. There was nothing for it but to follow up the single lead he had. He needed more information on this Andrew Crosse fellow, and the nature of the strange experiments he had apparently been conducting at his home in the Quantocks. Blackwood still considered it most unlikely that a recluse living in the wilds of Somerset would have been able to infiltrate the Martian Embassy and place the *Acarus galvanicus* larvae in R'ondd's breathing apparatus. Nor was a motive clearly apparent. Of course, Crosse must have been hurt and angered at his treatment by the Royal Society and may even have harboured the desire for revenge... but why would he visit that revenge upon a man from another world, who had taken no part in his humiliation?

Blackwood decided that there were three possibilities: one, Crosse had placed the larvae in the Ambassador's breathing apparatus; two, he had supplied the larvae to someone else, who had then committed the deed; and three, someone else had succeeded in creating *Acarus galvanicus* independently and had used the creatures to assassinate R'ondd.

In any event, Blackwood felt that a visit to Andrew Crosse was in order. He reached for the brass switch on the side of his new cogitator, flipped it, and was gratified to see a pale mist form in the scrying glass. The Helper had been true to his word: it looked like the contraption was up and running. The mist formed itself into words:

Welcome to the Tara III, powered by De Danann.
What would you like to do today?

Blackwood flexed his fingers, typed on the keyboard PLEASE CONNECT ME TO THE ÆTHER and pressed the carriage return key.

Almost immediately, the message in the scrying glass dissolved into mist again and then formed a new message:

You are now connected to the Æther.
Please type your next command.

Blackwood typed: I WOULD LIKE TO KNOW THE ADDRESS IN SOMERSET OF THE AMATEUR SCIENTIST MR ANDREW CROSSE.

A moment later, more words appeared in the glass:

Mr Andrew Crosse lives at Fyne Court,
in the village of Broomfield, four miles north of Taunton.
Would you care to view some photographs?

Good idea, thought Blackwood. *Won't hurt to get a feel for the layout of the place.* He typed: YES, PLEASE, pressed the carriage return key and sat back in his chair, thinking that cogitators weren't such a bane after all. He certainly couldn't deny the usefulness of this one.

This time, however, the words remained in the scrying glass. *Spoke too soon*, Blackwood thought, and pressed the carriage return again. *Oh, dash it all! Here we go again!*

He was about to press the HELP key, when the words abruptly vanished from the glass, and were replaced with another message in ugly, misshapen characters:

Error ... Error ... Error
Oh dear
Something seems to have gone wrong

'Oh, bugger it!' shouted Blackwood. He reached for the HELP key again. 'Where's that little blighter? I'm going to have it out with him!'

As he glanced into the scrying glass, he saw that the error message had vanished. In its place was a darkness that swirled and eddied strangely. Blackwood had the impression that he was looking into a bottomless pool of murky water, in which indistinct shapes writhed and twisted, flitting in and out of the depths.

'What the deuce...?'

Blackwood made to turn away but found that he could move neither his body nor his eyes, which remained locked upon the scrying glass. The malfunctioning cogitator began to hum; it shook and rattled upon its ornate brass gryphon's feet.

Again Blackwood tried to look away, but it was useless: whatever moved within the glass seemed to have reached out to his mind, defeating his volition, *forcing* him to remain where he was.

Oh no, he thought, as another message began to flicker intermittently in the glass.

*This cogitator has been infected
with an œtherial virus.
You are advised to vacate the area immediately.*

Suddenly, a tendril of writhing darkness swept through the message, transforming it into a swirling mist, which quickly dissipated. In the next instant, the tendril thrust out from the scrying glass and lashed at Blackwood, knocking him backwards off his chair. As he landed on the floor, jarring his shoulder painfully, he felt the temperature in the room drop suddenly by at least ten degrees.

Looking up at the cogitator, he saw more tendrils of darkness whipping back and forth in a horrible, unnatural silence. They appeared to be composed of filthy-looking smoke, in which pinpoints of lurid crimson light flashed and quivered obscenely. He tried to avert his horrified gaze, but it was held fast by the tentacle-like things emerging from the scrying glass.

Blackwood gazed helplessly into the smoke-tendrils and felt the lightless depths of his own mind being laid bare, his darkest thoughts and fears, the black terrors that lurk at the heart of every human being, exposed and molested in revolting ways.

He saw the lightless void of the Æther filled with gibbering stars; he saw spiked chains puncturing the flesh of screaming infants, their mouths filled with writhing maggots; he saw Precambrian oceans churning with the Earth's first terrified consciousness, while Jesus Christ hung from the Cross, laughing hysterically; he saw columns of fire and whirling spheres of ice strung with pulsating vessels. He saw self-contemplating shadows whispering to each other across gulfs of Eternity, dreaming of the hole at the centre of the Universe, and a vast, lipless mouth shouting frantically at the bottom of Space and Time...

Somehow, in the chaos of his terror, Blackwood knew that his mind was being torn apart by the ætherial virus, and that very soon it would be eaten, leaving him a quivering lump of insensate flesh, fodder for the madhouse.

Somehow, Thomas Blackwood knew that the frenzied screams that had begun to issue from his contorted lips were the last thing he would ever hear...

PART TWO

---

*In Which an Agent Provocateur
Reveals Himself*

CHAPTER ONE:
A Charming Rescuer

Thomas Blackwood opened his eyes, unsure of where he was, unsure even of *who* he was. He seemed to recall a dream – no, a *nightmare*, filled with terrible visions of monstrous things writhing upon blasphemous alien landscapes. He recalled something unclean and invisible clawing at his mind – at his very soul – with hideous insistence, and he recalled experiencing the absolute certainty that his mind and soul were about to be devoured...

As he lay there, the memory of his own identity and location gradually returned, and he took in a great heaving breath and raised a hand to his throbbing head. 'Good grief!' he whispered hoarsely. 'What the dickens happened?'

'Mr Blackwood?' said a woman's voice, somewhere off to his left.

'Mrs Butters?' he replied, turning his head.

'I am Lady Sophia Harrington,' said the woman, who had moved to his side. When he tried to sit up, she laid a hand upon his chest. 'No, lie still. You need to rest. You have had a very narrow escape.'

'Escape? From what?'

'From the ætherial virus with which your cogitator was infected.'

At these words, the memories flooded Blackwood's awareness, and he cried, 'The virus! My God, we must get out, now!'

'Hush, Mr Blackwood!' she said sternly, pushing him firmly back onto the couch on which he lay. 'The danger has passed, I assure you.'

'Passed? How?'

Lady Sophia indicated the cogitator sitting on Blackwood's desk. The scrying glass had been smashed. Jagged shards lay upon the desk and the floor around it. 'I broke the glass,' she explained, 'with the small clock on the table by the door. I fear,' she added with a rueful smile, 'that both the clock and the cogitator are beyond repair.'

'Apologies are quite unnecessary, Lady Sophia,' said Blackwood as he slowly sat up, waving away her protests. 'They are a small price to pay for my life and soul. I owe you my profoundest thanks.'

She nodded, and Blackwood regarded her more closely. He guessed her to be somewhere in her late twenties. She was dressed conservatively but elegantly in a grey jacket and long skirt, but it was not her dress which captivated his attention. The concerned frown which clouded her features could not hide the fact that she was one of the most beautiful women he had ever seen. Her dark hair shone with a rich, almost jewel-like lustre, and her deep brown, almond-shaped eyes gleamed with intelligence, compassion and – Blackwood thought – a subtle humour.

Discomfited somewhat by these impressions, Blackwood shook them from his mind and stood up unsteadily.

'I really do think you should lie still for a while longer, sir,' said Sophia. 'To experience something like this...'

'I assure you I'm quite all right,' said Blackwood, harshly. He brought himself up and smiled at his guest. 'Forgive me, your Ladyship; I didn't mean to speak so. But

I dislike being fussed over; I have enough of that from my housekeeper...'

'The Mrs Butters you mentioned?'

'Indeed...'

At that moment, they heard the apartment's front door opening and closing, and bustling footsteps sounding along the corridor leading to Blackwood's study. As if summoned by the very mention of her name, Mrs Butters poked her large, matronly head around the study's half-open door.

'Ooh! Pardon me, Mr Blackwood, I didn't realise you was...' Her voice trailed off as she took in her employer's haggard expression and the shards of glass scattered everywhere. 'Oh, my! Whatever 'as 'appened?'

'Nothing, Mrs Butters,' Blackwood replied. 'A minor accident – do not concern yourself.'

'But there's glass everywhere!' the housekeeper exclaimed. 'An accident it may well be, but minor it most certainly ain't! Oh my, oh my! Now, you take the young lady into the sitting room, while I fetch a dustpan and brush...'

'Mrs Butters,' said Blackwood in a tone which struck Sophia as grimly determined, 'fetch the dustpan and brush by all means, but *I* will clean up the mess.'

The housekeeper looked at her employer askance for a moment and then bustled out of the room, muttering, 'Oh well, 'ave it your own way, Mr Blackwood. I'm quite sure I was only trying to be of service...'

'And bring me the laudanum,' Blackwood called after her, 'for I have a damnable headache!'

Sophia's eyes widened a little at the profanity, and she raised a long-fingered hand to hide the smile that played suddenly upon her lips.

Mrs Butters brought the cleaning implements and a little dark-brown bottle, which Blackwood took off her before ushering her out of the room. He went to a table by the window, on which stood several glasses and decanters, and poured himself a large brandy, to which he added a drop from the little bottle. Sophia watched him in silence. He seemed to have regained his vigour with remarkable speed, considering the horrific ordeal he had just endured. She waited patiently while he downed the brandy in two large gulps.

Without looking at her, he said, 'Let me assure you, Lady Sophia, that I don't usually take this type of refreshment at this time of day.'

'Not at all, Mr Blackwood.'

'But I fear my manners have deserted me. Would you care for some tea, coffee?'

'Thank you, no.'

Blackwood brought forward a chair from a far corner of the room. 'Please sit.'

Sophia nodded her thanks and sat on the chair, while Blackwood, suitably fortified by the brandy and laudanum, busied himself with sweeping up the jagged shards of the cogitator's scrying glass.

As he worked, he said, 'Notwithstanding my gratitude, I must confess I'm puzzled...'

'In short, you're wondering who I am and what I am doing in your rooms,' said Sophia.

Blackwood nodded.

'The doorman let me into the building,' she explained, 'and when I reached the door to your apartments, I heard screaming coming from within. I entered as quickly as I could and found you in here, on the floor, with that... that unspeakable thing emerging from the cogitator's glass. I knew that the only way to sever the link with the Æther was to smash the glass, so I took up the first object that came to hand, and...'

'And saved me from shrieking madness,' said Blackwood with a grim smile. 'Again, thank you. But how did you get in so quickly?'

Sophia opened her purse and withdrew a small metal device from which several sharp prongs sprouted.

'A lock-pick?'

Sophia nodded, a mischievous smile playing upon her lips.

'Intriguing... but not as intriguing as the reason for your being here in the first place.'

The smile faded as Sophia replaced the device in her purse. Lowering her voice to little more than a whisper, she replied, 'I was given your address by Grandfather...'

Blackwood barely hesitated as he swept the last of the shards into the dustpan. 'Who?'

'There is no need to feign ignorance, sir. You know of whom I'm speaking. I came here from the Bureau, at Grandfather's suggestion.'

Blackwood stood up and regarded his guest with a frown. 'If you'll forgive my saying so, Lady Sophia, you are full of surprises.'

'An observation which I shall take as a compliment, Mr Blackwood.'

He gave a slight bow, a sardonic glint in his eye, and was about to say something more, when a slight movement over Sophia's left shoulder caught his attention, and he froze. One of the books on a far shelf had shifted a little, as if nudged forward from behind.

Sophia saw the expression on Blackwood's face. 'Sir...?'

He held up a peremptory hand, pressing one finger to his lips. *Is something there?* he thought. *Could something from that God-forsaken world have remained when the glass was broken?* Suppressing a shudder, he approached the bookshelf with slow, careful steps, his nerves drawn tight as strings, his breath held in his breast.

The book – a slim leather-bound edition of Bulwer-Lytton – was at his eye level. Reaching out, he placed his index finger on top of the spine and pulled the book suddenly from the shelf.

There was a miniature explosion of tiny wings and lilac haze, and a loud *thrrrrrrr!* as a diminutive, human-like figure flew from the shelf with a raucous screech.

Shocked, Blackwood recoiled halfway across the room, nearly colliding with Sophia, who had stood up and was watching him intently. '*What the deuce?*' he shouted.

'A denizen of Faerie!' exclaimed Sophia in delight.

'It's not my fault, sir!' cried the little man as he whirred about the room in the utmost agitation. 'Please don't blame me! There was nothing we could do!'

'The Helper!' cried Blackwood. 'What happened to my cogitator, you little oaf?'

'Mr Blackwood!' said Sophia. 'Kindly lower your voice. The poor little thing is half out of his mind with fear.'

'He'll have a good deal to be fearful *of* if I get my hands on him. Come here, you little blighter!'

'Mr Blackwood, notwithstanding the fact that this is your home, I assure you I will hear no more talk like that.'

Blackwood stopped trying to catch the little man, who was still flitting here and there in panic, and turned to look at his guest. She was standing with hands on hips, regarding him with furious, unblinking eyes, her lips set in grim determination. The Special Investigator felt his own resolve draining out of him in the face of this striking example of womanly fortitude, and he realised, belatedly, that he must have cut a quite ridiculous figure, hopping and jumping around the room like a boy chasing a butterfly.

'My apologies, Lady Sophia.'

'That's better,' she said, and raised her eyes to the ceiling, where the Helper was still fluttering. 'Come here, little fellow,' she called gently. 'I won't hurt you.'

'It's not you I'm worried about!' cried the little man.

'He won't hurt you either... *will* you, Mr Blackwood?'

Blackwood sighed. 'No... no, of course not. Come down from there, there's a good chap.'

After several moments' hesitation, the Helper descended from the ceiling, alighting in Sophia's outstretched hand. 'There now,' she said with a smile of great affection. 'I take it you are from Mr Blackwood's cogitator?'

'That I am, ma'am,' replied the little man with a low, theatrical bow.

'He's the Helper,' said Blackwood. 'Although I'm bound to say that appears to be something of a misnomer.'

'If you please, sir!' said Sophia in an exasperated tone. 'Now, my little friend, won't you tell us what happened?'

'Begging your pardon, ma'am, but I'm awful parched. Do you think I might prevail upon you for a thimbleful of milk?'

'Of course. Mr Blackwood, would you be so kind?'

Blackwood sighed and stalked from the room, wondering whether the Helper might also like a slice or two of roast beef and half a dozen oysters to go with it. Sophia and the Helper listened to him exchange a few curt words with Mrs Butters, who was in the kitchen preparing the vegetables for dinner.

'It wasn't my fault!' said the Helper in a frightened whisper.

'Hush now,' Sophia replied in a gentle voice.

Blackwood returned to the study, holding one of his housekeeper's thimbles between thumb and forefinger. He handed it to the Helper, who held it before him and breathed in deeply. He thanked Blackwood and handed the thimble back to him. Blackwood noted that the milk was still in it, although it appeared to have taken on a greenish tinge, as if it had suddenly gone sour.

'That is how faeries drink in our world, Mr Blackwood,' Sophia explained.

'I see,' he said, placing the thimble carefully on his desk beside the ruined cogitator. 'Now, my good chap,' he continued. 'Perhaps you could tell us what happened here.'

'First,' said Sophia, 'tell us your name, for I am quite certain it is not "Helper".'

'Indeed not, ma'am. My name is Shanahan.'

'A fine name,' Sophia smiled. 'It means "ancient" in the Gaelic tongue, does it not?'

'That it does, my lady!' exclaimed Shanahan, clearly delighted. 'And may I enquire as to your own name?'

'My name is Sophia.'

'A pleasure to make your acquaintance!' said Shanahan, bowing again.

Blackwood raised his eyes to the ceiling and gave a loud sigh. He felt his headache returning and considered another drop of laudanum... and then considered downing the whole bottle. 'If the pleasantries are concluded,' he said, 'might we now return to the matter at hand?'

'Very well, sir.' With a brief flutter of his dragonfly wings, Shanahan sat himself down in the palm of Sophia's hand. 'We completed the initialising procedure on the cogitator yesterday, just after you left, sir. All was well and in good order with the machine, and so we returned to the realm of Faerie to await your summons...'

'My summons?'

'Indeed, sir. We don't spend *all* our time inside a cogitator. Only when the machine is switched on do we return and resume our duties within the processing chamber, according to the terms of our contract.'

'I see,' said Blackwood. 'So how did my machine become infected with an ætherial virus? I thought you fellows had taken great pains to avoid such an occurrence.'

'We did, sir, I assure you! But the one that came through when you connected to the Æther... well, that was a monstrously powerful one. It flooded the processing chamber and swept my colleagues back to Faerie in an instant! There was nothing we could do in the face of its hideous potency.'

'Why weren't you swept back to Faerie along with the others?' asked Sophia.

'I managed to escape into this room through the maintenance hatch in the side of the cogitator. I couldn't allow myself to be sent back... I had to stay here. I couldn't leave Mr Blackwood!'

'You couldn't leave Mr Blackwood,' Sophia echoed, shaking her head at her host in such a sad and admonitory fashion that he averted his eyes in embarrassment. 'Even though you could do nothing to help, and might very well have been destroyed along with him... you stayed.'

'That I did, ma'am,' Shanahan replied, with a furtive glance at Blackwood.

'I think perhaps you owe our little friend here an apology, sir,' said Sophia.

Blackwood opened his mouth to protest, caught the look in Sophia's eyes, and thought better of it. In any event, the odd little chap *had* shown remarkable courage. 'Oh, very well,' he sighed. 'I apologise for my earlier behaviour, Mr Shanahan. I acted peremptorily, and without due thought to the reality of the situation.'

Shanahan stood up and bowed to him. 'Your apology is gladly accepted, sir!'

'Can you tell me what kind of virus came through?'

'From the looks of it, sir, it was a djinn, summoned by means of Arabian Star Magick.'

Sophia gasped, and put her free hand up to her mouth.

'Good grief,' said Blackwood, glancing at the dustpan containing the shards of glass. 'Star Magick... the most powerful and dangerous form of magick known to man.'

'And it was meant for you, sir,' said Shanahan.

Blackwood glanced at him. 'What? How do you know that?'

'This was no ordinary ætherial virus, sir. The djinn was summoned with the express purpose of destroying you, by someone with a profound knowledge of Arabian Star Magick. I know about these things, Mr Blackwood. I know what I'm talking about.'

'Yes,' Blackwood murmured. 'Yes, I'm sure you do.'

'But who would want to do such a beastly thing to you?' asked Sophia, appalled.

Blackwood gave a humourless laugh. 'In my line of work, Lady Sophia, one makes more than one's fair share of enemies... although I must admit that the timing is most intriguing.'

'The case you're working on at the moment,' Sophia said.

'Yes. Has Grandfather told you about it?'

'He has. And it is the very reason I came to you today.'

Blackwood stood up. 'We clearly have much to discuss, your Ladyship, but we will have to do so *en route*.'

'*En route*? To where?'

'To Cottingley's Cogitators of Mayfair.'

'Are you... going to tell them what happened here?' asked Shanahan tremulously.

'Of course I am, sir! If I can get to the bottom of this, I may be a step closer to a solution to the other matter.' Blackwood looked at the Helper, and continued in a softer tone, 'But you may be assured, Mr Shanahan, that I will comment favourably on your conduct.'

Shanahan heaved a tiny sigh of relief. 'I'm much obliged to you. Things wouldn't have gone well with me, otherwise.'

'How so?' asked Sophia.

'It never looks good when a Helper loses an operator. In fact, when it does happen, the chances of keeping one's job are slim to say the least – in *this* world, that is.'

'Then we shall do our very best to ensure your continued employment,' said Sophia, rising from her chair. 'In the meantime, what do you wish to do?'

'I would like to come with you, if I may,' said Shanahan. 'In fact, I really should show my face there, after what has happened.' He looked at the ruined cogitator and shook his head despondently.

Blackwood looked from Shanahan to Sophia. 'Very well,' he sighed.

CHAPTER TWO:
Cottingley's of Mayfair

Blackwood was surprised when Shanahan declined to join them in the hansom. However, when the Helper said that he would go on ahead and would see them at Cottingley's, promptly vanishin in a puff of lilac smoke, Blackwood remembered that faeries did not need to take cabs.

He helped Sophia up the steps and joined her on the seat, calling their destination up to the driver as he did so. As the cab pulled away from the curb and began its clattering journey to Mayfair, Blackwood placed the large black valise which he had procured from his dressing room, and into which he had put the cogitator, on his knee and said, 'Perhaps you should tell me a little about your conversation with Grandfather and your involvement with the present matter, your Ladyship. And let us converse quietly,' he added, indicating the unseen cab driver with an upward glance.

'Very well, Mr Blackwood. For some time, we at the Society for Psychical Research have been investigating the activities of the villain known as Spring-Heeled Jack...'

Blackwood immediately recalled his conversation with Peter Meddings the previous day and made a dismissive sound.

'I'm well aware that many people consider Jack to be no more than a figment of ill-educated and over-active imaginations,' Sophia continued pointedly. 'But I can assure you, sir, that he is quite real and every bit as evil and dangerous as the reports claim.'

'Indeed,' muttered Blackwood.

'In fact, I can personally attest to his savagery...'

Blackwood glanced at her. 'Good grief, my dear – you don't mean to say...'

She shook her head. 'No, I have not personally suffered at the hands of the brute, but I have spoken to a family of good standing, whose house was laid siege to by him only yesterday evening.'

'Really?'

'Really.'

Blackwood decided that it would probably be better to humour the young lady than to contradict her openly, so he asked her to continue.

Sophia related the dreadful incident which had befallen the Alsops and the interview she had conducted with Mr Alsop and two of his daughters. 'On examining the wreckage of the front door,' she concluded, 'I discovered a fragment of very strange metal...'

'What do you mean "strange"?'

'It was – how shall I put it? – *iridescent*; its surface displayed very unusual colours. In fact, it was quite unlike anything I have ever seen.'

'And you believe that this metal fragment came from one of Spring-Heeled Jack's talons,' said Blackwood.

'Indeed I do.'

'Where is the fragment now?'

'At the headquarters of the SPR. It is at present undergoing analysis by metallurgists and psychometrists.'

'Psychometrists? Then you hope to ascertain something of the object's nature and history through psychic means?'

'We do.'

Blackwood nodded. 'I must commend you on your thoroughness, Lady Sophia.'

She threw him a sidelong glance and smiled. 'Thank you, Mr Blackwood.'

'Now, perhaps you would tell me what all this has to do with the assassination of the Martian Ambassador, which, after all, is what you came to see me about.'

'I must admit that coming to see you was not my idea,' she replied. 'My intention in contacting the Bureau was to alert them to the possibility that we are not dealing with some run-of-the-mill ruffian, and that the singular abilities Jack is alleged to possess are quite genuine, as evidenced by the shard of metal which apparently came from one of his talons. Grandfather is intrigued at the possibility that the creature is not of this world and suggested that I join you in your own investigation of Lunan R'ondd's assassination.'

Blackwood grunted and shook his head. 'Just like Grandfather...'

Sophia gave him an enquiring look.

'It's his habit to make tenuous connections in complex cases such as this,' he explained. 'Grandfather has a way of throwing apparently disparate items into the pot, giving them a good stir and seeing what comes out at the end. It's a curious method, but I must allow that it's given capital results in the past.'

'Intuition can be a powerful tool,' Sophia agreed. Her voice had suddenly grown strange and dreamy; she turned from her companion and gazed through the window at the passing streets.

Blackwood glanced at her, noting that she seemed to have become a little distracted. He wondered at the cause but decided not to pursue it. 'Timing is everything,' he continued, 'and I learned long ago not to believe in coincidence. The death of the Ambassador, the infiltration of my cogitator by an ætherial virus, your evidence for the reality of Spring-Heeled Jack and the possibility that he is not a human being... these things may or may not be connected, but I believe that we should proceed under the assumption that they may well be.'

'Then you don't mind my accompanying you?' said Sophia, her voice still distant.

'Not at all, my dear. The Society for Psychical Research and Her Majesty's Bureau for Clandestine Affairs have collaborated on many investigations in the past. There is no reason why they should not do so now – especially since Grandfather has deemed it appropriate that they should. I shall be most interested to see the results of the analysis of that metallic fragment. When do you think they will become available?'

Sophia didn't reply, and Blackwood turned to her. 'Lady Sophia?'

She glanced suddenly at him, as if startled out of a profound dream. 'Oh... forgive me, Mr Blackwood. My mind was elsewhere. You were saying?'

'About the metal fragment: when may we expect the results of the analysis?'

'In a day or so.'

Blackwood hesitated before asking, 'Are you all right, your Ladyship?'

'I'm quite all right, thank you, Mr Blackwood. And since we are to be working together, I believe that titles may be dispensed with. I should appreciate it if you would call me Sophia.'

Taken aback, Blackwood replied, 'But we have known each other for barely an hour...'

'All the same, I would consider it a kindness.'

'Very well... er... Sophia. And you must call me Thomas.'

She nodded her thanks and returned her attention to the passing streets, again lost in reverie, leaving Blackwood to ponder the rather curious behaviour of his new acquaintance.

*

Cottingley's Cogitators Limited was situated in Albermarle Street, between one of several art galleries lining the thoroughfare and the Albermarle Club. The club had become rather less fashionable in the four years since the Marquess of Queensberry left his infamous calling card for Oscar Wilde while the latter was holidaying in Monte Carlo with Bosie. Following the conviction of the unfortunate genius for gross indecency, the Albermarle Club had begun its steady decline into disrepute and now claimed only a fraction of its previous members.

As Blackwood and Sophia alighted from the cab, a paperboy walked past on the other side of the road, shouting, '*Read all abart it! Full steam ahead for the Greater Exhibition! Martian exhibits arrive at New Crystal Palace! Read all abart it!*'

'Will you be attending the Greater Exhibition, Mr Blackwood?' asked Sophia, who seemed to have recomposed herself.

'Oh, I should think so,' he replied. 'Assuming, of course, that we can solve the present problem before then.'

'I must say that it does promise to put the original in the shade,' Sophia observed as she approached the shop, which was small and quaint, with a single bay window beside the entrance. Both the door and the window frames were painted a rather fetching shade of bright green. Through the window could be seen the establishment's wares, arranged on several tiers of polished oak. There were keyboards, scrying glasses and processing engines, all of which displayed admirable craftsmanship. Sophia peered in with undisguised admiration.

'How marvellous!' she said. 'One wonders if there are any limits to science.'

'There are certainly no limits to the dangers it may invoke,' observed Blackwood as he opened the door and held it for her.

As they entered, the sales clerk looked up from his task of polishing a scrying glass and said, 'Good morning to you, sir, madam. How may I be of assistance?'

Blackwood took in the interior of the shop in a single glance – the counter at which the clerk sat, the heavy oak shelves displaying more cogitating equipment that lined the walls, the open doorway in the far wall, leading to a narrow ascending staircase – and replied, 'Good morning to you. I have a complaint to make, regarding a machine I purchased from this establishment yesterday.' He hoisted the valise onto the counter and opened it.

The sales clerk, a short, middle-aged man with a receding hairline and a long, hooked nose which gave him the appearance of a tropical bird that had fallen upon hard times, took the jeweller's loupe from his eye and placed it on the counter beside the scrying glass. 'A complaint, sir?' he asked with a hint of incredulity.

'Yes,' said Blackwood. 'A complaint. My Tara III nearly drove me insane this morning. It became infected with an ætherial virus of a particularly dangerous and malignant type, which very nearly devoured my mind.'

The clerk swallowed loudly. 'Good Lord,' he stammered, peering reluctantly into the valise. 'Would... would sir and madam mind waiting for a moment, while I fetch the proprietor?'

'Not at all, my good man,' Blackwood replied in a measured tone.

The clerk hurried through the door and up the staircase and returned a few moments later, followed by a squat, rosy-cheeked woman in a rather loud pink dress, frosted like a vulgar confection with profusions of white lace around the neck and arms. After introducing herself as Mrs Daphne Cottingley, she said, 'Mr Jenkins informs me that you have had an unfortunate experience with one of our products... a Tara III?'

'Quite so,' said Blackwood.

'And you are unharmed, sir?' Mrs Cottingley enquired, with what appeared to be quite genuine concern.

'Pretty much, no thanks to your contraption.'

Mrs Cottingley produced a fan from somewhere within the folds of her dress, and proceeded to waft it to and fro with agitated flicks of her wrist. 'Oh my,' she said. 'This has never happened with a Tara III, I can assure you: the De Danann control system was designed to prevent such malfunctions...'

At this, Sophia nudged Blackwood with her elbow.

'What? Oh yes. I should inform you that the De Danann Helper showed remarkable courage and fortitude in trying to fend off the virus, but it was far too powerful for him to cope with. I, er, just thought I'd mention that.' He glanced at Sophia, who gave him a barely-perceptible smile.

'Well,' said Mrs Cottingley, who appeared to relax somewhat, 'the De Danann Helpers are renowned for their conscientiousness.'

'Be that as it may,' Blackwood said with some force, not wanting to lose ground to the proprietor, 'the fact remains that you sold me a dangerous contrivance. Need I remind you that other purveyors of cogitating equipment have fallen foul of the law for the same reason?'

The rosy hue faded somewhat from Mrs Cottingley's cheeks as she replied, 'Oh, but sir! We pride ourselves on the safety of our products, and I can provide you with ample testimony to the quality of both the Tara III *and* the De Danann control system.'

'And *I* can provide *you* with ample testimony to the contrary. The Helper informed me that the thing which came through from the Æther was an Arabian djinn.'

'Oh, Gawd!' exclaimed the sales clerk.

'Shut up, Jenkins!' snapped Mrs Cottingley. 'May I ask where the Helper is now, sir?'

With a soundless puff of lilac smoke, Shanahan appeared in the air over Sophia's left shoulder. 'Er, here I am, ma'am,' he said.

'Mr Shanahan! What the dickens were you playing at, allowing a djinn into the gentleman's cogitator? Explain yourself!'

Sophia bridled at this, and stepped forward. 'You may be unaware, madam, that an Arabian djinn is one of the most powerful astral entities known. This poor little fellow and his colleagues didn't stand a chance against it. The fault *must* lie with the hardware, with the cogitator itself.'

Mrs Cottingley drew herself up to her full (not considerable) height and pursed her lips in annoyance. 'Well, then! If that is the young lady's hypothesis, we can certainly test it.' She glared up at Sophia, turned back to the counter, took the cogitator from the valise and began to examine it. 'Yes,' she muttered, 'we'll soon get to the bottom of this.'

As the others watched, she opened the door covering the processing chamber and peered inside. 'Ah, yes, that's fine... uhum, nothing out of place there... that's all in order as well... this is all ship-shape and Bristol fashion...'

Blackwood tapped his foot on the floor and glanced at Sophia, who shrugged at him.

'Oh, just a moment,' said Mrs Cottingley. 'Jenkins, hand me your loupe.'

The clerk handed the eyeglass to his employer, who placed it in her right eye and bent close to the opening. 'Now this is rather odd...'

'What is?' asked Blackwood, stepping forward.

'The dream catcher appears to have been removed from the astral funnel.'

'What the devil is an astral funnel?' demanded Blackwood.

'It's the main conduit through which information from the Akashic Records enters the cogitator,' explained Shanahan. 'The dream catcher is designed to prevent the entry of malicious influences from the ætherial realms, or at least to delay them long enough for us to deal with them.'

'Could the dream catcher have prevented the djinn from infecting the cogitator?' asked Sophia.

'Most doubtful,' Shanahan replied, 'but it might have delayed it long enough for one of us to leave the machine and smash the scrying glass, just as you did, you Ladyship, which would sever the link with the Æther, and prevent the entity from fully entering this world.'

'In short,' said Blackwood, 'you're saying that this machine was sabotaged.'

'Precisely, sir.'

'By whom?'

Mrs Cottingley turned from the counter to face them. 'The answer is quite obvious, my good sir. By one of the De Dananns... although I must admit that the thought is absolutely outrageous.'

'I must agree with Mrs Cottingley,' said Shanahan ruefully, 'on both counts.'

The proprietor shook her head and sighed. Suddenly, she seemed on the point of tears. 'This will be the ruin of Cottingley's.'

'Not necessarily,' said Blackwood.

She glanced at him, a glint of hope in her eye.

'There is every reason to suppose that this was a one-off event.'

'Do you think so, sir?' said Mrs Cottingley. 'May I enquire as to how you–'

'No, you may not. For now, I think we will leave the matter here, and I will take no further action against your establishment.' Blackwood turned to Shanahan. 'How would you like to take a little sabbatical from your duties here?'

'A sabbatical, sir?'

'I may have some use for you, and I assure you I'll make it worth your while.'

'Why, I'd be delighted, sir!' enthused Shanahan, as he flitted back and forth in front of Blackwood's eyes. 'That is... if Mrs Cottingley has no objections.'

'Oh, I'm sure she'll have none at all... will you, madam?'

'None whatsoever, sir,' said the proprietor, still counting her blessings.

'Then it's settled. Come along!'

And with that, Blackwood turned and strode out of Cottingley's Cogitators Limited.

CHAPTER THREE:
On the West Country Omnibus

'What kind of work did you have in mind for me, sir?' asked Shanahan, who had seen fit to perch himself on Blackwood's left shoulder as they sat in the cab, headed for Paddington Station.

'Lady Sophia and I are going on a trip to Somerset, to interview a man who is almost certainly a material witness in this case – if not a direct participant in it – and while we are there, I would like you to return to Faerie and see if you can dig up some information on what happened to the dream catcher in my cogitator.' Blackwood craned his neck to look at the Helper, feeling like a pirate conversing with his parrot. 'If it *was* sabotage, I want to know who did it, and on whose orders. Can you handle that, Mr Shanahan?'

'Indubitably, sir!' cried the Helper.

'One other thing: how will I call you if I need you?'

Shanahan shrugged. 'Simply say my name, with your voice or your mind, and ask me to come, and I shall arrive forthwith.'

'Very good. Off you go.'

Shanahan bowed, launched himself from Blackwood's shoulder and vanished through the roof of the cab.

Sophia glanced at the Special Investigator and noted his pensive frown. 'If someone did arrange for your cogitator to be damaged, what does it mean?' she asked. 'What is the larger picture that is being painted?'

'I've been wondering that, myself, Sophia, and I don't like where my train of thought is leading,' Blackwood replied. 'The timing of all this is strange – off-kilter, you might say. I have no doubt that I was targeted for death because of my involvement in the investigation of Lunan R'ondd's assassination. And yet, I bought the cogitator a few hours *before* Grandfather summoned me and put me on the case.'

'That *is* rather odd,' Sophia agreed.

'Shanahan said that the De Danann operators don't stay in cogitators while they're switched off...'

'That's right: they only return from Faerie when the machines are activated.'

'So it would presumably have been a simple matter for one of the De Dananns – or an entity masquerading as a De Danann – to enter the machine after Shanahan and his colleagues had completed the set up procedure, and remove the dream catcher, thus leaving the cogitator vulnerable to infection.'

'And presumably,' added Sophia, 'the djinn was then purposely directed at the machine, with the intention of destroying your mind.'

'Quite so.' Blackwood and Sophia looked at each other. 'Still doesn't quite add up, does it?'

'Unless...' said Sophia, and then gave a small gasp. 'Unless someone knew that you would be assigned to the case, which means–'

'Which means that there is a traitor in Her Majesty's Bureau of Clandestine Affairs!' said Blackwood in a grim, bitter voice. 'It's the only explanation that makes sense. The events must have run like this: on the evening of the twenty-second, Lunan R'ondd dies during the banquet at Buckingham Palace; a post-mortem is performed the following day, during which the *Acarus galvanicus* larvae are discovered in his body; while I am buying my cogitator, Grandfather decides to put me on the case and sends for me; while I am away from my rooms, Shanahan and the other De Dananns complete the set up procedure and leave the cogitator; sometime thereafter, *something* enters the machine and removes the dream catcher.'

'You say "something", but couldn't it have been a person who broke into your apartments and sabotaged your cogitator?'

'I think not, for although you yourself have proved how easily a lock can be picked, I have ways of detecting unauthorised entry to my home: telltale signs which I will not go into now. Suffice it to say that when I returned from Buckingham Palace this morning, I saw no signs of a break-in. But regarding the train of events I have described, the only hypothesis that can account for them is that someone at the Bureau knew of Grandfather's intention to give the case to me.'

'Do you have any idea who that could be?' asked Sophia.

'Peter Meddings.'

'Who?'

'The man who delivered Grandfather's summons to me. Meddings obviously knew that the Bureau was about to begin an investigation, and he clearly guessed the reason for his own assignment.'

Sophia sat quietly for a moment, digesting this. 'Do you think that Meddings could be the one who murdered the Ambassador?' she wondered.

Blackwood shook his head. 'I doubt it. I suspect that he is merely somebody's flunky. As to who that somebody is...

well, it's certainly someone with a profound knowledge of the occult.'

'Including Arabian Star Magick.'

'Indeed.'

'But surely we are headed in the wrong direction!' exclaimed Sophia. 'Surely we should apprehend this Meddings fellow immediately and question him.'

Blackwood smiled at his companion. 'I admire your readiness to spring to action, but I don't believe that would be wise – at least, not yet. Assuming that Meddings is indeed culpable in this affair, it may be better to let him believe he is not under suspicion for a little while longer, during which time we may be able to gather more evidence against him.'

'And in the meantime,' added Sophia, 'Mr Shanahan may be able to come up with additional information.'

'Quite right. I will, however, telegraph Grandfather from Paddington, to let him know of our suspicions and to ask him to keep an eye on Mr Meddings.'

'Wouldn't you run the risk of alerting Meddings by doing so?'

'I think not. Grandfather has his own telegraph machine in his office, to which no one else has access – not even Miss Ripley...'

'Miss Ripley? Grandfather's secretary?'

'The same.'

'Is it not possible that *she* might be the traitor?'

Blackwood guffawed at this, then recovered himself and apologised. 'Forgive me, Sophia. It's *possible*, of course, but most unlikely, I assure you: Miss Ripley has served the Bureau faithfully and admirably for many years.'

'I see,' Sophia smiled. 'In that case, you must forgive me for impugning her good character.'

'Not at all, my dear. We must consider all options, after all.' And then Blackwood hesitated, and fell silent. *Yes*, he thought, *we must consider all options...*

*

As the cab approached Paddington Station, Blackwood and Sophia caught a glimpse of the great, grey bulk of an intercity omnibus rising above the platforms. Its pillar-like legs were folded up around it, giving it the appearance of a gargantuan insect, poised and ready to pounce upon some unsuspecting prey. The rear quarter of the hull displayed an advertisement which depicted a pair of Martians relaxing in armchairs in front of a roaring fire, each holding a large mug in his long-fingered hand. Above them, huge red letters declared: MARTIANS LOVE BOVRIL!

'Is that the West Country omnibus?' asked Sophia.

'It is,' replied Blackwood as he fished in his pocket for the cab fare.

'I must confess I'm rather looking forward to this journey. I do so love travelling by walking machine,' she cried as she opened the door and descended to the street with an elegant little jump, leaving Blackwood to hurry after her. 'I really should do it more often.'

Although he generally disliked frivolity, Blackwood found himself smiling at Sophia's sudden girlish enthusiasm, finding it as charming as it was surprising. He didn't particularly care for this new mode of transportation himself; he didn't feel it was quite natural to travel two hundred feet above the landscape, like some bizarre circus performer on stilts. Nevertheless, it would get them to Somerset in pretty short order.

The West Country omnibus was due to depart within a few minutes, so while Blackwood stepped into the telegraph office to send a message to Grandfather, Sophia bought two first class return tickets to Taunton. They met at the end of the platform and walked to the foot of the wrought iron gangway leading up into the main hull of the vehicle.

As they climbed up the gangway, along with the few other remaining passengers, Blackwood took in the huge hydraulic pistons protruding from their housings in the disc-shaped engine section beneath the hull. They looked to him like the components of a steam locomotive that had been designed by an opium addict and then constructed by a maniacal engineer with delusions of grandeur. Above the engine section was the complex gimbal assembly which kept the hull stable while the machine was walking. Above that, the lozenge-shaped hull itself, one hundred feet long and sixty wide, loomed with a weird magnificence against the overcast sky.

The passengers entered through the main hatch behind the gimbals, and Blackwood and Sophia followed them through and onto E Deck, the lowest level, which contained the control room and various items of electrical equipment pertaining to the running of the vehicle. They then climbed a wide spiral staircase, ascending through D Deck, which was given over to luggage storage, and then C and B Decks, which contained third and second class accommodation respectively, before terminating on A Deck, which contained the first class seating, restaurant and observation gallery.

Blackwood would quite happily have settled into his seat and not moved for the duration of the journey, but he took note of Sophia's expression and suggested that they observe their departure through the wide promenade windows at the front of the cabin. She readily agreed, and they walked past the restaurant section, in which a couple of liveried waiters were flitting between tables, laying out cutlery ready for lunch.

As they stood looking out at the rooftops around Paddington, they heard a faint hum from somewhere far below in the depths of the vehicle, which rose steadily in pitch until it was a faint but continuous whine. They both took hold of the brass railing beneath the windows as the floor lurched slightly, and Sophia gave a small gasp as the vast metal legs to the left and right of the observation gallery slowly unfolded, dropping out of view as the great walking machine rose upon them.

'It's like being in an airship that is somehow alive,' whispered Sophia, as she looked down upon streets and buildings that rapidly diminished in size until they looked like a child's toys.

'Hmm,' said Blackwood, as the machine moved off from the station, its rubber-shod feet treading with uncanny delicacy along the shallow trenches of the omnibus lanes, with a barely audible *WHUMP... WHUMP.*

'Have you ever been to Mars, Thomas?' Sophia asked, her eyes now fixed upon the horizon.

'No, although I must confess that I am tempted to make a trip there one of these days. Have you?'

She shook her head. 'Although, I also would like to go. One can barely imagine the wonders to be discovered there.' Her gaze drifted up towards the sky. 'And one wonders how many other worlds are inhabited... out there in the Æther, and what *their* inhabitants are like.'

'It's an intriguing question,' Blackwood conceded, noting once more the strange, dreamy quality in his companion's voice. 'There may well be many inhabited worlds out there in the dark depths of the firmament. After all, our own Solar System possesses two...'

'Only two?' Sophia murmured.

'I beg your pardon, my dear?'

She smiled at him, but the expression was small, sad and somehow cryptic. 'Nothing. Shall we take luncheon?'

They entered the restaurant section, where a few other first class passengers were already seated, and were shown to a table by a waiter. Hanging from the curved ceiling above them, a small chandelier tinkled faintly and swayed almost imperceptibly as the walking machine strode across southwest London.

As Blackwood and Sophia perused the menu, a large, horn-shaped loudspeaker mounted above the forward observation window crackled to life, and a voice said, 'Good afternoon, ladies and gentlemen. Welcome aboard the 12.45 West Country omnibus to Plymouth. I am Captain Gordon Cavendish, and my co-pilot is Lieutenant Duncan Broadbent. We shall be calling at Woking, Basingstoke, Andover, Warminster, Glastonbury, Taunton, Tiverton and Launceston, before reaching Plymouth at 3.15 this afternoon. We do hope you will enjoy your journey with us. Thank you.'

A waiter approached with a bottle of mineral water, which he opened and poured for them both. 'Are sir and madam ready to order?' he asked.

'I think I'll have the Indian Omelette,' said Sophia. Blackwood glanced at her, and felt the blood draining from his face.

She returned his look, and frowned. 'Thomas... are you all right?'

'Yes... yes, I'm fine,' he replied. *Oh God*, he thought. *Eggs!*

'And sir's choice?' said the waiter.

'I, er, I'll have the lemon sole. And a bottle of your best white wine, whatever it is.'

'Very good, sir,' said the waiter, and left.

'Are you quite sure you're all right?' Sophia persisted, her frown deepening into genuine concern. 'You have gone quite pale.'

'A very slight case of motion sickness. I get it sometimes on trains and walking machines. Please do not be concerned; it will pass.'

Blackwood decided to try to take his mind away from what was being prepared in the kitchen. 'Tell me, Sophia: how did you become involved with the Society for Psychical Research?'

'I joined the Society five years ago, at the invitation of the President, Sir William Crookes, who is a great friend to the Harrington family.'

'I know Sir William; he is a fine man and a brilliant scientist.'

'Indeed.'

'And so, in five years, you have risen to become the Society's Secretary. A most impressive achievement. I was under the impression, however, that Dr Henry Armistead was Secretary...'

'Dr Armistead left a few months ago to pursue a lecturing opportunity at Brown University in Providence, Rhode Island. Sir William did me the honour of offering the vacant position to me.'

'I see,' Blackwood replied, regarding her carefully.

Sophia returned his gaze, and again offered that small, cryptic smile. 'Let me guess: you are finding it difficult to believe that a woman of my tender years should rise so quickly through the ranks of such an august institution as the SPR, even under the patronage of its President.'

Blackwood gave an embarrassed laugh. 'Well, I wouldn't have put it in so many words, myself...'

'It is a reasonable question,' Sophia replied levelly, 'and since we are to be working together, I believe it deserves a reasonable and truthful response, and so I shall tell you a little of my history. How much do you know of the Harrington family?'

'I was aware of the name, of course, but beyond that, I'm afraid I must admit to almost total ignorance – although I naturally read of the mysterious disappearance of Lord Percival Harrington some ten years ago.'

Sophia nodded. 'He was my father. A natural explorer and hunter, his fascination with the world and curiosity as to its remotest locations consumed him, and it directed the course of his entire life. I inherited that love of strange and distant places, and by the time I was eighteen, I had accompanied him on numerous safaris in Africa and India and had become passably acquainted with the singular lands of the Far East.'

'Did your mother accompany you on these excursions?' asked Blackwood.

Sophia took a sip of her water. 'Although my parents were devoted to each other, my mother never shared this wanderlust, and so she remained on the estate while my father and I were off on our various travels.' She smiled. 'Never once did Mama begrudge us our interests, and when we returned, she would always ply us for stories of our experiences in far regions.

'However, as time passed, I began to grow weary of oppressive heat, of sand and dust and tropical forests. I have always loved the snows of winter in England, its deep frosts, the immaculate stillness of its coldest mornings when the very world seems carved in alabaster, and I suggested to my father that I should like to explore the pristine lands of the Arctic north. He readily agreed and straight away began to make arrangements for a hunting trip to the Canadian wilderness, which he himself had not visited for many years.

'We set sail on my eighteenth birthday. I still recall the excitement I felt at the thought of pitting myself against the implacable, frozen world that awaited us.' Sophia hesitated as the memories returned, and Blackwood was struck by the expression of profound sadness that had crept upon her features. 'Little did I know how implacable that strange world would turn out to be.' She stopped again and took another sip of water, and Blackwood had the impression that she would much rather be drinking something a little stronger at that moment.

The waiter arrived with the wine, and Blackwood thanked him and waved him away before he could pour it.

He filled their wine glasses himself as he said to her, 'That was when your father disappeared.'

'Yes.'

'Sophia, I promise you I will understand if you do not wish to speak of this further. I hadn't intended for you to revisit the pain of earlier years...'

She took a long sip of wine before replying, 'It's quite all right, Thomas. I have gone over the horrors of that journey so many times in my mind since then... to describe them to you will place little further strain upon me. And somehow...' She gave him a strange look. 'Somehow it feels appropriate that I should tell you.'

Blackwood inclined his head slightly. 'In that case, please do go on, my dear.'

'We had been in the depths of the forest for three days, along with our two guides – men of rough manners but good character, who had been recommended to my father for their knowledge of woodcraft and bush-lore. One of them was a Canuck, a native of the Province of Quebec, who possessed a profoundly superstitious frame of mind. In spite of the season, the hunting was not good, and try as we might, we could not come upon a single moose trail. Our Canuck guide claimed to know the reason, and it was only with the greatest insistence that my father was able to drag an explanation from him, although the explanation, when it came, was more problematical than the scarcity of moose which had inspired it.

'The Canuck claimed that the animals had been driven away by the presence in the forest of something abnormal and unholy, something incomprehensible to human thought, which had ventured forth from its own mysterious and horrible realm to trouble this frozen world. He added that, had it not been for the handsome remuneration my father had offered, which would see him and his poor family in good order for many months to come, he would not have ventured into the wilderness on this occasion – for he had begun to suspect the presence of this monstrous thing as soon as the forest closed about us on the first day.

'Both my father and the other guide laughed at this and dismissed it as no more than quaint legend. This angered the Canuck, and he declared that the wilderness was no place for a woman, and that my father would be well-advised to take me back to the comforts of our grand house in England, where I belonged.'

Although he refrained from saying as much, Blackwood found himself in agreement with this sentiment and wondered to himself what could have possessed Lord Percival to place his daughter in the path of such peril, supernatural or otherwise.

Sophia herself answered the question for him. 'My father declared indignantly that I was fully the equal in courage and ability of any boy my age. "My daughter," he said, "has looked into the eyes of charging tigers and brought them down with a single shot. She will meet any challenge this forest of yours can present to her, and she will prevail!"'

'He was clearly very proud of you,' said Blackwood.

Sophia was about to reply, but she fell silent as the waiter approached with their lunch. He placed their plates before them, gave a slight bow and withdrew.

Blackwood's lemon sole smelled delicious, but his attention was exercised far more by Sophia's Indian Omelette. It mattered little to him that most other people might have looked favourably at the tomatoes, chopped green chillis and coriander which made up the main flavors of the dish; however, the fluffy yellow mass of beaten eggs made Blackwood's flesh crawl and his breath catch in his throat, and he would have fled from the restaurant and the first class cabin and hidden amongst the luggage on D Deck if he could have done so without arousing the alarm of the haunted young woman sitting opposite him.

Sophia breathed in the aroma and smiled, clearly grateful for this momentary respite from the terrible memories she had been revisiting. 'I developed a taste for this while on safari in India,' she said. 'It's a most interesting and unusual variation on the traditional recipe. Would you care to try some, Thomas?'

'Thank you, no,' he replied between two large gulps of wine, trying to banish his own hideous memories. *Calm yourself!* he thought. *It's in the past. The Cosmic Spheres are gone – never to return, if there be any mercy in the universe!*

Sophia ate in silence, while Blackwood half-heartedly prodded at his fish, taking the occasional small bite. His appetite had completely deserted him, and he found his attention seeking escape towards the promenade windows and the seating aft of the restaurant. Thankfully, Sophia didn't notice, or if she did, she chose not to comment.

Presently, she laid down her knife and fork. 'That was rather good – although not quite enough chilli. But then, I suppose care must be taken with the parochial English palate.'

'Indeed. Would you care for dessert?'

'No, thank you. Coffee will suffice, I think.'

Blackwood ordered coffee for them, and breathed a sigh of relief when the waiter took their plates.

'Yes, my father was very proud of me,' Sophia continued, as if no interruption had occurred. 'And my heart swelled at the thought of it, and I resolved to be worthy of his praise. I resolved to be the first to bag a moose.' She gave a small, bitter laugh. 'Had I but known that we were not the hunters in that God-forsaken forest, but the hunted!'

'Hunted?' said Blackwood. 'By what, or by whom?'

'By the thing of which the Canuck spoke... for he was right: the forest *did* contain something ungodly and awful...'

'Forgive me, Sophia,' said Blackwood, leaning forward. 'But it sounds to me like you are speaking of the Wendigo.'

Sophia visibly shuddered at the word, and Blackwood reached out and took her trembling hands in his. 'You've heard of it?' she whispered.

'Cogitators may not be my speciality... but I *do* know something of the abnormal and supernatural. My line of work, you understand.'

'Then you know what it is... the thing that rides the night wind in far, cold hinterlands. You know that the American Indian tribes of the north know it and fear it, that it is an evil, cannibalistic spirit, a skeletal apparition whose desiccated skin is like cracked parchment, and that the smell of death and decay hangs upon it like a cloak of corruption. You know these things,' Sophia said, fixing Blackwood with her agonised gaze, 'and I know them too: for the Wendigo came for us while we were in that forest. It dragged my father, kicking and screaming, out of our tent one night, and I heard his anguished cries fading into the night sky above our camp. I never saw him again.'

'Good God,' whispered Blackwood. 'How did you escape?'

'Our two guides took me and dragged me bodily from the camp, even as I screamed my father's name again and again into the night. We fled back along the trail we had followed, for two days and two nights, the Canuck leading us. And through each of those two nights, my protectors watched over me, shunning sleep, ever alert for the approach of the monster. I owe them my life, for their roughness of demeanour could not hide their decency and stoutness of heart. On the third day, we reached civilisation and raised the alarm. A search party of volunteers was assembled in short order and headed off into the forest to look for my father... but no trace of him was ever found.'

Blackwood gazed at her in silence. He could think of nothing useful to say.

'Upon my return to England, I fell into such a state of despair that our friends and relatives feared for my sanity. It was my mother who saved me – ironically, you might think – for so utterly heartbroken was she by the loss of her beloved husband that she underwent a sudden and terrible decline in health, and I realised that it was up to me to pull both of us through that awful period.'

'Which you did,' said Blackwood.

'Yes. Gradually, my mother and I recovered, with the help and support of our family, and friends such as Sir William Crookes. He was the only one with whom I felt able to discuss what had really happened to my father, and it was he who supported me in my resultant desire to study the supernatural.'

Blackwood was shocked by this. 'One would have thought that after such a tragic and ghastly experience, you would never again want to *hear* the word "supernatural", much less study it.'

'Oh, but I did! I wanted to know its ways and the means by which it interacts with our world. I wanted to seek out the darkness, to do battle with it and defeat it, and I wanted also to seek out the light, to learn from it and gain strength from it – for as I'm sure you know, the realms of the supernatural contain much that is good, as well as much that is wicked and destructive.'

'True enough,' Blackwood nodded.

'And so this is what brought me to the Society for Psychical Research, the institution which is allowing me to fulfil my vocation. With my permission, Sir William shared my experience with certain other key members, and they had no objections to my becoming Secretary.'

'And well they might not!' declared Blackwood. 'For I have no doubt that you are a great asset to the organisation. You have already proved your qualities to me, for otherwise I would have been carted off to the madhouse by now!'

Sophia lowered her eyes. 'You are kind to say so, Thomas.'

Kindness has nothing to do with it, thought Blackwood. *With a woman like this by my side, and the little chap from Faerie helping out as well... why, we'll get to the bottom of this caper in no time!*

CHAPTER FOUR:
At Fyne Court

The omnibus arrived at Taunton a little after half past two. With a hiss of hydraulics and a bell-like clang of moving metal, its great piston-driven legs folded up, and the hull settled toward the station's platform. Blackwood and Sophia were already at the main hatch on E Deck, and they waited patiently as the gangway was wheeled into position by a trio of station porters.

As she stepped lightly onto the platform, Sophia breathed in deeply. 'Ah!' she said. 'Smell the air, Thomas! It's so lovely to get out of London for an afternoon.'

Blackwood agreed: the air was cool and clear, with none of the taint that constantly afflicted the atmosphere in the capital.

'How far is it to Fyne Court?'

'The Crosse estate is a little over four miles north of here, near the village of Broomfield. I'm sure we shall be able to secure some transportation, if we ask in the right place.'

'And where would that be?' asked Sophia as they left the station and emerged onto North Street, the main thoroughfare through Taunton.

Blackwood pointed directly ahead, at a tavern whose sign proclaimed it to be the Waggoner's Arms. They crossed the street and entered the low-ceilinged saloon, in which a few locals were taking some early afternoon refreshment. Everyone turned in their direction, as local people are wont to do when newcomers arrive, and the scattered conversations died down to an occasional murmur of curiosity.

They approached the bar, behind which the rotund, florid-faced barkeep gave a slight bow and said, 'Arternoon, sir, madam. What'll it be?'

Blackwood withdrew his wallet and placed a guinea on the counter. 'Your help would be much appreciated, my good man. My companion and I would like to procure transportation to Broomfield. Do you know of anyone who might take us there without delay?'

The guinea vanished into the barkeep's pocket with almost supernatural speed, and he nodded in the direction of a far corner of the room. 'Old Davey's headin' up that way, ain't you, Davey?'

'That oi be,' came the reply from the corner, in which sat a wiry old man with a thin, straggly beard and bright, humorous eyes. 'If the gentleman'll toss one o' them guineas my way, oi'll be 'appy to take him and the lady... if they don't moind spendin' 'alf an hour in an 'ay cart, that is.'

'Splendid,' said Blackwood. 'A guinea it is, then.'

Old Davey drained the last of the ale from his tankard and stood up, a trifle unsteadily, Sophia thought with a suppressed smile. 'Cart's 'round the back,' he said as he tottered through the front door.

'Good day to you all,' said Blackwood to the other patrons as he and Sophia followed their new driver out into the street. Davey led them around the corner of the building and into a small yard at the rear, where his horse and cart were waiting.

Blackwood helped Sophia up onto the bench, and then climbed up as Davey took the reins and said, 'Come on, boy!' to the horse. With a clap-clapping of hooves, they left the Waggoner's Arms behind and, a few minutes later, were heading north out of Taunton through the rolling Quantock Hills.

*

'This is such a delightful part of the country,' said Sophia as they made their way along a narrow lane with lush green hills rising towards a cloud-feathered sky. 'Have you lived here all your life, Davey?' she asked the old man.

'Aye, that oi 'ave, ma'am,' he replied.

'In that case,' said Blackwood, 'you will know something of Mr Andrew Crosse.'

Sophia, who was sitting between Davey and Blackwood, felt the old man tense, as if he had received a shock.

When he made no reply, Blackwood glanced across at him. 'Davey?'

'All the folks 'ereabouts knows about Mr Crosse, sir,' he said in a low grumble. 'We calls him the Wizard of the Quantocks.'

'A most peculiar nickname,' observed Sophia. 'Why do you call him that?'

'Because that's what he is, ma'am. Keepin' himself locked away on that ramshackle estate o' his, in that *workshop* o' his, doin' all them things that man weren't meant to do! Aye, he be a wizard all right, and folks 'round here'd be right glad if he'd take himself off and never come back!'

Sophia and Blackwood glanced at each other. 'What *kind* of things?' asked Blackwood.

'He calls up ghosts and devils, he does! The people o' Broomfield know all about it, and they take care to steer clear o' Fyne Court after dark. You can see the lights at night: queer, blue dancin' lights upon the hills around the estate, an' a terrible sparking sound, like nearby thunder. Some people calls 'im the thunder an' lightnin' man, as well, and there's

115

some as believe he uses black magic to call the thunder down out o' the sky – and other things, besides!'

Blackwood stole a quick look at Sophia, wishing that the old man hadn't spoken in such terms, but she seemed unperturbed, and was regarding their confidante with an expression of intense concentration.

Old Davey continued in a low voice, speaking more to himself than to his passengers. 'Aye, whatever he's doin' up there, it ain't natural... it be against God is what it be!' As he said this, something seemed to occur to him, and he turned suddenly suspicious eyes on Blackwood. 'By the by, sir – who be you and the young lady goin' to see up in Broomfield, if it ain't out o' turn to ask?'

Blackwood smiled at him, and replied, 'Why, we're going to see the very gentleman of whom you speak.'

Sophia gave a little gasp and looked at him as Davey brought the cart to a sudden halt.

Blackwood took out his wallet, flipped it open and showed his identification to Davey. 'We are agents of the Crown, and are conducting an investigation into Mr Crosse's activities, of which, I might add, Her Majesty takes a very dim view. I shouldn't be at all surprised if, one day quite soon, you and the other good people of Broomfield are free of him forever.'

Davey peered at the contents of the wallet and scratched his beard. 'Agents of the Crown, you say?'

'Indeed. And you, sir, have already been of great service to us, which I assure you we will not forget. Now... may we continue on our way?'

Davey hesitated for a moment and then nodded and flicked the reins.

Half an hour later, they reached the edge of Broomfield. Davey brought the cart to a halt and pointed towards a narrow path between two fields of rich, dark soil. 'Fyne Court be that way,' he said. 'I'll be sure to say a prayer for you both.'

'Much obliged,' Blackwood replied, as he helped Sophia down. 'I'd also be obliged enough to give you five guineas if you're here in two hours' time. We'll be needing a ride back to Taunton when we have completed our business.'

'Five guineas?' Davey marvelled. 'Oi'll be 'ere, sir!' And with that, the cart clattered off into the village.

As they began to walk in the direction Davey had indicated, Sophia said, 'I must admit, Thomas, that I was most surprised when you told him where we're going.'

'I had no choice: we know no one in Broomfield, and I'll wager Old Davey knows everyone. He would have seen through a lie immediately. This way, at least he is assured that we are on the side of good, and that we shall take action against "the Wizard of the Quantocks" if necessary.'

As their course took them up the shallow rise of a low, rounded hill, Sophia seized Blackwood's arm and pointed into the field to their left. 'What is that?'

'I see it,' he said, and without further ado, he jumped across the ditch and turned, with his arms spread to catch Sophia. She had already jumped across, however, and now stood beside him once more, a delightful smirk on her face. 'Capital,' chuckled Blackwood as they entered the field and walked toward the line of strange objects that marched off into the distance.

As they drew near, they saw that the objects were wooden posts, each about five feet tall, which had been sunk into the soil, and between which a number of strands of copper wire had been strung. The whole arrangement comprised a sort of incomplete fence, which extended beyond their field of view around the shoulder of the hill.

'What on earth is it?' wondered Sophia.

'My bet would be that it is the origin of the ghostly blue lights Old Davey was telling us about – not to mention the strange sparking sounds which he likened to thunder.'

'An experiment in electricity?'

'So I should judge. Come, let's continue on our way. I'm anxious to make the acquaintance of the "thunder and lightning man"!'

*

The path led over the brow of the hill and down to a wide lawn, at the centre of which stood Fyne Court. Blackwood estimated the main part of the house to date from the early eighteenth century, although the two-storey structure had been added to much more recently, with a single-storey annex running across the gravel courtyard to a smaller outbuilding. The whole complex was constructed of light tan stone which reflected the intermittent sunlight quite fetchingly.

'What a charming place!' declared Sophia. 'It's difficult to imagine that this could be the origin of so much fear and dark rumours.'

Blackwood took his revolver from the pocket of his Ulster and checked that all five chambers were full. 'Fear and darkness can be found in the unlikeliest of places, as we both well know,' he replied as he strode across the courtyard to the front door of the main house. He rapped loudly upon the peeling paint with his cane, and they waited patiently for a response.

When none came, Blackwood nodded, as if he had been expecting this.

'Perhaps he is in his laboratory,' suggested Sophia.

'A fair assumption.'

They turned away from the door and walked back along the wall of the annex, looking in through the windows as they went. Presently, they came to the door of the outbuilding, upon which Blackwood rapped.

'Who's there?' came a voice from within.

'My name is Thomas Blackwood, Special Investigator for Her Majesty. I am here on Crown business. Open the door, sir!'

'I don't care who you are!' cried the voice. 'Go away! I don't wish to be disturbed.'

'Oh, you don't, do you?' Blackwood muttered. He called out, 'Your wishes are irrelevant, Mr Crosse. Open this door at once, or I will not hesitate to knock it down and arrest you for obstruction of a Crown Investigator! You have ten seconds.'

There were sounds of movement from within, as of someone shuffling back and forth. Sophia imagined the man pacing rapidly, wondering whether the interloper were bluffing or would make good on his threat.

'Five seconds!' shouted Blackwood.

'All right, all right!' came the voice, its tone suggesting a curious mixture of panic and resignation.

There was a click as the latch was lifted, and the door swung aside to reveal Andrew Crosse. Sophia was struck by his fine-featured handsomeness; for some reason, she had been expecting some grizzled ogre, an expectation which had not been countered by the obvious youthfulness of his voice. But here, clearly, was a man of refinement and good breeding, with pale skin and a neatly-trimmed moustache, carefully-combed hair and bright, clear eyes in which she detected warmth and decency.

Blackwood stepped forward. 'Mr Crosse. Thomas Blackwood...'

'So you said.'

'This is my colleague, Lady Sophia Harrington.'

In spite of his obvious agitation, Crosse did not neglect his manners and gave a slight bow to Sophia. 'What do you wish to see me about, Mr Blackwood?'

'A matter pertaining to the security of the Empire,' Blackwood replied, stepping across the threshold with such authority that Crosse was forced to retreat a few steps. 'And perhaps to the security of the entire world. Do you still wish to send us on our way?' he added in a dark and threatening tone.

Crosse's shoulders sagged, and his face wore a defeated expression as he replied, 'No... no, of course not.' He turned and walked away from them, motioning them inside with a listless wave of his hand.

Sophia followed Blackwood into the room and closed the door behind her. She looked around, and was astonished at the profusion of arcane equipment and curious devices which lined the walls and occupied the long workbench which dominated the centre of the laboratory. Strange lumps of machinery, festooned with pipes and wires and gauges, occupied every available horizontal surface. Some were connected to each other with strands of copper wire, similar to that which they had seen out in the nearby field. The air in the room was warm – due, Sophia surmised, to the running of the electrical apparatuses – and was suffused with a low hum, which disturbed and unsettled her in a way that she could not quite define.

Crosse turned and faced his visitors. 'Well, Mr Blackwood, what is this matter which concerns the security of the world?'

'I take it you are aware that Ambassador Lunan R'ondd of Mars died three days ago.'

'I do read the papers.'

'Then you will also be aware that there has been speculation regarding the nature of his death – that he was the victim of an assassin.'

Crosse swallowed but said nothing.

'That speculation, sir, is well-founded, for Ambassador R'ondd *was* murdered.'

Crosse regarded Blackwood with wide, unblinking eyes. 'How?' he whispered.

'He was suffocated. His breathing apparatus was sabotaged... by the insertion of *Acarus galvanicus* mites!'

Crosse stepped back suddenly and seemed to stagger, as if Blackwood had just struck him. 'Oh, dear God!' he cried.

Blackwood moved forward slowly towards the scientist, his tall frame subtly menacing. 'The mites fed directly on the life-giving gasses circulating through the apparatus, before they could reach the Ambassador's lungs. Whoever placed them there murdered him, just as surely as if they'd put a bullet through his brain!'

'No!' whispered Crosse.

'There is no such organism as *Acarus galvanicus* in Nature: they are artificial life forms, grown from inanimate matter through the application of electro-chemical techniques... techniques which *you* perfected, Mr Crosse!'

The scientist's hands flew up to his face, hiding it, and he turned away from Blackwood and Sophia, bent over his workbench, and began to weep. 'I didn't know!' he said, between snivelling gasps. 'God help me, I didn't know!'

'Didn't know *what*, Mr Crosse?'

Sophia moved forward, intending to comfort the man, but Blackwood put out an arm and stopped her. 'Thomas,' she whispered angrily, 'he's broken – *look* at him.'

Blackwood glared at her and shook his head firmly.

'I didn't... didn't know they'd be used for such a foul purpose. How *could* I have known?'

'Used by whom?' demanded Blackwood. 'Tell me now, man, or it will go very badly for you!'

Although he had stopped Sophia from comforting Crosse, Blackwood understood her compassion. This man, he was quite sure, was no criminal: he was a seeker after the truth of the world, a pilgrim in search of knowledge. He was an explorer, after a fashion, charting the unknown realms of electricity and chemistry, seeking out the mysterious processes by which they had combined, in aeons past, to produce life on Earth. He was to be respected – applauded! – for his vocation, but clearly, like many men of science, he was naïve and ill understood the darker ways of humankind. Blackwood saw through to the root of the matter: someone had visited Crosse recently and had taken advantage of his research in ways the scientist would never have sanctioned, had he but known the truth. But who?

Blackwood did not like using threats, but regrettably there were occasions when there was no other way to get to the truth. Andrew Crosse appeared to be on the point of collapse: Blackwood would only have to sneeze to make him crumble completely and spill everything he knew.

He lowered his voice as he said, 'I have to tell you, sir, that you are looking at the hangman's noose unless you cooperate with us entirely and without hesitation. Even then, it'll be the devil's own job to keep you out of prison for a very long time.'

'But I had no intention of...' Crosse began to protest.

'Your intentions are what we have come to ascertain,' Blackwood interrupted. 'Your work was dismissed by the Royal Society, was it not? They considered you a charlatan and a buffoon.'

'You think I acted out of a desire for revenge?' asked Crosse incredulously.

Blackwood did not answer immediately. Instead, he began to examine the various items of electrical equipment with which the laboratory was packed. 'How did you do it?' he asked presently. 'How did you manage to create life from lifelessness? Tell us everything. And tell us now!'

Crosse sighed deeply, and leaned against the workbench as if exhausted by some terrible labour. 'It happened while I was conducting certain experiments on the artificial formation of crystals by means of weak electrical currents applied over long periods of time. I was attempting to produce crystals of silica by allowing a suitable fluid medium to seep through a piece of porous stone, while applying an electric current from a voltaic battery. The fluid was a mixture of hydrochloric acid and a solution of silicate of potash.

'On the fourteenth day from the commencement of this experiment, I observed through a lens a few small whitish excrescences, projecting from about the middle of the electrified stone. On the eighteenth day, these projections enlarged and stuck out seven or eight filaments, each of them longer than the hemisphere on which they grew.'

'The *galvanicus* mites?' said Blackwood.

Crosse nodded. 'On the twenty-sixth day, these appearances assumed the form of a *perfect insect*, standing erect on a few bristles which formed its tail. Until this period I had no notion that these appearances were other than an incipient mineral formation. On the twenty-eighth day, these little creatures moved their legs. I must admit that I was not a little astonished. After a few days they detached themselves from the stone and moved about of their own volition.

'Over the course of the next few weeks, about a hundred of these creatures appeared on the stone. I examined them closely under a microscope, and saw that the smaller ones appeared to have six legs, and the larger ones eight. I decided that they must be of the genus *Acarus*, but wondered whether they were a known species or one never seen before.

'At first, I was unable to venture an opinion on the cause of their birth, and for a very good reason: I was unable to form one. The simplest solution of the problem which occurred to me was that they arose from ova deposited by insects floating in the atmosphere and hatched by electric action. Still I could not imagine that an ovum could shoot out filaments, or that these filaments could become bristles, and moreover I could not detect, on the closest examination, the remains of a shell.

'I next imagined that they might have originated from the water and consequently made a close examination of numbers of vessels filled with the same fluid; in none of these could I perceive a trace of an insect, nor could I see any in any other part of the room.'

Blackwood and Sophia listened to Crosse's explanation in silence. They both felt their flesh crawling at his matter-of-fact description of the creatures' unexpected emergence out of inanimate matter. Although Sophia had been struck by the scientist's respectable appearance, she couldn't help but sympathise with the people of the area who viewed him with such terror and loathing. She likewise noted how he seemed to have lost his own fear and anguish – or at least had succeeded in ignoring them for the moment. As with all true men of science, Crosse seemed able to banish the problems and vicissitudes of life from his awareness while considering the abstract, scientific and theoretical. In that respect, she thought, science was very close to art.

'What happened then?' asked Blackwood. 'Presumably, you attempted to perfect your technique.'

'That's correct,' Crosse replied. 'I modified the method: I discarded the porous stone, and found that I could produce the *Acarus* mites in glass cylinders filled with concentrated solutions of copper nitrate, copper sulphate and zinc sulphate. The creatures usually appeared at the edge of the fluid surface; however, in some cases the creatures appeared two inches *under* the electrified fluid, but after emerging from it, they were destroyed if thrown back.

'In one experiment, the mites appeared on a small piece of quartz, immersed at a depth of two inches in fluoric acid holding silica in solution. I arranged for a current of electricity to pass through this fluid for just over a year, and at the end of some months three of the *Acarus* mites were visible on the piece of quartz, which was kept negatively electrified.

'Their first appearance consisted in a very minute whitish hemisphere, formed upon the surface of the electrified body, sometimes at the positive end, and sometimes at the negative, and occasionally between the two, or in the middle of the electrified current, and sometimes upon all. This speck gradually enlarged and elongated vertically, and shot out filaments of a whitish wavy appearance, easily seen through a lens of very low power.

'Then commenced the first appearance of animal life. If a fine point was made to approach these filaments, they immediately shrank up and collapsed like zoophytes upon moss, but expanded again sometime after the removal of the point. Some days afterwards these filaments became legs and bristles, and a perfect *Acarus* was the result, which finally detached itself from its birthplace, and if under a fluid, climbed up the electrified wire and escaped from the vessel.

'If one of them was afterwards thrown into the fluid in which it was produced, it immediately drowned. I have never before heard of *Acari* having been produced under a fluid, or of their ova throwing out filaments; not have I ever observed any ova previous to or during electrization, except that the speck which throws out filaments be an ovum, but when a number of these creatures, in a perfect state, congregate, ova are produced.

'In a later experiment, I managed to produce an *Acarus* in a closed and airtight glass retort, filled with an electrified silicate solution. On connecting the battery, I observed that an electric action commenced; oxygen and hydrogen gases were liberated; the volume of atmospheric air was soon expelled. Every care had been taken to avoid atmospheric contact and admittance of extraneous matter, and the retort itself had previously been washed with hot alcohol.

'I discovered no sign of incipient animal formation until on the 140th day, when I plainly distinguished *one Acarus* actively crawling about *within* the bulb of the retort.

'I found that I had made a great error in this experiment, and I believe it was in consequence of this error that I not only lost sight of the single insect, but never saw any others in this apparatus. I had omitted to insert within the bulb of the retort a *resting-place* for these *Acari,* and as I had observed, they are always destroyed if they fall back into the fluid from which they have emerged. I thought it very strange that, in a solution *eminently caustic* and under an atmosphere of *oxihydrogen gas*, one single *Acarus* should have made its appearance.'

'It sounds to me like these organisms are incredibly resilient and thrive in conditions which would be the end of ordinary organic life,' observed Blackwood.

'What now for the ideas of Mr Darwin?' wondered Sophia. 'Your successes fly in the face of Evolution, sir.'

'An interesting statement, madam,' Crosse replied. 'But one with which I cannot concur. The Theory of Evolution is quite intact, I assure you, and is not in the least undermined by my own work – any more than the reality of walking is undermined by the existence of steam locomotives! Just as Mr Watt invented a short cut between locations through the application of artificial speed, I discovered a short cut from inanimate matter to the substance of life, through the artificial application of life-creating principles.

'But you, Mr Blackwood, noted the extreme resilience of the creatures,' he continued. 'And I was most curious as to the *limits* of that resilience. I found myself wondering what would happen if I placed them in environments analogous to those of other planets...'

'Other planets?' said Sophia. 'Including Mars?'

'Mars was the first alien world I chose for the next phase of my experiments,' Crosse replied with a vigorous nod. 'As you may know, the Martian atmosphere consists of 95 percent carbon dioxide, 2.7 percent nitrogen, 1.6 percent argon, and just over a tenth of a percent oxygen, along with a number of other gases in trace amounts. I introduced these gases in the correct proportions into one of the sealed retorts containing several *Acarus* mites, and found that they metabolised the atmosphere at an incredible rate!'

'Fascinating,' said Blackwood, with a glance at Sophia. 'But I fail to understand the *reason* for this research. What could it avail a man to reproduce artificially what Nature achieves as a matter of course?'

'There are two answers to that question, Mr Blackwood. First, original research – enquiry *for its own sake* – is always desirable, and may become useful in ways unimagined by the person conducting it. And second, it occurred to me that there might very well be practical applications for my work. If a way could be discovered of compelling the *Acari* to absorb dangerous gases and metabolise them into harmless or beneficial ones...'

'I see your point,' said Blackwood. 'For one thing, the mining industry would be transformed: the danger from volatile gases in coalmines would be removed, allowing men to work in greater safety than they do now.'

'Precisely!' cried Andrew Crosse. 'And that is merely one among many possible applications.'

'But the Royal Society didn't agree,' said Sophia.

Crosse's enthusiastic expression collapsed into a downhearted frown. 'No, they didn't. They concluded that I had allowed my apparatus to be contaminated, that my discoveries were spurious. And yet, I didn't hold it against them...'

'No?' said Blackwood.

Crosse shook his head and offered them a sad smile. 'Such is the way of humankind. The first discovery is often dismissed by those who have not witnessed it with their own eyes, and such is their prejudice that they will not even countenance an attempt to reproduce the discovery themselves. It is human nature to fear and mistrust the new,

127

the unknown, the unexpected or unexplained. The Akashic Records, for instance, were once dismissed as Oriental fantasy, and the realm of Faerie was likewise considered to be no more than medieval superstition... until their existence was verified and gave rise to the science of artificial cogitation. One day, perhaps, my own work *will* be reproduced and verified... although I wouldn't lay a bet on whether I am still alive when that day comes.'

'And yet,' said Blackwood, moving to stand directly in front of Crosse, so that their faces were mere inches apart, '*someone* took your research seriously, didn't they?'

The enthusiasm which had galvanised the scientist's explanation of his work was now completely at bay. His gaze fell away from Blackwood's, and to Sophia it appeared that he shrank a little in on himself, as if the vital forces which animated his own body had diminished.

'Yes,' he said. 'About two weeks ago, a man came to see me. He told me that he had read of my work, in particular my paper "The Creation of Life from Lifelessness", and that he was interested in developing my process for the purpose of improving the lot of humanity. He claimed to represent an association of entrepreneurial individuals who were profoundly concerned with philanthropy and ethics, and who felt it was their duty to divert industry and technology away from the dehumanising path they have taken for the last hundred years. He said that this branch of human endeavour has become our master, rather than our servant: a statement which can be verified by anyone who walks through the tenements of any industrial city and sees the utter squalor, degradation and human misery which afflict them.

'Human beings, he said, have become fuel for the machines which they themselves created, and as such have been reduced to the status of mechanical components in that much larger and subtler machine called Progress.

But progress is not what most people see, whose lives are blighted and shortened by disease and fatigue. What *they* see is hardship beyond endurance; meanness of spirit, the total absence of human compassion. The world is becoming a mass of seething activity, frenetic, trivial and pointless. Our bond with the world is being broken; the air is becoming thick with pollution and decay while we blindly continue, stoking the fires of our new cathedrals of metal, praying to an idiot deity that exists only in the sullied minds and cold hearts of our fallen species.

'He said many things like this – he was very persuasive. He convinced me of the altruistic intentions of the group which he represented: how they wished to turn aside this great, dehumanising tide and divert it into channels that would lead to the betterment of human life, rather than its degradation. He said that I could help, if I chose, and added that he was in the process of gathering likeminded individuals into the fold – scientists, teachers, philosophers, engineers, artists. He begged me to allow him to take away a sample of *Acarus galvanicus*, so that his group might analyse the creatures and formulate ways in which they might be applied to the grand scheme.'

'And so you complied and gave him the sample,' said Blackwood.

Crosse shook his head helplessly. 'I believed him.'

'What was this fellow's name?'

'He called himself Indrid Cold.'

Blackwood frowned at the strangeness of the name. 'Did he say where he was from? His nationality?'

'No.'

'Can you describe his appearance?'

'He was tall and powerfully-built; his bearing was utterly confident – I might almost say there was something aristocratic about him. But his face...' Crosse hesitated.

'What about his face?'

'There was something strange about it. His skin was pale and seemed to be stretched very tightly across his skull. And his eyes... there was something hypnotic in them. I had the feeling that when I looked into his eyes, I was looking upon the profoundest depths of Space and Time. There was something otherworldly in those eyes, although I can't define it any more accurately than that. When he had gone, I was left with the feeling that I had been in the presence of something more than a man.'

Blackwood glanced at Sophia and was momentarily stunned by the expression of shock and fear on her face. He recovered himself immediately, and without commenting, turned back to Crosse. 'You have been very helpful, sir. I thank you.'

'Please understand, Mr Blackwood,' pleaded the scientist, 'I gave Indrid Cold those samples out of a desire to do good. He assured me that once his own people had analysed the organisms and begun to develop an application for them, he would contact me again to offer me permanent membership in his group. I have not heard from him, however...'

'Nor will you, I am sure. I now believe that your only crime was naivety – and that, in truth, is not a crime. However, we may need to talk to you again, and so I would appreciate it if you didn't leave the area for the next few days.'

'I assure you I have no intention of doing so, and of course, I will do all in my power to help.'

'Then we shall take our leave of you.'

Blackwood and Sophia left Crosse in his laboratory. The late afternoon air was cold; the day had begun to gather its cloak of twilight in preparation for its descent into night. As they walked back across the courtyard, their boots crunching on the gravel, Blackwood said, 'What do you think?'

'I think he is telling the truth,' Sophia replied quietly.

'As do I. But tell me: back there, I noticed a curious expression on your face when Mr Crosse described this fellow Indrid Cold.'

Sophia said nothing, and so Blackwood persisted. 'I had the impression that it was not merely shock at the singular description of his appearance.'

'It wasn't,' said Sophia.

'Then what was it?' '

'I have heard that description before, Thomas – or at least, something very like it.'

'Indeed?'

'Yes.' As she glanced up at him, Blackwood saw that same look of profound trepidation return to her eyes. 'I believe that Mr Crosse was describing Spring-Heeled Jack!'

CHAPTER FIVE:
'Mars Will Triumph!'

Crouching upon the vast dome of Saint Paul's Cathedral, the creature known by many as Spring-Heeled Jack, and by a few as Indrid Cold, gazed up at the infinitely greater dome of the night sky, at the stars flickering like gas lamps in the pitch blackness of the firmament. One star in particular caught his attention, and his strange eyes narrowed in contemplation, as if they would pierce the countless leagues of Space, carrying his mind through the endless dark, carrying it... home.

Indrid Cold's pale, tight-skinned face twisted into a grimace of pain and dread, for the star at which he gazed was *not* a star, but a world, distant and dying: once verdant and beautiful, but now barren and desiccated, on the edge of a planetary catastrophe from which recovery would be impossible.

Unable to bear the sight any longer, Indrid Cold turned away from the flickering pinpoint of light and directed his attention downward towards the labyrinthine swathe of London. With inhuman elegance, he stepped across the glass panes of the dome's light well, through which the sun illuminated the interior of the great edifice where the humans worshipped their strange god.

He looked south, at the glinting band of the River Thames threading through the heart of the city – how beautiful the water was! How sublime the subtle stirring of its crystalline surface! How terrible the crime of its pollution! – and his gaze took in the ugly spans of Blackfriars Bridge and Southwark Bridge, which offered insult to the gently flowing river beneath. He turned his eyes to the east, to the Bank of England, and then to the northwest, towards Holborn and Bloomsbury. Finally, his attention settled upon Whitehall and the Houses of Parliament to the southwest, and his smile returned – but it was not a smile of affection: it was a grimace of hatred and contempt for the arrogant buffoons who directed the course of their paltry empire from within those walls, all in the name of a bitch queen who should have been in her mausoleum by now...

No matter, for that would come soon enough. Death would come soon enough for all of them!

With a rasping hiss of foul anticipation, Indrid Cold began his evening's work.

Like a slender white ape in a jungle of concrete, stone and glass, he leaped from the dome to the roof of the cathedral, and then across Ludgate Hill to the rooftops opposite. His frightful, piercing eyes scanned the streets below, looking for victims.

On the Charing Cross Road, he spied a man and woman walking together, and jumped to the street in front of them. The woman screamed, and the man placed himself between her and the apparition that had suddenly descended before them. But his gallantry was to no avail, for the creature opened his mouth and belched blue fire into both their faces before taking hold of the man and dashing his head against the pavement. Too terrified now even to scream, the woman gazed disbelievingly at the fiend, her mouth wide open in shock and terror. With a single swipe of his metal-taloned hand, he turned her face to ribbons of dripping flesh, while fearful onlookers shouted, '*It's Spring-Heeled Jack! He's here. Oh, God, he's here!*'

With a single leap, Indrid Cold gained the roof of a town house and looked down at the gathering crowd. 'Mars will triumph!' he shouted at them. '*Mars will triumph!*' And then he was gone, bounding across the rooftops.

In the filthy slums of Bermondsey, he descended upon a young prostitute, lifted her bodily above his head and flung her into one of the stinking open sewers which blighted that unfortunate district. Drawn by her frantic screams for help, a crowd of people quickly gathered, and some tried to climb down the embankment to reach her – but there was no hope: the filth-clogged sewer was like quicksand. The poor waif struggled and cried for a few more moments, before vanishing into its depths. Men and women alike turned away in grief from the horrible sight, in time to see the murderer leaping up into the sky, screaming at them, '*Mars will triumph!*'

For the next hour, Indrid Cold sowed new terror through the streets of the capital. In a storm of unnatural blue fire and flashing talons, he stabbed and sliced and pummelled victim after victim, taking no heed of their social standing, for he offered violent outrage to rich and poor alike – all the while crying, '*Mars will triumph!*' as he went about his horrible business.

He headed west, out of the night-time heart of London, leaving blood and screams in his wake, into open countryside, where he attacked a pair of wagoners whom he encountered in the lonely darkness, leaving them battered and bloody in a ditch.

His last port of call was the army barracks in Aldershot in Hampshire, where he descended upon the roof of a sentry box and reached down to slash the face of the hapless soldier who was manning the post. The man screamed in agony, alerting two officers who were passing, and they arrived in time to see the ghost-like figure hurtling into the distance. One officer grabbed the injured sentry's rifle and loosed a couple of shots after him, but if the bullets found their target, they did not slow the fiend's escape.

*

Indrid Cold left Aldershot far behind, heading once more into the dark Hampshire countryside, bounding across fields and over hedges on powerful, tireless limbs. Eight miles from the town, he came upon a high stone wall bordering a large estate, over which he leaped with ease.

With his great strides, he ran towards a vast manor house that stood resplendently in the midst of a wide, elegantly tended lawn. A warm, orange glow emanated from many of the leaded windows. One in particular, on the first floor, was open, and it was towards this that Cold directed his course.

Without even breaking his stride, he launched himself at the window, and with cat-like elegance landed neatly upon the sill. Through narrowed eyes, he regarded the room – a luxuriously appointed office – and its single occupant. The man was standing with his back to the window, looking down into the flames dancing in the maw of a huge marble fireplace.

Cold stepped silently into the room and slowly approached the man, who was dressed in a burgundy velvet smoking jacket and dark grey trousers.

The man turned, regarded him, and smiled. 'Welcome, my friend. Have you delivered your message?'

Indrid Cold nodded. 'Verbal *and* physical.'

'Mars will triumph!' whispered the man and gave a low, soft chuckle.

'Do you really think it will work?' asked Cold. 'Are humans really so gullible?'

'Oh yes,' replied the man as he walked across the room to a large Louis XIV cabinet containing several crystal decanters. He selected one and poured some of the rich, amber liquid into an elegant tulip glass, which he raised to his guest. Cold shook his head. 'Are you sure? It's a Delamain, *Reserve de la Famille*. One of the finest cognacs – quite exquisite.'

'I'm sure it is,' replied Cold. 'But as you know, Lord Pannick, alcohol does not sit well with me – however exquisite.'

Lord Pannick chuckled again. 'I pity you your alien metabolism, my friend.' He took a delicate sip of the cognac. 'Yes... humans really are that gullible: they will believe what their newspapers tell them, and their politicians... and since I own so many – newspapers *and* politicians – I am in the perfect position to fill their heads with whatever I choose.'

'Including that I am a Martian terrorist, an *agent provocateur* sowing the seeds of war between Earth and Mars?'

'That, too.'

'I still find it hard to believe that their thoughts can be guided so easily, and down such unlikely avenues.'

'When words are combined with violence and the threat of more violence, people sit up and take notice. They *listen*, and they look to their leaders for guidance, for explanations, and remedies. This has always been so, throughout the history of this world. "Mars will triumph!" Ha! You have no idea how powerful a simple phrase can be. And soon, that particular phrase will be repeated throughout the city, and then the country, and then the Empire! And then the Martians, already feared and mistrusted by a few, will be feared and hated by all.'

'And war between your worlds will come a large step closer,' said Indrid Cold.

Lord Pannick laughed. 'As large as one of your own singular leaps, Mr Cold!'

'What about Blackwood? Your plan failed; he is still alive and sane.'

Lord Pannick waved this aside. 'Don't worry about Mr Blackwood. It's true that it would have been more convenient for us had he been removed from the picture, but even if he discovers our plan, he will not succeed in preventing its conclusion. And when *that* happens, my friend, it will not be Mars which triumphs... it will be Venus!'

CHAPTER SIX:
The Metal Fragment

'Venus?' Blackwood said incredulously. 'Are you sure?'

'I'm quite sure, Thomas,' replied Sophia.

They were sitting in Blackwood's office at the Bureau of Clandestine Affairs, having taken the late omnibus from Taunton to London the previous evening. The strange metal fragment left behind by Spring-Heeled Jack at the Alsop residence lay on the desk between them, its iridescent surface contrasting strangely with the green Moroccan leather of the desktop.

Sophia had just come from the Society for Psychical Research in Kensington and had brought the report on the fragment's analysis, which she handed to Blackwood. He leafed through the pages, raising his eyebrows in gradual increments until his expression was one of unalloyed astonishment.

'The chemical analysis correlates quite strikingly with the impressions experienced by our psychometrists,' said Sophia. 'They bear each other out to such an extent that I don't think there's any room for doubt: this piece of metal came from the planet Venus.'

'Quite so, my dear,' Blackwood murmured as he continued to scan the pages. 'Carbon dioxide... sulphur dioxide... inert nitrogen, silicates, carbonates, quartz. What a strange brew!'

Sophia leaned forward in her chair. 'The really striking parallels are between the psychometrists. We asked our three most talented ones to hold the fragment and describe the psychic sensations it evoked. Of course, we kept them isolated from each other and did not offer them any information whatsoever on how we came by the artefact.'

Blackwood nodded. 'A wise precaution.'

'As you will see if you read from page four onwards, their psychic impressions were virtually identical.'

He did as Sophia suggested, and read aloud, 'The air in the place from which this object came is hot and heavy... suffocating... unbearably oppressive. There is a livid yellow sky above me; I can see neither sun nor stars, for the firmament is obscured by thick, churning clouds. The ground below is hard and brittle... desiccated, with broken rocks strewn everywhere. It's a horrible place – a dying place! No trace of green paints the distant mountains, whose jagged peaks reach up to the yellow sky as if begging for escape. This is not Earth... although it might be what Earth will become in future aeons, when the ancient Sun reaches out angrily to smite its children. No, it is not Earth: I feel that I am closer to the Sun here... a little closer... oh, the heat! It beats upon me, stifling, relentless!'

Blackwood turned the page to the account given by the second psychometrist. 'I see vast ranges of orange dust and chaotically-strewn boulders... great valleys sweeping into indigo depths of hot shadow. Nothing moves on the plains: all is silence; all is death. But below... in the depths of the valleys, at the bottoms of deep gorges and chasms, and at the poles of this world... there are lights in the dark. There is life. Furtive, frightened, cloaking itself in eternal dusk, amidst the last of the boreal ice and in the darkness of vast caverns underground... there is life!'

Again, Blackwood turned the page and read the words of the third of the psychometrists who had held the metal fragment and opened their minds to the psychic impressions it generated. 'A mighty civilisation once dwelled upon this world. Rich in ability but poor in wisdom, it ate and drank of its resources, stripping the world bare with its ceaseless activity. Its industry was an insatiable maw into which all was hurled, until all was machine, and the machine breathed in the air of life and exhaled the miasma of death, and the world was covered with it … and all the while the nearby Sun continued to pour its light and warmth upon the surface of the world, until the world became overheated with the ceaselessness of the machine and the brightness of the Sun… and began to suffocate. And the people looked with hatred upon their ruined world, for they did not regret their excesses and believed the world to have betrayed them, and they retreated to the poles and into caverns they made with their great machines, which had become no more than shovels to dig their ultimate graves. And there they wait, wondering what will become of them…'

Blackwood laid the pages aside and gave a deep sigh. 'Good grief, Sophia, what a strange and terrible picture your psychics have painted!'

'Monstrous, isn't it? I could barely bring myself to read those descriptions. What a horrible, tragic place it must be!' Sophia suppressed a shudder and sipped at the tea which Blackwood's secretary had prepared for her.

'I see that there's no actual description of the Venusians themselves,' said Blackwood. 'Why is that? Were the psychic impressions not powerful enough to provide even a glimpse?'

'Yes, they were,' Sophia replied. 'But not one of the psychometrists could bring himself to write down a description of them.'

'Why not?'

Sophia hesitated, and Blackwood now saw genuine fear in her eyes. 'Because of what they looked like. They were horrible beyond words – indescribably awful. I spoke with the psychometrists myself, and asked them to give me just a vague description... but they wouldn't, and they became visibly distressed even at the question.'

Blackwood raised his eyebrows. 'I see.'

At that moment, there was a high-pitched whistle, and a small cylinder of paper dropped from the vacuum tube beside Blackwood's desk into a tray at his elbow. He took the cylinder, unrolled it and read the brief message it contained. 'Grandfather would like to see us,' he said.

*

'Have you seen the papers?' Grandfather growled. He was leaning over his desk as Blackwood and Sophia entered his office. Several newspapers were spread out before him, including *The Times*, *The Telegraph*, *The Daily News* and *The Morning Post*. He took up *The Times* and thrust it at Blackwood, who accepted it and scanned the front page. The report's heading brought a frown of consternation to his brow:

SPRING-HEELED JACK STRIKES AGAIN

——

'MARS WILL TRIUMPH!' HE SHOUTS AS HE ATTACKS PASSERSBY ACROSS LONDON AND THE HOME COUNTIES
WHAT CAN IT MEAN?

——

NOW, HE ADDS MURDER TO HIS LIST OF CRIMES

——

'Murder?' said Blackwood. 'He killed a soldier?'

Grandfather shook his head. 'Some poor girl in Bermondsey: threw her into a sewer and watched her drown, he did!'

'Oh!' Sophia put a hand to her mouth in horror.

Grandfather glanced at her. 'Do forgive me, your Ladyship. I did not mean to shock you so. Please, take a seat, both of you.'

'Did he really say that?' asked Blackwood. 'Did he really say that Mars will triumph?'

'New Scotland Temple are investigating,' Grandfather replied. 'So far, they have testimony from at least a dozen witnesses that that is *exactly* what he said. But what the deuce it means, I have no idea, for the brute is clearly no Martian.'

'Indeed not,' Blackwood replied in a measured tone. 'In fact, we have evidence to suggest that he hails from Venus.'

'*What?*' Grandfather spluttered. 'What the dickens are you talking about, man?'

'It's quite true, I assure you sir,' said Sophia, as she handed the SPR report and the waxed envelope containing the metal fragment across the desk to him.

Grandfather took them both and glanced at the envelope. 'This is the thing you showed me yesterday.'

Sophia nodded. 'And you also have there the metallurgical and psychometrical analyses. Our chemists and psychometrists concur that the fragment originated on Venus.'

Grandfather read the report, periodically muttering to himself in amazement as he did so.

Blackwood waited for him to finish and then said, 'It looks like you were right, sir: there *does* seem to be a connection between the activities of Spring-Heeled Jack and the death of Ambassador R'ondd – a connection which is strengthened by what we were told by Andrew Crosse.'

'Explain,' said Grandfather.

Blackwood described their questioning of the amateur scientist the previous day, along with his description of his singular visitor, who had called himself 'Indrid Cold'.

'If this Johnnie *is* from Venus,' said Grandfather when his Special Investigator had finished, 'then why in God's name is he babbling about a Martian victory?' He picked up *The Times* again and waved it at Blackwood. 'Lord knows, I've no particular liking for journalists, but they ask a fair question: what *can* it mean?'

'I'm afraid that has yet to be ascertained, sir,' replied Blackwood with a sigh. 'As far as we were aware, there *was* no life on Venus – at least, no *intelligent* life. And yet, apparently there is…'

Grandfather grunted. 'Well, how could we have known for sure? Our new Æther zeppelins have yet to be tested in the depths of space, although of course there are now designs afoot to build craft capable of reaching Mars.' He slapped the paper down on his desk. 'One thing's for sure: this "Mars will triumph" business puts us in the wrong ditch, and we'd better climb out of it before people start thinking that the Martians are behind all this.'

'Can we be absolutely sure that they're not?' asked Blackwood.

Grandfather sat back in his chair and gave his Investigator an appraising look. 'What, you mean employ some ruffian from another planet to attack the centre of the British Empire, and then assassinate their own Ambassador? What could they possibly gain from such a plan?'

'Perhaps they need an excuse to attack Earth,' Blackwood replied.

Sophia glanced at him in shock. 'Thomas! I mean... Mr Blackwood! Do you really think so?'

'I really don't know. But we'll do well to examine all possibilities.'

'Hmm,' said Grandfather. 'Well, examine as much as you want, but do it quickly. Time is rapidly becoming our enemy.' He picked up a piece of paper from his desk and handed it to Blackwood, who read it.

'They've brought forward the departure of the interplanetary cylinder from the twenty-ninth!'

'Quite so,' said Grandfather. 'It lifts off from Biggin Hill Cosmodrome at ten forty-five tomorrow morning. Personnel from the Martian Embassy have already retrieved the Ambassador's body from us and are preparing it for its journey as we speak.'

'But why?' wondered Sophia. 'Why bring the departure forward?'

'Her Majesty wanted to prove to the Martian Government that we have made some significant progress with our investigation,' Blackwood replied. 'She wanted to include that information in her letter of condolence. Perhaps someone on Mars doesn't want that to happen: perhaps someone wants Lunan R'ondd's body to be sent home *without* an explanation.'

'That would certainly cause a great deal of upset,' conceded Grandfather.

'Even anger,' Sophia added.

'There is a great deal we don't know about the political situation on Mars,' Blackwood continued. 'There may well be factions there who don't want anything to do with Earth, or with Humanity. It's possible that there are influences at work of which we know nothing, but which are working against the continued forging of peaceful relations between the two planets.'

'But where does Venus fit into all this?' demanded Grandfather.

Blackwood fell silent, suddenly lost in thought.

Grandfather sighed. 'Well, whatever the answer, it's quite clear we're operating on two fronts. Blackwood, I'd like you to go to the Martian Embassy and have a chat with the Ambassador's Assistant… what's the fellow's name?'

'Petrox Voronezh.'

'That's the chap. Find out what, if anything, the Martians know of Venus. They're streets ahead of us when it comes to interplanetary travel, after all, and they may have some information that we could use to our advantage.'

Blackwood nodded.

'Shall I go too?' asked Sophia.

'No, my dear,' replied Grandfather. 'I would like you to liaise with New Scotland Temple. I believe they've put one of their best men on the Spring-Heeled Jack case – Detective Gerhard de Chardin…'

'I know Detective de Chardin,' Sophia said. 'We have collaborated once or twice in the past on cases of a supernatural nature.'

'Excellent. Then join forces with him once again and interview as many witnesses to last night's attacks as you can. I'm willing to wager that the oaf didn't just vanish into thin air once he'd had his fun! He must have gone somewhere. See if you can't gather any clues as to where that might be. We have about twenty-four hours until that cylinder departs. Let's see if we can put a little more information onboard!'

CHAPTER SEVEN:
At the Martian Embassy

Blackwood took a hansom to Chesham Place and got out in front of a large, elegant building overlooking Belgrave Square. The building was of five storeys, its walls whitewashed to pristine brightness, the columns about its portico tall and slender; in fact, there was nothing in its external appearance to suggest that it contained the diplomatic mission of a distant world.

This impression of normality was quickly dispelled, however, when Blackwood rang the bell beside the heavy oak door, which was firmly locked. A thin, high-pitched voice issued from the ornately-fashioned brass loudspeaker grille beside the bell-pull.

'Yes?'

'My name is Thomas Blackwood. I am here on Crown business.'

A moment later, there was a faint buzz and the sharp *clack* of a withdrawing bolt, and the door unlocked – apparently, Blackwood guessed, by means of some remotely-operated electrical mechanism.

The door swung open on soundless hinges, and he stepped into an expansive foyer, at the far end of which a Martian, formally dressed in a shimmering blue suit and wearing full breathing apparatus, sat behind a desk that appeared to be fashioned from a large slab of highly-polished mottled stone akin to onyx.

Blackwood walked across the marble floor and came to a halt before the desk. Even though the Martian was sitting down, his large head, which presented aspects of the avian and reptilian in equal measure, was on a level with Blackwood's.

'Good morning, sir,' said the Martian.

'Good morning.' Blackwood withdrew his calling card and placed it on the strangely-patterned surface of the desk. 'I am investigating the death of Ambassador R'ondd on behalf of Her Majesty's Government, and I wonder if it would be possible to speak with Mr Petrox Voronezh.'

The Martian lowered his huge, dark eyes to the card and regarded it in silence for several moments, as if trying to decipher the characters printed upon it. Then, suddenly, a piercing twitter escaped from the speaker grille set into the burnished neck ring of his breathing apparatus. Blackwood winced as the Martian language stabbed at his eardrums.

Almost immediately, another Martian appeared in a nearby doorway and ambled across the floor towards them. A brief exchange ensued in their bizarre, chirruping language, after which the new arrival took the calling card and vanished once again through the door.

'If you would care to take a seat, Mr Blackwood,' said the Martian behind the reception desk, 'my colleague will inform Petrox Voronezh of your desire to speak with him.'

'Thank you.' Blackwood glanced around at the Chesterfield standing against the wall to his left and sat himself down. While he waited, he allowed his mind to turn over the various aspects of the case which he and Sophia had so far uncovered. As was his habit, he thought in brief phrases, examining each in turn, much in the manner of an antiquary browsing amongst curious artefacts:

Ambassador murdered by means of artificial life forms... Andrew Crosse, their creator, visited by a strange man calling himself Indrid Cold... who may be Spring-Heeled Jack... apparently from Venus... takes a sample of the creatures... somehow introduces them into R'ondd's breathing apparatus... how does he do that? Past Martian security? Unlikely.

A Venusian attacking people in London... the heart of the Empire... shouting 'Mars will triumph!'... to what purpose? Is he in the employ of the Martians? Again... why? If they wanted to attack us, why not simply do so? Unless such an attack would be considered an outrage by the majority of the Martian people. An excuse, then: an agent provocateur *to sow seeds of mistrust and hatred between the two species.*

They know we're building new Æther zeppelins with a range sufficient to reach Mars. Do they want that? At the moment, we have to request passage on their cylinders if we want to go to Mars... that will soon change. Is that enough to make them want to destroy us? Is the forging of economic and cultural relations between our two worlds nothing more than a ruse, a means by which they can learn of our strengths and weaknesses? Perhaps... but what the deuce is the Venus connection?

Blackwood's thoughts were interrupted by the return of the Martian who had taken his card and who now stood towering above him. 'Petrox Voronezh will see you now, Mr Blackwood,' he said.

Blackwood got to his feet. 'Thank you.'

As they crossed the foyer, the Martian said, 'Have you ever been in our environment?'

Somewhat taken aback by the question, Blackwood shook his head. 'No... no, I have not.' He had expected Voronezh to don breathing apparatus and meet him in the atmosphere of Earth, as a courtesy. He was slightly irritated that the opposite was apparently the case. And yet, he supposed, this *was* Martian territory... *When in Rome*, he thought, philosophically.

It was only when he followed his guide through the door from which he had originally appeared that Blackwood realised the reason for this apparent incivility. The room in which he found himself was unremarkable save for the rows of breathing apparatuses hanging upon one wall, like the disembodied heads of weird automata, and the large, circular metal door which dominated the far wall.

An airlock, Blackwood thought. *Of course! The entire building must be given over to the Martian atmosphere. The rooms must be hermetically sealed to preserve the correct proportion of gases. Voronezh isn't being discourteous in bidding me enter the Embassy-proper – quite the opposite, in fact! It would have been impolite – not to mention indiscreet – to hold a conversation in the foyer.*

Blackwood's guide selected one of the smaller items of headgear and turned to him. 'If you will allow me, sir...'

'Of course.'

The Martian placed the bulbous helmet of the breathing apparatus over Blackwood's head and helped him into the harness supporting the air tanks. 'We keep several of these smaller types,' he explained as he began to manipulate knobs and switches beyond Blackwood's field of view, 'for humans visiting the Embassy. The tanks contain gases in the correct Earthly proportions, for a maximum duration of four hours.'

'I see,' said Blackwood. He was about to say more but was surprised into silence by the curious – and rather unpleasant – sensation of something pliable and slightly damp closing around his neck. 'Ugh!' he said.

'Please do not be alarmed,' said the Martian. 'That is merely the neck ring self-sealing.'

Damned thing feels alive! Blackwood thought, and then he added to himself, *Lunan R'ondd died in one of these...*

Suppressing a shudder, he followed his guide to the circular metal door, which reminded him somewhat of the entrance to a bank vault. The Martian began to turn the large, five-spoked wheel at the centre of the door, and as he did so, Blackwood heard the faint hiss of well-oiled precision machinery.

The door swung slowly open – Blackwood noted that it was more than a foot thick – and they passed through into a rather smaller chamber whose walls were covered with what looked like air vents. The Martian closed the outer door and went to a wall panel covered with complex-looking levers and dials, from which numerous metal pipes sprouted before disappearing into the floor and ceiling.

There was a loud hiss as the Martian completed his operation, and Blackwood felt goose pimples rise all over his body at the sudden touch of cold, unfamiliar air.

Presently, when the atmosphere of Earth had been replaced with that of Mars, Blackwood's guide opened the inner airlock door and beckoned him through to another dressing room, where the Martian divested himself of his own breathing apparatus.

To Blackwood, the sight was surprising – shocking, even – for although he knew perfectly well what Martians looked like and had viewed Lunan R'ondd's body in its dead nakedness, he had never seen a living Martian without his breathing apparatus. Although he hadn't realised it, the helmets they wore, while affording an unobstructed view of their features, nevertheless acted as a kind of screen or barrier separating them from their environment on a subtle emotional level as well as a crudely physical one. The fact that Blackwood himself was now ensconced within his own apparatus did nothing to lessen the intense impression of *alienness* which the bare-headed Martian now evoked in him.

The Martian gave him a look which he perceived as strange even for that singular race. What was behind that look? he wondered. Was it due to a sudden sense of vulnerability... or perhaps the opposite?

I am at you mercy...

The thought sprang unbidden into Blackwood's mind, and he could not banish it, for it struck him as profoundly true: just as the Martians in London were at the heart of the British Empire, so had he entered the heart of their presence on Earth. It was not a comfortable feeling, and it was only exacerbated by the self-sealing neck ring of the breathing apparatus which had closed so powerfully and cloyingly about his neck.

He followed his guide out of the dressing room and into a long corridor containing several doors. Blackwood noted the complete lack of Martian decoration; it might have been a corridor in any large and well-appointed house.

He mentioned this to his guide, who replied, 'We do not consider corridors to be living spaces; even in our cities, they are rare and are unfurnished and undecorated. However, we are also well aware of our status as guests on your world, and as such we consider it discourteous to alter the appointment of any rooms, in any houses, which we may use. You will see what I mean when you are in the Assistant's office.'

Blackwood tried to shrug, but it was no easy feat in the contraption he was wearing, and so he simply nodded and followed his guide to the end of the corridor, where the Martian chirruped loudly at a wide double door. An answering chirrup came immediately, and the Martian opened the door. 'Please go in,' he said and then, turning on his heels, started off down the corridor.

As soon as he stepped into Petrox Voronezh's office, Blackwood understood what his guide had meant with his brief explanation of Martian decorative practices while on

Earth. The room was tastefully furnished with a number of very fine pieces, and the intricately-patterned rug covering the parquet floor was evidently of Turkish provenance. Such was the elegance and harmony of the furnishings that Blackwood assumed that the choices must have been made by humans, perhaps at the behest of the building's interplanetary residents.

And yet, the room also contained a number of exceedingly tall screens, some of which reached right up to the ceiling fifteen feet above Blackwood's head. These screens, which were arranged about the room in a haphazard fashion (haphazard, at least, to human eyes), were painted with a variety of Martian scenes, which struck Blackwood as beautiful and *outré* in equal measure. There were desert scenes rendered in exquisite shades of red and ochre, sunsets of cloud-strewn pink and lilac, canals of glittering azure beneath million-starred night skies, and distant cities filled with pinpoints of light which seemed to flicker as Blackwood looked at them, their light catching and playing upon the strange geometries of the alien buildings.

'Beautiful, aren't they?' said Petrox Voronezh, who had risen from his desk and was now approaching Blackwood.

'Very.'

'I confess I spend a few minutes every morning simply standing here amid the scenes of my home world. It – what is the English expression? – it sets me up for the day.'

'You must miss it very much.'

'I do.' Voronezh offered Blackwood his hand and then indicated the single chair facing the desk. Blackwood noted that the desk was made of the same curious stone as the one in the foyer. He also noted that the cogitator which sat upon it was of a Martian design which appeared to operate on completely different principles to Earthly machines. In fact, there was only a complex keyboard and a scrying glass; of the cogitator itself, there was no sign.

'May I ask what type of stone this is?' asked Blackwood as he took the proffered chair.

'Its name translates to English as World Mind Stone,' replied Voronezh. 'A rather clumsy phrase, I admit, but then, if you will forgive me for saying so, English is a rather clumsy language.'

'World Mind Stone,' Blackwood echoed, ignoring the slight.

'We believe that our world is a conscious being and that its awareness is concentrated in certain minerals, including this.' Voronezh gently laid a long-fingered hand upon the polished surface of the desk. 'It gives us comfort to bring it with us when we visit other worlds.'

Other worlds, thought Blackwood. *Plural. Interesting.* 'Certain humans have similar beliefs,' he replied. 'The shamanic cultures of the Americas and the Far East believe that everything has a soul, including animals, trees, rocks…'

'I did not say "soul", Mr Blackwood: I said "awareness".'

'Is there a difference?'

The Martian responded with a curious expression, which Blackwood took to be a smile. 'Why do you wish to see me? Have you made any further progress in your investigation?'

'Indeed we have. Tell me, have you read this morning's papers?'

Voronezh nodded.

'Then you will be aware of the attacks perpetrated by the creature known as Spring-Heeled Jack across London last night, and what he is reported to have said to the witnesses.'

The Martian gave another nod – albeit a more tentative one, Blackwood thought.

'Do you have any idea what he could have meant by that?' the Investigator asked.

'None whatsoever,' came the reply.

'I see. Are you similarly unaware that this creature comes from the planet Venus?'

Voronezh blinked at him. 'How do you know that?'

Blackwood smiled. 'The details are unimportant, Mr Voronezh, but we *do* know.'

Voronezh stood up and went to a nearby table, on which stood a large, bulbous decanter fashioned in a highly unusual shape, as if the glass had been blown from several different directions at once. He poured a pale blue liquid into an equally bizarre tumbler and sipped it contemplatively.

Playing for time, Blackwood thought. *He knows more than he's letting on.* 'We were unaware of any intelligent life on Venus,' he said. 'Were *you*?'

Voronezh sighed. 'Yes, Mr Blackwood. We are well aware of what lives on Venus.'

'It's been only six years since contact was established between our two worlds,' said Blackwood. 'And in that short time, we have already begun to forge strong links – scientific and cultural.'

Voronezh gave a brief nod.

'One would think that the existence of a third civilisation in the solar system is of such significance that you would have shared the knowledge with us more or less straight away. May I ask why you haven't?'

Petrox Voronezh drained his glass and replaced it carefully on the table. He turned to Blackwood. 'We kept the knowledge from you to protect you.'

'Protect us?'

'From the terrible things which inhabit that sad and dying world.'

'Hostile intelligences?'

Voronezh sat down at his desk. 'You said that the details of how you came by this knowledge are unimportant, Mr Blackwood, but I would appreciate it if you would tell me, nevertheless.'

'Very well. My colleague, Lady Sophia Harrington, has been investigating the attacks perpetrated by Spring-

Heeled Jack. While interviewing a family who had recently encountered him, she discovered a fragment of metal, which had apparently broken off from one of his talons. That fragment has been analysed by chemists and psychometrists at the Society for Psychical Research, and it has been established beyond all reasonable doubt that it comes from Venus.'

'I see.'

'I therefore believe it to be vitally important that we learn all we can of that world and its inhabitants.'

Voronezh considered this for several moments. 'Very well,' he said presently. 'I will tell you something of Venus. As I said, it is a dying world. Once, in ages long past, it was a kind of paradise: verdant and warm, with lush forests in the northern and southern latitudes, and thick jungles in the equatorial regions. Life was abundant there – all manner of life. Its skies were painted with the thousand-hued plumages of great birds, and its vast oceans glittered with a countless myriad fishes, their scales catching the rays of the sun like living jewels, making the water alive with light and movement.

'On the land, great civilisations rose and fell with the passing of millennia – much like on your world and mine. Gradually, the people of Venus developed technologies of greater and greater power: they were confident and industrious – one is bound to say *too much* so, for they saw their world, in all its beauty and magnificent abundance, as nothing more than a resource to be used as they saw fit. They had great intelligence, but they were also prey to great foolishness.'

Blackwood nodded, thinking of the words one of the psychometrists had used. 'Rich in ability, but poor in wisdom,' he said.

'Precisely.'

'And their industry grew out of control, until it had consumed their world's resources, tainting its air and poisoning its soil.'

Voronezh nodded. 'They made a desolation and called it Progress.'

'Are there many of them left?'

'At its height, the planetary civilisation of Venus numbered in excess of nine thousand million, but their numbers are vastly reduced. We estimate there can't be much more than a thousand million left, living at the poles, which are still tolerably cool, and in deep valleys and gorges…'

'And in subterranean caverns,' said Blackwood.

'Yes. Their civilisation is in ruins, but their intelligence remains, as does their arrogance and acquisitiveness. You may think me callous to speak in such terms, but an animal is most dangerous when it is under threat… and the Venusians are threatened with extinction. They have damaged their world to such an extent that it will soon kill all who remain. Every year, the atmosphere grows hotter, as if Venus itself has sought collaboration with the Sun to rid itself of its children, who have turned against it.'

'How do you know all this?' asked Blackwood. 'Have Martians visited Venus?'

Voronezh nodded.

'Haven't you tried to help them? You have technological expertise *and* wisdom. Didn't you try to…?'

Voronezh held up his hand. 'Yes, Mr Blackwood, we tried. Our first exploratory cylinders reached Venus decades ago. They were met with a hostility that has not diminished in the intervening years, in spite of our efforts to forge diplomatic relations. We tried to offer them our guidance in rebuilding their world and their civilisation – perhaps that was arrogance on *our* part, but it was born of the most benign intentions. Our overtures were rebuffed in quite unequivocal terms. They saw our desire to help as mere condescension, perhaps masking colonial ambitions, and they threatened death to any Martian who set foot on Venus again.'

Blackwood considered this in silence. Assuming that Petrox Voronezh was telling the truth, he felt rather guilty at having suspected the Martians of underhand dealings. It was the Venusians who were up to something – and something pretty serious at that.

He thanked Voronezh for his candour and added, 'All of this brings us to the present question: why is there a Venusian on Earth? What's he up to?'

'Isn't it obvious?' said Voronezh. 'We are well aware that many humans view us with fear and mistrust; it is only natural, after all, for any being to fear the unknown, the other – especially when that other possesses power and technology far in advance of one's own. We appreciate the friendship extended to us by some, while sympathising with the trepidation of others, and we have read enough of your history to note how contact between human civilisations at different stages of development has ended badly for the less developed. Contact between Europe and what was once called the New World, for example, resulted in the catastrophic decline of those cultures which were "discovered".'

'You think the Venusians have sent an agent to sow discord between Earth and Mars?' said Blackwood.

'It is a reasonable assumption, wouldn't you say?'

'But why? For what purpose?'

'I am not sure. Nor do I believe that a few random attacks are all that this creature and his masters have planned. It seems to me that they are merely the groundwork – a preamble to other events which have yet to unfold.'

Blackwood nodded. 'By the way, I believe the brute's name to be Indrid Cold. At least, that's the one he gave to Andrew Crosse when he visited him in Somerset.'

'That is indeed a Venusian name,' Voronezh replied.

Something else occurred to Blackwood just then. 'If the Venusian civilisation is in ruins,' he said, 'how did Indrid Cold get to Earth?'

'It was noted during our initial expeditions that they still have the capacity to produce Æther ships,' Voronezh replied. 'I suspect that Indrid Cold arrived in a one-man vessel, which is hidden somewhere near London. That, however, is the least important of the questions facing us.'

'True enough,' Blackwood nodded. 'Mr Voronezh, may I ask another question?'

'Of course.'

'Why has the departure of the interplanetary cylinder been brought forward from the twenty-ninth to tomorrow?'

'Our Government has received a request from Ambassador R'ondd's family that his body be brought home as soon as possible.'

'Is that the only reason?'

Voronezh regarded his guest with unblinking eyes. 'I'm not sure I understand.'

Blackwood took a deep breath, wondering how wise it was to say what he was about to say. He supposed that he would soon find out. 'It was the intention of the Queen to provide your Government with a full and comprehensive account of what happened to Ambassador R'ondd, along with her letter of condolence. I was wondering whether there might be certain individuals on Mars who don't want that to happen: individuals who would rather he be returned with little or no explanation…'

'So that humans might be seen as dangerous fools by the people of Mars, who would then demand that diplomatic relations be broken off,' said Voronezh. 'An interesting theory.'

'Please forgive my candour, sir, but I can't help thinking of what you said during our meeting with the Queen. You threatened direct intervention in this investigation unless results were achieved very quickly.'

'We are merely anxious to resolve this matter without delay, Mr Blackwood,' Voronezh replied. 'I am certain you would too, were our positions reversed.'

'What *is* the Martian attitude to Humanity? How are we seen on your world?'

'You are viewed with curiosity – *benign* curiosity – and the desire for friendship. I assure you that there is no one on Mars who harbours any animosity whatsoever towards the people of Earth, the present situation notwithstanding. We are all children of the star you call Sol, the life-giver at the centre of this Solar System. We value your presence, we rejoice in the existence of fellow intelligent beings… for we have caught glimpses of what lies beyond the outermost planets, in the dark depths of Space, and we believe that all should cling to each other in bonds of friendship and support in the face of what dwells… out there.'

Blackwood was taken aback by this utterance. Voronezh noted his surprised expression, and made the gentle chittering sound that was Martian laughter. 'Do not look so shocked, Mr Blackwood. You understand that of which I speak, for you yourself have caught a glimpse of it.'

'What do you mean?'

'I am speaking of what you call the Cosmic Spheres, of course.'

Blackwood's expression became one of outright astonishment. 'You know about that? How?'

'We obtained access to your file; we claimed that right when we learned that you would be handling this investigation, and your Government conceded it and allowed us to view your professional history. Five years ago, you investigated a series of mysterious deaths at a secret research laboratory on the west coast of Scotland. The scientists were attempting, with the full support of your Government, to harness the ætherial force known as Vril, the force which powers our interplanetary cylinders.'

'They wanted to use it as a weapon,' muttered Blackwood, shuddering inwardly at the memory. 'They hoped it would consolidate the military power of the Empire… but they failed. Catastrophically.'

'On the contrary, they succeeded,' said Voronezh. 'But there are areas of enquiry which are so dangerous that success *is* failure. Your scientists managed, for an infinitesimal moment, to open a fissure between this world and the astral realm containing the Vril force, but they did so carelessly, with the wrong intentions, and without taking the necessary precautions, with the result that one of the denizens of that realm, a Sha'halloth, was able to deposit its eggs in the laboratory.'

Don't, Blackwood thought, struggling against the temptation to shut his eyes tight and flee the room. *Please don't say any more!*

But Voronezh continued, 'The eggs of the Sha'halloth are intelligent and ravenous; they fed on the scientists' minds in order to fuel the growth of the abominations they contained. They drove the men insane, and when you were sent to the laboratory, and saw what they had done to each other, your own mind was nearly unhinged. And yet, you conquered your terror and revulsion; you destroyed the eggs, neutralised the threat…'

'I destroyed the scientists, too,' Blackwood whispered. 'I… I killed them all.'

'You had no choice, for they were already lost.'

Blackwood shook his head. 'God… the things they'd done!' He felt tears welling in his eyes at the memories which had risen to prominence in his mind, memories he had tried desperately to rid himself of in the five years since those

160

terrible events, but which now lay exposed once again in their filthy nakedness before his mind's eye. He remembered the eggs: pulsating globs of glistening jelly, faintly glowing with impossible colours, covered with writhing tendrils that seemed to fade in and out of visibility, as though still connected somehow to the realm from which they had come. To look upon them had been intolerable; to feel them probing his mind had been utterly unbearable, akin to a sexual molestation, but far more intimate. He felt his stomach churning at the memories, threatening to void itself there and then. He put a hand up to his mouth, and was surprised when it collided with the faceplate: he had completely forgotten that he was wearing the breathing apparatus, so powerful were the memories. He forced himself to breathe deeply and evenly. He looked at Voronezh and saw that the Martian was watching him intently.

'You did a great service to your country,' said Voronezh, 'to your Empire, to your world. If the Sha'halloth eggs had hatched, it would have been the end of all of you. After reading your report, your Government decided to place an indefinite moratorium on Vril research. It was a wise decision. The people of Earth have much to thank you for. But we have digressed considerably. We were speaking of the Martian attitude to Earthmen. I repeat: we bear you no animosity whatsoever; we consider you as friends.'

'But that attitude could change,' said Blackwood, grateful that they had returned to the matter at hand.

'Yes,' replied Voronezh. 'Of course it could change, given sufficient impetus.'

'The Venusians *want* it to change. They want us to become enemies. Why?'

'I do not know. But it does seem likely that they will continue with their agenda. Their activities, I think, will escalate in seriousness.'

'I agree,' said Blackwood with a sigh. 'I think you're right that these attacks by Spring-Heeled Jack, or Indrid Cold – whatever you want to call him – are only the first phase of some dark plan. The assassination of Lunan R'ondd was the second phase. He isn't finished yet, not by a long way. But the question is: what does he intend to do next?'

'The only thing that can be said with any certainty,' replied Voronezh, 'is that he will do *something*.'

CHAPTER EIGHT:
De Chardin of New Scotland Temple

While Blackwood was discussing Spring-Heeled Jack and his nefarious plans with Petrox Voronezh, Sophia's carriage turned from Richmond Terrace onto Victoria Embankment and came to a halt outside New Scotland Temple. Beyond the Gothic ramparts, which were banded in red brick and white Portland stone, the elegant spire of the great Clock Tower rose from the Palace of Westminster in the growing murk of another London particular. Through the veil of dun-coloured fog, the Tower took on a sinister, spectral aspect, which Sophia found entirely in keeping with her present mission.

She asked her driver, John, to wait for her; then, gathering the collar of her coat tight about her neck to ward off the dank chill, which she found most inconvenient despite its aptness, she walked quickly to the main entrance and through the arched granite portico.

The desk sergeant smiled and nodded to her as she approached, for Sophia was well-known and respected by the Metropolitan Templar Police. 'Good morning, your Ladyship,' he said. 'How may I be of assistance?'

Sophia returned his smile. 'Good morning to you, sir. I wonder if I might speak with Detective de Chardin? Is he here?'

'He's in his office, I believe.'

Sophia indicated the door leading from the entrance lobby into the interior of the building. 'May I?'

'Of course, Lady Sophia,' replied the sergeant. 'I'm sure he'll be very happy to see you.' There was a subtle note of sadness or regret in the man's voice, which suggested to Sophia that the Spring-Heeled Jack investigation was not going particularly well, and that de Chardin would indeed be pleased to see anyone who might shed further light upon it.

She nodded her thanks, went through the door and walked briskly along a series of corridors leading further into the warren-like depths of the building. Here and there, she passed police officers who recognised and greeted her cordially, and despite the sinister strangeness of the case upon which she was engaged, she felt a sudden, powerful sense of safety and wellbeing.

Along with all other decent, law-abiding citizens of the British Empire, Sophia believed the Metropolitan Templar Police to be one of its greatest assets. The organisation had changed frequently and radically in the nearly eight centuries since its creation in 1119, when a knight of Champagne named Hugh de Payens bound himself, along with eight trusted companions, in a perpetual vow to defend the Holy Land and the pilgrims who travelled there.

Within two hundred years, this knightly order, which became known as the Poor Fellow-Soldiers of Jesus Christ and the Temple of Solomon, or simply as the Knights Templar, became one of the richest and most powerful organisations in the world, possessing lands and wealth beyond the wildest dreams of most, together with a military power to rival that of many nations. Their success was not to last much longer, however, for it bred jealousy and animosity in the hearts of many, including Philip the Fair of France. Bankrupt, fearful and envious of the enormous power and wealth wielded by the Knights Templar, Philip contributed to the spreading of dark and terrible rumours about the Order: that they fought for no other reason than to swell their own coffers; that they were secretly in league with the Saracens against whom they had ostensibly sworn to fight; that they secretly worshipped the Devil, and so on, and so on.

Philip the Fair ordered the arrest of the Grand Master, Jacques de Molay, along with sixty of his fellow knights, who had accepted Pope Clement V's invitation to go to Paris to discuss a new Crusade with the kings of Armenia and Cyprus. While de Molay and the other Templars were suffering the most hideous tortures designed to elicit confessions of devil-worship and other blasphemies, Philip took possession of the Paris Temple and sent word to the English King Edward II, advising him to take similar action against the Order there. Edward replied that he had serious doubts as to the veracity of the charges levelled against the Templars and wrote to the kings of Portugal, Castile, Aragon and Sicily, asking if there were any truth to the accusations. Although the replies Edward received maintained the Templars' innocence of all such charges, Pope Clement assured him that they were true and ordered him to suppress the Order.

In 1314, after years of imprisonment, Jacques de Molay was burned alive on a charcoal fire on the Ile-des-Javiaux in the Seine, and many of his fellow Templars fled their lands, seeking safe havens across Europe. One of these was western Scotland, where they allied themselves with Robert the Bruce in his war of independence against the English, contributing to his victory at the Battle of Bannockburn, in return for which they were allowed to remain in that country unmolested. Thus did the unhappy and unjustly victimised Order maintain its presence in the British Isles.

In the centuries that followed, the Knights Templar gradually re-established themselves as bankers, entrepreneurs and philanthropists in Britain, ever mindful of their betrayal by the Catholic Church, declaring themselves the enemies of social injustice and the oppression of the weak by the powerful.

Such was their reputation for decency and fairness that when Sir Robert Peel was appointed as Home Secretary in 1822, and put forward his plan to standardise the police and make it an official paid profession, his thoughts turned first to the Knights Templar. Until then, inefficiency and corruption, combined with the lack of proper organisation, had largely robbed the public of its faith in the volunteer parish constables, watchmen and Bow Street Runners who had hitherto policed London's streets. The Knights Templar, Peel believed, were the perfect group from which to recruit his new force. Thus was the Metropolitan Templar Police Act passed in 1829, and the Order which had begun its life protecting pilgrims on their journeys through the Holy Land in the twelfth century, now protected law-abiding citizens going about their business in the heart of the British Empire in the nineteenth.

Sophia came to a halt at the door of de Chardin's office and gave a knock.

A voice drifted out to her. 'Come!'

Gerhard de Chardin was sitting at his desk with his head in his hands when Sophia entered. On seeing her, he sprang to his feet, a look of surprise on his finely-chiselled features. 'Lady Sophia!' he cried. 'Do please come in.'

'Thank you, Detective de Chardin,' Sophia replied, watching in amusement as he hurriedly moved a small pile of papers from a chair and placed it before his desk, and then (with a rather charming self-consciousness) smoothed his neatly trimmed goatee.

'Would you care for some refreshment?' he asked, taking his own seat again. 'A cup of tea, perhaps?'

'Thank you, no.'

'Well… to what do I owe the honour, your Ladyship?'

'I have come to offer you my assistance in the case you are currently investigating.'

'The Spring-Heeled Jack business?' he asked, surprised.

'The same.'

'I see. May I ask what interest the SPR has in the affair?'

'Our interest was piqued by the apparently supernatural abilities which he seems to possess,' she explained. 'As a result of my own investigations, I have come into possession of a piece of metal from one of the villain's talons.'

De Chardin sat forward suddenly. 'You have? May I see it?'

'You may indeed, sir – but not now, for I do not have it with me; it is at present at the SPR headquarters, where it has been examined by our best chemists and psychometrists.'

'And what were their conclusions?' de Chardin asked.

When Sophia told him, the detective gazed at her, open-mouthed, for several moments. 'Venus?' he managed to say, presently.

'Venus,' she replied.

'Good grief.' De Chardin stroked his beard, contemplatively this time. 'What does it mean?'

'That is what I'm endeavouring to find out, along with Mr Thomas Blackwood of Her Majesty's Bureau of Clandestine Affairs.'

De Chardin nodded. 'I know Mr Blackwood. He's a good man, a credit to the Empire.'

'Indeed,' Sophia replied, suppressing the smile which seemed to have begun to spring unbidden to her lips whenever she thought of the Special Investigator. As de Chardin listened with mounting interest, she related everything that had happened thus far in the affair of the Martian Ambassador's assassination, and how it appeared to be intimately connected with the activities of the mysterious attacker. 'I take it,' she concluded, 'that you will be interviewing witnesses to last night's assaults.'

'Certainly. In fact, I was about to make my way to the scene of the first incident. Would you care to accompany me?'

Sophia smiled. 'I'd be delighted. We can use my carriage.'

*

In spite of the trust and esteem in which the Templar Police were held, Sophia and de Chardin found it surprisingly difficult to find witnesses, or to persuade them to talk when they did find them.

'It's as if they're still terrified of the miscreant,' the detective commented as they rode in Sophia's carriage towards Bermondsey and the scene of the previous night's murder of the young prostitute. 'Terrified that if they talk, he will know and return to exact his vengeance upon them.'

'One cannot blame them for being so afraid,' Sophia replied. 'They believe Spring-Heeled Jack to be possessed of supernormal powers – and they are right.'

'Supernormal, yes,' said de Chardin, 'but not supernatural. If this Indrid Cold is from another world, then he is a physical being, and as such he is mortal and capable of being apprehended.'

Sophia glanced at her companion. 'Let us hope so, Detective de Chardin... let us hope so.'

The carriage passed a line of warehouses and factories, established in recent years along the banks of the Thames in an effort to rescue the district from the filth and squalor that had afflicted it and its people. The project had only been partially successful, however, for there were still large areas of Bermondsey where human misery and despair maintained their grip, an incurable disease of body, mind and soul that seeped from the flaking, sagging buildings and rose like a hellish fume from the sewers that threaded cancerously through the area.

It seemed to Sophia, as she looked out at the newer buildings which hid the spiritual and material darkness beyond, that there were parts of the city that possessed their own peculiar evil, their own special degradation that no amount of regeneration would ever entirely banish or even ameliorate. Built by human beings, it had turned against them, in the manner of the creature assembled by Dr Frankenstein some years ago, which had cursed its creator for inflicting unwanted existence upon it. *Is it progress you want?* the city seemed to say. *Very well; behold your progress. Look upon it and weep!*

The carriage left the warehouses and factories behind and entered a narrow street flanked by decrepit buildings that slumped as if in exhaustion, their time-worn bricks sweating and glistening in the fog's dank caress. Here and there, figures moved in the gloom, each a sad Theseus wandering through a labyrinth from which there was no escape, for there was no Ariadne to offer a ball of string by which they might find their way into the light.

The carriage moved on, watched by dull, hooded eyes, until it came to the edge of the sewer where Indrid Cold's victim had met her atrocious end.

As Sophia and de Chardin stepped down from the carriage, two rough figures approached from out of the shifting tendrils of fog.

'Well well, what 'ave we 'ere?' said one.

'Looks like a fine lady an' gentleman, come to pay us a visit,' said his companion.

Sophia shuddered as she took in their appearance: their ragged, filthy clothes, their beady eyes glinting in hostile, hungry faces. One of them looked her up and down, grinned foully at her and licked his lips.

The first speaker chuckled and said, 'If the gentleman will kindly hand over his valuables, which includes the young lady, we'll be on our way. Ain't that right, Bert?'

'Oh yes, Alfie,' said the other. 'That's right enough. You may rest assured, sir, that we'll spend your money wisely… and spend ourselves on the young lady!' They both chuckled lasciviously.

De Chardin unbuttoned both his Ulster and the grey coat beneath to reveal the large cross that was stitched in crimson silk upon the breast of his shirt. 'Templar Police,' he said in a quiet, measured tone which nevertheless hinted at great power and greater ruthlessness. 'Begone, or suffer the consequences.'

The expressions on the two ruffians' faces were transformed instantly from greed and lust to uncertainty and fear. One scratched his stubbly chin, clearly debating with himself whether to chance his arm against the stranger. The other, however, allowed himself no such equivocation, and tugged at his colleague's sleeve, drawing him away into the murk from which they had emerged.

Sophia let out the breath she had been holding as de Chardin turned to her. 'Are you all right, your Ladyship?'

'Yes, I'm quite all right, Detective de Chardin,' she replied, glancing up at her driver. John nodded to her as he put away the large revolver which he had withdrawn as soon as the ruffians appeared. 'I don't believe I was ever in any danger.'

De Chardin gave a wry smile, for he had also noticed John's weapon. 'Indeed not. In fact, I believe this abysmal stench offers more peril than any of Bermondsey's denizens.'

By way of agreement, Sophia took a handkerchief from the sleeve of her coat and pressed it to her face. *These poor people!* she thought. *To live one's entire life breathing this filth.*

'Look,' said de Chardin suddenly, pointing into the gloom.

Sophia did as he asked and dimly spied a lone figure, small and hunched, standing a little way off in the distance at the edge of the sewer.

'Come, your Ladyship,' the Templar Knight said, and together they approached the figure, which, they presently saw, was that of an old woman, beaten down by age and unimaginable hardship into a tiny bundle of rags and bones and withered flesh.

As they drew up alongside her, they saw that the old woman was silently weeping, her tears falling into the river of brown sludge that steamed faintly at her feet. She sighed and shook her head periodically, ignoring the newcomers, lost in her grief.

'You knew her,' said de Chardin quietly, for the cause of the old woman's distress was quite plain.

'Poor Emily,' the woman whispered. 'Oh, my poor little thing!'

She seemed not to notice their presence, seemed to be talking to herself, and so de Chardin added, 'Emily Taylor… that was her name.'

'Yes,' the woman replied, still gazing down into the fetid depths of the sewer. 'Emily Taylor was her name.'

'Are you a member of her family?' asked Sophia quietly. Perhaps it was the sound of another female voice which made the woman look up at Sophia and de Chardin. 'I'm her grandmother,' she said. 'Her parents died when she was a little girl… I did my best to take care of her… but the money… never any money. She worked… you know, on the streets. I didn't want her to, but she said there was no other way. And now… now, gone!' Her frail old body was wracked anew with sobs, and Sophia placed a hand on her shoulder.

'I promise you we shall apprehend the man who did this,' said de Chardin. 'We shall apprehend him and punish him with the utmost severity of the law.'

'Those Martians,' the woman said, having recovered herself a little. 'Those foul, beastly things! It's their fault! They're the ones that should be punished! "Mars will triumph," he said. "Mars will triumph!" while he threw my poor Emily down there. And he laughed while she was pulled under. Laughed, he did!'

Sophia cast an anguished look at de Chardin. The tall, powerfully-built Templar Knight looked hazy and indistinct, and Sophia wondered whether it was the presence of the fog or the thoughts of utter helplessness drifting through her own mind that turned him into a phantom rather than a man.

De Chardin leaned forward and whispered in her ear, 'We should go.' Then, to the old woman he said, 'The sewer will be dredged today. We will not allow your Emily to remain there.' Then he took a note from his wallet and placed it in the old woman's hand. 'For flowers, when she is laid to rest.'

The old woman accepted the money, whispering, 'Bless you, sir.'

De Chardin crossed himself, and then he and Sophia returned to her carriage. 'This villain's agenda has begun to work itself out,' he said as they settled themselves into the seat. 'Did you mark what she said, your Ladyship?'

'I did,' Sophia sighed. 'In the blink of an eye, she has come to hate Martians, because of what Indrid Cold said. How many others heard him say that as they watched him commit his atrocities?'

'I fear that question is no longer relevant,' the detective replied, 'since it is now all over London, thanks to the papers, and it will only be a matter of hours before it is all over the country. The word will spread like wildfire that the Martians are to blame for these crimes – even though Spring-Heeled Jack looks nothing like a Martian; even though he doesn't even come from Mars!'

'We should notify the press immediately, apprise them of the true situation,' Sophia declared.

De Chardin nodded. 'Absolutely, although I suspect that the Bureau will have the final word on that matter. Nevertheless, I'm not certain how much good it will do.'

Sophia gave him a questioning glance. 'What do you mean?'

'This would be the first the public has heard of intelligent life on Venus. Lord knows, it was enough of a shock when it became apparent that there was such life on Mars! I'm not sure that they will believe it. It's much easier to tilt at an enemy one can see, an adversary whom one *knows* to exist. Even if we tell the press that this ne'er-do-well hails from Venus, I doubt that it will make any difference.'

'In that case,' said Sophia as the carriage began to make its way out of Bermondsey, 'it is all the more imperative that he be apprehended and his true identity revealed to all!'

*

The carriage took them west, out of London and into the rolling countryside of Hampshire. In spite of the change in their surroundings, Sophia couldn't shake the feeling of deadly depression that had settled upon her, couldn't rid herself of the memory of the poor old woman standing on that grimy bank, looking down into the fetid depths that had swallowed her granddaughter.

As if in response to her mood, the lush, verdant landscape gave way once more to the harshness of brick and stone, as they entered the Barracks at Aldershot. Their destination was the Talevara Barracks south of the Basingstoke Canal, which had been named after Wellington's hard-won victory during the Peninsular War in 1809. Designed to accommodate a battalion of infantry, the Barracks consisted of two large, three-storey buildings facing each other across a wide parade ground.

De Chardin and Sophia presented themselves at the sentry box, stated their business, and were allowed to pass. The Army held the Templar Police in high esteem due to their martial history, and it was therefore a simple matter to convince the Commanding Officer to allow them to interview the soldiers who had encountered Spring-Heeled Jack the previous evening, one of whom was still in the infirmary being treated for face wounds sustained during the altercation.

'Like a demon from Hell, he was, sir,' said Private Buckley, his face dressed in bandages. 'Never seen the likes of him before.'

De Chardin and Sophia took the two chairs which had been brought to his bedside by a nurse. 'Can you describe him in a little greater detail, Private Buckley?' asked de Chardin.

'Oh yes, I can do that,' replied the soldier with a visible shudder. 'I've seen battle, out in the Sudan, and I don't mind admitting that I've known fear, *terrible* fear; it's natural, it can't be avoided, sir, no way, and any soldier who'd tell you different ain't being truthful. But there's different types of fear, I'd say. There's fear of dyin', o' course, fear of the enemy that's tryin' to kill you... but there's *another* type of fear, a type I'd never felt before – but I felt it last night.'

'What type of fear are you talking about, Private Buckley?' asked Sophia.

The wounded soldier hesitated before replying, 'Fear of what's unknown, ma'am, *that's* the type of fear I'm talkin' about. The thing that came to the Barracks last night.' He raised a hand to his ruined face. 'The thing what did *this* to me... it weren't no man. And I tell you straight I ain't *never* felt such a fear before. Like a little boy I was, a little nipper out in the cruel world with no defence against what the world was throwin' at him, no… no *understandin*' of it.'

'Describe him,' said de Chardin, 'please.'

Private Buckley sighed. 'Tall, he was, sir. And built powerful, like a boxer, maybe. And he was dressed in a white suit that looked like it was made of oilskin or something similar. And he had something on his chest, like a box with a light on it… and his face… his *face*…'

'Go on,' said Sophia gently. 'What about his face?'

'Horrible, it was. Pale and stretched… like the skin didn't fit proper over the skull. And the eyes, God, those *eyes*. Like a devil's eyes, they were, full of hatred, full of burning hate! But I think the skin was the worst. I had the feelin', even while my mates and me was fightin' with him, I had the feelin' that it wasn't skin at all: that it was… I dunno, some kind of *mask*.'

'A mask?' said de Chardin, glancing at Sophia. 'Interesting,' he added in a whisper.

Private Buckley nodded vigorously and winced at the resulting pain. 'Yes sir, that's what I thought. And even while I was lying there, bleeding, I wondered what I'd see if I pulled the mask off…' The soldier's voice drifted into silence, but his eyes told eloquently of the horrors he was imagining.

'Your companions shot at him as he made his escape, didn't they?' said de Chardin.

'Yes sir, they did. But if they hit him, he showed no sign of it, for he bounded off across the fields. I've never seen anythin' like that! The way he leaped, like… like some huge frog! Unnatural, it was. He wasn't no man.'

'And the thing he said…'

'Oh yes, the thing he said. "Mars will triumph!" But he wasn't no Martian, so I don't know why he said that… unless…'

'Unless?' prompted de Chardin.

'Unless he's in league with 'em. Unless they're plannin' something. I don't know. It don't make no sense… for they're our friends, ain't they? I mean, that's what they *say*.'

'Yes,' said de Chardin. 'That's what they say, and I've no doubt that it's true.'

'Then what does it *mean,* sir?' asked the soldier desperately.

'I'm afraid I don't know,' replied the Templar Knight. 'Not yet.'

'Are we goin' to war with Mars?' said Buckley.

De Chardin smiled. 'No, my lad, we are not.'

'I don't believe we'd come off very well if we did,' said the soldier. 'I've heard tell that they've got strange weapons: guns that can blow up whole cities, and things that can destroy men's minds…'

'Fanciful rumours,' said de Chardin. 'The Martians are a peaceful people. They don't want to hurt us.'

But Private Buckley was no longer listening. He muttered to himself, 'No, we wouldn't do very well against that… but neither would they against us! We'd give 'em a good show, by God we would! They wouldn't walk away without a few bloody noses and black eyes.'

The nurse came over to them. 'Begging your pardon, sir,' she said, 'but I think Private Buckley needs to rest now.'

De Chardin nodded. 'Of course. I think we have finished here, anyway.' He laid a hand on Buckley's shoulder and said, 'You're a credit to the Empire, lad. Get well soon.'

But still the soldier wasn't listening. He was still mumbling to himself when de Chardin and Sophia thanked the nurse and left the infirmary, fighting an imaginary war which no one else could see, somewhere within the blasted landscape of his mind.

*

They interviewed Private Buckley's fellow soldiers, but gleaned no further information from them, other than the direction in which Spring-Heeled Jack had headed after his attack on the sentry box. He had disappeared, they said, into the north west, and so that was the direction in which Sophia's carriage headed, following the lanes that threaded between wide, rolling fields beneath the ash-coloured sky.

'That poor man,' said Sophia. 'He has been quite undone by his experience.'

'Yes,' said de Chardin, 'but he will recover, for I saw great resilience in his eyes, the strength of a simple yet brave soul.'

'I hope so.'

'I was intrigued by his impression that Spring-Heeled Jack was wearing a mask,' de Chardin continued.

'It would certainly explain the discrepancy between the eyewitness accounts of his appearance and the impressions gleaned by our psychometrists. But why would he wear a mask?'

De Chardin shrugged. 'Perhaps because, were he to show his true face, people would immediately realise that he is not from Mars.'

Sophia nodded. 'Perhaps.'

The carriage continued along the lane, which gradually widened until it became the main thoroughfare through a village whose sign proclaimed it to be Furfield.

'How pretty,' observed Sophia as she looked out at the ancient but beautifully-maintained buildings: the village shop, the post office and the public house, ranged around a tiny, neatly-tended green. 'I suspect it would look wonderful in a covering of winter snow…'

At that moment, there was a shattering of glass and de Chardin clutched at his forehead with a grunt. The carriage came to an immediate stop as John reigned in the horses.

'Detective!' cried Sophia, as de Chardin took away his hand, which was smeared with blood. She was about to take his head in her hands, to get a better look at the wound he had just sustained, but before she could move, he was out of the carriage and giving chase to a small figure which was running away across the green.

The Templar Knight caught up with the figure almost immediately, seizing him by the scruff of the neck and dragging him back to the carriage. Sophia climbed down as de Chardin held the boy up and examined him, in the manner of a naturalist examining an interesting but violent little animal. 'Well, my lad! Is it common sport around these parts to throw stones at passers-by?'

'Let me go!' cried the boy.

'What, and let you put through the remaining windows in this lady's carriage? I think not!'

'Let me go!' the boy cried again. 'Let me go, Martian!'

'Martian?' De Chardin gave Sophia a shocked look, but he maintained his grip on the lad. 'I am no Martian, my boy!'

'You are! You are! Help, help! The Martians have come back! They've got me!' The boy began to scream and cry with such force and anguish that de Chardin released his grip, but instead of making his escape, the boy collapsed in a sobbing heap on the ground.

Sophia went to him and gathered him up in her arms. 'There there,' she said. 'It's all right; there's nothing to be afraid of.'

The handful of villagers who were outside were now joined by several others who, alerted by the commotion, emerged from the surrounding buildings. They all approached the carriage with hostile, frowning faces.

'Leave the boy alone!' shouted one.

Another cried, 'Leave us all alone, whoever you be!'

The villagers drew up alongside the carriage. There were perhaps a dozen of them; several were brandishing knives and cudgels, and their faces were twisted with anger and fear.

'What's going on here?' demanded de Chardin.

'Just go,' said the man who had spoken first. 'We don't want no strangers around here, not anymore.'

The Knight gazed at the man with unblinking eyes, and said, 'I am Gerhard de Chardin of the Metropolitan Templar Police, and I will stay for as long as I please. And mark me well, sir: you *will* tell me what is going on here.'

The villagers glanced at each other uncertainly, and Sophia noted with surprise how the fight seemed to drain from them.

'The... Templar Police?' said one.

De Chardin indicated the boy, who had stopped crying and was now looking up at him, wide-eyed and panting. 'This young ruffian put a stone through our carriage window.' He pointed to the wound on his brow. 'As you can see, it found its mark. No mean feat to injure a Templar, my lad!'

Sophia's surprise grew as she saw the smile spreading across de Chardin's face. She had no idea whether he was genuinely angry or as amused as he appeared to be. She suspected that it was a combination of both, for such was the reputation of the Templar Police for implacability and fighting prowess that a show of humour – especially in a fraught situation such as this – could be as disarming as a show of strength.

Not for the first time, Sophia decided that Gerhard de Chardin knew exactly what he was doing.

'Now then,' said the Templar Knight, 'lower your weapons, for while I mean you no harm, you may be assured that harm will come to you if you continue to threaten us.'

The villagers looked at the smile which was still playing upon his lips, and then they looked at his eyes, and what they saw there made them obey.

A woman came forward and took the boy in her arms. 'He didn't mean no harm, sir,' she said. 'He was afraid, that's all. He thought he was protecting us, didn't you, Tommy?'

The boy said nothing, for he was still captivated by the tall, powerful Knight.

'You're his mother?' asked de Chardin.

'That I am, sir.'

'What was he protecting you from?' asked Sophia.

'From the fiend who came through here last night!' declared one of the men, and the others muttered loudly their agreement.

'Let me guess,' said de Chardin. 'He was tall and powerfully built and dressed in a white suit with a curious box attached to his chest. And his face was taught and pale, as if it were stretched over his skull.'

A momentary silence fell upon the gathering, which was then broken by exclamations of assent mingled with snatches of observation and opinion:

'Like nothin' I've ever seen.'

'Horrible, he was!'

'He was a Martian.'

'He wasn't a Martian!'

'How do *you* know what he was?'

'A devil out of Hell!'

'He was a man.'

'A man can't jump like that!'

De Chardin held up his hands, saying in a loud voice, 'Good people, I pray you be silent! What you saw last night was not a man – but neither was he a Martian…'

'What was he then?'

'He was a Martian!'

'Didn't you hear what the gentleman just said, cloth ears?'

'Well, he weren't no Hampshire lad!'

De Chardin sighed and held up his hands again. 'What did he do? Did he hurt anyone?'

'No sir, he didn't,' said the boy's mother. 'But many people saw him come bounding through Furfield – bounding along, like he didn't weigh nothing at all! It was unnatural, sir, that's what it was.'

Once again, the other villagers offered loud confirmation.

'And we saw where he went, too!' declared one.

This brought a surprising reaction from the others: they all turned to him, some with wide eyes, others with frowns of irritation. Voices were suddenly raised against him:

'Shut up, Arthur!'

'We don't know that!'

'Why did you tell them that?'

'Don't listen to him, sir. He's deranged!'

'He's an 'alf-wit!'

'Listen, you! I'm no 'alf-wit! Say that again, and I'll knock you down!'

'That's enough!' cried de Chardin. 'You, man. Arthur. Come here.'

With obvious reluctance, Arthur stepped forward under the hostile gaze of his fellows.

'You saw where he went?'

'That we did, sir.'

'No we didn't!' someone cried.

'Enough!' said the detective. 'Where did he go?'

Arthur's resolve seemed to drain from him as he stood before de Chardin, and it was quite plain that he was now beginning to question his own wisdom in offering the information. 'The others, sir… they don't want me to say.'

'But *I* want you to say. And believe me, that is what you must hold uppermost in your mind. You have already decided to tell. You cannot go back. I will not allow you to.'

'All right, sir,' Arthur sighed, and pointed to the west, towards a high wall which surmounted a distant hill. 'He went to the place this village is named after.'

'No, Arthur!' cried the villagers.

'He went to Furfield... He went to Lord Pannick's estate.'

CHAPTER NINE:
Strange News from Another World

'Well, de Chardin, you look like you've been in the wars!' Blackwood said, indicating the cut above the Templar Knight's right eye.

'A young lad, a good eye and a sharp stone: a dangerous combination,' de Chardin replied. 'How are you, Blackwood?'

'Never better.' Blackwood asked de Chardin and Sophia to be seated and took his own chair behind his desk. It was three o'clock, and they had just returned from Hampshire, coming immediately to the Bureau of Clandestine Affairs.

Blackwood's secretary brought in a large tray bearing a pot of Earl Grey for his guests, one of Blue Mountain coffee for him and a plate of macaroons, and without further ado they got down to the matter at hand.

'Did you see Petrox Voronezh, Thomas?' asked Sophia.

'I did. Your psychometrists were quite right, as we expected them to be. But the situation is much more serious and unsettling than even their brief glimpses suggested. Voronezh confirmed that there *is* intelligent life on Venus, and that the Venusians have all but destroyed their world through the unbridled development of technology and industry.'

'Why didn't the Martians tell us this before?' asked de Chardin, handing Sophia a cup of tea.

'I asked him that very question,' Blackwood replied. 'He said it was to protect us…'

'Protect us?'

'From potential contact with a hostile and acquisitive species. It seems that the Venusians aren't the types to fall in with: they're extremely aggressive and arrogant beyond all reason. They believe that it was their *right* to consume their world and turn it into a suburb of Hell. I must admit, I was wrong about the Martians: Voronezh assured me that they harbour no animosity whatsoever towards humans, and I believe him. The real danger lies on Venus, not Mars.'

'You may well be right,' said de Chardin. 'But I fear that the people we spoke to would not agree with you, even if they were told the truth.'

'Thomas,' said Sophia, 'we were thinking that it would be a very good idea to inform the public that there is hostile life on Venus, and that we have nothing to fear from Mars.'

Blackwood smiled. 'I was thinking the very same thing. In fact, I suggested it to Grandfather as soon as I returned from the Martian Embassy. He's going to discuss it with Her Majesty and the Prime Minister, and put forward the case for releasing this information.'

'I hope they agree,' said Sophia. 'It seems plain enough that the Venusians are engaged in some kind of propaganda war, sowing fear and mistrust amongst the people of Earth…'

'And fear and mistrust amongst the people of Mars,' Blackwood added. 'Voronezh believes – as I do – that this Indrid Cold chap is far from finished, that he has something else up his sleeve… perhaps a lot of things.'

Sophia was about to speak, but she was interrupted by a sudden puff of lilac smoke in the air above Blackwood's desk.

'Good afternoon, everyone!' said Shanahan.

'Good afternoon, Shanahan,' said Sophia. 'How lovely to see you again.'

The faerie alighted on the desk, gave a deep bow and, dragging one of the macaroons off the plate, proceeded to munch on it enthusiastically. 'You don't mind, do you, Mr Blackwood?' he said between mouthfuls.

'Be my guest.' Blackwood briefly considered allowing him to finish the biscuit, but since its size was to Shanahan what a cartwheel would have been to a human, he decided that the interval would be too great. 'Would you mind telling us what you have learned about the sabotaging of my cogitator, if anything?'

'Ah! In fact I learned something very interesting while I was away in Faerie,' Shanahan replied. 'Although I'm not entirely sure how much use it will be to you.'

'We shall be the judges of that,' said Blackwood. 'Pray tell.'

Shanahan licked his fingers and sat himself down cross-legged on the desktop. 'Well, as soon as I arrived home, I set about finding my colleagues, who had been commissioned by Mrs Cottingley to run your machine. They were all in a fine state, sir, I can tell you, torn between relief at having avoided destruction by the djinn and remorse at what they believed to be your unfortunate fate. I can't tell you how glad they were when I informed them that you were safe and well, thanks to the quick thinking of the beautiful young lady here.' He indicated Sophia, who smiled and blushed.

'Anyway,' he continued. 'I gathered the De Dananns together, and persuaded them to help me track down the miscreant who removed the dream catcher from your cogitator.'

'And?' said Blackwood.

'We found him, sir!' Shanahan declared, his tiny chest swelling with pride.

'Who was it?'

'Not "who", sir – "*what*"! It was a kobold: a nasty little sprite of Germanic extraction…'

'And he managed to infiltrate your team?' said de Chardin.

'Well… yes,' Shanahan replied in a slightly hurt tone. 'Mr…?'

'Gerhard de Chardin, of New Scotland Temple.'

'A pleasure to make your acquaintance, sir! Yes, he *did* manage to infiltrate the De Dananns – but only because kobolds are shape-shifters and can appear as any person, animal or object they choose.'

'How did you manage to track him down?' asked Blackwood.

'Ah, Mr Blackwood, would that I were able to tell you! But I can't.'

'Why not?'

'It's a rule amongst the Good People of Faerie that we never discuss our world with the people of this one. Were I to explain the details of our investigation, I would be in breach of that rule, and things would not go well for me back home. I hope you understand.'

Blackwood sighed. 'Of course. So, you found and apprehended the kobold. What then?'

'We questioned him, but we weren't able to get very much out of him, I'm afraid, for he had a pellet of iron secreted upon his person, which he managed to swallow…'

'Good grief!' said Sophia in shock. 'He *killed* himself?'

'That he did, your Ladyship. It's my guess that he was terrified of what his employer would do to him if he found out that he had been captured. Death, it seems, was preferable.'

Blackwood tutted in disappointment. 'What *did* he tell you?'

'That he had been summoned and employed by a very powerful man…'

'In what way "powerful"?'

'In *every* way, Mr Blackwood. Powerful enough to summon him; enough to bind him to his will; enough to summon a djinn; enough to walk the human world with impunity. Very powerful and very rich.'

'But he didn't give a name,' said Blackwood.

'I'm afraid not, sir,' replied Shanahan regretfully.

Blackwood noticed Sophia and de Chardin glancing at each other. 'What is it?' he asked.

'We may already have a name, Thomas,' said Sophia.

'Indeed?'

'We passed through a village in Hampshire this afternoon, where we encountered people who were in a state of great fear and agitation. Last night, they said, Spring-Heeled Jack passed through, and such was the impression he made upon them that they no longer welcome strangers there.'

'Was he still babbling about Martian victories?'

'He was. Detective de Chardin received his wound from a young boy who hurled a stone at my carriage, believing us to be Martians. He was terrified, as were the rest of the villagers, for they came to meet us carrying makeshift weapons. In fact, I believe that it was only the forcefulness of the detective's character that saved us from a most unpleasant encounter.'

Hmm, thought Blackwood. *Bravo to the detective.*

'One of the villagers,' Sophia continued, not noticing the slight sourness that had crept into Blackwood's expression, 'told us that they saw Spring-Heeled Jack bounding over the wall surrounding the neighbouring estate. So dismayed were his fellows when he told us this, that they very nearly turned their weapons on him.'

'What's the name of this village?' asked Blackwood.

'Furfield,' Sophia replied.

Blackwood leaned forward suddenly. 'Furfield? But that's Lord Pannick's estate!'

'It is,' said Sophia.

'Who is Lord Pannick, if I may ask?' said Shanahan.

'A powerful man,' Blackwood muttered. 'A *very* powerful man.'

CHAPTER TEN:
The Interplanetary Cylinder

The small Æther ship was well hidden in the depths of the wood. Its dark metal hull, blackened and pitted by the vehicle's entry into the Earth's atmosphere, lay half buried in the soft humus covering the ground, beneath a thick camouflage of leaves and branches. The ship had not come with a gaudy fanfare, like the Martian cylinders; it had crept in silence upon the world, carrying its hunger and envy within it, like a perversely-cherished malady.

The humans had not noticed its arrival, for their eyes and their minds were firmly fixed upon another point in the sky. They looked to Mars when they thought of the future, never suspecting that their final destiny might arrive from Venus.

Indrid Cold, who had piloted the Æther ship to Earth, shivered in the delicious chill of morning. What a beautiful climate this was! To breathe the autumn air was like quenching one's thirst with fresh, cold water. Even the summers were a delight: a soft, tentative warmth that caressed the body and lifted the spirit, making one want to walk forever over the lush green landscape, with face turned up to the gentle blue sky. They were nothing like the summers on Venus, where the livid sun breathed fire upon the empty, blasted world, and the only chance of survival was to remain at the poles and in the deep cavern-cities, cowering like animals while the rocks above grew hotter and hotter. One day, even the caverns and the poles would offer no refuge, and when that day came, the people of Venus would roast.

It was inevitable that that day would come, but it was *not* inevitable that the Venusians would still be there when it did.

Indrid Cold removed the camouflage of branches from the Æther ship's hatch and opened it. Leaning inside, he retrieved the object for which he had returned to Leason's Wood. The wood lay to the east of the Biggin Hill Cosmodrome in the heart of the Kent countryside, between London and Sevenoaks. It was from Biggin Hill that the humans were taking their first tentative steps into the infinite Æther, and it was here that they had built the world's first Cosmodrome to receive the interplanetary cylinders which were coming more and more frequently from Mars.

Cold cradled the object in his arms, examining the long, pipe-festooned metal tube carefully, making certain it was in good working order.

Then he took off the pale mask that covered his true face, and when he did so, the birds fled in panic from the surrounding trees...

*

Blackwood and Sophia arrived at the Cosmodrone at ten o'clock, forty-five minutes before the cylinder was due to depart. Detective de Chardin was already there, along with a large contingent of Templar Police, who had cordoned off the area and stationed themselves at various points around the complex and its central launching platform.

The platform was a circle of grey concrete a hundred and fifty yards in diameter, at the centre of which was a deep depression, its vertical sides containing a spider web of support gantries and a number of electrical connection points, fed by three large generators of Martian design.

Within the depression stood the interplanetary cylinder, the upper half of its one-hundred-yard length protruding above the ground, its smooth hull, the colour of burnished copper, glinting in the weak morning sunlight. From his vantage point near the edge of the launching platform, Blackwood gazed up at the craft. He could not deny that it was a fabulous sight, a marvel of engineering prowess, and yet he could not help thinking that it looked like a vast zeppelin that had taken a blackly comical nose-dive into the ground, half burying itself in the tranquil English countryside.

De Chardin saw them and walked over. 'Good morning, Blackwood, Lady Sophia.'

'Good morning,' said Blackwood. 'Is everything in order?'

'My men have checked and re-checked the perimeter of the Cosmodrome. The area is secure. We are standing by.'

'Excellent.'

De Chardin cast his gaze from the faintly humming tower of the cylinder to the surrounding buildings, which included the Æther traffic control centre and the reception lounges, and gave a nervous sigh. 'Do you think it likely that Indrid Cold will try something here, today?'

'You must admit that it's the perfect opportunity to cause more mischief. Then again, perhaps our very presence will deter him.'

'Let us hope so,' said Sophia, as she watched the arrival of the cylinder's flight crew. The four Martians – Captain, Co-Pilot, Astrogator and Engineer – walked past them without even a glance in their direction, strode across the access walkway connecting the launching platform with the craft's main entry hatch, and vanished into the dimly-lit interior.

'Good morning to you, too,' muttered de Chardin.

Blackwood turned away. 'The Ambassador is here,' he said.

In silence they watched the arrival of a Martian self-propelled carriage, which mounted the ramp leading up to the launching platform and trundled slowly across the concrete towards the waiting cylinder. Here was another marvel of Martian ingenuity, thought Blackwood as he observed the vehicle's progress. It was about the size of a horse-drawn omnibus, but its motive force was more advanced even than the internal combustion engines of the motor cars which were beginning to make their appearance in the streets of London and the larger towns. It was powered by electricity stored in several batteries, smaller versions of the ones aboard the cylinder, which were at present being recharged by the surrounding generators.

Its design was at once ineffably beautiful and startling in its strangeness. Its six wheels, which had rubberised pneumatic tyres, were hidden behind a sweeping cowl fashioned from the same copper-like metal as the interplanetary cylinder – although this was adorned with intricate curlicues of silver which caught the light and made it dance across the vehicle's flanks. The passenger cabin sat atop this arrangement, its strange geometry echoing the elegant lines of the cowl, giving the impression of one frozen wave rising from another. The windows were irregularly shaped, their dark-tinted glass hinting at further wonders of design within.

The vehicle moved past without altering its stately pace, and Blackwood, Sophia and de Chardin walked along beside it until it had reached the access walkway. Here it stopped, and a door opened upwards like a giant bird's wing. Five Martians emerged and descended to the concrete platform, among them Petrox Voronezh. The Assistant to the late Ambassador looked down at the humans, his dark eyes utterly inscrutable.

'Good morning, Mr Voronezh,' said Blackwood.

'Good morning to you all.'

'A very sad day, sir,' said de Chardin.

Voronezh ignored the comment, his attention remaining fixed on Blackwood. 'I am glad to see that your security arrangements seem to be in order.'

Blackwood nodded to de Chardin as he replied, 'We have the Templar Police to thank for that. Her Majesty sends her apologies for being unable to attend, as does the Prime Minister…'

'I quite understand,' said Voronezh. 'It would be foolish to risk their safety, no matter how tight the security.'

De Chardin visibly bridled at this but kept silent.

'Will you be accompanying Ambassador R'ondd on this sad journey, sir?' asked Sophia.

'No. I must remain on Earth to make preparations for the arrival of the new Ambassador. I accompany my friend this far to bid him farewell.'

While they were speaking, the other four Martians opened the rear of the carriage and slowly withdrew a plain sarcophagus, alabaster-pale and unadorned by any markings or ornaments. As Blackwood and the others watched, the pallbearers carried the Martian Ambassador across the access-way and into the cylinder.

The three humans crossed themselves as the hatch slid shut with a barely perceptible whine, and withdrew to a safe distance, followed by the electric carriage.

As the cylinder made its final preparations for lift-off, a vivid green glow emerged from the depression in which the craft stood, accompanied by a deep rumble which the onlookers felt through the soles of their shoes. Sophia felt the breath catch in her throat at this manifestation of the fantastic power harnessed within the machine, and instinctively she took Blackwood's arm. There was a *basso profundo* crackle, the teeth-jarring concussion of nearby thunder, as the Vril energy powering the vessel was directed downwards and released, and the cylinder began to emerge majestically from its steel and concrete nest.

Although all three humans had witnessed the departure of interplanetary cylinders before (in the six years since the Martians' arrival, it had become a great and eagerly-watched spectacle, to which people came from all over the country), they were stunned anew by the display as the vehicle, as elegant as it was massive, emerged fully from the ground, its copper skin shining in the anaemic autumn light, and climbed into the sky on an emerald pillar of pulsating Vril energy.

What fools we were to believe that we could harness such power, thought Blackwood. *How many centuries are to come before we can stand as equals to these beings?*

The air grew thick with the low-frequency growl of the cylinder's engines, and instinctively Sophia drew further away from the rising behemoth. Blackwood placed an arm around her shoulders and whispered in her ear, 'It's all right, my dear. We are quite safe.'

She looked up into his eyes – eyes that were as green as the terrifying Vril energy emerging from the cylinder – and for a moment her heart beat even faster, and her breath shuddered in her throat.

At that moment, de Chardin suddenly cried out, 'Hark!' – and pointed up at the glowing base of the craft, which by now had risen perhaps a thousand feet into the air. A needle-thin beam of blue light had lanced up from the ground, and connected with the mass of energy seething upon the vessel's underside. De Chardin looked at Voronezh. 'What is that?'

The Ambassador's Assistant made no reply; he simply stood, gazing up at the beam of light.

'Mr Voronezh,' de Chardin persisted, 'what *is* that?'

'It is coming from the northeast,' said the Martian. 'And it is *wrong*.'

The blue beam had the same effect on the Vril energy as water poured into a pan of boiling oil. With a deafening roar, the lower half of the cylinder tore itself asunder, disgorging a vast fireball which bloomed and expanded like a hideous flower, engulfing and incinerating the upper section.

Sophia screamed and clapped her hands upon her ears in a futile effort to shut out the cacophony, while Blackwood took her in his arms and shouted, '*Great God!* The thing is destroyed!'

'As are we!' de Chardin cried, pointing up at the million glowing fragments which were all that remained of the great vessel, and which were now raining down upon the Cosmodrome like molten lava from an erupting volcano. The sky was filled with them, for they had been cast outward by the force of the explosion to a distance of several hundred yards. 'We'll never get clear in time!' de Chardin shouted, his voice boiling with rage and despair. 'We're done for!'

PART THREE

In Which the Shadows of War Begin to Gather

CHAPTER ONE:
The Destruction of Biggin Hill

The sky was torn with the thunder of the interplanetary cylinder's destruction; the air above them was rent by the expanding fireball of livid red and green, which swelled like some strange new star in the pangs of its birth. All around them the ground was pummelled and set afire by the glowing fragments of the great craft, which descended in an incandescent, meteor-like rain over the Cosmodrome.

'We're done for!' de Chardin repeated, his voice all but lost in the cacophony.

Blackwood glanced around, his desperate gaze seeking cover – anything that might offer some protection from the death bearing down upon them. But the buildings of the Cosmodrome were too far away to be reached in time, and in any event they were now being battered into blazing ruin by the wreckage of the cylinder. He caught a glimpse of people running in blind panic from the Æther traffic control centre, the reception lounges and the maintenance hangars which bordered the launching platform. Many fell victim to the debris, and Blackwood turned his eyes away in despair as their fleeing bodies were smashed to burning smithereens by the deluge of glowing metal.

There was nowhere to hide, nothing to offer shelter…

Except…

He pointed to the electric carriage which had brought Lunan R'ondd's body to the Cosmodrome. 'All of you, in there!' he shouted, taking Sophia by the hand and hauling her along after him.

De Chardin and Petrox Voronezh followed. The humans were running at full tilt, but so tall was the Martian that his elegant strides took him to the vehicle well ahead of them. He pulled a lever in the flank, and the door lifted up. As Blackwood was helping Sophia up into the carriage, Voronezh said to him, 'This will offer protection from the smaller fragments, but if a larger piece should fall upon us…'

'I understand,' Blackwood replied as he shoved de Chardin in after Sophia. 'How fast can this contraption go?'

'Quite fast,' said the Martian.

Blackwood climbed in and glanced around. The rear of the passenger cabin was now empty, having been previously given over to the Ambassador's sarcophagus; the forward section contained six large seats, upholstered in blue-green Martian leather. Up front were two more seats, in one of which sat the driver, who looked at his new passengers with wide, unblinking eyes. Although he found it difficult to interpret Martian expressions, Blackwood guessed that the driver was as shocked and dismayed by the disaster as everyone else.

'Drive!' Blackwood shouted as Voronezh closed the carriage's door. 'Get us away from here, now!'

The driver turned to his controls and began to pull brass leavers and throw jewel-like switches. A low hum filled the cabin, punctuated by loud, sickening crashes as flaming debris hit the ground all around them.

'As fast as you can, Ghell'ed,' said Voronezh as he took the seat next to Blackwood.

The hum quickly rose in pitch to a frantic whine as the driver opened the throttle on the carriage's electric engines. The vehicle surged forward, and Blackwood heard the squeal of pneumatic tyres on the shuddering concrete beneath them.

Sophia screamed and covered her head instinctively as the cabin's ceiling reverberated with sizzling cracks, and Blackwood looked up and prayed that the roof would be able to withstand the debris that was now striking it repeatedly. They were thrown violently back and forth in their seats as the driver swerved to avoid the incandescent clumps of wreckage. Blackwood looked out of the window and was both astonished and gratified at the terrific speed the carriage had attained in just a few moments. The concrete of the launching platform, now scarred and pitted like a battlefield, was rushing by in a blur of grey and glowing crimson, and, craning his neck a little, he could see that they were fast approaching the edge of the platform.

'Brace yourselves,' said Ghell'ed as he gripped the steering column.

Blackwood took hold of his seat's armrests and felt the entire vehicle tilt forward as it left the edge and sailed through the air. The platform was eight feet thick, and there was a bone-crunching impact. Blackwood felt as if he had been kicked in the rump by a horse. The vehicle's shock absorbers groaned and squealed in protest as it hit the ground, but the carriage was undamaged and continued on across the flat grassland surrounding the Cosmodrome.

'Keep going, Ghell'ed,' said Voronezh. 'We are not out of danger yet.'

It was true, for so powerful had been the detonation of the cylinder's Vril engines that the entire area was prey to the deadly rain from the sky. The carriage sped on across the grass, between piles of wreckage and half-melted components which burned and smouldered upon the charred ground.

As their distance from the destruction increased, Blackwood turned and looked through the carriage's rear window. A great pall of smoke hung over the ruined Cosmodrome. The titanic explosion had now spent itself, leaving a vast grey ball of gas and atomised metal from which long streamers descended to the ground like the legs of a monstrous spider. The greatest danger had retreated now, for the heavier pieces of wreckage had fallen, leaving only the lighter fragments to float down, cooling as they went.

Ghell'ed brought the carriage to a halt near a stand of ash trees, and all in the cabin breathed ragged sighs of relief as the whine of the engines subsided, leaving an eerie silence.

Blackwood reached out and took Sophia's hand. 'Are you all right, my dear?'

She nodded. 'Yes, Thomas, I am. But the Cosmodrome! Those poor people!'

'I know.' He turned to Voronezh. 'Does this carriage have a telegraph?'

'It does.'

'Would you please send a message to the emergency relief services?'

'Of course.' Voronezh left his seat and moved forward to the driver's section, while de Chardin opened the door and stepped down from the carriage. Blackwood and Sophia followed him out. De Chardin stood with balled fists resting on his hips. 'My God, Blackwood,' he said through gritted teeth. 'Look at that... look at the carnage!' He shook his head, and his voice cracked as he said, 'My men...'

'I'm sorry, de Chardin,' said Blackwood, laying a hand on the Templar Knight's shoulder.

Petrox Voronezh appeared in the doorway, and stepped down. 'Ghell'ed is sending the message, Mr Blackwood.'

'Thank you.'

De Chardin shook his head. 'What the devil happened? What caused the explosion?'

'That beam of blue light,' said Blackwood. 'What was it?'

'An energy beam,' replied the Martian. 'A weapon.'

'Fired by whom?' demanded de Chardin.

'I think we all know the answer to that question,' said Voronezh.

Blackwood glanced at him. 'Indrid Cold?'

'He's playing us off against each other,' said de Chardin suddenly. 'Earth and Mars.'

Sophia nodded her agreement. 'First he attacks the innocent citizens of the Empire, sowing seeds of terror throughout London, while planting in the minds of the people the notion that Mars is somehow responsible. Then he murders the Ambassador by means which are guaranteed to cause a primal revulsion to seize all Martians. Now, he destroys an interplanetary cylinder, which will further outrage the people of Mars, once they receive the news. Detective de Chardin is right: Indrid Cold is attempting to foment mistrust and hatred between our two worlds.'

'He's trying to start a war,' muttered Blackwood. 'But why? For what purpose?'

'I suggest that we ask him,' replied Voronezh.

'How may we do that, Mr Voronezh?' asked Sophia.

The Martian pointed towards the northeast. 'The beam came from that direction, and from its steep angle, of which I took note, I would say that it was fired from quite close by.'

'That's Leason's Wood,' said de Chardin.

'I believe it is possible that Indrid Cold might still be there, especially if he assumes that his handiwork has left no survivors.'

'Then there's not a moment to lose!' declared de Chardin. 'Come, let's see how quickly this contrivance of yours can get us there!'

CHAPTER TWO:
The Æther Ship

The trees on the edge of Leason's Wood were far enough apart to allow the easy passage of the electric carriage, and its progress was swift. Even when the tree trunks became more densely-packed, Ghell'ed's driving skills were such that he negotiated them with ease, turning this way and that while sacrificing little in the way of speed.

Presently, however, the wood became too dense to allow the passage of the large vehicle, and reluctantly the driver brought it to a halt. 'I fear that this is as far as we may proceed,' he said.

'No matter,' Voronezh replied as he opened the door. 'I believe we are close to the position from which Cold fired his shot.'

Blackwood turned to Sophia. 'I think it best that you remain here…'

She raised her eyebrows. 'I shall do no such thing, Mr Blackwood!'

'But Cold may still be out here. The danger–'

'Is something I am more than capable of facing, I assure you.' She smiled and took his hand. 'Don't worry about me, Thomas. I can look after myself.'

'I don't doubt it, but…' He hesitated, noting her resolute expression. 'Oh, very well.'

Voronezh instructed Ghell'ed to remain in the carriage, and then alighted, followed by de Chardin, Sophia and Blackwood.

The wood was still and silent, and as they walked away from the vehicle, their shoes crackled upon the fallen leaves. 'We're giving away our presence,' observed de Chardin, his voice quiet nonetheless. 'If he's still here, he'll know we're coming.'

'Then let's make haste,' replied Blackwood. 'Mr Voronezh, are you still able to guide us?'

'I am,' said the Martian. 'But a thought occurs to me: if Indrid Cold is here, and is aware of our presence, we will make an easy target for him.'

Blackwood had a sudden vision of the blue beam flashing out from the depths of the wood and incinerating them all in an instant. 'Dash it all,' he muttered, 'you're right.'

'Well, we'll just have to keep our wits about us, eh?' said de Chardin. He turned to Sophia. 'Your Ladyship, are you quite sure you will not remain in the carriage?'

'Do you think I would be any safer there, Detective de Chardin?' she said.

The Templar Knight sighed. 'No, I suppose not.'

'Then let us stop concerning ourselves with my wellbeing, and turn our attention to the matter at hand.'

Blackwood could not help but smile at her words, and the tone in which she uttered them. *Remarkable woman*, he thought. Something occurred to him, then, and he said, 'Shanahan… Shanahan, come here.'

A few moments later, the faerie Helper appeared before them. 'Here I am, sir!'

Petrox Voronezh started visibly and took a step back. 'Relax, sir,' said Blackwood. 'He is our friend.'

Voronezh looked from Blackwood to Shanahan and back again. 'He is… your *friend*?'

'Indeed.'

'Mr Blackwood, you grow in my estimation!' said Voronezh, and gave to Shanahan a deep bow.

The little man seemed mightily pleased at the gesture. 'A pleasure to make your acquaintance, Mr Voronezh,' he said. 'Oh yes, always a pleasure to meet a Martian, for they are so much more polite than Earth people.'

'The honour is mine,' said Voronezh. Blackwood gave him a nonplussed look.

'As I said to you before, sir,' said Shanahan, 'just say my name aloud, and I shall come to offer whatever assistance I may. Now… what can I do for you?'

'The interplanetary cylinder carrying the Martian Ambassador's body has just been destroyed. We believe that the Venusian Indrid Cold is responsible and may still be here in the wood. We are going to try to apprehend him, but we fear he may destroy us first. Can you see your way clear to pinning down his location?'

Shanahan nodded. 'I'm aware of all these things, sir. The power required to bring down a craft of such size is considerable. It's more than likely that the weapon used will need to be recharged before it can be fired again…'

'That's all very well, little chap,' said de Chardin peremptorily. 'But he probably has other weapons at his disposal.'

Voronezh turned to the Templar Knight, and this time Blackwood had no doubt about his expression: it was one of great anger. 'Do not speak to him so!'

They all looked at him in surprise, except for Shanahan, who merely smiled. 'See what I mean? So much more polite than humans.'

De Chardin said, 'I apologise for my tone. I merely meant to…'

'No matter,' said the Helper. 'I will scout out the area and report back to you.' And with that, he vanished in a puff of lilac smoke.

Voronezh looked at de Chardin and shook his head. 'You do not know to whom you speak,' he said.

'If you please, Mr Voronezh, I know very well,' the detective retorted. He was about to say more, but Blackwood held up his hand.

'Who is he?' he asked.

The Martian regarded him in silence.

Blackwood continued, 'He claims to be the Helper from my cogitator, and he was certainly there when the contraption went wrong. Do you know something that we don't?'

Voronezh turned away from them. 'If you do not know, it means that he does not want you to know, and I will not go against his wishes. Come... the weapon was fired from this direction.' And with that, the Martian walked away into the depths of the wood.

'What the deuce was that all about?' muttered de Chardin as they followed him.

'I don't know,' replied Blackwood, taking out his revolver. 'But it seems that there is more to Mr Shanahan than meets the eye.'

*

Voronezh was true to his word, for presently they came upon a small clearing, hardly more than twenty yards wide, at the centre of which stood a low mound covered with branches, leaves and clods of humus.

'That doesn't look natural,' said Blackwood. 'Let's take a closer look.'

De Chardin glanced at the clearing and the surrounding trees with a penetrating eye. 'I don't like it. We'll be terribly exposed.'

'Shanahan will warn us of any danger,' Blackwood assured him. He turned to Sophia. 'All the same, I think it's best if you remain here.'

'Thomas, I–'

'Just until we make sure that it's safe,' he interrupted her gently. 'I'm sorry, but I'll hear no arguments. Mr Voronezh, will you remain here also?'

'I will,' the Martian replied. 'Just until you make sure it's safe. Then her Ladyship and I will join you.'

Sophia folded her arms and gave Blackwood a stern look, her brow furrowed over her deep brown eyes. He found the expression delightful but forced himself not to smile. 'Come on, de Chardin,' he said.

With their revolvers at the ready, the Special Investigator and the Templar Knight stepped into the clearing, moving slowly and carefully. Although he tried to focus his attention entirely on his surroundings, Blackwood couldn't help thinking about Voronezh's reaction to the appearance of Shanahan. He knew him, or at least knew *of* him, and had displayed a deference Blackwood had never seen a Martian display before – not even to Her Majesty. It was really quite extraordinary.

This, however, was a puzzle for another time, he told himself, and returned his attention exclusively to the matter at hand. He listened intently for any unusual sound, and watched for any furtive movement in the trees surrounding the clearing, ready to drop to the ground and take aim at a moment's notice. But he was aware of nothing but trees and silence…

Silence, he thought. *No sounds at all…* That struck him as odd, for there should have been the rustlings of woodland animals, the occasional chirrup of a bird. It was as if they had fled…

De Chardin gave voice to Blackwood's thoughts. 'The animals have been frightened away,' he whispered. 'The villain is still here... somewhere.'

'Keep your eye out, de Chardin,' said Blackwood. 'I'm going to have a look at that mound.'

De Chardin nodded and swept the barrel of his revolver back and forth, covering the line of trees on the far side of the clearing, while Blackwood edged towards the mound.

There was something under there, that much was evident – but what? Blackwood recalled Voronezh's suggestion that Indrid Cold had come to Earth in a small vessel, which he had probably concealed somewhere near London.

Blackwood peered closely at the pile of branches and leaves. Something glinted faintly beneath them. He reached out and pulled away some of the vegetation.

'Good God,' he said.

'What is it?' asked de Chardin, his eyes still firmly fixed upon the surrounding trees.

'Voronezh was right. It's Indrid Cold's Æther ship!'

'The devil you say!'

'Come and see for yourself,' said Blackwood as he flung aside the clods of humus and cleared away the rest of the branches and leaves.

De Chardin took a quick glance at the object thus revealed. 'Saints preserve us, what an odd-looking device!'

The Templar Knight was right: never in his life had Blackwood seen such a strange contrivance. The Æther ship was perhaps fifteen feet long, and shaped like a teardrop. From the stern (or what Blackwood supposed was the stern) extended a complex agglomeration of pipes and funnels, entirely enclosed within an elongated dome of some material akin to glass or crystal. The main body of the craft was fashioned from an iridescent metal which reminded Blackwood of the fragment which Sophia had retrieved from the Alsop family's front door.

Blackwood moved around to the blunt nose of the ship and peered into the interior through the single round porthole.

'What do you see?' asked de Chardin.

'Nothing. Looks like it's empty.' Blackwood began to inspect the vessel's flanks, searching for some means of gaining entry. Before long, his eye fell upon a lever set flush with the metal, and he pulled it gingerly.

With a hiss of hidden hydraulics, a small hatch opened.

'Good man,' said de Chardin. 'Now, if we can–'

He was interrupted by the appearance of Shanahan in the air before them. The tiny man flew back and forth in extreme agitation. 'Mr Blackwood! Mr de Chardin! Have a care, sirs, for he is returned! In fact, he was here all the time – he has led you into a trap!'

At that moment, the silence was pierced by a scream from the edge of the clearing. Both men span around and looked in the direction from which they'd come. The sight which greeted them made their blood run cold.

Petrox Voronezh was on his knees, an ugly black rent in his chest. He pitched forward onto his face and lay still, while Sophia cried, 'Thomas! De Chardin!'

'*Sophia!*' Blackwood bolted towards the line of trees, brandishing his revolver.

The fiend appeared from amongst the trees, bounding along with unnaturally long strides towards Sophia. Blackwood fired once, twice. He felt de Chardin's bullets whizzing past his head as the Templar Knight let fly with his own weapon, but if the bullets found their target, there was no sign of it.

With a final leap, Indrid Cold fell upon Sophia. She screamed again, struggling frantically to free herself from his loathsome grip, but he was far too strong, and her desperate efforts were in vain.

'*Sophia!*' Blackwood cried again, still running at full tilt towards the dreadful scene. He had emptied his revolver's cylinder, but even had the weapon been fully loaded, he would not have been able to fire it again without risk of hitting her.

'Let her go, you blackguard!' shouted de Chardin.

Blackwood had nearly reached them. He caught a glimpse of narrow, hate-filled eyes – eyes that were as hostile and implacable as the unplumbed depths of the Æther – before Indrid Cold, still clutching his captive firmly by the waist, leaped up into the branches of a tree. He paused for a moment, gazing down at Blackwood and de Chardin. Then, with a contemptuous sneer he said, 'My ship for her Ladyship. A fair exchange, don't you think? Ha ha!'

And with that, he was gone, swinging through the trees like some hideous monkey. Blackwood was about to give chase, but he saw immediately that it would be useless, for the villain's passage through the wood was far too swift. 'Shanahan!' he cried. 'Shanahan!'

'Here, sir!'

'Follow them. Find out where he takes her, but don't let him see you.'

'That I will,' said the faerie, and hurtled off into the depths of the wood.

Blackwood turned and saw de Chardin kneeling beside the prone body of Petrox Voronezh. 'How is he?'

The Templar Knight looked up and slowly shook his head. He had turned the Martian over onto his back, and a single glance told Blackwood the horrible truth. The gaping wound smoked in the cold air, its edges ragged and cauterised. The great barrel chest rose and fell fitfully, and Voronezh's body twitched with intermittent spasms as the last of life's breath prepared to leave it.

Blackwood leaned over and looked into Voronezh's eyes. Even in the shadow of death, they remained inscrutable, guarding their mysteries. 'I'm sorry,' he murmured.

'Do not... blame... yourself,' said Voronezh. 'Find... Cold. Save... your friend. Save... Earth... and Mars.'

And with those words, Petrox Voronezh breathed his last, and the glinting lustre of his great dark eyes gradually faded to a thin, dry crust.

CHAPTER THREE:
Station X

They carried Voronezh's body back through the wood to the electric carriage. So light was he that by the time they had done so, they had barely broken a sweat. Even so, it was the longest journey Thomas Blackwood had ever made, for the heaviness of his heart more than made up for the lightness of his physical burden. Countless times he cursed himself for having allowed Sophia to accompany them: he should never have brought her into Leason's Wood; he should have made her wait on the edge of the Cosmodrome while he and the others faced the danger.

Sophia had saved his life, but when she stood in dire need of his protection, he had been unable to save her. Now, she was in the clutches of the Venusian fiend, who was taking her God knew where, to do to her God knew what.

And now, Petrox Voronezh was dead, the second Martian to be murdered on Earth in less than a week. Blackwood could imagine the look on Grandfather's face when he told him, and as for the Queen…

As he and de Chardin spied the carriage amongst the trees, some intuition told Blackwood that there was another tragedy yet to be revealed. Ghell'ed should have hurried out to meet them when he saw that they were carrying Voronezh's body… but there was no movement in the vehicle's front windows as they approached.

'Something's wrong,' he said.

They laid the body down beside the open door, then took out their revolvers once again and entered the vehicle.

Ghell'ed was slumped over his controls, dead, the charred hole in his back still smoking slightly.

'Great God,' said de Chardin with bitter sadness. 'How easily this fiend takes life.'

Without a word, Blackwood went to the telegraph machine which was set into the dashboard and began to send a message in Morse code.

De Chardin came and stood beside him. 'The Bureau?' he said.

Blackwood nodded. 'I'm sending a request for the Unearthly Phenomenon Unit to come out here and retrieve the Æther ship. They'll take it to one of our Research and Development laboratories for study…'

'Blackwood… I'm sorry about Lady Sophia.'

The Special Investigator stopped what he was doing. 'It's my fault, de Chardin. I shouldn't have allowed her to come.'

'She has a rather forceful personality. She insisted.'

'That's no excuse.'

'No… I suppose it isn't.'

'But I'll get her back. So help me God, I'll get her back, and make Indrid Cold pay for all the evil he's done.'

*

Within an hour, the Unearthly Phenomenon Unit arrived in Leason's Wood. Blackwood and de Chardin watched impatiently as two four-wheel carriages, each drawn by two horses, came into view, followed by a large, steam-driven lorry with a wide flatbed. Mounted directly behind the driver's cab was a crane with block and tackle and a folded tarpaulin.

The vehicles came to a halt beside the Martian carriage, and a tall, imposing figure stepped down from one of the four-wheelers. Blackwood shook hands with him and introduced him to de Chardin as Colonel Caxton-Roper, Chief Operations Manager of the UPU.

Caxton-Roper took one look at Petrox Voronezh's body, and signalled to the other four-wheeler. Three black-suited men emerged with a stretcher. They carefully lifted the Martian onto it, carried it back to their carriage and placed it inside.

'Where are you taking him?' asked de Chardin.

'To the Home Office pathologist,' replied the colonel in a clipped voice. 'Protocol must be observed, even in extraordinary circumstances – *especially* in such circumstances.'

'Has Her Majesty been informed?' asked Blackwood.

Caxton-Roper nodded. 'Indeed she has.' He gave Blackwood a brief smile which was partly sardonic, partly sympathetic. 'I daresay you have some explaining to do, sir.'

Blackwood sighed. 'I daresay I have.'

'Hmm. Now then, to the business at hand. Where is the vessel?'

Blackwood and de Chardin guided the steam lorry towards the clearing containing the Æther ship. Colonel Caxton-Roper walked beside them, looking around all the time, as if he expected Indrid Cold to come bounding through the trees once again, eager to have another crack at them.

The lorry was less bulky than the baroque Martian carriage and was able to reach the clearing with little trouble. The driver parked it beside the alien vessel, climbed down from his cab and immediately set to work untying the crane. The other four-wheeler followed behind but only made it to the edge of the clearing before the horses became agitated, whinnying and stamping their hooves upon the ground.

'Curious,' said Caxton-Roper. 'They don't seem to like this gadget.'

While the carriage driver climbed down and tried to placate the horses, murmuring comfortingly to them and stroking their necks, four more men emerged from the vehicle and joined the others in the clearing. They examined the Æther ship without hesitation, their faces expressionless, their manner utterly professional and lacking in anything which might remotely be called surprise. Blackwood wouldn't have expected anything else, for the Bureau's Unearthly Phenomenon Unit was used to dealing with such sudden departures from the normal run of things.

In short order, the Æther ship was secured with heavy canvas straps and hooked up to the block and tackle, which was a threefold purchase designed for heavy lifting. The men pulled on the hauling line and lifted the vessel from its nest of earth and branches, then the lorry driver pulled the crane's boom around so that it was directly above the flatbed.

'That was straightforward enough,' said de Chardin as the lorry's strange new cargo was tied down with more canvas straps. Finally, the men unfolded the tarpaulin, threw it over the Æther ship and secured it to the steel rings bolted along the sides of the flatbed.

'Where are you taking it?' asked de Chardin.

Caxton-Roper flashed his ephemeral smile once again and replied, 'I'm afraid that's classified information, Detective.'

De Chardin cast a glance at Blackwood, who shrugged apologetically. 'Sorry, old chap. Need-to-know only, I'm afraid.'

The detective looked at the black-suited men, who met his gaze with expressionless faces, and nodded. 'I quite understand, gentlemen. Well, I'd better get back to the Cosmodrome. There's a great deal to be done there.'

Blackwood smiled and offered him his hand. 'I appreciate your help, sir.'

'Not at all. Will you let me know of any further developments?'

'Without a doubt.'

De Chardin nodded. 'Then I shall bid you all good day.'

With that, he walked, a little stiffly, out of the clearing and disappeared amongst the trees.

'Shame,' muttered Blackwood. 'I didn't enjoy rebuffing him like that.'

'I understand,' said Caxton-Roper. 'He's clearly a good man... but he's not Bureau.'

'So,' Blackwood sighed. 'Were *are* you taking it?'

'To Station X, Bletchley Park.'

*

Bletchley Park was situated fifty miles northwest of London and consisted of three hundred acres of Buckinghamshire countryside next to the London and North-Western Railway line. It had been acquired in 1883 by Her Majesty's Government from Herbert Samuel Leon, a wealthy London financier and Liberal MP, who had developed sixty of those acres into his personal estate. Now it was home to the newest and best-equipped of the Bureau's research and development laboratories.

Blackwood rode in Caxton-Roper's carriage. He was silent during the entire journey from Leason's Wood and was grateful that the colonel was a man of few words, who did not attempt to engage him in conversation. He kept thinking of Indrid Cold's words as he made off with Sophia: *My ship for her Ladyship. A fair exchange, don't you think?* It was quite clear that the Æther ship was no longer of any use to him, which meant that Cold had come on a one-way trip to Earth, and had no intention of escaping and returning to his own world. This in turn implied that the Venusian plot was nearing its completion.

And then he thought of Sophia's words in the immediate aftermath of the interplanetary cylinder's destruction. He believed she was absolutely correct in her inference that Cold's ultimate objective was to start a war between Earth and Mars, by creating a powerful sense of fear, mistrust and revulsion amongst each planetary population for the other. It did not matter that he looked nothing like a Martian; his words following each attack in the crowded streets of the British Empire's capital were enough to equate Mars with violence and terror in the public mind. Then, the nature of Lunan R'ondd's death was calculated to make the Martians equate Earth with parasitical infestation, of which they had a powerful racial terror – a primal revulsion. Blackwood had no doubt that the cylinder's destruction (and the murder of two more Martians) would cause further outrage on the Red Planet, whose inhabitants would see it as an act of revenge for the attacks in London.

And yet, even these events were surely not enough to make the two worlds go to war… surely, a final catalyst was required, a final outrage to tip them into the abyss. What that catalyst would be, Blackwood had no idea, but he was quite certain that he would have to find out in pretty short order.

And what of his motive? Blackwood thought, as the carriage entered the Bletchley Park estate. *Why does Cold want Earth and Mars to go to war? What possible use could it serve to Venus?*

He recalled Private Buckley's words when he, Sophia and de Chardin had spoken with him in his hospital bed at the Aldershot barracks: *Are we goin' to war with Mars?… I don't believe we'd come off very well if we did… but neither would they against us! We'd give 'em a good show, by God we would! They wouldn't walk away without a few bloody noses and black eyes.*

'Neither would they against us,' Blackwood murmured.

Colonel Caxton-Roper glanced at him. 'I beg your pardon?'

And then Blackwood recalled the final words Petrox Voronezh said to him, before succumbing to his injuries: *Save... Earth... and Mars.*

All at once, the answer came to him. 'My God, that's it!' he cried. 'How could I have been so stupid? How could I have been so blind?'

'What is it, Mr Blackwood?'

'I've just realised what the Venusians' plan is. It's been staring me in the face all along, but like a dullard, I've only just seen it.'

'What is their plan?' said the colonel.

Blackwood spoke quickly, giving voice to his thoughts as soon as they entered his mind.

'The planet Venus is facing an environmental catastrophe which threatens to destroy its civilisation. Its industrial emissions have triggered an irreversible warming of the planet. Venusian society is highly secretive and isolationist: even the Martians, with their superior methods of interplanetary flight, know very little about it. Venusians are also aggressive and acquisitive. Their plan is to sow seeds of discord between Earth and Mars, which will, they hope, result in war between the two worlds.

'But here's the thing: they know that they would not be able to defeat Mars unless the Red Planet had already been weakened in a conflict with Earth. The Venusians intend to ignite a war between Earth and Mars, in which human civilisation will be destroyed, *and Martian civilisation weakened to the extent that the Venusians will be able to invade both planets*, thus ensuring the continuation of their own civilisation!'

'Good grief!' said Caxton-Roper. 'Can that really be what they're up to?'

'It *must* be, Colonel. In an all-out war between our worlds, Earth would lose, but our new Æther zeppelins are nearing completion, which means that we would be able to inflict heavy losses on Mars. We wouldn't be able to defeat them, but we *would* be able to weaken them enough for the Venusians to step in and finish the job.'

'My God,' said the colonel, appalled. 'The *audacity* of the brutes!'

'Audacious, indeed,' agreed Blackwood, who then voiced his conviction that something more, some final atrocity, would be required to goad the worlds of Earth and Mars into a state of war.

'A final push,' nodded Caxton-Roper. 'But what?'

'I don't know, Colonel,' Blackwood sighed. 'But I mean to find out.'

'How?'

'I believe that Indrid Cold has more than one ally on Earth…'

'You mean humans? *Traitors?*'

'Precisely. And one of them is very powerful – in more ways than one. I think I shall pay him a visit this evening.'

Perhaps, he added to himself, *that is where Sophia has been taken.*

*

The Bletchley Park mansion had been built in a curious mixture of architectural styles. As the carriage approached, Blackwood frowned at the disparate elements of Gothic, Tudor and Dutch Baroque which gave the building a rather schizophrenic appearance not at all to his liking – although the impression of conflict it conveyed was entirely in keeping with the building's function as the headquarters of the Bureau's Unearthly Phenomenon Unit.

It was here that research was undertaken into the fields of the paranormal, the spiritualistic and the extraplanetary, where supernatural and supernormal threats to the British Empire were identified, studied, and defences against them formulated. Blackwood had been here on a number of occasions and had been struck each time by the ingenuity and dedication of the staff, which included astronomers, physicists, biologists and engineers, not to mention alchemists, spiritualistic mediums, white witches, and shamans. This combination of the physical and occult sciences, this viewing of the Universe in all the aspects of its great totality, made the Unearthly Phenomenon Unit one of the most potent weapons in the Bureau's arsenal.

That potency became apparent to Blackwood as he stepped down from the carriage, which had stopped outside the mansion's portico. He had the feeling of eyes upon him… eyes that were not human, that were not even animal in any meaningful sense. The house and the wide lawns surrounding it appeared perfectly normal on the surface, but Blackwood was keenly aware that beyond or beneath that surface, he and Caxton-Roper were being watched by something unseen, something immensely powerful and utterly implacable.

After a few moments, however, this unsettling feeling passed, for whatever had been regarding them recognised them as having authorisation to enter Station X, and the sensation of being under intense scrutiny vanished from Blackwood's mind.

Caxton-Roper breathed a sigh of relief and muttered, 'I can never quite get used to that.'

'A necessary precaution,' replied Blackwood, 'but I know what you mean.'

The two men mounted the steps to the front door, while the colonel's carriage continued around the side of the house, followed by the steam lorry and its strange cargo. Caxton-Roper took out his latch-key and unlocked the door, and Blackwood followed him inside.

The interior of Bletchley Park was several orders of magnitude stranger than the exterior, and Blackwood wondered whether he would ever become accustomed to this, either. The structure of the entrance hall was more in keeping with the external architecture of a cathedral than the foyer of a mansion. The internal space was a maze of flying buttresses and pinnacles, clerestories and triforia. Here and there, gigantic gargoyles snarled from the centres of complex traceries, their hideous visages apparently inspired by the fauna of distant and unknown worlds. It would have struck the casual visitor (had he managed to get past the watcher outside) as curious that such sentinels should be posted within the house rather than on the outside, since the purpose of a gargoyle is to ward off evil encroaching from without. At any rate, Blackwood could not prevent himself from shuddering as he regarded these frightful carvings, and gave an uncomfortable thought to the nature of the things they were intended to hold at bay.

The attention of the two men was drawn to one of the far walls, which had begun to warp and ripple as if made of thick liquid. Presently, the warping and rippling resolved itself into a human form, which detached itself from the wall and walked towards them. As it approached across the intricate parquetry of the vast floor, the undifferentiated and featureless paleness of its form took on colour and texture until, by the time it reached them, it had become fully resolved into a distinguished-looking man of late middle age, dressed in black trousers and a black Nehru jacket, with grey-flecked hair and a neatly-trimmed goatee.

This was the Comte de Saint Germain, immortal adept and Director of the Unearthly Phenomenon Unit. Saint Germain had ceased to be a corporeal being some years ago; now, his home was Bletchley Park, where he oversaw the tireless efforts of the staff to protect the Empire from all comers – natural and supernatural.

'Good afternoon, gentlemen,' he said in a voice rich and resonant with the untold centuries of his life.

Blackwood gave a slight bow. 'Good afternoon, sir. I trust you are well.'

Saint Germain smiled absently, and Blackwood had the distinct impression that he was devoting only the merest fraction of his mind to the here and now, the rest lost in contemplation of concepts barely imaginable by normal human beings.

'I understand you have brought us a curious artefact, Mr Blackwood.'

'I have: a Venusian Æther ship…' Blackwood watched for signs of surprise in Saint Germain's expression, and when he detected none, he added, 'With all due respect, sir, you seem… unperturbed by this discovery.'

'Discovery? Why, Mr Blackwood, the discovery is yours, not mine.'

'I have the impression that you were aware of the presence of intelligent life on Venus, before the present situation. Am I correct, sir?'

'You are.'

'And you never informed Her Majesty's Government of the fact?'

Again, that enigmatic, absent smile. 'I agreed with the Martians that it was something mankind did not need to know. Indeed, there are some things it is better *not* to know. However, recent events have rendered such precautions academic, haven't they?' Saint Germain regarded Blackwood in silence for a few moments. When he next spoke, it was the Special Investigator's features which broadened in surprise. 'You have recently encountered a djinn, haven't you?'

'How did you know?'

'I can smell it on you. It was summoned by one with a profound knowledge of Arabian Star Magick. You are very lucky to be alive and sane.'

Thoughts of Sophia crowded Blackwood's mind once again, and he murmured, 'I know.'

'I have the suspicion that you will encounter such Magick again before this business is over. We'll have to do something about that. In the meantime, why don't we have a look at our new toy?'

Blackwood and Caxton-Roper followed Saint Germain through a door which led into the depths of the house. They passed drawing rooms, libraries, studies, a dining room and telegraph room, before passing through a large conservatory and out into the grounds at the rear. A number of people were converging on one of several large huts ranged across the neatly-tended lawns.

'As you can see, gentlemen,' said Saint Germain, 'Station X is abuzz with your discovery. There are a lot of people here who are most anxious to get their hands on the Æther ship.'

'I don't doubt it,' Caxton-Roper replied.

The hut was painted white and was about twenty feet by fifty. Through the open double doors at one end, a glow of electric light shone brightly in the cloudy murk of the mid-afternoon. As they approached, Blackwood caught glimpses of frenetic activity within: people were hurrying to and fro before the half-obscured bulk of the vessel.

'Her Majesty has already sent word to Mars by Æther telegraph,' said Saint Germain. 'The Martians are also anxious to examine the vessel, since this will be their first opportunity to do so.'

Blackwood felt his heart sink. 'Has she also informed them of the latest developments in this case?' he asked, thinking of Voronezh and Ghell'ed.

'She has.'

'Do you know what her reaction was?'

Saint Germain glanced at him, and he cursed himself for having uttered such a stupid question. 'Don't tell me. She is not amused.'

'No, Mr Blackwood, she is not. In fact, a doubt that there has ever been a time in her long life when she has been *less* amused.'

'I've been trying to think of what to say to her, and to Grandfather,' he confided. 'I fear that I haven't done terribly well, so far. And to cap it all, my friend and colleague is now in the clutches of a Venusian, thanks to my carelessness.'

'You are too hard on yourself. Your record of service is exemplary.'

'Thank you, but that is cold comfort. In fact, an agent of the Crown is only as good as his performance in the current case: past successes count for little if he loses his edge.'

'And you think you are losing yours?'

'I've begun to wonder.'

'Why do you think that is?'

'I don't know.'

'Really? I think you do.'

'What do you mean?'

Saint Germain shrugged. 'Perhaps your judgment is becoming clouded by thoughts of a more… personal nature.'

Blackwood snorted. 'Are you suggesting that my feelings for Lady Sophia… go beyond the professional?'

Saint Germain smiled. 'Those words are yours, not mine.'

'Ridiculous,' Blackwood muttered as they entered the hut.

'Perhaps… but in any event, I advise you to put all such thoughts to the back of your mind, at least for now – for there is a much more pressing matter to attend to.'

Blackwood immediately saw what Saint Germain meant. His heart quickened and the blood left his face when his gaze fell upon the two people standing before the Æther ship.

Grandfather was scowling at him, puffs of steam emerging in angry little spurts from his artificial legs, and beside him, Queen Victoria stood, her face expressionless but her eyes bright with Martian fire.

No, Blackwood thought miserably. *She most certainly does* not *look amused.*

CHAPTER FOUR:
An Ultimatum

Blackwood steeled himself and walked forward. He noted that Grandfather's jaw muscles were working furiously, as if he were chewing on a tough piece of meat. He bowed to Victoria. 'Good afternoon, Your Majesty... Grandfather.'

'Blackwood! What the devil do you think you're doing, man?' thundered Grandfather. 'Two more Martians dead, Lady Sophia abducted, and still we're no closer to getting our hands on this Indrid Cold Johnnie! You're making a shambles of this whole blasted affair.' He glanced at the Queen. 'Apologies for the language, ma'am.'

'Think nothing of it, sir,' Victoria replied. She spoke in quiet, measured tones, but it was clear from the timbre of her voice that she was barely suppressing an explosive rage. 'Mr Blackwood,' she continued, gazing up at the Special Investigator with her heavy-lidded eyes, 'we had hoped to bring this unfortunate situation to a speedy conclusion, but thanks to your most unsatisfactory performance, we are now witness to yet more death and destruction. We can only speculate as to the reaction this will provoke on Mars.'

'An interplanetary cylinder destroyed. Biggin Hill all but obliterated,' continued Grandfather. 'This is rank buffoonery, Blackwood!' From the colour of his cheeks, he looked about ready to explode himself. 'What are we going to tell the Martians, eh? What are we to tell them?'

Blackwood took a deep breath. 'We are to tell them that the Venusians wish Earth and Mars to go to war: everything that has happened so far is geared towards that end. The Venusians wish to leave their dying planet and colonise our two worlds, but they know that this is impossible unless both Earth and Mars are weakened to the point where resistance becomes impossible. It's quite obvious that this is Indrid Cold's mission: he is an *agent provocateur* who has been sent to Earth on a one-way trip, and his intention is to ignite a war between Human and Martian. As a result, so he hopes, Earth civilisation will be destroyed, and Mars will be left without defences adequate to repel a Venusian invasion.'

Victoria and Grandfather glanced at each other as Blackwood continued, 'But that is not the worst of it. We have at least two traitors in our midst: men who are in collusion with Indrid Cold, and who are willing, for whatever reason, to betray their world and their species.'

'*What?*' Grandfather blustered. '*Traitors*, you say?'

'Yes, sir.'

'Who are they?' demanded the Queen.

'I believe one of them to be Lord Pannick of Furfield.'

'Preposterous!' declared Grandfather.

'I am well acquainted with Lord Pannick,' said Victoria. 'This is a very serious allegation you make against him, Mr Blackwood. Are you quite sure of what you are saying?'

'I am reasonably confident, Your Majesty.'

'Reasonably confident?' echoed Grandfather. 'What's that supposed to mean? Where's your evidence?'

Blackwood hesitated. In fact, the evidence was circumstantial at best, but his intuition told him that Pannick was his man. Unfortunately, he suspected that his intuition didn't carry much weight with either Grandfather or the

Queen at this point. He recalled Saint Germain's comment regarding his record and felt a brief flaring of anger, which he quickly fought down.

Taking a small step forward towards Grandfather, he said quietly, 'My evidence, sir, is admittedly circumstantial, but my intuition is, I believe, as sound as it has ever been. It has served both me and Her Majesty's Bureau of Clandestine Affairs extremely well over the years, as my service record will amply attest.'

He half expected Grandfather to erupt again at this, but instead he was surprised to detect a flicker of amusement pass across his lips. 'I suppose that much can't be denied,' he conceded.

'Who do you believe is the other traitor?' asked Victoria.

'Peter Meddings.'

Grandfather raised his eyebrows. 'Meddings? He's a decent enough chap, Blackwood. Not very dynamic, I grant you – not much in the way of gumption… but a traitor?'

'Meddings delivered your summons to me three days ago. He clearly knew that the Bureau had been instructed by Her Majesty to begin an investigation of Lunan R'ondd's assassination – and he had gumption enough to realise that I was about to be put on the case. And lo and behold, the following day I find that my cogitator has been sabotaged, allowing an Arabian djinn to enter the machine. I believe Meddings to be in the employ of Lord Pannick, who is in league with the Venusians.'

Victoria thought about this for some moments. 'It is true,' she said presently, 'that Lord Pannick is a man of wide-ranging interests… and those interests include the occult.'

'And Indrid Cold was seen entering Pannick's estate on the evening of the twenty-fifth.'

Grandfather looked at the Queen, who gave him a barely-perceptible nod. 'All right, Blackwood,' he said.

'You've won yourself a reprieve. What do you intend to do next? What are your recommendations?'

Blackwood indicated the Æther ship behind them. 'First of all, I would suggest that we make a gift of this to the Martians. It would be an act of considerable good faith: it would acknowledge their superiority in the science of space travel and would display our own refusal to keep anything from them.'

Grandfather looked at the Queen.

'Agreed,' said Victoria.

'Thank you, Your Majesty.'

'What about you?' asked Grandfather. 'What's *your* next step?'

Before Blackwood could answer, Shanahan appeared in the air before them. *Perfect timing, my little friend*, he thought.

'Good afternoon, sir!' he said. 'I'm very sorry to drop in unannounced.'

'Think nothing of it,' said Blackwood, who then introduced the faerie to Victoria and Grandfather.

Shanahan landed on Blackwood's left shoulder and gave a deep bow to the Queen. 'An honour to make your acquaintance, Your Majesty!'

Victoria quickly overcame her surprise, and replied, 'We are pleased to meet you, Mr Shanahan.'

'What news?' asked Blackwood.

'I followed Indrid Cold, as you instructed, sir. My goodness but he moved fast! But I was able to keep up.'

'Excellent, excellent,' said Blackwood impatiently. 'Where did he take Sophia?'

'To Lord Pannick's manor house, sir!'

'Good grief,' said Grandfather. 'Well, I suppose that clinches it. There's nothing for it but to arrest His Lordship without delay.'

'With respect,' said Blackwood, 'that may not be the best option. Don't forget that he is holding Sophia…'

'I understand your concern,' Grandfather interrupted, holding up his hand. 'But we are talking about the security of the British Empire – not to mention that of the entire world – and that must take priority over the safety of any one individual. We must put an end to Pannick's plan as soon as possible.'

Saint Germain, who had been listening in silence to the conversation, turned as a man approached him with a slip of paper. The man's expression was one of grim concern. The Comte took the paper, read it and frowned.

'Monsieur le Comte,' said Victoria. 'What is it?'

'A telegraph message, Your Majesty,' he replied.

'From whom?' asked Grandfather.

'I don't know,' Saint Germain replied, 'but I think I should read it out.'

'Please do,' said Victoria.

The Comte cleared his throat and read, 'To Her Majesty's Bureau of Clandestine Affairs, for the attention of Grandfather and Mr Thomas Blackwood, Special Investigator. I must inform you that Lady Sophia Harrington is now my guest, and that I shall treat her with all due care and courtesy, provided that you cease and desist from your investigation into the assassination of Lunan R'ondd, late Ambassador for Mars to the Court of Saint James's. Should you choose to ignore this communication, I shall have no option but to take Her Ladyship's life, in a manner most unpleasant.'

'Oh… that poor girl!' said Victoria.

'We must stand firm, Your Majesty,' said Grandfather. 'I assure you that I am equally appalled by this. But I say again that the Empire and the world are at stake.'

'What do *you* think, Mr Blackwood?' asked Victoria.

Struggling with the fear and rage that had risen like a tidal wave in his heart, Blackwood replied, 'Grandfather is right: we *cannot* place the safety of a single individual above that of the Empire. However,' he added after taking a deep breath, 'we should also note that this telegraph message is anonymous.'

'Meaning?' said Grandfather.

'Meaning Lord Pannick doesn't realise that we know he's the one behind this. He's still playing his cards close to his chest, believing that his identity is still unknown. I must say I'm very glad I didn't arrest Meddings.'

'Hmm,' said Grandfather. 'I think I know where you're going with this.'

'The fact that Pannick doesn't realise we know he's the traitor is very much to our advantage. But we're still in the dark as to the fine detail of his plan...'

'On the country,' said Grandfather, 'we know *exactly* what the blighter's plan is: he's pushing Earth and Mars into a state of war!'

'Yes, but *how*? Indrid Cold has sown the seeds of fear and mistrust between the two worlds, but that in itself is not enough to ignite an all-out interplanetary conflagration. Something more is required – but we still don't know what that something *is*. Arresting Pannick now may well rob us of the opportunity to find out. We may be unable to get him to talk, and the plan may be such that it reaches fruition without his direct involvement. And of course, Sophia will die – in a horrible way, apparently.'

Grandfather chuckled grimly. 'You want to go in alone, don't you?'

'I do, sir. My suggestion is that I enter his estate under cover of night and see if I can find out what his endgame is: how he plans to push Earth and Mars over the edge and into the abyss of interplanetary war.'

'And rescue Lady Sophia in the process?'

'If at all possible, yes sir.'

'Won't that tip our hand just as surely as arresting Peter Meddings would have done?'

'Only if I'm seen... or caught. But if I succeed, then it won't matter.'

Grandfather thought about this, then nodded. 'Very well. Are you going in tonight?'

Blackwood nodded.

'What about Meddings? Shall we take him in for questioning?'

'I don't think that would be advisable: we don't want to do anything that might alert Pannick to the fact that we're onto him. If he realises that we have Meddings, he'll assume that the man will talk and betray him, and then we'll be up a tree. Leave him be for now, but keep a close watch on him. And be very careful what you say aloud back at the Bureau.'

'Gentlemen,' said Victoria, 'I believe our business here is concluded. I shall send an Æther telegraph to Mars, explaining everything that has happened. Let us hope that the Martian Parliament takes us at our word.'

'That *is* to be fervently hoped, Your Majesty,' said Blackwood. 'I have a feeling that if it isn't, then the Parliament will make good on Voronezh's threat, and seek to intervene directly in this affair.'

'Do you really think they would?' asked Grandfather.

'Would we do any different, sir, in any of our colonies?'

Grandfather sighed. 'No, I suppose not. But we are not a colony of Mars.' His brow furrowed, and he cast a furtive glance at Victoria as he added, 'At least... not yet.'

The Queen gave him a reproving look. 'We will not hear such talk, sir! We still have confidence that Mr Blackwood will bring this affair to a satisfactory conclusion and that Earth and Mars will continue to forge their bonds of friendship and mutual respect once it is over.'

'Of course, ma'am,' Grandfather nodded. 'My apologies.'

The Queen nodded in satisfaction. 'Now, we must return to the Palace. See us to our carriage.'

When Victoria and Grandfather had left, Saint Germain clapped a hand on Blackwood's shoulder. 'Well, my dear chap, it looks like you've got your work cut out.'

Blackwood gave him a sardonic smile. 'Do you think so?'

'Come, let's go back to the house. There's something I think you should take with you to Furfield this evening.'

CHAPTER FIVE:
Dinner with His Lordship

Sophia had finally stopped shaking, although the memory of that dreadful journey from Leason's Wood to the room in which she now sat tormented her still. Her screams echoed in her memory, a raucous, tuneless song of terror and despair, and she hated herself for having uttered them. She hated herself for having been hauled away like a sack of vegetables, like an *object*, with no consciousness or volition of its own, utterly powerless, utterly *weak*.

Was this how her father had felt on that night all those years ago, in that wild and lonely place, in the depths of that disastrous winter? When the unknown and indescribable thing which some called the Wendigo had descended from the pitiless sky and snatched him away, had he felt that same self-hatred glowing balefully in the dark miasma of his horror? The unbearable supposition was that it depended on what the Wendigo had done to him. Had his death followed swiftly? Had it been lingering? Had it occurred at all?

These questions chased each other through Sophia's mind as she sat in the opulently furnished room, looking at herself in the elegantly-framed oval mirror which stood atop the dressing table. And as she gazed at her reflection, the tears came again, and now they were not for herself, but for her father, and they were not really new tears, but old ones – as old as the Canadian forest in which he had met his fate.

She had thought she was going to die: that Indrid Cold would take her to some secluded spot in Leason's Wood and carve her to ribbons at his leisure. But he had not. With unearthly agility he had swept through the trees, clutching her tightly and painfully with his left arm, and she recalled little beyond the flash of branches, the blur of tree trunks, the occasional glimpse of cold, grey sky… and then they were out of the wood and hurtling across the countryside, the captive helpless, the captor tireless and implacable. She had screamed until her throat was raw and finally succumbed to her terror and exhaustion. She had lost consciousness…

And had awoken here, in this large and beautifully-appointed bedroom, with a man whom she immediately recognised as Lord Pannick looking down at her, smiling.

'Rest, my dear Lady Sophia,' he had said, 'for you have had a frightful experience.'

'And you are responsible, sir!' she had cried, her eyes darting about the room, looking for the monster who had seized her.

Lord Pannick's smile grew broader. 'Do not be concerned. Mr Cold is not with us: he is seeing to matters elsewhere on the estate.'

Struggling to gather her wits, Sophia sat up in the vast four-poster bed and said, 'Then we are at Furfield?'

'Indeed we are. Welcome to my home.'

'Why have you brought me here?'

'I will explain later, but for now, take some time to recover. I normally dine at eight, and I would be honoured if you would join me.'

Sophia had the distinct impression that this was rather more than a mere invitation. 'It would appear that I have little choice, your Lordship.'

'That much, I am bound to say, is true,' he replied, and his smile broadened yet further into a feral grin, which unsettled Sophia so much that she was forced to look away.

Lord Pannick indicated a beautiful silk evening gown, which had been laid upon the bed beside Sophia. 'I took the liberty of ordering this for you. I do hope you find it to your taste.'

'I prefer my present apparel, thank you, Lord Pannick,' Sophia muttered, giving the gown a cursory glance.

'That may be, but I'm sure you will agree that it is a little too utilitarian for evening wear. Please… indulge me.' And with that, he had turned on his heel and left the room, saying over his shoulder, 'My man will come for you at eight and will escort you to the dining room.'

Sophia heard the sound of a key being turned and smiled in spite of the grimness of her predicament. She waited a full five minutes and then reached into the pocket of her coat for her purse. Taking out her lock pick, she bent down and inserted it into the lock of the bedroom door, her intention being to do a little exploring of Furfield and to gather as much information for Blackwood as she could before making her escape.

But her plan immediately came to nought, for at the instant she inserted the instrument, a spark of livid blue light shot out from the lock, throwing her backwards onto the floor. She cried out in pain and rubbed her throbbing hand. It seemed that Lord Pannick's reputation as an experienced investigator of the occult sciences was well-founded indeed, for he appeared to have sealed the bedroom door through some arcane, supernatural means.

Sophia sighed, glanced again at the evening gown, and decided that, for the time being at least, she would be forced to play this game according to Lord Pannick's rules.

*

She was still sitting at the dressing table, looking into the mirror and struggling with thoughts of a horrible past and an awful present, when she heard the faint click of the bedroom door being unlocked. A moment later, there was a discreet knock.

'Enter,' she said.

The door opened to reveal a tall, cadaverous-looking man in immaculate butler's livery. 'Dinner is about to be served, your Ladyship,' he said. 'If you will kindly follow me?'

She followed Lord Pannick's man along a series of corridors, down the house's main staircase and along the grand gallery past portraits of severe-looking ancestors, before finally arriving at the dining room.

Pannick was already seated at the head of the long table; he stood up when he saw Sophia enter. 'Good evening, my dear,' he said with a bow.

Sophia demurred from answering as she was led to her seat at the other end of the table.

'May I say,' said Pannick as he retook his own seat, 'how very charming you look.'

'Considering it was you who chose this gown, sir,' she replied frostily, 'you flatter yourself, not me.'

Pannick gave a satisfied chuckle, and Sophia regarded him across the oak landscape of the dining table. Although he was in his late fifties, Lord Pannick looked much younger: his skin had the smoothness and rosy sheen of youth, and his limpid blue-grey eyes shone like those of a man in his twenties. He was not slim, but his paunch and the plumpness of his face were more redolent of the healthy chubbiness of the infant than the middle-aged man gone to seed. He wore his hair fairly long, and its luxuriant brown curls added the final touch to his cherubic appearance.

As his man poured claret for Sophia, he said, 'I do hope you find this evening's repast to your liking… I also hope that it will be the first of many.'

'You may hope what you like,' Sophia replied, ignoring her wineglass. 'For my part, I hope you realise the mistake you have made in committing this outrage.'

Pannick took up his own glass and sniffed the wine contemplatively, then took a sip. 'My dear Lady Sophia, it would only be a mistake if I were to allow you to leave before the present business is concluded. Her Majesty's Bureau of Clandestine Affairs still do not know that Ambassador R'ondd's death was my doing – although it is surely only a matter of time before Thomas Blackwood's bumbling investigations lead him to my door. That's why it is useful to me that you remain here as my guest for a while.'

'I am a hostage,' said Sophia, a strong hint of distaste in her voice.

'If you wish to put it so, yes. I have already sent a communication to the Bureau, suggesting that they curtail their investigations forthwith… on pain of your demise.'

Sophia suppressed a shudder at these words, for she had little doubt that Pannick would make good on his threat if necessary.

Their conversation was momentarily interrupted by the arrival of the first course, a smoked salmon mousse. It looked delicious, and Sophia was reminded of the fact that she had not eaten since breakfast. There was little to be gained from the petulant act of starving herself, so she began to eat. The mousse tasted as delightful as it looked. 'My compliments to your cook,' she said.

Lord Pannick beamed at her.

'Tell me, your Lordship, how did you do it?'

'Do what, my dear?'

'How did you arrange for the *Acarus* mites to be placed

inside Lunan R'ondd's breathing apparatus? It couldn't have been easy, considering that security is so tight at the Martian Embassy.'

'On the contrary, it was quite simple,' Pannick replied, his mouth full. 'I enlisted supernatural aid: the same kobold who sabotaged Mr Blackwood's cogitator infiltrated the Embassy and the rest, as they say, is history.'

Sophia was sorely tempted to inform Pannick that the kobold was dead, but she decided that it was better to offer him as little information as possible. Instead, she said, 'Why are you doing this? Why murder R'ondd? Why the attacks in London and Hampshire? Why the destruction of the interplanetary cylinder?'

Pannick gave her a quizzical look. 'Do you mean to say that you don't know?'

'Mr Blackwood is a fine man, but he is having great trouble making headway: you yourself have seen to that, sir.'

'Thank you, my dear.'

'That was not a compliment.'

'Nevertheless, I take it as such.'

'Then will you repay it by telling me the reason for all this death and mayhem?'

Lord Pannick took another thoughtful sip of his wine, regarding Sophia over the rim of his glass as he did so.

Come, your Lordship, she thought. *Surely your arrogance will not fail now. I am your captive, after all.*

As if he had read her thoughts, Pannick put down his glass, sat back in his chair and smiled broadly at her. 'I am going to start a little war,' he said.

'A war?'

'Earth's first interplanetary conflict… and its last.'

Sophia gasped – convincingly, she hoped. 'War with Mars? For what purpose?'

'To make way for a successful invasion of both worlds by the planet Venus.'

'You… you make fun of me!' Sophia stammered.

'I would not dream of it, I assure you.'

'But… there is no life on Venus – the climate is too hot to sustain it.'

'Ah! I see that astronomy is one of your many talents. It is true that Venus is an unbearably hot, dying world… but there *is* life there, intelligent life. In fact, you have already met a Venusian.'

Sophia carefully controlled the dawning of realisation upon her face. Her fork fell to her plate with a loud clatter as she exclaimed, 'The fiend who abducted me!'

'The very same. His name is Indrid Cold. He and I have been working to create a climate of fear and mistrust between Earth and Mars… and war will be the inevitable result of our efforts.'

Sophia shook her head in dismay. 'In God's name, *why?*'

'Isn't it obvious? Venus is dying; her people need to vacate their world or face extinction. The Earth is the obvious choice for their relocation, but such is the morality of the Martians that they would never allow such an invasion to occur: they would quickly step in to prevent it. The solution is equally obvious: Mars must be eliminated as a threat to Venusian expansion; however, Mars is too powerful to go against directly. A war between Mars and the Earth will serve a twofold purpose: it will destroy the Earth's ability to defend itself, and it will also weaken Mars to the extent that it will be unable to resist a further invasion. *Both* worlds will fall to Venus.'

Sophia had been trying to mask her knowledge of Lord Pannick's involvement with Indrid Cold, but now she was genuinely shocked. While she had suspected that interplanetary conflict was the goal of these villains, she was stunned anew by the sheer audacity of their plan. To ignite a war between the worlds of Earth and Mars, to prepare both for an invasion from Venus... it was outrageous, utterly revolting.

At that moment, Sophia realised that it was more important than ever to escape from Lord Pannick's clutches as soon as possible and bring this dire news to Blackwood and the Bureau.

Their plates were cleared away, and the main course arrived: a roast haunch of venison. In spite of the delicious aroma that filled the dining room, Sophia found that her appetite had completely deserted her. She watched dumbly as the medium-rare slices were placed delicately upon her plate. Lord Pannick fell upon his with relish.

Sophia gave him a disgusted look, and said, 'So you would betray your world, your species... and for what? What will you do when the Earth falls under the dominion of Venus? Do you think you will be rewarded?'

'Oh yes,' Pannick replied. 'I will be rewarded most handsomely, I assure you.'

Sophia shook her head. 'Can you really be so foolish?'

Pannick laughed. 'I assure you I am nothing of the kind, my dear. When the Venusians arrive, they will require help in acclimatising themselves to their new home: they will need to learn of its geography, the distribution of its cities, the locations of its natural resources, the psychology of its people...'

'And you will be the one to help them.'

'Of course.'

'And your reward?'

'My reward will be power and riches beyond the imagination of any human in history.'

Sophia looked around the room. 'Have you not power and riches enough, Lord Pannick?'

The smile left his face, and his expression grew dark as he replied, 'No man who attains my position is ever satisfied with what he has. It is a law of Nature – immutable and inviolable. Put simply, it is the survival of the fittest in a hostile Universe.'

Sophia shook her head. 'If you are *not* so foolish – and believe me, sir, I do not concede that for one moment – then you must consider the governments of Earth and Mars to be so. Do you really think it will be that easy to goad them into declaring war upon each other? What you have done so far is beastly, to be sure, but it is equally certain that they will realise what is happening, the foul plan behind it, and will not allow themselves to be manipulated in this crude fashion.'

Pannick drained his wineglass and refilled it from the decanter by his side. 'A very good point, and one which I cannot gainsay. That is the reason why this "foul plan" as you put it has yet to reach its conclusion. What has passed so far is merely groundwork: a preamble, the overture to the main movement which is to come.'

Sophia regarded him in silence for a long moment. 'A preamble?'

'Indeed. Of course, a few acts of violence and sabotage are sufficient only to open the abyss. Something else is required to pitch Earth and Mars into it.'

'And what might that something be?'

'Two things, actually: two highly significant events, which will be so awful, so utterly catastrophic, that they will completely change the way the people of Earth and Mars see each other. They will be matches thrown into the powder keg which Mr Cold and I have created…'

'Movements, abysses, powder kegs? I believe you are mixing your metaphors, your Lordship.'

Pannick laughed. 'Quite so, my dear; I beg your pardon. But if I do so, it is only to impress upon you the irresistible power of our intent.'

In spite of the warmth in the dining room, Sophia felt herself growing gradually colder. 'And what *are* these "highly significant events"?'

Pannick smiled and shook his head. 'There will be time for that tomorrow, Lady Sophia. For now, I see that you have not touched your venison. Is it not to your liking? Perhaps you would prefer something else?'

'No, thank you.'

'Will you at least take dessert?'

Sophia did not answer.

Lord Pannick sighed. 'Ah, well. In that case, it is time to impress upon you the seriousness of your situation and why you should not even consider attempting to leave this house, even if that were possible.'

Sophia sensed a movement behind her and turned to see that Indrid Cold had entered the room. She gasped in spite of herself at his powerful bulk; at the white suit he wore, which glistened repulsively in the gaslight like the skin of some subterranean beast; at the pale, wax-like mask that covered his head; at the eyes which burned within.

'Forgive me, my dear,' said Pannick. 'But I must show you what will happen if you prove troublesome to me in any way, or if Thomas Blackwood ignores my request to cease his investigations. Behold, Lady Sophia, the instrument of your destruction!'

Slowly, deliberately, Indrid Cold reached up with both hands and removed the waxen mask from his face… his true face.

When Sophia saw what lay beneath, she felt the breath leaving her lungs, not allowing her even a single scream before unconsciousness overcame her. She heard Lord Pannick laughing maniacally before merciful darkness descended.

CHAPTER SIX:
At Midnight, a Revelation

The stars shone brilliantly in the moonless sky as Blackwood approached the high wall bordering the Furfield estate. He was dressed all in black, and his face was darkened with camouflage paint: a stealthy wraith of a man whose eyes were the only clue to the anger burning invisibly within him. He knew that in a situation such as this, anger was the most dangerous of emotions, for it made one reckless and clouded one's judgement, but he could not help himself. Sophia was in there, somewhere, and while the telegram had stated that she would be treated well, for the time being at least, the very thought of her captivity brought a rage upon him that he could barely contain.

Two nights ago, according to the people of Furfield village, Indrid Cold had cleared this eight-foot-high wall in a single leap. Blackwood would need to negotiate it by more conventional means. He took off his black canvas backpack and withdrew from it a rope and grappling hook, which he flung upwards. The hook found purchase immediately and, hastily putting on the backpack again, Blackwood heaved himself up and over, his muscles gaining further strength from the adrenalin pounding through him.

He dropped to the ground and fell instantly into a crouch, scanning the pitch-dark grounds before him. 'Shanahan,' he whispered.

'Here, sir,' said a voice, which seemed to come simultaneously from inside his mind and an inch from his left ear.

'You know what you have to do.'

'That I do, sir: find Lord Pannick's cogitator, get inside, and see what he's planning, if I can.'

'Good. Now, keep your wits about you, and don't show yourself unless it's absolutely necessary.'

'Understood.'

Blackwood hesitated, feeling through his black woollen sweater at the large amulet which he wore about his neck. Saint Germain had given it to him before he left Bletchley Park, telling him that it was a ward against Arabian Star Magick, that it would allow him to enter Lord Pannick's house undetected and would offer some protection once he was inside. Blackwood had not liked the use of the word 'some', but had thanked the Comte nevertheless. The amulet was about three inches in diameter and had been fashioned from meteoritic iron. Upon each of its faces was a curious design: an irregular pentacle with an eye at the centre. Although he was not particularly keen on Magick, preferring more traditional methods of dealing with his enemies, Blackwood was glad of it on this occasion – even if it did weigh rather heavily about his neck.

Maintaining his crouch, he moved off into the night, swiftly, silently and, he hoped, invisibly. His best tactic, he decided, was to circle the main house at a respectable distance, using the surrounding stands of trees as cover whenever possible. In this way, he would be able to gain some ides of the layout of the place and find the best means of entry.

The house was vast, a veritable mountain of Gothic masonry, festooned with gables and turrets, from which a score of chimney stacks sprouted like a miniature forest of petrified stone. As he circled the house, Blackwood had the distinct impression that the stars were concentrated in a great, globular mass directly above it, as though they were colossal bees attracted by some ætherial scent within. But when he blinked and looked again, the stars were not like that at all: they still occupied their normal positions in the firmament.

The house is protected by Star Magick, he thought. That particular form took its power from the stars themselves, in a way that was still a bafflement to science. It was the most powerful form of Magick known to mankind – so powerful that its very presence seeped into the mind and altered its perceptions, allowing brief glimpses into an ætherial realm of which most people were, blessedly, unaware.

Blackwood touched the heavy lump beneath his sweater once again and hoped that it would be enough to get him in and out of Furfield alive.

He pressed on through the dark, alternately keeping a watch on the house while paying attention to the ground beneath his feet. There was but one light burning in a large upper floor window, and he guessed that Lord Pannick was in that room. *Good evening, your Lordship*, he thought. *I'm looking forward to our first meeting...*

As he continued his circumspect progress around the house, Blackwood became aware of a structure in the near distance: a large folly – although it was like no folly he had ever seen before. It appeared to be nothing more than a misshapen pile of masonry, the product of a mind beleaguered by the distorted dreams of opium. There was no rhyme or reason to its design, no harmony or symmetry in its lines: in fact, the closer Blackwood drew to it, the more intense his conviction became that this thing had not been built at all, but rather... *grown*.

That is no folly, he thought. *Great God, what manner of place is this?*

As if in response to his thoughts, the pile of masonry – or whatever it really was – gathered itself into strange movement, extending thick tendrils of stone and flexing them upon the ground, in the manner of some monstrous starfish. There was a hollow, brittle grinding sound as of bricks rasping against each other, and the entire ghastly agglomeration shifted in Blackwood's direction.

He froze, partly at the approach of the hideous, unnatural thing, and partly because the amulet he wore had begun to grow warm against his skin. He surmised that the Magickal ward had been activated, and was now working to protect him.

The unearthly sentinel lurched forward again, and then appeared to hesitate. It moved in a different direction, and then stopped again. *It knows something is not quite right*, Blackwood thought. *But it can't detect me. The amulet is working!*

After a few more desultory lurches back and forth, the pile of masonry became still once more, and slowly and carefully, Blackwood edged around it. As he did so, he had the powerful impression of an alien awareness casting strange senses into the night, trying to catch the scent of whatever had roused it. He hardly dared breathe as he passed the thing, and at his closest approach, he felt the amulet grow uncomfortably hot against his chest.

As he left the sentinel behind and continued around to the rear of the house, Blackwood felt the temperature of the amulet gradually reduce, until it had become quite cool once again. But all thoughts of the amulet and the dark and noxious powers against which it was intended to offer protection were forgotten when he saw what lay on the other side of Furfield. Two buildings stood upon the wide lawn. Blackwood hesitated and took them in. They looked

247

like prefabricated zeppelin hangars, although one was much larger than the other.

Blackwood decided to make for the larger one, which was perhaps seventy feet high and as many wide. The vast double doors were sealed, and he moved around to the side of the building and tried the handle of the small door he found there. It was locked as well – a superfluous precaution, he thought, given the nature of the bizarre monstrosity which stood watch in the vicinity of the house.

He reached into his trouser pocket and withdrew his lock pick, which he quickly and deftly inserted into the lock and twisted. There was a satisfying click, and the door swung open on soundless hinges. Blackwood slipped inside and closed the door behind him.

The interior was dimly lit by several gas lanterns that had been left burning, and by their subdued light, Blackwood gazed up at what the hangar contained, his lips parted in awe.

The Æther zeppelin was more than three hundred feet long from needle-pointed prow to elegantly-finned stern and bulged to more than sixty feet at its midsection. Its silver skin glinted faintly in the gaslight, and the long, slender gondola which was slung beneath it was flanked by two oversized engines, their delicate, frond-like propeller blades designed to gain purchase on the Luminiferous Æther of deep space. Blackwood was stunned by the beauty of its lines, the sense of vast propulsive force embodied in the huge engines. He had seen the plans for such vessels and was well-acquainted with their design, but this was the first time he had actually stood before one, and the effect was quite breathtaking. These ships were designed to fly much further than any location on Earth: they were ships of *space*, and were intended for the exploration of other worlds in the solar system.

They were the first harbingers of mankind's presence off the Earth.

But what was Lord Pannick doing with one?

Blackwood approached the gondola and peered in through one of the portholes. The light from the gas lamps was not strong enough to penetrate through to the interior, which was in near-total darkness. He reached into his backpack and withdrew a miniature electric lantern, which he switched on and held up to the thick glass of the porthole. The powerful beam played upon the gondola's contents, and at first, Blackwood was unsure what he was looking at.

There was row upon row of small, fragile-looking canisters, neatly arrayed on shelves which stretched from floor to ceiling, and which appeared to extend for the entire length of the main cabin. Blackwood intensified the beam of electric light and peered closer. Each canister was filled with a murky yellow substance, which seemed to be smeared across the glass surface.

Blackwood recalled seeing that strange, unclean colour before, in the morgue where Lunan R'ondd's body had been kept; he recalled the pathologist, Dr Felix Cutter, showing him a test tube containing a smudge of tainted yellow…

'*Acarus galvanicus*,' Blackwood whispered. 'Good God!'

The tiny smudge Dr Cutter had shown him was composed of thousands of larvae, and there appeared to be hundreds of canisters loaded aboard the Æther zeppelin, each full to the brim with the microscopic creatures.

There could be one reason for this, and one reason only.

Pannick is going to take these to Mars, Blackwood thought. *He's going to contaminate the entire planet with them!*

He switched off his electric light and left the hangar. Outside, all was as it had been: the stone sentinel was still there, unmoving, perhaps asleep once more. The house and its grounds were still in darkness, steeped in the silence of the night. A little way off, the second of the two prefabricated buildings stood, and without delay Blackwood moved swiftly across the grass towards it. He noted how its design differed curiously from the hangar containing the Æther zeppelin: its main access doors were not set into its side, but rather appeared to form part of its roof.

Blackwood went straight to the side door and again picked the lock in a few seconds. He had no idea what he would find inside this smaller hangar, and at first he was a little disappointed to see a small Martian walking machine crouched upon the floor with its three slender legs folded up around it. The hull was only about fifteen feet long and perhaps ten wide. In fact, he had never seen such a diminutive example of these vehicles and suspected that it was actually for Lord Pannick's private use – the Martian equivalent of a two-wheeler drawn by a single horse.

He was about to turn and leave when something caught his eye, and he stopped and regarded the vehicle more carefully. There was a curious bulge on the dorsal surface of the hull, a feature he had never seen on any other walking machine. He had no idea what its function was, but it certainly ruined the otherwise elegant lines of the vehicle. From the front of the bulge, a short cylinder protruded. The cylinder appeared to be composed of a crystalline material, perhaps ruby.

Stepping around the nearest of the machine's three-lobed feet, Blackwood stood directly in front of the control cabin and looked up past the cyclopean eye of the observation blister at the strange feature.

What the dickens is that? he wondered.

The answer, he knew, would have to wait, for he had more pressing business to attend to. Leaving the hangar behind, he headed off into the darkness towards the house. He hadn't got very far when the temperature of the amulet began to increase again. It was clear that the house was protected by the same dark Magick which had given life to the pile of masonry outside, and Blackwood wondered what would have happened to him had he not been carrying the ward.

He also wondered how much hotter it would get, and if he could stand to keep wearing it once inside…

CHAPTER SEVEN:
His Lordship's Plan

Why the devil didn't Saint Germain warn me about this? Blackwood wondered as he reached a door at the rear of the house. The amulet was becoming quite uncomfortably hot, so much so that he was tempted to take it off and put it in a pocket. He decided, however, that such an action would probably not be wise.

The door was clearly for servants and tradesmen, and the lock was defeated as easily as those in the two hangars. As he opened the door, Blackwood felt a painful flaring of heat in his amulet, and surmised that, had he not been wearing it, he would have died there and then.

He took out his electric lantern and cast a low-power beam into the room beyond. It was a large scullery, containing two slate sinks and numerous shelves on which sat a vast array of copper pans. At the centre of the room stood a worktable, and in a far corner a large, evil-looking mangle squatted like another bizarre sentinel.

Blackwood passed quickly through the room and on into the vast kitchen, where he played his beam upon the black-and-white-tiled floor and the tables, oven and cooking range, and finally the shelves containing all the arcane accoutrements of cookery, which he had always considered to be as impenetrably mysterious as the contents of any scientific research laboratory. He cast a brief glance at the shelves containing pie forms, pastry jiggers, patty pans, sugar nippers, larding pins and sculpting tools and a dozen other types of culinary contrivance, before leaving the kitchen and moving swiftly along the dark corridor beyond and ascending a steep flight of stairs.

From his external survey of the house, Blackwood had a rough idea of its basic layout and of the direction he should take in order to reach the room in which he had seen the single light burning, which he suspected to be Lord Pannick's study. As he moved silently along the corridors of the first floor, he called out to Shanahan with his mind.

Presently, a voice – or rather, the mental impression of a voice – replied, *Here, sir.*

Did you manage to get inside Pannick's cogitator?

I did indeed, sir, and I have some very interesting information for you.

That can wait. For now, I need to know where he is and what he's doing.

He has just retired. I can direct you to his study, if you wish. I'm sure you'll find much of interest there.

No doubt. Lead the way.

With the faerie's voice to guide him, Blackwood quickly arrived at a stout oak door.

You're sure he's not in here?

Quite sure, sir.

Blackwood tried the handle; the door was unlocked. He pushed it open, entered the room and turned up the gaslights a fraction. In the dim light, he could see that Lord Pannick's study was vast and opulently furnished with an eclecticism which bordered on bad taste. Indeed, Blackwood's first impression was that he had stepped into the world of fifty years ago, when the vogue in Victorian society was for all manner of clutter. But the clutter in this room came from the four corners of the globe, and from periods remote in history.

Blackwood's astonished eye quickly took in the room's contents. It was a veritable museum of artefacts from many ancient civilisations, both familiar and mysterious. There were examples of the first technological fumblings in flint and sandstone produced by humanity's forebears, relics from the era of civilisation's first primordial flickering; there were priceless artefacts from Mesopotamia and Egypt and mysterious, distant Asia; there were exquisite examples of pottery, sculpture and metalwork from the Hellenistic world and from fabulous Rome and from the Arab empires and glorious Byzantium; there were delicate marvels from the far side of the world, from China and Japan; there were glimpses of the intellectual flowering of the Renaissance, embodied in oils and marble and illuminated manuscripts; and there were idols and figurines from the New World, the violent strangeness of their aspect offering eloquent testament to the singular history of those distant people.

As he surveyed these treasures, Blackwood modified his opinion of Lord Pannick's taste in furnishings: he had chosen well, with a highly educated and discerning eye, and if his enormous study was cluttered, it was cluttered with the very best of mankind's striving towards the divine. It was an incongruity strange and sad, Blackwood reflected, that such beauty belonged to a man of such malevolence.

Shanahan became visible as Blackwood closed the door. 'Over here, sir,' he said as he fluttered across to a large, ornately carved oak cabinet. 'Top drawer.'

Blackwood opened the drawer, which contained a number of sheets of paper. He took them out and carried them to the desk that stood at the centre of the room. The first sheet contained a complex and highly detailed diagram of a Martian walking machine. 'Good Lord!' he whispered. 'This is the one I saw in the hangar outside.'

'Quite so, sir,' agreed Shanahan. 'But this is different from any other. Look here.' He indicated the strange, unsightly bulge on the upper surface of the machine's hull.

'Yes,' Blackwood nodded. 'I noticed that... but what is it?' Hardly had he voiced the question before his eye took in the annotation on the diagram. 'A... Heat Ray?'

'A weapon, sir,' said Shanahan. 'A projector of violent destruction. Its power is vast and lethal...'

'And Lord Pannick possesses it. But how did he get hold of it? The Martians must have given it to him... but why the deuce would they do that?'

'The answer lies in his cogitator, sir,' replied Shanahan, indicating the machine on the desk. 'Lord Pannick is brokering an arms deal between Her Majesty's Government and the Martian Parliament...'

'An arms deal?'

Shanahan nodded. 'This is merely the first of many such fighting machines, which are to be shipped to Earth in order to consolidate the power of the British Empire. It is quite secret, for the moment at least, since knowledge of such a deal would drastically destabilise international relations.'

'I don't doubt it,' Blackwood muttered.

'But this is not our most pressing concern at this point,' Shanahan continued. 'Please look at the next sheet.'

Blackwood folded aside the diagram of the Martian fighting machine, and the frown that had clouded his features deepened still further when he saw what lay beneath. 'This is a map of Hyde Park,' he said. 'And the New Crystal Palace...'

'Do you recall, sir, what you said back at Station X?' said Shanahan. 'Indrid Cold has sown the seeds of fear and mistrust between Earth and Mars, but that in itself is not enough to start a war. Something more is required, you said, and you are right.'

'Yes,' Blackwood whispered. 'A powerful catalyst, a final outrage to tip us over the brink... except that there are *two* catalysts: the first is the planned infestation of Mars with *Acarus galvanicus*… and the second… oh, dear God!'

'That's right, sir,' said Shanahan. 'The second is the destruction of the Greater Exhibition by Martian Heat Ray, in two days' time!'

Blackwood felt sick to his stomach as he said, 'The Queen is going to be there, at the grand opening.'

'That is when Pannick and Cold will mount their attack, for they will certainly not miss the opportunity of assassinating the British monarch and symbol of the Empire.'

Blackwood quickly gathered up the drawings, folded them and put them in an inside pocket of his coat. 'I'm taking these back to Station X,' he said. 'If we give them the plans, perhaps our technical chaps will be able to find a weakness in the fighting machine.'

'I doubt it, sir, but it's worth a try,' said Shanahan.

'Now, can you tell me where Lady Sophia is being held?'

Shanahan smiled. 'That I can, sir.'

*

Sophia lay on the bed, still dressed in the evening gown which Lord Pannick had had the impudence to provide for her. She had no idea how long she had been unconscious, only that when she had finally awoken, she was back here in the bedroom. As soon as awareness had returned, she felt a scream of terror rising in her throat, and it was only with the greatest of determination and self-control that she had prevented herself from letting loose with it. Instead, she had buried her head in the pillow and sobbed.

The memory of Indrid Cold's true appearance was awful beyond imagining, and try as she might, she could not rid herself of it. It was emblazoned upon her mind as if branded there, an indelible image which tormented her with the horror of its uttermost alienness.

She knew that she had to find some way to escape from Furfield, but such was her fear and anguish that it seemed to drain the strength from her muscles and the air from her lungs. And so she had lain there upon the bed, panting and sobbing, utterly unable to move, while the minutes seemed to turn into hours, and the hours into days and weeks of misery and terror.

When she heard the soft click of the lock on the bedroom door, she moaned aloud and thrust her face deeper into the pillow. Had the alien fiend returned? If he had, she knew she would die. She felt rather than heard the door opening, and braced herself to face the unendurable...

And then, a familiar voice, deep and strong.

'Sophia!'

She raised her head, and saw Blackwood standing there in the doorway.

'Thomas! Oh, Thomas!'

Instantly, he was at her side, holding her in his arms and drawing her dishevelled, tear-damp hair from her face. 'Great God, what did they do to you?'

'Nothing... but Indrid Cold is here... and he showed me his true face... and...' She shut her eyes tightly and gave a shuddering moan.

'Come, Sophia: we are getting out of here, right this moment!' And with that, he lifted her off the bed and placed her on her feet. 'Be strong, my dear.'

'Yes, be strong, my dear!' said another voice from the doorway.

Sophia gasped, and Blackwood spun on his heels to see Lord Pannick standing on the threshold, a revolver in his hand. 'Be strong indeed,' he added, a broad, satisfied smile on his corpulent face. 'Although no amount of strength will serve you now.'

'Lord Pannick,' Blackwood began, but Pannick raised the gun, and he fell silent.

'Good evening, Mr Blackwood,' he said. 'How unfortunate it is that you chose to ignore my warning. I would have been true to my word, you know: I would have returned her Ladyship to you unharmed, once all this was over. But now…' He shook his head sadly. 'Now you force me to a most unpleasant course of action.'

'Your little plan will not succeed, Pannick,' Blackwood said with barely suppressed rage. 'You'll swing for this, you filthy bounder!'

Pannick gave a low chuckle. 'I would dispute that, my dear sir… but even if I do, I assure you that you and Lady Sophia will not live to see it!'

PART FOUR

---

*In Which the Greater Exhibition
Does Not Go Entirely to Plan*

CHAPTER ONE:
On the Plain of Yoh-Vombis

The Martian moons Phobos and Deimos, twin fragments of glittering light, emerged from behind the rolling red horizon to continue their dance through the firmament. The countless stars which formed a backdrop to the moons' eternal courtship were harder and brighter here than when viewed from distant Earth: without a dense atmosphere to impede their light, they fractured the darkness of space like gleaming blades driven through the ice of a black, frozen lake. That vast and unplumbed darkness seemed to seep down from the sky, slowly filling the valleys and canyons which surrounded the Plain of Yoh-Vombis, edging stealthily towards the gently lapping, star-reflecting waters of the great canals which threaded the land.

A thousand years ago, Yoh-Vombis himself, the World-Builder, who united the peoples of Mars into a single planetary civilisation and left them their greatest poetry, had likened the monstrous darkness of deep space to a great beast, hungry and silent, which coveted the mountains and the rolling plains, the waters and the bright, warm lights of the scattered cities, and which descended each night to sate its hunger on Martian dreams.

At the centre of the vast, mesa-pillared plain, amid a complex of five-sided temple pyramids, stood a singular building. Two miles long and a mile and a half wide and carved from the living rock of a mountain as old as Mars itself, the structure soared nearly three thousand feet into the air in the form of a colossal face, gazing up impassively at the stars: the Face of Yoh-Vombis, eternal shrine to the World-Builder, and seat of the Martian Parliament.

On this evening, the Parliament had been called to an emergency session, representatives having been summoned by the High Minister from each of the planet's ten satrapies. Their skyships now lay at anchor on the landing field to the south of the temple complex, and the electric braziers in the eyes of the Face, which were normally extinguished at night, now cast twin beams of crystalline light into the black sky.

In the surrounding cities, the people gazed uneasily at the great upturned face with its serene expression and blazing eyes. They knew why the Parliament was in emergency session – or thought they did. They were aware that the Martian Ambassador to Earth had met with an untimely end, that in all likelihood he had been murdered, and that the Parliament was deeply troubled. They did not, however, know just how troubled their leaders were, for the news had yet to reach them that two more Martians had been slain.

The Chamber of Thought and Voice was located at the centre of the Face, and was the place where matters of government were debated. Its elegantly curving inner wall was panelled with rose-hued marble, and was bathed in the subdued light of numerous electric braziers. The circular floor of polished granite was divided into eleven segments, one for each of the ten satrapies, and the eleventh for the High Minister, whose responsibility it was to oversee the debate, and to make a final decision on which course of action should be followed.

The satraps entered the chamber quickly and without fanfare, and they took their seats with barely an acknowledgment of each others' presence. The final satrap to arrive, from distant Ultima Volantis in the far northern lands, hurried to take his position, and then the High Minister rose and addressed the assembly.

'I welcome you,' he said, spreading his long arms wide. 'I welcome all the satraps of Rhenquahar. I welcome the Satrap of Ultima Volantis, of Ghot'anozhor, Kharkarras, Sten'dhek, S'aghitar, Bell'abrax, Sansarras, Fhontarras, Kharkaraphon and Khututhah. I invite to speak whomever so wishes. Who will begin?'

'With the Minister's indulgence, I will speak first,' said the Satrap of Kharkarras. 'I will give voice to the thoughts of many: many in this chamber, and many in the lands beyond. It was a dire mistake to initiate contact with the people of the Blue Planet Azquahar. We acted precipitously. We should have waited and gathered more information on the humans and their ways. The price of our unthinking haste is the death of three of our people.'

'It was not we who made contact,' countered the Satrap of Fhontarras. 'The humans sent a radio broadcast across the Æther; we merely responded.'

'If you must concentrate on mere detail, Fhontarras, so be it. The mistake was still ours in responding.'

'I disagree,' said the Satrap of Bell'abrax. 'The people of Azquahar are not to blame for what has happened. Nor are we to consider them a danger to the peace and security of our own world of Rhenquahar.'

'Bell'abrax is right,' declared the Satrap of Kharkaraphon. 'In the six Azquaharan years since contact was established, the humans have never given us any cause to mistrust them or to suspect them of ill will towards us. The intelligence we received from Petrox Voronezh bears this out. It is the people of Zhinquahar who are our enemies, for it was their agent who took the life of Lunan R'ondd.'

'With the help of a human,' the Satrap of Khututhah interjected. 'Let us not forget that it was human science which developed the parasites which invaded the Ambassador's body and stole the air from his lungs.'

All in the room shifted uncomfortably at this, the thought stirring horrible memories of the catastrophe which had nearly destroyed their race in the distant past.

Khututhah continued, 'I am not so eager to give Humankind the benefit of our doubts. We have learned much of their ways since contact was made – contact which I, too, consider a mistake. They are an acquisitive and warlike race, always taking what their fellows own as if it were their right, and meeting all resistance with force of arms. The empires of their history all tell the same story. They are following the same path as that followed by Zhinquahar; every passing day brings new inventions, new industrial processes, new ways of consuming their world's resources. Their technology is still in its infancy, and yet it has the potential to grow beyond their ability to control – even should they wish to control it.'

'Quite so,' nodded Kharkaraphon. 'But that is not what we are here to discuss. Our proper topic of debate should be Zhinquahar and its intentions.'

'Very well,' replied Khututhah. 'Although I believe the two subjects to be inseparable, let us follow Kharkaraphon's advice and confine ourselves, for now at least, to the matter of Zhinquahar. Their plight is obvious, as is the strategy they have formulated to escape the doom which hovers over them. In short, they wish to engineer a conflict between Rhenquahar and Azquahar, and in so doing weaken both planets to the extent that we and the humans will fall easily to a subsequent Zhinquaharan invasion. They have betrayed the world which gave them life, so that it will no longer accept their existence, and so they plan to take our worlds for their own.'

'Khututhah summarises the situation admirably,' said the Satrap of Ghot'anozhor. 'However, he neglects to mention that we will not allow ourselves to fall so easily into the trap. We will not be manipulated in such an obvious manner by a desperate and dying race. The Zhinquaharan plan will fail.'

'Will it?' said the Satrap of Ultima Volantis.

All eyes turned to him.

'Of course it will,' said Ghot'anozhor irritably. 'Do you think us such fools as to walk into a trap which we can plainly see?'

Ultima Volantis gave a soft, chirruping laugh. 'The best trap is the one which is unavoidable, even when its existence is known. The Zhinquaharans are playing a clever game; they are using our fears against us, fomenting revulsion in our hearts. Why else would they choose such a method to assassinate Lunan R'ondd than to make every Rhenquaharan shudder at the very mention of humanity? And let us not forget that Indrid Cold's other activities perform the same function: many humans think that we are behind his attacks in the capital of their world's most powerful empire and that the gaze of fear and hatred should be turned upon Rhenquahar. It is more than likely that Indrid Cold was responsible for the destruction of the interplanetary cylinder which was to have brought Lunan R'ondd's body home. But how many of *our* people will believe it? There are many amongst us who agree with Kharkarras and Khututhah that we should not have responded to the humans' radio message, that we should have been more careful and not revealed our existence to them quite so peremptorily.

'There are those among our people who maintain that we should expel the human Ambassador and his entire Embassy, while others are pressing for their immediate internment as a dangerous alien element. And meanwhile, on Azquahar, there is a similar attitude spreading rapidly amongst the general public. Many of their news journals declare that diplomatic relations with Rhenquahar should be suspended, or even abandoned altogether, that we are covetous of the Blue Planet, and wish to take it for our own.'

'Do they really believe that?' wondered Ghot'anozhor, 'In spite of the fact that we cannot live unaided in their atmosphere?'

'You forget, my friend,' replied Ultima Volantis, 'that just as we have learned much of the humans from our diplomatic mission, they have learned much of us from theirs. They know that we possess the biological technology to alter the atmosphere of a planet. They know of the Red Weed, by which our own atmosphere is maintained. Many humans believe that, were we to transplant the Weed to Azquahar, it would transform their world into an analogue of Rhenquahar.'

'That's outrageous!' said the Satrap of Sten'dhek. 'How can they believe us capable of such a terrible act?'

'They believe us capable of it because they themselves would be capable of it, were they to possess such technology,' replied Ultima Volantis. 'Their thoughts and attitudes are limited: they find it very difficult to think in terms other than those which are familiar to them.'

'Another reason why we should not have responded to their radio broadcast,' muttered Kharkarras. 'They are not ready to assimilate the knowledge that their tiny world is not the only seat of intelligence in the Æther. The knowledge fills them with fear and mistrust: fertile ground for the Zhinquaharans. I wonder how many amongst us still think it was wise to begin sending fighting machines to Azquahar?'

'That treaty,' said Bell'abrax, 'was intended to ensure the security of the Blue Planet against threats from outer space: an act of good faith and fellow feeling on our part. The humans have already caught a glimpse of the horrors which lurk in the depths of the Æther, but still they have no idea of what is really out there in the ultimate darkness.'

'And when the rest of the fighting machines arrive,' retorted Kharkarras, 'do you really think that Queen Victoria will reserve their use for that purpose only? Do you really think that she will not use them for the domestic consolidation of her empire's power?'

Bell'abrax hesitated, then looked away. 'That is a matter for her and her government.'

Kharkarras gave a short, contemptuous laugh. 'Ah! How quickly and easily we transfer responsibility for our weapons' use to those who have acquired them from us! Perhaps we should not stop at fighting machines: perhaps we should offer them our newest technology, perhaps we should offer them the Sun Cannon!'

Bell'abrax cast an appalled glance at Kharkarras. 'I am not suggesting that for one moment!'

'Why not?' Kharkarras asked with a rhetorical shrug, looking around the chamber at the other satraps. 'The Sun Cannon is the ultimate weapon of defence. Should we not share it with our new friends?'

'I believe you have made your point, Kharkarras,' said Ghot'anozhor. 'The humans are certainly not mature enough as a civilisation – nor even as a species – to be allowed access to such a device. They would in all likelihood destroy themselves with it. But we are drifting away from the topic of discussion and the central question that we have come here to debate: how should we proceed in the present situation?'

'We should withdraw from Azquahar,' said Kharkarras decisively. 'We should turn our backs on the humans and attend to our own affairs. There is nothing to be gained from continued relations with the Blue Planet.'

'Not even the joy of knowing another civilisation?' said the Satrap of Fhontarras. 'The fascination of learning its history, its arts and sciences, the biological diversity and evolution of its world? Does none of that hold any allure for you, Kharkarras?'

'If the price of such knowledge is the lamentable situation in which we now find ourselves, Fhontarras, then the answer is no.'

'And what of Zhinquahar?' asked the Satrap of Sansarras. 'How will its strategy play out? My friends, we are holding this debate in a state of ignorance, for we do not know precisely how they plan to ignite conflict between Rhenquahar and Azquahar. Their psychological tactics have been quite effective thus far... but what form will the final blow take? And will we be able to resist it when it falls?'

'More to the point,' said Kharkarras, 'will the *humans* be able to resist it? Khututhah is quite right: their technology is growing rapidly in power and sophistication. Already they have developed a means of travelling through space with their new Æther zeppelins. Very soon, they will no longer be dependent on us for interplanetary travel; our cylinders will no longer be of any use to them – they will be able to reach Rhenquahar by themselves. And if the conclusion of Zhinquahar's strategy makes war inevitable, as Sansarras implies, what then? Will Azquahar launch an armada of zeppelins against us?'

Silence descended upon the Chamber of Thought and Voice, as each satrap considered the question.

Presently, Ultima Volantis spoke. 'If that happens, we shall be forced to defend ourselves.'

'Of course we shall,' said Kharkarras, 'but not in the way Zhinquahar is expecting...' He paused, allowing the thought to settle within the minds of the others. 'Not by *conventional* means, for a conventional war *would* have the effect they are hoping for, and weaken us to the point where we are no longer capable of defending ourselves.'

Ultima Volantis turned his eyes to Kharkarras, and they were filled with the horror and despair of a terrible realisation. 'You… you are suggesting that we bring the Sun Cannon to bear upon Azquahar.'

At this, the chamber erupted with a sudden clamour of voices. Some of the satraps rose to their feet and began shouting at Kharkarras, while others hurled loud and angry words at those who were standing. Kharkarras remained in his seat, gazing impassively at his fellows and listening to the words which filled the room like a sudden swarm of fireflies.

'Outrageous!'

'Impossible!'

'We cannot do such a thing!'

'We may have no choice.'

'Turn the Sun Cannon on our fellow beings?'

'We may have no choice.'

'That is not why we created it.'

'We created it to defend ourselves.'

'Against threats from the deep Æther!'

'Azquahar may become such a threat.'

'Unacceptable!'

'We would not deserve our continued existence, were we to commit such an atrocity.'

'One shell is all that would be necessary.'

'One shell is too much!'

'One shell, aimed at London, the capital of Victoria's empire.'

'No!'

'What is the alternative? To walk into the Zhinquaharan trap? To conduct a conventional war with Azquahar?'

'To do so would be to invite our own destruction.'

The exchanges continued in this vein for another minute or so before the High Minister stood up and raised his arms. Immediately, silence was restored.

'We have a clear choice,' he said. 'Neither Azquahar nor Zhinquahar are aware of the Sun Cannon's existence: it is *they* who are conducting themselves from a position of ignorance, not us. A shell from the Cannon, aimed at Azquahar, and one aimed at Zhinquahar, would certainly extinguish their hostile intent. But the question is: should we use it?'

The satraps returned to their seats as the High Minister continued, 'The time has come to make our decision. I will have your answers to this question:

'Should Azquahar consider it necessary to launch an attack on Rhenquahar... will we respond by using the Sun Cannon?

'Khututhah.'

'Yes.'

'Kharkaraphon.'

'No.'

'Fhontarras.'

'No.'

'Sansarras.'

'Yes.'

'Bell'abrax.'

'No.'

'S'aghitar.'

'No.'

'Sten'dhek.'

'Yes.'

'Kharkarras.'

'Yes.'

'Ghot'anozhor.'

'No.'

'Ultima Volantis.'

The satrap hesitated, looked around at the others, and then gave a great sigh. 'Yes,' he said.

'Five in favour, five against,' said the High Minister. 'It therefore falls to me to cast the deciding vote.'

Each of the satraps leaned forward in his chair, waiting for the Minister's decision.

'This,' he said, 'is the most momentous and terrible decision any Rhenquaharan has ever had to make. There is a part of my mind which recoils from the Sun Cannon and wishes our scientists had never discovered the atomic principles which govern its function. But it is futile to do so, for the Cannon now exists, and cannot be un-invented.

'It is indeed appalling that we should have created such a weapon. It is appalling that we should have *needed* to... but the Things which our Far Seers have glimpsed in the depths of the Æther make it necessary. Who among us could have foreseen the possibility that we might be required to bring it to bear upon our fellow creatures in this Solar System?

'But what is the alternative? We have the wisdom to see through the machinations of Zhinquahar; we have the discipline and the forbearance to avoid the snare of conflict which they have laid in our path. Can we say the same of the Azquaharans? Can we trust that they are mature enough to step back from the abyss of war? More pertinently, should we wager the security of our world and the continuation of our civilisation on such trust?

'I believe we all know the answer to that question. For ten generations, since the time of Yoh-Vombis the World Builder, we have lived in peace and turned away from the folly of conflict; we have applied our minds and energies to the cultivation of knowledge and to the contemplation of Nature's wonders and mysteries, while remaining ever mindful of its dangers.

'We have come too far and built too much to tolerate the hostility of others – even those others who are our siblings in this, our solar cradle. We must protect Rhenquahar: this is the covenant our ancestors made with the World Builder, the unbreakable promise; this is the vow taken by all who serve our Parliament.

'It may be that ultimately the Azquaharans will see no alternative but to act against us. Yes… that may be the case, for as Ultima Volantis has observed, a sufficiently clever trap cannot be avoided, even when one is aware of its existence. If that happens, we must be prepared to respond with all the power at our disposal. The alternative is defeat, death, subjugation. The alternative is unacceptable.'

'High Minister, if I may…' said Ultima Volantis, who had risen to his feet.

'Speak,' said the Minister.

'Could we not warn the Azquaharans that we possess a weapon capable of destroying their world? Could we not send word to them that they must not allow themselves to be manipulated by Zhinquahar? That if they do, the consequences would be terrible beyond imagining?'

'And if we were to send such a warning, what do you think their reaction would be? Even if the present crisis were averted, they would consider us potential aggressors for evermore. Relations between our worlds would be irreparably damaged.'

'Will they not believe us to be eternal aggressors if we rain atomic destruction upon one of their cities?' the satrap persisted.

Fhontarras rose to his feet. 'High Minister, if I may…'

'Speak, Fhontarras.'

'We are assuming that this crisis will continue towards the conclusion planned by Zhinquahar. That may not be the case, for there are agents of Azquahar who are, even as we speak, working towards its peaceful solution.'

'You are speaking of the one called Thomas Blackwood.'

'And his companion, Sophia Harrington. It is quite clear that Queen Victoria has the utmost confidence in their abilities. We should not forget that it was their investigation which revealed the existence of a Zhinquaharan on their world, and they who were instrumental in uncovering the plot to foment war between Rhenquahar and Azquahar.'

'And your point, Fhontarras?' said the High Minster.

'My point is that we should continue with our present policy of non-interference, that we should allow Blackwood and Harrington to continue with their investigation. If they apprehend the Zhinquaharan Indrid Cold, if they reveal him to their own people to be an enemy of both our worlds, rather than an ally of ours, then I am certain that the crisis *will* be averted, and peace will continue. There will be no need to use the Sun Cannon, against either Azquahar *or* Zhinquahar. We need to give them more time.'

The High Minster nodded. 'Your words make sense, Fhontarras. Very well, we will do as you suggest – but know you all that my vote is this: should Blackwood and Harrington fail, should this matter end in a declaration of war, then we *will* launch a shell from the Sun Cannon at the Azquaharan and Zhinquarahan capitals, for the sake of our own survival!'

CHAPTER TWO:
The Return of the Djinn

Blackwood looked down the barrel of Lord Pannick's revolver and gave a silent but vehement curse.

'Such a shame,' said Pannick, 'that you saw fit to continue meddling in my affairs.'

'*Your* affairs?' said Blackwood. 'It is *you*, sir, who are meddling in the affairs of Earth, and in so doing are sealing the fate of every man, woman and child upon it.'

'And securing my own future in the process,' Pannick said with a satisfied smirk.

'He's going to betray us all, Thomas,' said Sophia, who was still clinging to Blackwood, but she was regaining her strength and resolve with every passing moment. 'He's made a deal with the Venusians: they're going to bestow power and riches upon him, while the rest of us are reduced to slavery, or worse.'

'The rest of *them*, my dear – not you. As I said, you and Mr Blackwood will not live to see the future of Earth. In fact, you will not live beyond the next few seconds.' He pulled back the revolver's hammer.

'What's the purpose of that Æther zeppelin you've got outside, Pannick?' asked Blackwood suddenly. He was keenly aware of the need to stall his enemy by any means possible, while he tried to figure a way out of this fix. He was not confident that he could do so.

'Ah! The Æther zeppelin. You saw it, did you?'

'I did.'

'And presumably you saw what it contains?'

'Hundreds of canisters, filled with what looks like *Acarus galvanicus*.'

'Quite right. It seems to me that you already know the answer to your question, sir. I intend to send the zeppelin to Mars, where it will enter the atmosphere and release the *Acarus* mites. Of course, they won't kill *all* the Martians, but enough of them will succumb to guarantee their rage and desire for revenge upon the Earth.'

'And who will fly the zeppelin? You?'

'Oh dear me, no!' Pannick laughed. 'That's much too dangerous for me, and besides, I've never particularly cared for the notion of space travel. I will leave that particular job to my man here. I believe you know Mr Meddings?'

Peter Meddings appeared in the doorway behind Pannick. He was also brandishing a revolver, which he pointed at Sophia. 'Good evening, sir, madam,' he said. 'Good to see you again, Mr Blackwood.'

'I assure you the feeling is not mutual, sir,' muttered Blackwood. 'How much is he paying you to betray your entire world?'

Meddings smiled. 'Enough to make me want to betray it.'

'It sounds to me like his Lordship has you marked down for a suicide mission.'

'Do you think so?'

'I certainly do. How far do you think you'll get, once you've entered the Martian atmosphere. Do you really think they'll let you fly around, polluting their world with deadly organisms?'

'But they won't know, Mr Blackwood,' Meddings replied, his smile growing broader. 'Lord Pannick will place a glamour upon the zeppelin. Do you know what that is?'

'A Magickal disguise.'

'Precisely. When the Martians look at the craft, they will see one of their shantak birds – nothing more.'

'Very clever,' said Blackwood sarcastically.

'I think so,' said Pannick.

'Where's your other lackey?'

'Lackey?'

'Indrid Cold. Where is he?'

'In London, causing more mayhem. He's stepping up his campaign of psychological torment. There will be many more deaths in the capital this evening, I assure you.'

'You wretch!'

'Now, now, sir. Insults will get you nowhere.'

'And what about the Greater Exhibition? What do you plan to do there?'

Pannick laughed. 'My! We *have* been busy, haven't we? If you saw the Æther zeppelin, then you must also have seen the Martian fighting machine in the neighbouring hangar. It's the first of a planned shipment of heavy armaments from Mars to Earth…'

'A secret weapons treaty,' said Blackwood.

'Quite so, and one which I helped to broker. The Martians believe that they are offering us the means to defend our planet against threats from the deep Æther, about which they seem to know rather a lot. But I have quite different plans for this particular contraption.'

'You plan to attack the Exhibition.'

'Indeed I do. In 1851, the Great Exhibition represented the pinnacle of human technological and cultural achievement. The Greater Exhibition, which will be opened by Her Majesty the day after tomorrow, will surpass even that grand enterprise – not least because it will include a number of Martian exhibits. It is seen as the culmination of the first phase of Martian-Human contact – the first and *last* I might add.'

'Because you intend to attack it with the fighting machine.'

'The machine's Heat Ray will turn the New Crystal Palace – not to mention the whole of Hyde Park – into a charred wasteland. I hardly need describe the reaction of the British people to such an event, especially since Her Majesty will be among the dead.'

'They will believe that the Martians are to blame and demand a declaration of war upon Mars.'

'And the Government will accede to their demand. And of course, in the meantime, my Æther zeppelin will be headed to Mars to deliver my calling card, which the Martian people will take in a similar vein.'

'You beast!' said Sophia, shaking her head in disgust.

Lord Pannick ignored her. 'Now, I will ask you to come with me.'

'To where?' asked Blackwood.

'You are standing on a particularly beautiful Persian rug, and it will be impossible to get the bloodstains out, so we shall retire to the entrance hall, which has a stone floor.'

Blackwood was tempted to stay where he was, but he had no doubt that Pannick would sacrifice his precious rug if necessary. 'Come, Sophia,' he said gently.

'Thomas…'

'It's all right, my dear. Come.' As Pannick and Meddings backed out of the room, Blackwood led Sophia into the corridor. Pannick gestured with his revolver, and they began to walk towards the main staircase.

As he walked, Blackwood's eyes darted between the walls, searching for some means of escape or defence. There were antique swords and battle axes mounted at intervals upon the oak panelling, but there was no way he would be able to grab one and use it before Pannick fired. He would have to wait until they reached the hall, and then…

And then he would have to think of something pretty sharpish, or he and Sophia would surely die…

As he began to descend the staircase, Blackwood realised that there was no way for both he and Sophia to get out of this fix alive. From his vantage point, he could see nothing in the entrance hall which might be brought to bear as a weapon. His only option was to make a lunge for both Pannick and Meddings as soon as they reached the foot of the stairs. They would surely cut him down in short order, but it might just provide Sophia with the opportunity to make a run for it. He only hoped that she would do so and not waste her chance by staying with him as he fell.

'Well,' said Pannick, 'here we are. I do so hate long goodbyes, so…' He raised his revolver and took aim between Blackwood's eyes.

At that moment, Blackwood heard a familiar voice inside his head. The voice said, *Get ready to run, sir.*

In the next instant, the entire house vibrated with a dull concussion, as though a colossal hammer had pummelled the ground nearby.

Pannick hesitated. 'What was that?' he whispered.

Shanahan, thought Blackwood. *What* was *that?*

As I said, sir, get ready to run.

The floor trembled beneath their feet as the house was shaken by another massive *thud*.

'What's happening, your Lordship?' asked Meddings, looking up at the ceiling with fear in his eyes.

'Shut up,' said Pannick. He took renewed aim at Blackwood. 'What have you done?'

'Nothing. I'm as mystified as you, I assure you.' Blackwood was about to say more, but his voice died in his throat as a searing pain lanced through his chest. For a fleeting moment, he thought that Pannick had fired at him – but the source of the pain was not a bullet. The amulet which Count Saint Germain had given him felt suddenly red hot upon his skin. He grimaced.

The floor shuddered again at a third impact, and this time it was accompanied by the distant sound of splintering wood.

'My God, what's happening?' cried Meddings.

'I told you, be silent!' shouted Pannick, but Meddings was already edging across the hall towards the front door, his eyes darting this way and that, looking for the source of the concussions.

Blackwood was not surprised: Lord Pannick's lackey had probably seen more than his fair share of dark Magick in this place. No wonder he was so inclined to terror.

Pannick glanced down at Blackwood and saw the look of pain on his face as the house shook yet again. This time, there was the sound of shattering windows from somewhere above them. Pannick's face twisted into a grimace of fear and rage. 'No,' he said. '*No!*'

A crack appeared in the ceiling and rapidly spread from one side of the hall to the other. As Pannick looked up, Blackwood saw his chance. Grabbing Sophia's hand, he rushed away from the staircase towards Meddings, who had nearly reached the front door. Swinging Sophia behind him, he pivoted Meddings around and took him in a powerful neck lock with his left arm, while with his right he grabbed the man's wrist and pointed the revolver at Lord Pannick.

'Open the door, Sophia!' he cried.

He squeezed Meddings's hand tightly, forcing him to fire the gun, but Meddings was struggling so much that the two shots went wide of their mark. Pannick crouched low and fired a single shot. Blackwood cursed him for the trueness of his aim as the back of Meddings's head exploded, spraying him with blood and brains. The man went limp instantly, and the muscles in Blackwood's left arm screamed in protest as he strove to maintain the sudden dead weight. He tried to wrest the gun from Meddings's hand, but his finger was curled tightly around the trigger, and Pannick was already firing again. Blackwood felt his macabre, makeshift shield jerk horribly with the impacts of the bullets.

'Sophia!'

'It's open, Thomas!'

'Get out, now!'

Pannick had fired his six shots, and was already reloading with bullets pulled rapidly from a pocket of his waistcoat. Blackwood was about to rush him, for he was confident he could cover the distance to the staircase before the revolver was brought to bear upon him again, but Shanahan's voice echoed through his mind.

No, sir. You must leave now and get as far away from the house as you can. You must leave right now!

The searing pain in Blackwood's chest grew yet more intense, and he felt himself grow lightheaded, as though he were about to pass out. Panting and grimacing against the agony, he decided that he had to follow Shanahan's entreaty. He dropped Meddings's bullet-riddled corpse and dashed out through the door, slamming it shut behind him. No sooner had he done so than the wood cracked and splintered as Pannick fired through it. He lunged at Sophia, forcing her to the ground and lying on top of her, shielding her with his body while he counted the number of shots.

One, two, three, four, five, six.

'Up!' he barked, dragging her to her feet. They ran together across the lawn, away from the house.

'Curse this infernal dress!' Sophia gasped, as she gathered the lower part of the evening gown around her knees to make running a little easier.

When they had reached what Blackwood judged to be a reasonably safe distance, they stopped before a stand of trees and looked back at the house.

'Good grief!' cried Sophia. 'What's happening to it?'

All of the windows on the first floor appeared to have been shattered, blown outwards by some strange force, and from them a fierce blue glow emanated, flooding the surrounding lawn with an unnatural flickering light.

Blackwood was bent double from the pain, his hands grasping his knees, his legs threatening to buckle at any moment. 'Oh God!' he panted.

Shocked and terrified, Sophia put her arms around his shoulders. 'Thomas, you've been hit! Where did the bullet strike?'

'It… it isn't a bullet,' he said through gritted teeth. 'The amulet…'

'What amulet?'

'A form of protection… against…'

'Thomas, it's killing you. Take it off!'

'I wouldn't do that, if I were you, sir,' said a voice in the air above them.

'Shanahan.' Blackwood gazed up at the faerie, his eyes filling with tears. 'I can't stand it… I have to take it off… it's going to kill me.'

'No it isn't, sir. It wouldn't be much of a protective charm if it did, now, would it?'

'But the pain!'

'The pain is only in your mind. It isn't harming your body: in fact, it's keeping you and Lady Sophia alive. Hold that thought in your mind, sir: the pain is not physical…'

'It feels pretty bloody physical to me, damn it!'

'Shanahan, *do* something!' cried Sophia.

'Listen to me, sir. The pain exists in your mind, not your chest. Concentrate on it…'

'Concentrate? I don't have much choice.'

'Draw the pain upwards... draw it up to its true location. You can do it, sir.'

Blackwood did as the faerie instructed, and to his astonishment, the pain *did* seem to be moving up out of his chest. He gagged as it passed through his neck, and screamed as it entered his head. He felt as if his brain was boiling and imagined a great gout of steam belching from his mouth. 'It's in my head,' he moaned. 'Great God, it's in my head!'

'Good, sir. Now you're perceiving it as it really is: a sense impression in your mind.'

'What... what do I do now?'

'Why, sir, you simply stop thinking about it,' Shanahan replied.

'Easier said than...' Blackwood stopped.

The pain had completely vanished.

'Done.'

'You see, sir? Simple.'

Blackwood was about to ask how he could possibly have banished the pain so suddenly and completely, but as he glanced back at the house, he knew that that question would have to wait. 'What's happening there? It looks like it's being destroyed from the inside out. How?'

'Ah, well, I must admit that's my doing, sir.'

'*Your* doing? What the blazes did you do?'

'As soon as Lord Pannick got hold of you,' Shanahan replied, 'I knew you were in a tight fix, sir... so I created a little diversion, to give you and Lady Sophia a chance to get away.'

'How?' asked Sophia.

'I went back inside his Lordship's cogitator and took out the dreamcatcher.'

'You sabotaged it,' said Blackwood. 'You took away its protective device, leaving it vulnerable to an ætherial virus.'

'Correct, sir – and not just *any* virus.'

'What do you mean?'

'When her Ladyship smashed the scrying glass of your own cogitator a few days ago, the djinn that had come through was banished back to its own realm. It was denied its prey – *you*, sir. And it wasn't very pleased, I can tell you!'

'Do you mean to say that the djinn which tried to devour me is now attacking Lord Pannick's house?'

'I am, sir. Djinns are like that: they'll do your bidding, if you know how to manipulate them, but if they don't get their reward, they will vent their wrath upon the summoner – in this case, his Lordship.'

'I see,' said Blackwood with a grim smile. 'I suppose one would call that poetic justice.'

'Yes sir, I suppose one would.'

Blackwood and Sophia watched in horrified fascination as a mass of writhing tentacles erupted from the roof, while more spilled out in loathsome grey tides from the shattered windows. It was as though a tree made of living flesh had sprouted beneath Furfield and was growing with terrifying speed, splitting walls, demolishing towers, writhing and wrenching and destroying. And the noise it made while it did so was like nothing Blackwood or Sophia had ever heard in their lives before, nor ever wished to again: a great, earth-shaking, trumpeting blast; an insensate scream of rage from the ultimate gulfs beyond the ramparts of the ordered Universe.

'I believe we had best retreat a little further, sir,' said Shanahan. 'In fact, I believe we had best retreat a *lot* further.'

'It's still growing, Thomas,' shouted Sophia, pointing at the wildly flailing tentacles which had now all but obliterated the house. 'Look! It has someone!'

They saw a tiny figure clutched in one of the fleshy cords, which uncoiled high into the cold night sky. And then, horror of horrors, a gibbering, lipless mouth opened at the base of the tentacle, and the figure was dropped inside.

'Oh!' Sophia turned away, her eyes tightly shut. 'Was that Lord Pannick?'

'I don't think so,' Blackwood replied, feeling bile rising in his throat. I think it was Meddings.'

'Please, sir,' said Shanahan urgently. 'Let us be gone.'

'Wait!' Blackwood pointed to the left of the churning pile of rubble that had once been Furfield. 'Look there.'

A figure was running at full tilt towards the two hangars which stood nearby. As it reached the larger building, another figure emerged from out of the darkness, a pale, leaping caricature, bounding with unnaturally long strides across the lawn.

'That's Pannick, heading for the Æther zeppelin,' Blackwood said. 'And Indrid Cold heading for the fighting machine. I've got to stop them!'

Sophia took hold of his arm. 'There's no time, Thomas. Those horrible things will fall on you before you can get there.'

'Her Ladyship is right, sir,' said Shanahan. 'There's nothing more we can do here. It will be the death of you to go after them.'

As if to punctuate Shanahan's point, one of the longer tentacles reared up against the sky and slammed into the ground less than ten yards from where they stood. The impact knocked Blackwood and Sophia off their feet.

'Perhaps you're right,' said Blackwood. 'We'd best make a run for it.'

'In which case,' said Sophia, 'I'll do far better without this.' Much to Blackwood's surprise and discomfiture, she proceeded quickly to divest herself of her evening gown. Now clad only in a short slip, she stood up straight and met his unblinking gaze. 'I can't run in that infernal thing.'

'Quite so, my dear... quite so,' replied Blackwood, as courtesy vanquished shock and he averted his eyes from Sophia's long-legged, exquisitely-proportioned form. *My goodness*, he thought. *Oh my goodness*.

'This way,' said Shanahan as he flew off through the trees. 'Follow me sir, your Ladyship. Quickly!'

They withdrew into the stand of trees as more tentacles reared up and smote the ground, while other, thinner tendrils thrust amongst the trees, wrapping themselves around their trunks and uprooting them with all the ease of a gardener pulling weeds. Without the evening gown to encumber her, Sophia was as fleet of foot as a gazelle, and quickly drew ahead of Blackwood as she sprinted after Shanahan.

'What about my amulet?' he shouted.

'What about it?' the faerie called back.

'Won't it protect us?'

'Not against direct contact with a djinn, sir! That would overload it in an instant.'

'Splendid.'

They left the stand of trees behind and continued across a wide expanse of open lawn towards a dense area of woodland which fringed the estate. Risking a glance over his shoulder, Blackwood saw the Æther zeppelin rising majestically from its hangar, while the Martian fighting machine rose suddenly, shattering the roof of its own enclosure. Instantly, a brace of tentacles lashed out at the vehicles, but when they got to within a few feet of their targets, they were thwarted by what appeared to be a bubble of crackling blue energy, against which the flesh of the Outer Being fizzed and bubbled. The djinn roared in pain and fury as the zeppelin gained altitude and vanished behind a thick bank of cloud, while the fighting machine strode off across the grounds, each vehicle impervious to the djinn's assaults.

Must have some kind of protection, thought Blackwood. *Although whether Magickal or technological, who knows? At any rate, that'll put the djinn in an even fouler mood.* He drew level with Sophia and tried not to stare at the hypnotic movement of her slim, supple thighs. *Oh... my goodness.*

They gained the edge of the woodland, just as a lance of fearsome red light struck the ground a few yards away, ploughing a huge furrow across the meticulously tended grass. Sophia screamed, tripped, and fell heavily, so that the wind was knocked from her lungs. In an instant, Blackwood was beside her, gathering her up in his arms.

'I'm... I'm all right, Thomas,' she panted. 'What *was* that?'

'Martian Heat Ray, I'll be bound. It seems that Cold has decided to join forces with the djinn and wipe us from the face of the earth.'

No sooner had he spoken than another lance of energy flashed overhead, shearing the tops from the trees and showering them with burning leaves and charred branches. Blackwood shielded Sophia with his body and then drew her to her feet. 'Can you continue?'

'Of course I can, you fool!' she cried. 'Look what's after us!' Her face was caked in dirt, and her hair had come untied and was falling upon her heaving shoulders like a great dark waterfall; as her eyes blazed at him with fear and anger, like those of an Amazon prepared for battle, Blackwood felt something stirring in his chest which was not remotely as uncomfortable as the amulet had been, but which was profoundly unsettling nevertheless.

'Excellent, my dear. Excellent.'

'Mr Blackwood! Lady Sophia!' cried Shanahan from somewhere up ahead. 'Hurry yourselves – there's not a moment to lose!'

'Where are we going, Shanahan?' Blackwood shouted.

'Anywhere but here,' said Sophia.

'Yes, but with a hundred-foot-high fighting machine and an entity from another dimension after us, "here" is a very big place.'

Sophia sprinted off once again. 'Come along, Thomas,' she called over her shoulder. 'No time to dawdle.'

Dawdle indeed! he thought as he set off after her.

As they made their way deeper into the woodland, Blackwood glanced up repeatedly through the treetops, dreading the sight of the fighting machine's armoured hull rearing above them. But for the moment, Indrid Cold had lost them, for he seemed to be firing the Heat Ray indiscriminately, blasting trees to oblivion to the left and right of them. The greater danger lay with the djinn's tendrils, which were whipping amongst the trees directly behind them, as if possessed of some infernal perception. The creature knew where they were, and the tendrils were gaining rapidly upon them. Blackwood spurred himself on, with the whip-like snapping of the tendrils in his ears and the horrific screaming and roaring of the djinn seeming to tear the very sky apart. *We're not going to get out of this alive*, he thought and immediately had a vision of Sophia being dropped into the djinn's gibbering maw. *No. No no no!*

'Shanahan, where are you?' he called.

'Here, sir. Quickly!'

Blackwood followed the sound of the faerie's voice and burst through the trees into a wide clearing whose long grass shone like emerald in the darkness. 'What's here?' he demanded. 'Why did you bring us here?'

'It's plain enough that there's no escaping our pursuers, sir.'

'Agreed.'

'Nevertheless, I've arranged for a means of escape.'

The whip-crack of the djinn's tendrils was now joined by the WHUMP, WHUMP of the fighting machine's tripod legs striking the ground nearby.

'You're talking in riddles, Shanahan,' said Blackwood. 'Whatever cards you have up your sleeve, now's the time to play them.'

'My thoughts exactly, sir,' said Shanahan, with a heavy hint of satisfaction in his voice.

Blackwood heard Sophia gasp. She was pointing at the centre of the clearing, which had begun to rise into the air, as if an upturned bowl was pushing the grass and earth upwards. The ground continued to rise, until it had formed a hemispherical dome.

'What the devil is this?' whispered Blackwood.

'This, sir,' replied Shanahan, 'is the means of escape I mentioned.'

'It's… it's a faerie mound,' said Sophia in wonderment.

The grass which covered the mound began to glitter and glow as if it really were made of emeralds, until presently the glow filled the entire clearing. So shocked was he that Blackwood only dimly registered the fact that the djinn had fallen silent. Now, the only sound was that of the approaching fighting machine.

Shanahan hovered above the mound, his delicate dragonfly wings glittering like the emerald grass. He beckoned to them. 'Come, my friends,' he said, and suddenly his voice seemed deeper and more powerful than before.

Blackwood took Sophia's hand in his. She gripped it tightly. 'Where are you taking us, Mr Shanahan?' she asked, her voice trembling.

'To the only place where you will be safe, beautiful Sophia,' he replied in that deep, powerful, resonant voice. 'I am taking you to the Realm of Faerie.'

CHAPTER THREE:
In the Faerie Realm

As Blackwood and Sophia watched, captivated, scarcely believing their eyes, the mound opened – or rather, it *seemed* to open: for while their physical vision told them that the surface of the green hemisphere remained intact, some other sense, of whose existence they had always been dimly aware and yet had never truly acknowledged, told them that a door had opened, from which a light emerged, pale, crystalline, pure and indescribably beautiful.

They began to discern movement within the light, which gradually resolved itself and became three human-like figures, which were as small as butterflies and as tall as men. They possessed the same delicate wings as Shanahan and were completely naked, their bodies strong and supple and exquisite to behold. As the figures walked out of the mound, Blackwood and Sophia saw that they were carrying long, slender objects which looked like the branches of trees, and at the ends of the objects were many-petalled blooms which rippled with a myriad unknown colours.

The figures bowed to Shanahan, just as Petrox Voronezh had done, Blackwood noted, and they raised the branch-like objects towards the writhing tentacles of the djinn, which towered above the surrounding trees. From each of the many-coloured blooms, a silent beam emerged, but the beam was not composed of light – rather, it was a *clarity*, as if the material, human world were a pane of glass caked with dust and grime, and the beams were wiping it clean, and within each beam, scintillating motes danced like raindrops in moonlight.

The beams cut through the cold night air and struck the djinn, and wherever they touched, the flesh of the Outer Being vanished without a sound; nor did the monstrosity utter the smallest murmur as it was pushed out of the world and the Universe, back to the terrible place from which it had come.

As the djinn was expelled, Blackwood felt a curious sensation in his chest. For a moment, he feared the resurgence of the dreadful burning pain, but in fact the very opposite was the case: the sensation he felt was one of unalloyed sweetness and wellbeing. Mystified, he felt for the amulet beneath his sweater, and was astonished to discover that it was no longer there.

Their task completed, the three faerie men lowered their weapons and returned to the mound. Shanahan beckoned to Blackwood and Sophia. 'Come, my friends, quickly. We cannot linger here.'

The sound of the Martian fighting machine's footfalls came closer, and once again the Heat Ray flashed out, incinerating great swathes of woodland, from which dark columns of smoke and flame erupted. Blackwood took Sophia's hand again, and together they followed Shanahan through the door that was not a door, into the faerie mound.

*

Blackwood was unsure what he was expecting to see – perhaps a stairway leading down to a hidden world of caves and subterranean cities, perhaps a misty realm of ethereal cloudscapes with weightless faerie castles floating in a rarefied atmosphere... But he saw neither of those things:

instead, he and Sophia found themselves in a twilit glade not entirely dissimilar to the woodland clearing they had just vacated. Glancing behind him, he saw the mound and sensed the invisible door through which they had come. Looking up, he saw the sky as he would have expected it to appear from Earth; the only difference was that he no longer felt the chill of an English October: the air was sweet-smelling and pleasantly warm. Somewhat guiltily, he realised that he was rather disappointed with the place.

'Not very different from your own world, is it?' said Shanahan's voice in his ear.

'Not really, no,' he replied.

'Wait.'

'For what?'

'For your mind to re-orientate itself. Just as the human body acclimatises itself automatically to a new environment, so the mind must undergo a similar process, here in Faerie.'

'I'm not sure I understand.'

'In a few moments, you will.'

As Blackwood and Sophia waited, they felt something stirring in their minds: a feeling, a memory, lying buried beneath all the thousands of years of human history, until it had all but vanished, lost in the bright glare of conscious thought. It was the same intuition which had allowed them to perceive a door in the faerie mound where no door existed; it was the same faculty which was once so vibrant and powerful in the human mind, when the mind was brand new, and shone with delicate light and the innocence of animals. It was the primal beauty and purity of perception, the loss of which was the price humanity had paid for civilisation.

The feeling, the memory, grew stronger in the minds of the humans as they stood in the faerie glade, and as they looked about them, the stars became bright jewels set within an obsidian sky; the glade opened upon a landscape that was infinite in extent, rolling away and away towards a horizon which was a naïve assumption rather than a reality, and within this landscape, which was home to snow-capped mountains of impossible height, to floating forests bright with a million shades of green and many-towered cities glowing in pastel hues, they became aware of people – millions upon millions of people, in the cities, in dwellings nestling within the floating forests, in villages resting upon the foothills of the mountains. They sensed each mind... and each mind sensed them and welcomed them.

And then they turned to Shanahan and saw that he was no longer a tiny, flitting creature dressed in clothes that might have been fashionable a century ago, but tall and powerful and naked, and beautiful beyond words, and his dragonfly wings were vast in the light of the jewelled stars.

'Shanahan?' Blackwood said.

'That is not my real name, and I beg your forgiveness for deceiving you, but it was necessary.'

'What *is* your real name?' asked Sophia.

He smiled at them and answered, 'Oberon.'

Sophia gasped and whispered, 'The King of the Faeries!'

His eyes blazed in the starlight, and the humans felt their knees buckle, and they sank to the grass that was softer than cotton wool and averted their eyes, for it was painful to look upon him, at the power and purity of him.

Oberon stepped forward and laid a hand upon their heads, saying, 'Do not kneel before me, my friends. Come. Stand. Look at me.'

Rising unsteadily to their feet, Blackwood and Sophia looked again into those blazing eyes, but now the pain was gone, leaving in its wake only the dull sadness of their crude physicality – sadness, and in Blackwood's case a burning shame at the condescension with which he had frequently treated Shanahan. *I treated him like a lackey*, he thought.

And all the while, he could have destroyed me with a single thought or turned my life into a nightmare of pain and misfortune.

'Time was when I walked often with humans,' Oberon said. 'Time was when the Earth was another home to us.'

'But not anymore,' said Sophia.

'No. That time is long past, for the human mind has chosen a path which has taken it far from us, from the friendship we once shared, the commonality of perception and feeling.'

'We have lost much,' said Blackwood.

Sophia shook her head. 'We have lost *everything*.'

Oberon smiled again. 'You are of the material world, children of matter. It was always to be, from the moment when the first life-chemicals bound themselves together in the primordial waters of Earth. Yes, it was always to be… and yet we still help you when we can.'

'You have helped us a great deal,' said Blackwood, 'for which I offer you my humblest thanks. But why did you disguise yourself? Why did you, Oberon, King of the Faeries, pretend to be a Helper from a human cogitator?'

'I will answer that question and the others you doubtlessly have. But first you will be guests in my home.'

'Where is that?' asked Sophia.

'In the Fortress of Apples.'

*

Oberon led Blackwood and Sophia out of the glade and across the fantastic landscape of Faerie, and as they walked, it seemed that they were not walking at all, but gliding above the soft grass, propelled by a sweet-scented breeze. And the people of the land bowed to Oberon as he passed, upon the plains and in the floating forests and on the sides of the mountains, and it seemed to the humans that even the jewelled stars watched his passing, and that they loved him as much as his people did.

292

At the centre of a vast field of swaying green, a great tree stood taller than any mountain on Earth, its colossal branches stroking the obsidian sky, so that the stars above nestled like fruit in its uppermost leaves. Its trunk rose like a wall before them and curved off on either side into the far distance. Blackwood guessed that it was as wide as the city of London. Entire buildings stood within the deep furrows of its trunk, and in the high branches, the lights of a million torches shone in perfect counterpoint to the light from the jewelled stars.

'This,' said Oberon, 'is the Fortress of Apples, where I live with my Queen Titania.'

Both Blackwood and Sophia wanted to say something, but they had no idea what to say: no human words could do justice to this magnificence, this exquisite immensity that was at once both unreal and infinitely more than real.

Oberon took in the expressions on their faces and gently touched the tears that had begun to fall from Sophia's eyes, and then he gathered the humans in his arms and ascended into the air on his vast, glittering wings, taking them higher than the tallest of Earth's buildings, the tallest of its trees, the highest of its mountains or clouds, into the branches of the Fortress of Apples. Within the tree's canopy, they passed villages of beautifully fashioned wooden buildings, standing upon the twisting lanes formed by the branches, until they came to a vast castle of wood at the living heart of the tree. Whether the castle had been fashioned by the faeries or by the tree itself, they didn't know. That it was alive, they had no doubt, for as they approached, the gigantic leaves which formed its gates opened, spreading wide to reveal a great hall within.

Oberon alighted upon the floor and released Blackwood and Sophia. Perhaps they would have commented on the singular nature of the chamber – the elegant and complex curves of its living walls, the intricate seraglios of wood grain which at once confused and delighted the eye, the graceful arches of the doorways which led deeper into the castle, and which were located at various heights above the floor – had not their attention immediately been seized and held fast by the vision standing before them.

Of such staggering beauty was she that both Blackwood and Sophia wondered whether they were hallucinating, for it seemed to them that no creature, whether in the material world or the Realm of Faerie, could be so exquisite, so perfect in every way. The humans stared at her openly, unable to draw their gaze from her face, from the long, dark-auburn hair which framed it, from the flawlessness of her pale skin, from the delicate lace wings which spread out behind her, from the gentle magnificence of her slender, naked body.

'Titania, my Queen,' said Oberon, stepping forward.

'Oberon, my husband,' she replied, and her voice was like the wind and rain, like the whisper of distant thunder and the opening of a flower in the swift sunlight of dawn.

They embraced each other and kissed, and Blackwood and Sophia felt the kiss upon their own lips, and their hearts pounded with the delight of it.

Taking his wife by the hand, Oberon said, 'These are my friends, Thomas Blackwood and Lady Sophia Harrington. Thomas, Sophia, I present to you my Queen, Titania of Faerie.'

'You are very welcome here,' Titania said, as she stepped forward towards them.

'Thank you,' whispered Blackwood. Unsure of what else to say or do, he gave an awkward bow. Sophia glanced at him and did the same.

Titania broke into a smile, and her eyes shone like the jewels drifting through the sky above. Blackwood's mouth was dry, and he felt himself stirring in a way which caused him the utmost consternation. The image of Titania filled his mind and brought the blood rushing to his cheeks, and he fervently hoped that neither she nor Oberon was aware of the waves of passionate adoration that were flowing through him at this moment.

Although he didn't know it (and it would not have surprised him in the least if he had), Sophia found herself in the tender clutches of a similarly overwhelming sweetness as she regarded Oberon. Her breath came in quick gasps of delight, which she struggled vainly to control, and she wished to be away from here without delay, while simultaneously wishing to stay here forever.

Titania's smile grew broader as she said, 'Your friends are embarrassed, Oberon. Could it be because we are unclothed?'

'I suspect so,' replied the Faerie King.

'Why is that, I wonder?'

'They believe that the human body is tainted by a sin committed at the beginning of Time, and for which all subsequent generations of their race must pay with shame and despair at their own physical nature. They do not appreciate the beauty of the forms in which their souls are embedded.'

'Ah,' said Titania, her voice bright with amusement. 'You are speaking of *modesty* – the modesty which is born of that mythical infraction which casts a shadow even upon their newborns.'

'I am.'

She shook her head and addressed their guests. 'What a pity it is, for you are both beautiful and should rejoice in your physical existence. Your bodies glow with the beauty of Being, a beauty which is undeservedly dimmed by the obscurity of clothing, born of a shame as false as it is puerile.'

'I... that is to say, we,' stammered Blackwood. 'We are products of our culture and history, I'm afraid. It's... just the way we are.'

'Thomas wishes to make love to me,' said Titania, her amusement growing in her voice. 'And Sophia wishes to make love to you, Oberon.'

Sophia gave a little gasp at this, and Blackwood said, 'Your Majesty! I assure you the thought never crossed my mind!'

Oberon and Titania laughed at Blackwood's discomfiture, and the Faerie Queen said, 'Your denial is as charming as it is ridiculous.'

'Come, my friends,' said Oberon. 'Do not allow yourselves to be put out of sorts by my wife's sense of humour. She is merely teasing you, for she is often amused by the antics of humans, by their strange beliefs and attitudes.'

'We are often amused by them ourselves,' said Sophia.

'I have no doubt. But for now, we must lay such things aside, for we have important matters to discuss.'

Apparently in response to this statement, the floor stirred, and from it arose four chairs with cushions and backs of soft leaves. 'Be seated,' said Oberon. As they sat in the chairs, he added, 'I would offer you refreshment, but were you to partake of it, you would never be able to leave the Realm of Faerie.'

'Then human folklore is true in that regard?' said Sophia. 'It's often said in wild and remote communities that faerie food should never be eaten.'

'It is true,' Oberon replied, 'as is much of your folklore. Now, Thomas, you asked me a question earlier: why did I disguise myself as a humble faerie Helper?'

'Indeed.'

'But first, there is another question you wish to ask.'

'I'm not sure I follow.'

'You are wondering how you were able to banish the pain from your amulet so easily.'

Of course! thought Blackwood. The marvels he had experienced in the last few minutes had made him forget entirely about the amulet and the agony it had so recently caused him – not to mention the fact that it had apparently disappeared. 'I suspect,' he said 'that I had your help in that.'

Oberon shrugged and indicated Blackwood's chest. 'Open your shirt.'

Blackwood did so, and looked down at his chest. Sophia looked also, and gasped in shock. The amulet had not disappeared; nor, however, did it remain hanging around his neck. The irregular pentacle with the staring eye at the centre was now – incredibly, unbelievably – embedded in his skin, its silvery lines glittering in the lamplight.

'Good grief,' Blackwood whispered. 'How did this happen?'

'The Comte de Saint Germain gave you a useful tool; I have merely made it *more* useful. Now, it cannot be taken from you, and it will alert you – without pain – to the presence of Magick and will offer a certain amount of protection.'

'I'm very grateful,' said Blackwood. 'Although I'm bound to say that I don't come up against Magick all that often.'

'In the past, no,' Oberon replied with a faint, mysterious smile. 'But in the future… who can say?'

'Do you, by any chance, know something I don't?' Blackwood asked.

Oberon's smile grew broader, but no less enigmatic. 'My friend, I know a great many things which you don't.'

'I have no doubt, sir.'

'But to return to your other question, regarding my disguising myself. That is easily answered. I did it to offer you aid in your current assignment.'

'May I ask why?'

'Because the future of your world is at stake. We will not allow Earth to fall into the hands of the Venusians, who have all but destroyed their own planet, and now wish to take possession of yours. The Earth is beloved by us, for as

297

I have said, we once walked openly and often there, and we maintain our connection with it. In fact, the connection can never be broken, for in a sense, Earth is still our home as much as it is yours, and we love it and the vast diversity of its life – a diversity which you have yet to appreciate or fully understand, even with your rapidly developing sciences.'

'If that's the case,' said Sophia, 'then why don't you come to our world *en masse* and engage the Venusians openly?'

'A fair and simple question,' Oberon nodded. 'The answer, however, is a little more complicated. When we left the Earth behind in ages long past, when human consciousness was new and civilisation was first stirring in its cradle, we made a Covenant with the material Universe that we would allow custody of the planet to pass to humanity and never interfere directly with the course of human history. We maintain that Covenant to this day and keep our interventions to a minimum. We help humanity when we can, in small ways: we help to run the information processing systems in your cogitators, for example, and we sometimes give aid to those who grow things upon the land. And there are other ways in which we lend a hand to humans on occasion, although they need not detain us here.'

'But major interventions are forbidden,' said Blackwood.

Oberon nodded.

'Is that the reason you brought us here, rather than allowing your men to engage the fighting machine and the Æther zeppelin directly? From the looks of those weapons of theirs, they would have made short work of them.'

'That is correct, and I must apologise, for we could indeed have destroyed them.'

'But you would have been doing our jobs for us, and you're not allowed to do that.'

'We are not. We engaged the djinn because it is not a creature of the material Universe. Our Covenant permits us to intervene where Magick is involved, and the djinn would certainly have pursued Lord Pannick until it had found a way to exact its vengeance upon him; in so doing, it would have wreaked untold havoc upon your world, perhaps ultimately consuming it entirely. Of course, I could not allow that to happen. I brought you here to Faerie because it was the only way I could protect you from the fighting machine, which even as we speak is destroying the woodland around Lord Pannick's house in its search for you.' As he said this, a great anger and bitterness entered Oberon's voice, and his expression grew dark at the thought of what the machine was doing to the trees.

'We thank you for that,' said Blackwood. 'But if it's our job to prevent war with Mars, then it's just become a lot more complicated. The fighting machine is in Indrid Cold's hands, and the Æther zeppelin has likewise made its escape and may well be *en route* to Mars at this very moment. Even if I took another zeppelin equipped for space travel and set off in pursuit, I wouldn't be able to catch up with it until it was too late.'

'And in the meantime,' added Sophia, 'the fighting machine may well have been hidden at another location, making it impossible to find before the Greater Exhibition opens. Lord Pannick is not the type of man to leave any contingency unplanned for.'

Titania turned to her husband. 'Oberon, you must help them, and if necessary, you must put aside the terms of the Covenant to do so.'

Oberon shook his head. 'My Queen, you know I cannot do that. We are bound to the Covenant for all future time; we cannot break it.'

'What would happen if you *did* break it?' asked Blackwood.

Oberon looked at him in silence, and Blackwood saw something in his eyes which made him look away and wish that he had not asked the question.

'Then they are lost,' said Titania. 'For they cannot intercept the Æther zeppelin, and they will not be able to find the fighting machine before it rains destruction upon the Greater Exhibition. Queen Victoria will die, as will thousands of others, and thousands upon Mars will succumb to the terrible plague that is being carried to them. The burgeoning friendship that exists between the Blue Planet and the Red will wither and be transformed into fear and hatred. War will be declared, and each civilisation will decimate the other, while Venus looks on in satisfaction.'

'That will not happen,' said Oberon, and there was something in his voice which made Titania hesitate and regard him closely.

'Why do you say that, my husband?'

'I have listened to the Æther, and have heard the whispering of the Planetary Angels of Mars. They are beings very much like us: the first inhabitants of the Red Planet. The Martians – some of them, at least – have a much closer relationship with them than humans do with the Faeries of Earth. That is how Petrox Voronezh was able to recognise my true identity when he met me in Leason's Wood. The Planetary Angels are saying that the Martians have developed a new and terrible weapon, which will ensure their survival if war breaks out.'

'A new weapon?' said Blackwood. 'What kind of weapon?'

'They call it the Sun Cannon. Each shell it fires contains within it the energy of a star. Were these shells to be fired at Earth's cities from Mars or dropped upon them from interplanetary cylinders orbiting above the planet, they would destroy them, instantly and completely.'

300

'Instantly?' said Blackwood. 'Completely? But no such weapon exists… surely no such weapon *can* exist!'

'I assure you, it does, and if they perceive their world, their civilisation to be under threat, the Martians will use it.'

'Then what are we to do?' said Sophia, her voice tremulous.

'Oberon, please…' said Titania, taking her husband's hand.

'I cannot intervene directly,' the Faerie King whispered.

'Then there must be another way,' said the Queen. 'There must be a way to help them to save their world and its people.'

Blackwood leaned forward in his chair. 'I will give my life to prevent the disaster that is threatening my world. But if that Æther zeppelin really is headed for Mars as we speak, and if the fighting machine with its Heat Ray really has been hidden beyond our sight or reach, then I can do nothing. King Oberon, there must be *something* you can do, some way you can help me to perform my duty.'

Oberon looked at Blackwood and Sophia, and then at his Queen. 'There is something I can do,' he said presently. 'But the timing of it will be critical, and I cannot guarantee that it will enable you to succeed. And it will be extremely dangerous.'

'I am used to danger,' said Blackwood. 'And death has been my constant companion for many years. What do you propose?'

CHAPTER FOUR:
The Æther Zeppelin

Lord Pannick sat at the controls of the great space craft as it left Earth behind and headed into the depths of the Luminiferous Æther. Upon acquiring the machine, he had acquainted himself thoroughly with its workings and knew the function of every dial and switch with which the ornately fashioned oak and brass instrument panel was festooned. Through the gondola's front windows, the stars shone brighter and more intensely than he would have imagined possible, and notwithstanding the foulness of his mood and the trepidation which gripped him, he gazed upon them with astonishment and wonder. Far behind him, the vast, frond-like propellers gripped the Æther and pushed the zeppelin onward, into the endless night of deep space.

His bad temper was caused partly by the weightlessness of the Æther, which was causing havoc with his stomach and which necessitated the wearing of the rather ugly and uncomfortable magnetic boots which kept him firmly upon the deck, but mainly by the destruction of his beloved Furfield and all it contained by the djinn. He had taken the zeppelin up to a thousand feet and had watched his home being ripped asunder by the entity, and as he watched, he had thought of all the beautiful things he had collected over the years, all the priceless artefacts which now lay in ruin at the centre of his estate. Blackwood, he supposed, had not come to Furfield alone: he'd had help – someone or something had allowed the djinn to return to this world, and a thwarted djinn was not to be trifled with, even by one as versed in the arcane as Pannick.

As the zeppelin had hovered high above the chaos, he wondered how Blackwood had managed it, and as he watched Indrid Cold take the Martian fighting machine out of its hangar and begin blasting the grounds with its Heat Ray, he hoped that somewhere down there, Blackwood and little Miss Harrington were frying…

He'd been about to leave the scene, preparing to take the zeppelin out of the Earth's atmosphere and into the Luminiferous Æther, when something had caught his eye, and he had stayed his hand over the large twin throttles at the centre of the instrument panel. Someone was firing a beam of something that was not light at the monster, forcing it back through the rift in time and space through which it had come. He quickly recognised the beam as coming from a faerie weapon, and with that realisation, the mystery resolved itself in his mind, and he couldn't help smiling grimly in appreciation. He had arranged for Blackwood's cogitator to be sabotaged by the removal of its dreamcatcher, and that was precisely how the djinn had been allowed entry into Furfield.

Blackwood had indeed had help – faerie help.

Touché, Mr Blackwood, Pannick thought.

In spite of his annoyance at the loss of his home, Pannick had to admit that the arrival of the faerie warriors had solved the problem of the rampaging djinn: at least now he wouldn't have to worry about it coming to look for him. They really were most tenacious in the pursuit of their prey. That thought, however, immediately gave rise to another concern: Oberon, King of the Faeries. Had he become directly involved in this? Pannick doubted it, for he knew of the Faerie Covenant and how they had forbidden themselves from intervening in important human affairs. All the same, he might find some more subtle way of meddling...

Pannick glanced behind him, through the hatch and into the gondola's main compartment, at the shelves packed with canisters containing the *Acarus galvanicus* mites, and he smiled in satisfaction. Neither Blackwood nor Oberon would be able to stop him now. He was well on his way to Mars, and even if Blackwood or some other fool launched an Æther zeppelin in pursuit, they would have no hope of catching up with him before he reached the Red Planet and dropped his calling card upon the good people of that world.

The only hiccup in his plans was the death of Peter Meddings. The idiot had lost his nerve at a crucial moment, had tried to flee and blundered straight into Blackwood's hands. He deserved the bullet that had blown his head to pieces, the cowardly dolt! Now Pannick had no choice but to pilot the zeppelin himself and hope that he could drop the cylinders and get back into the Æther before the Martians knew what had hit them.

And while the little *Acarus* blighters hatched and grew and stole the air from their lungs, and the Martians died in fear and horror, Indrid Cold would stride across London in the fighting machine, to Hyde Park and the Greater Exhibition, where he would rain fiery destruction upon all who had gathered there. Two catastrophes, two great cries of outrage, two worlds turning in rage upon each other. The Æther zeppelins would fly, a vast interplanetary armada loaded with the most powerful weaponry at Earth's disposal, while the cylinders would come from Mars, carrying battalions of fighting machines...

And then the war to end all wars would begin.

Pannick leaned forward and looked through the eyepiece of the zeppelin's telescope at his destination. The flawless clarity of the Æther allowed a magnificent view of the tiny orb floating in the black infinity. It struck him that the Red Planet was not actually red at all: its hue was more that of pale orange Carnelian, with inclusions of Aventurine-green. Those little swathes were, he knew, the regions of vegetation which were maintained by the planet-wide system of irrigation canals which brought fresh water from the north and south poles.

'Pretty little world,' Pannick whispered...

And then there was a sound behind him, and the hairs on the back of his neck rose as he became aware that he was no longer alone on the zeppelin.

He spun around to see Thomas Blackwood floating in the hatchway between the flight deck and the gondola's main compartment. With his left hand he gripped one of the many supporting handles bolted to the walls and bulkheads, while in his right he gripped a revolver.

'Good evening, your Lordship,' he said. 'Or is it morning? Difficult to tell out here, isn't it?'

'How did you get on board?' Pannick growled.

'You're the occultist; you tell me.'

Pannick hesitated, and then, as realisation dawned, he smiled and said, 'Ah... I think I understand. The faeries who engaged the djinn in battle took you back to their realm, didn't they? And then they opened a portal directly to here. Very clever.'

Blackwood gave him a sardonic smirk. 'Thank you.'

'Tell me, how is Oberon these days?'

'He's very well – and extremely annoyed at your antics, I might add.'

'I don't see why: after all, the Earth doesn't belong to them anymore. Why should he care what happens to it?'

'He cares because he still loves it, and he understands that humans are its caretakers now. He doesn't want to see it become like Venus, and neither do I. Now, turn this craft around immediately and return us to Earth.'

Pannick chuckled. 'I'm afraid that won't be possible, Mr Blackwood. You see, I have a delivery to make, and I assure you I intend to make it. And by the way, I wouldn't even think about firing your gun in here: the results would be most unpleasant for both of us.' As he spoke, Pannick's hands slowly and carefully moved behind his back, until they came to rest upon the engine throttles and the joystick.

Blackwood raised the gun, pointing the barrel between Pannick's eyes. 'Keep your hands where I can see them...'

But his order was too late. With a single movement, Pannick pushed down on the throttles and the joystick. Instantly, two things happened: the engines flew into a screaming frenzy of overdrive, and the zeppelin's prow pitched upwards. Blackwood was thrown backwards by the wildly-inclining deck, through the hatch and into the main compartment. Pannick pulled another lever, and the hatch slid shut with a hiss of hydraulics.

He turned to the instrument panel and quickly corrected the zeppelin's course, putting it once again on a heading for Mars; then he took a key from his pocket, inserted it in the panel and twisted, locking the controls in their current position. He glanced back at the hatch, cursing it for its lack of a locking mechanism. In another few moments, Blackwood would open it, and they'd be back to square one. Pannick, however, had other ideas. He withdrew the key, put it back in his pocket and stepped away from the instrument panel.

*

Blackwood had been flung backwards against a steel supporting brace, cracking his head and momentarily dazing himself. When he opened his eyes, he saw the compartment spinning wildly about him, and for a moment he couldn't tell whether it really was spinning or he was suffering from vertigo induced by the blow to his head. He had never experienced weightlessness before, and it was a deeply unpleasant sensation: his internal organs felt like they had grown tired of their locations in his torso, and had decided to go for a wander in search of more amenable surroundings, while his brain told him that up was down, down was up, left was right and right left, before finally giving up and leaving his body to its own devices.

His flailing hands connected with another brace, and he held on and steadied himself, realising that he had been cartwheeling end over end. His stomach felt like it was jostling his heart for its position in the middle of his chest, and for a few moments he was certain that he would be physically sick. He closed his eyes, realised that that was a bad idea, and opened them again, taking deep breaths in an attempt to steady his innards.

He looked around for his revolver, which had flown from his hand, but it was nowhere to be seen, and with a curse, he decided that he didn't have the time to go looking for it. Nor could he see any of the magnetic boots which he had noticed Pannick wearing. He supposed that there might be some in a locker somewhere, but once again, time forbade a search. In any event, he felt more comfortable without them. He decided that unencumbered speed would be more of an ally than the ability to walk upright.

As he began to pull himself towards the flight deck hatch, his brow damp with nausea-induced sweat, Blackwood looked down and noticed something odd about the floor of the main compartment. He glanced back at the ranks of canisters. *Ah*, he thought. *I see...*

He reached the hatch, pulled the lever set into the bulkhead next to it and was surprised and gratified when it opened immediately. The flight deck was empty. Blackwood pulled himself inside and glanced around. *Where have you got to, you blackguard?* On the starboard side, there was a metal ladder ascending to a trapdoor in the ceiling – probably a maintenance hatch allowing access to the interior of the balloon. Clearly, this was Pannick's escape route.

Blackwood cast a quick eye over the instruments, which were not so different from those of a conventional zeppelin, except that in place of a magnetic compass, which was of no use away from the Earth, there was a curious spherical instrument mounted in a water-filled cylinder on top of the panel. Blackwood took note of the numerals etched into the surface of the sphere – which apparently referred to degrees – and then took hold of the joystick, intending to guide the vessel through a 180-degree yaw away from Mars and back towards Earth.

The joystick, however, refused to budge. Blackwood looked down and saw the keyhole. Above it was a label marked INSTRUMENT LOCK. *Damn and blast!* he thought. As he turned towards the ladder, his eye caught another control and the label above it. And then he was up the ladder and through the maintenance hatch.

Pannick was nowhere in sight. From his vantage point, Blackwood quickly took in the layout of the balloon's interior. He was at the forward end of a metal catwalk which appeared to stretch for the entire length of the zeppelin. Eight feet above the catwalk was the lowest row of gasbags, gigantic and bulbous, like whales floating in midair, and strapped together with heavy canvas webbing. Blackwood peered along the three hundred feet of catwalk. At fifty-foot intervals, ladders ascended – he guessed to the axial corridor running through the centre of the balloon. Pannick had to be up there, somewhere.

Blackwood listened intently, trying to catch the faintest sound which might alert him to Pannick's location. He pulled himself slowly along the catwalk, past the first ladder and on to the second. All was silence. He moved on towards the third ladder, halfway along the zeppelin's length.

A barely-audible metallic clank brought him to a sudden halt. A few moments later, another clank sounded from somewhere above. Pannick was up there, apparently directly above Blackwood's position – although such were the acoustics in this singular place that he could not be entirely sure. He grabbed the rungs of the third ladder and hauled himself upwards through the vertical shaft connecting the catwalk with the axial corridor.

The shaft was oppressive in its narrowness; its walls were the dark ruddy yellow of the surrounding gasbags and seemed to stretch upwards uniformly to their vanishing point. So uniform were the walls that Blackwood realised too late that he was fast approaching the axial corridor, and before he could do anything to slow himself down, he was within it. Pannick was standing directly in front of him, swinging a massive spanner at his head. Blackwood barely had time to put up his left arm to fend off the blow, and he felt both his ulna and radius shatter in an explosion of pain as he was knocked out of the shaft and began to tumble along the corridor.

His crippled arm floating uselessly at his side, Blackwood reached out with his right hand, grabbed one of the girders lining the corridor and brought himself to a halt. The pain was sickening, unbearable, and combined with the effects of weightlessness, it was nearly enough to make him pass out.

Pannick laughed out loud and clanked towards him in his magnetic boots, brandishing the spanner. 'Quite a handy weapon, don't you think? Especially when there's no gravity. But although it has no weight, it still has mass – as you may have noticed. Ha ha ha!'

Blackwood was growing increasingly light-headed from the pain in his shattered arm. *Stay awake, damn you!* he screamed inwardly at himself. *Lose consciousness, and you lose your life!* 'I warn you, Pannick,' he said, 'I may not be able to take you in alive, now. I may have to kill you just to stop you from being a nuisance while we return to Earth.'

'Return to Earth? And how, pray tell, are you going to do that?' asked Pannick, still moving clumsily forward like a clockwork toy soldier.

Blackwood panted and blinked the sweat from his eyes. 'I know… I know you've locked the flight controls…'

'Precisely.' Pannick tapped his trouser pocket. 'I have the key to unlock them, but you'll have to *get it from me first!*' he ended the sentence in a scream as he furiously swung the spanner again. This time, however, Blackwood anticipated the trajectory of the movement and dodged the blow easily, pushing himself across to the other side of the corridor. He struck it with his left arm, however, and howled as a new wave of agony swept through him.

'My dear Mr Blackwood, how long do you think you can keep this up? I know how long *I* can – until we reach Mars!'

Another vicious blow, which once again Blackwood was able to dodge – although this time only just. Pannick was right: he wouldn't last much longer like this. As he drifted across the corridor, he quickly thrust his hand into his pocket and pulled out his pocket knife, unsheathing the blade with a deft movement of his thumb while he kept it behind his back, out of Pannick's view.

Pannick swung the spanner again, and this time Blackwood felt the air stir as it missed his forehead by less than an inch. Gritting his teeth against the pain, Blackwood launched himself forward as Pannick completed the swing, which had left his upper body exposed, and buried the knife just below his collarbone.

Pannick screamed in pain and shock, and released the spanner, which whirled off along the corridor, bouncing and clattering between the girders.

With lightning-fast movements, Blackwood withdrew the knife, put its bloodied blade between his teeth, thrust his hand into Pannick's trouser pocket, grabbed the key and put it in his own; then he took the knife and slashed the gasbag beside which he was floating. Pannick tried to grab him, but the resulting blast of helium propelled him back along the corridor towards the prow of the ship and beyond his opponent's reach.

As he neared the end of the axial corridor and the first of the access ladders leading down to the lowest level of the balloon, Blackwood spied the dim figure of Pannick clutching at his injured chest with one hand and his face with the other, before clanking towards the third ladder.

Knowing he had mere seconds in which to act, Blackwood grabbed the topmost rung of the ladder and hauled himself down. Not even bothering to slow himself as he reached the bottom, he emerged from the shaft and slammed into the catwalk, taking the impact with his right shoulder. He pulled himself along to the maintenance hatch leading to the flight deck and hauled himself through, closing it behind him.

He turned and looked through the hatch leading to the gondola's main compartment and saw Pannick pulling himself through a similar trapdoor to the one on the flight deck. Pannick's cherubic face was twisted into a rictus of pain and hatred as he clanked towards the flight deck between the serried ranks of glass cylinders.

'Blackwood!' he screamed. 'I'm going to *kill* you, Blackwood! You shan't stand between me and my destiny.'

'I regret to inform your Lordship,' Blackwood called as he took hold of the lever by the hatch, 'that I most certainly shall!'

He threw the lever, and the hatch hissed shut. The clanking of Pannick's magnetic boots continued, albeit muffled now by the steel door. Blackwood went to the instrument panel and pulled the lever he had seen earlier.

The lever was marked PAYLOAD RELEASE.

There was another hiss of hydraulics, accompanied by a single high-pitched scream as the bottom of the gondola's main compartment opened, evacuating the compartment and everything it contained: the canisters, the atmosphere, and Lord Pannick.

The entire vessel shuddered horribly as the evacuating air shunted it upwards. Girders creaked and moaned in protest, while the deck plates tried to shake themselves loose from their rivets. Blackwood thrust the key into the instrument panel and twisted it. Instantly, the joystick began to jerk chaotically forwards and backwards, left and right. Wincing at the pain in his left arm, Blackwood grabbed the joystick in his right fist and managed to steady it; then he brought the craft around until the blue-green orb of Earth was squarely in the front windows.

As he did so, something glittered off to starboard, and he peered through the side windows. In the far distance, drifting against the vast starscape, Blackwood saw hundreds of tiny flecks of glass, and among them the unmoving figure of Lord Pannick.

'The canisters are yours,' Blackwood whispered. 'You keep them.'

CHAPTER FIVE:
The New Crystal Palace

Sophia stood at the edge of Hyde Park and cast a fearful gaze at the vast edifice of the New Crystal Palace, which glittered in the bright morning sunlight. The building was utterly magnificent, half as big again as the original, which had played host to the monumentally successful Great Exhibition of 1851, and which had been moved to Sydenham Hill three years later. Although there had been a number of World's Fairs in the intervening decades, the Greater Exhibition of the Works of Industry of all Nations was the first to include contributions from the civilisation of Mars. It was therefore a unique event, and the number of attendees was expected to surpass the six million who had come during the five-and-a-half months of the 1851 Exhibition.

Beside Sophia, Detective Gerhard de Chardin of New Scotland Temple stood with his hands clasped behind his back, watching the thousands of people milling about in the distance, wandering into and out of the great building, strolling through the park or sitting in large groups upon the grass. Somewhere within the New Crystal Palace, Queen Victoria and the Prime Minister were being shown around the exhibits, and this, more than anything else, gave de Chardin pause for concern.

'Did Her Majesty agree to see you, Lady Sophia?' he asked.

'Yes,' she replied, her eyes still fixed upon the gargantuan steel and glass building. 'As soon as I returned from Faerie, I requested, and was granted, an audience. I informed Her Majesty of Lord Pannick's plans and begged her to order the postponement of the Grand Opening – or if she were unable to do so, at least to postpone her own attendance.'

'Her reaction is evident,' de Chardin muttered.

Sophia gave a brief, grim smile. 'Indeed, Detective. She told me that she could not countenance hiding from the danger and assured me that she had full confidence in Mr Blackwood and me.'

'I'm sure that confidence is well-placed... but Mr Blackwood is not here.'

At this, Sophia caught her breath, and the frown of concern which had clouded her brow turned briefly into a grimace of dread. 'No, he is not here. He is at present in the depths of space – precisely where, I have no idea – nor even if he is alive or dead.'

De Chardin placed a comforting hand upon her shoulder. 'I am sure he is alive. He is a capable man. Lord Pannick will be no match for him.'

Sophia forced a weak smile and nodded her thanks.

'Nevertheless, I must maintain that the decision to attend was a serious mistake on the part of Her Majesty.'

'I have to agree, although I can understand her resolve. She reminded me that she and the Royal Family left London prior to the mass demonstration of the Chartists in 1848, and sought refuge at Osborne on the Isle of Wight. She confided to me that she had vowed never to flee the city again after that.'

'She is indeed courageous.'

'How have you fared with your own preparations, Detective?'

De Chardin gave a frustrated sigh. 'Very well, although I'm ashamed to say that my men have been reduced to the status of ushers, such is the nature of the threat. If and when Indrid Cold makes his move, there will be little we can do, save to coordinate an immediate evacuation of the site. The real battle will be between the fighting machine and the Army.' He proceeded to point out the locations around the New Crystal Palace where artillery had been set up. 'In all,' he said, 'there are fifty cannons, with gunners standing by.'

'Will they be enough, I wonder, against such a fearsome weapon of war?'

De Chardin chose not to answer.

'The Exhibition should have been postponed – or cancelled altogether!' Sophia said bitterly.

'I understand your anger,' said the Templar Knight in a gentle tone. 'But to do so would have shown weakness on the part of the Empire. We cannot turn tail and run in the face of danger, and certainly not in the heart of our own capital. And we cannot allow a threat from outside to force us to abandon the best of our civilisation, to change the way we live.'

'No... I suppose not.' Sophia sighed. 'In any event, Detective, I'm sure you are anxious to join your men. Shall we?'

De Chardin nodded, and he and Sophia began to walk across the park towards the New Crystal Palace.

*

The Earth was growing larger and larger in the forward windows of the Æther zeppelin's flight deck. Already, Blackwood could make out the shape of the British Isles, and he would have allowed himself a certain satisfaction were it not for the infernal pain that was coursing through his left forearm, as if the very blood in his veins had been transformed into molten metal. He wished he had a bottle of laudanum to take the edge off it and briefly considered locking the flight controls and looking for a first aid locker.

Reluctantly, however, he decided against it: the drug would have too deleterious an effect upon his senses, which he needed to maintain at razor-sharpness, and so he gritted his teeth and held fast to the joystick as the huge, fronded propellers of the Æther engines continued to thrust him homewards.

*

Indrid Cold sat at the controls of the Martian fighting machine and looked out through the forward observation blister at the pitch-dark murk that surrounded him. In some respects, the bottom of the Thames was like night on Venus, where the hot, thick atmosphere reduced visibility to a minimum. The similarity elicited no feelings of homesickness or nostalgia, however, for Cold hated his world and was glad to be away from it.

Following the destruction of Furfield and the subsequent vanquishing of the djinn by means unknown to Cold, he had laid waste to the woodland on the estate with the machine's Heat Ray. In spite of his thoroughness, however, he could not be absolutely certain that he had despatched the meddlesome pair of Blackwood and Harrington, and furthermore, he knew that he had to get the machine to a safe and secure location. And so he had left Furfield behind and headed north, tripping like a colossal insect across the landscape from Hampshire across Berkshire and into Oxfordshire, where he had entered the river between Henley and Marlow.

If Blackwood and Harrington had indeed managed to escape, they would have alerted the authorities to Lord Pannick's plans, and they would in turn have arranged for defensive measures to be taken in Hyde Park, so Cold spent the next few hours preparing the machine for battle, recharging the Heat Ray and making certain that all of the vehicle's systems of locomotion were in perfect working order.

Once he was satisfied, he had restarted the machine's engines and begun the solitary march along the riverbed towards the capital.

*

As she walked through the central exhibition hall with de Chardin, Sophia was so impressed with the contents of the New Crystal Palace that she almost forgot the fear and anxiety that had gripped her heart ever since her return from Faerie. When Oberon had suggested opening a portal directly to the interior of Lord Pannick's Æther zeppelin, she had felt a dark flowering of terror for Blackwood's sake, but he had agreed immediately, and she had had only the briefest of moments to say goodbye to him and to wish him luck before he was gone, into the night of space and an uncertain destiny.

The central hall was a truly colossal space, some 3,000 feet long and 400 wide. From her vantage point at the centre of the hall, Sophia looked up at the four tiers of secondary exhibition spaces and observation galleries, at the elm trees reaching towards the elegant arched ceiling of steel and glass, and at the gigantic Grand Orrery, which formed the centrepiece of the entire exhibition.

The Orrery followed the design of a device originally conceived in 1780 by the Scottish astronomer and instrument maker James Ferguson; however, whereas the original had been a few inches in diameter, the contrivance before which Sophia and de Chardin now stood was fully sixty feet across, an astonishing masterpiece of both large-scale and precision engineering. The base, which came up to Sophia's shoulders, was of highly-polished yew, and was surmounted by a collection of vertically mounted cog wheels attached to the motor mechanism, which was contained within a large brass box engraved with intricate seraglios. Next to the motor was a clock face, nearly six feet in diameter, with elegant Roman numerals inlaid in ivory. Above the clock were three huge, concentric brass rings, which were supported by six radial spurs extending from the centre of the Orrery.

Looking up through this arrangement, Sophia tried to make sense of the fabulous and exquisite complexity of the horizontal cog wheel assembly which surmounted it, and which formed the mechanism by which the planets, mounted atop sturdy brass spars, revolved around the golden orb of the Sun. It was impossible, however, and she smiled in spite of herself at the incredible profusion of steel and brass components, all of which worked together in perfect synchronisation to make the gigantic model of the Solar System turn about itself.

'How utterly marvellous!' she said.

'Indeed,' de Chardin replied.

'Do you think the Universe really does work with such precision as this?'

The detective chuckled. 'Would that it did, my dear Lady Sophia.' He indicated a large wrought iron staircase which ascended to the first tier. 'Would you care to see it from a higher vantage point?'

'Thank you, I would.'

They climbed the staircase and joined the crowd, which was at present observing the operation of the Orrery. In recognition of the epoch-making events of recent years, the globes representing Earth and Mars had been mounted higher than the other planets of the Solar System, so that the twin worlds circled in apparent solitude through the air. The smile which brightened Sophia's expression as she watched their slow, graceful movements faded when she looked down upon the pale yellow sphere representing Venus. She thought again of Blackwood, out there somewhere in the Æther, perhaps alive and victorious, perhaps dead, his mission failed, while the zeppelin sailed on towards Mars to deliver its hideous cargo.

She glanced to her left and saw, away in the distance, the Queen and her entourage making their way along the exhibition hall towards the area devoted to the Martian exhibits. She turned away from the Orrery and said, 'Perhaps we should make a tour of the exits. I'd like to know their exact locations and the whereabouts of your men.'

*

The sickening pain in Blackwood's shattered forearm had diminished somewhat, until it was now merely an intense and distracting ache. As he moved the joystick a little this way and that, making minor course corrections to keep southeast England squarely in the centre of the forward windows, he allowed his left arm to float outstretched. He knew that the lessening of the pain was only a brief respite: the forearm was beginning to swell with the internal bleeding, and once he was back within the gravity field of Earth, he'd be in for a rough time once more – especially with what he was planning to do.

In spite of his intense discomfort, he watched in fascination as the green and ochre mottling of the landscape was gradually transformed by his approach into a fantastically complex patchwork of fields, partially obscured by drifting mats of cotton-white cloud. He felt a strange ache in his heart when he recalled seeing the Earth in its entirety from the depths of the Æther: how small and fragile it had seemed – unreal, somehow, as if it were merely a subtle and delicate representation of the world rather than the world itself. The idea that it was home to vast mountains and plains, wide oceans and sprawling cities, that it contained millions upon millions of human souls, was strange beyond countenance, and he felt a sudden rush of existential anxiety when he considered the brute fact that this tiny orb represented the entirety of the human presence in the Universe.

Whatever the trials and hardships that awaited him, Blackwood was immensely relieved and thankful to be returning, even after so brief a sojourn in the outer darkness.

The world, however, has a peculiar habit of responding to such feelings by hurling an unexpected obstacle into one's path. Suddenly, the joystick began to buck and twist in Blackwood's hand, so that he was forced to brace himself by thrusting his knees underneath the lower edge of the instrument panel to maintain his grip on it.

'What the devil...?' he muttered as he struggled with the joystick, which appeared to have taken on a life of its own. The Æther zeppelin began to pitch and roll wildly, so that Blackwood wondered fleetingly whether Lord Pannick had somehow sabotaged the craft through Magickal means, his final act of mischief.

A glance at the instrument panel quickly told him otherwise. The needles on several gauges were fluctuating chaotically, as the various systems of the vessel began to fail. The lights on the flight deck flickered dangerously, while from somewhere above him, Blackwood heard the sharp crack and hiss of bursting pipes.

He groaned as he realised what was happening. The sudden decompression of the gondola's main compartment must have damaged the structure of the vessel. The electrical lines connecting the flight controls with the engines and manoeuvring surfaces had been compromised, perhaps sundered altogether – and if that were the case, he would be unable to control the zeppelin's speed or rate of descent.

As the rapidly approaching landscape beyond the forward windows continued to whirl and gyre dizzyingly, Blackwood tightened his grip on the joystick, cursing loudly as he struggled to get it under control. As he twisted and writhed, the agony in his left arm returned with full force... and he began to wonder whether the last the world would see of Thomas Blackwood would be a fiery meteor hurtling into the ground somewhere in the south of England...

*

As Sophia and de Chardin walked through the vast spaces of the New Crystal Palace, the detective pointed out the locations of the exits and the positions that his men had taken up in order to keep watch over the throng. Sophia did her best to pay attention but was distracted by the riot of emotions she was experiencing. She was desperately worried about Blackwood and equally concerned for the safety of the thousands of people milling around in the gargantuan building. She had seen at first hand what the Martian Heat Ray could do, the utter destruction it could wreak. If the fighting machine took them by surprise, the carnage would be unimaginable – not only from its weapon, but from the panic which would ensue when the attack began. For this reason, they were relying on a number of lookouts who were positioned throughout Hyde Park and atop the surrounding buildings on Bayswater Road, Park Lane, South Carriage Drive and Kensington Palace Gardens. At the first sign of trouble, the lookouts would release signal rockets to alert the gunners standing by in their own positions, along with the Templar Police in the Exhibition itself, and an evacuation would begin immediately.

Sophia felt a profound sense of irritation at Victoria for having insisted that the Greater Exhibition should go ahead on schedule. And yet, she could not help but recall de Chardin's words: *We cannot allow a threat from outside to force us to abandon the best of our civilisation, to change the way we live.*

Nor could Sophia resist the sense of wonder and fascination which came upon her as she moved amongst the exhibits. There were astonishing examples of scientific and artistic endeavour from across the world, although the twin centrepieces were undoubtedly those of Great Britain and Mars. At the end of one gallery, which was given over to innovations in science and technology, she found herself facing a wall of cogitators perhaps twenty feet high and as many wide. 'Remarkable,' she said. 'But why are they all the same model?'

'Ah,' de Chardin replied. 'Unless I'm mistaken, this is the Michelson-Morley Concatenator. Those chaps really have gone from strength to strength since they proved the existence of the Æther ten years ago.'

'What does it do?' asked Sophia as she approached the gently humming wall of ornately-fashioned contrivances, which was all polished teak and glinting brass, threaded with jet-black rubber conduits and glass gauges in which indicator needles gently twitched.

'I believe Messrs Michelson and Morley have developed a way of getting a large number of cogitators to work together in unison, to increase the speed with which they process information. Or something like that: science, I regret to say, was never my strong suit.'

Sophia shook her head in wonder.

In another area, they came upon a meticulously detailed diorama of the lunar landscape. At its centre stood a beautifully fashioned model of an Æther zeppelin, surrounded by several tiny figures dressed in what looked like deep-sea divers' suits. This, Sophia knew, was a representation of the planned British expedition to the Moon, which was due to depart in a year's time.

The next section contained a working model, at one-tenth scale, of the new atmospheric railway system which was at present being installed on the London Underground. The system worked by means of a sealed tube running between the tracks, to which each carriage was attached. Powerful Vansittart-Sideley Ultra-compressors at various points in the system pumped air at fantastically high pressure through the tubes, thus propelling the trains. Such was the efficiency of the compressors that the cost of powering the Underground would be half that of the electricity which was currently used.

In spite of the profusion of singular and fascinating objects and exhibits, Sophia felt herself grow increasingly restless. She wanted this day to be over; she wanted the Martian fighting machine to make its appearance, to be engaged by the gunners and to be vanquished without anyone being killed or injured. She wanted Blackwood to return with news that he had defeated Lord Pannick...

She wanted all this to be *over*.

She sighed loudly as she looked around at the great internal space with its thousands of milling visitors.

'Are you all right, Lady Sophia?' said de Chardin.

'Yes. I just... Why doesn't that infernal machine come? If battle is to be joined, then let it be joined now!'

'I understand your frustration: in my experience, waiting for an inevitable fight is worse than the fighting itself. But be assured, your Ladyship, it *will* come.'

*

The fighting machine's powerful headlights turned the blackness at the bottom of the Thames into a fetid gloom filled with bits and pieces of unidentifiable detritus. The lack of visibility was no impediment to Indrid Cold, however, for the vehicle was fitted with a sophisticated gyroscopic compass and proximity detectors which, combined with his knowledge of the city's layout, allowed him to home in on his target with ease.

The machine's powerful piston-driven legs pushed against the soggy bottom of the river, their wide, three-lobed feet finding easy purchase upon the rank mud that covered it. Like some huge, unearthly crab, it moved with slow deliberation in the murky depths, unseen and unsuspected by the people bustling through the streets of the surrounding city.

Presently, the proximity detectors registered the place where the Thames turned north, past Millbank, towards Westminster and the Houses of Parliament. When he reached his intended location, Cold threw a large switch on the instrument panel, and each of the machine's splayed feet sprouted three metal claws.

Pulling back on the control wheel, he edged the machine up towards the surface, the shock absorbers cushioning the control cabin against each violent judder as the claws bit into the slimy stonework of the river's bank.

On the river's surface, the crews of barges, freighters and pleasure craft glanced westward towards the embankment below the Houses of Parliament as the water there began to bubble and surge. People near the river's edge rushed to see what was happening and called to other passersby, who joined them. From the land and the river, curious eyes were fixed upon the mysterious churning of the water.

The onlookers edged further forward, chattering to each other in intense curiosity... and then the chattering was transformed into a single cry of alarm as the bubbling water parted to reveal a lozenge-shaped object thrusting upwards from the depths. The crowd fell back as the object continued to emerge from the river and then clambered with terrifying speed onto the embankment to stand before them on its tripod legs.

Women screamed and men shouted anxious questions at each other, the more gallant among them stepping in front of their female companions to shield them against the mechanical apparition.

'A Martian walking machine!' cried one.

'What the dickens is it doing in the Thames?' shouted another.

'What are those blighters up to?'

'What does it mean?'

'We should call the police, by God!'

Inside the control cabin, Indrid Cold looked down at the mass of incredulous people, his hand hovering over the trigger of the Heat Ray, and he would have despatched them all to fiery oblivion there and then, had not another thought occurred to him. Instead, he twisted the control wheel, and the hull swivelled upon its gimballed mounting until it was facing the Palace of Westminster and the great Clock Tower. His eyes blazing with fiendish excitement, Cold pulled the trigger of the Heat Ray.

The crowd screamed in unison as a beam of intense red light flashed out from the machine and struck the Clock Tower, which trembled for an instant before exploding in a horrific shower of glass and masonry, which rained down upon the Palace, smashing through the roof and into the chambers below.

All was instant pandemonium; the crowd of onlookers disintegrated like a swarm of bees, each fleeing in a different direction, as the fighting machine strode off towards Westminster Abbey and Buckingham Palace beyond.

*

The gravity of Earth reasserted itself as the Æther zeppelin re-entered the atmosphere. Blackwood had ambivalent feelings about its return, for while at least now he could sit properly in the pilot's chair and wrestle more effectively with the flight controls, his left arm began to bang excruciatingly against the armrest, and with each jolt he shouted out in agony.

He had managed to effect a kind of compromise with the recalcitrant controls, so that in spite of the continuous pitching and yawing of the craft, it maintained its course in the general direction of southeast England. Shaking the sweat from his brow, Blackwood peered through the forward windows as the familiar landscape passed by beneath him. Wokingham… Ascot… Sunbury on Thames… Richmond… Kew Gardens.

He was directly over London now, heading in a north easterly direction towards Hyde Park.

Away in the distance, he caught sight of a grey cloud rising from the ground. While he kept a firm grip on the joystick with his right hand, he looked through the eyepiece of the zeppelin's telescope, adjusting the instrument as best he could with his left hand, wincing against the pain.

'My God,' he whispered. The cloud was issuing from the Palace of Westminster, in the place where the Clock Tower had once stood. As he peered in appalled fascination at the wreckage, he added to himself, *It's begun. Cold is on the move!*

He twisted the brass knobs controlling the angle of the telescope, searching for the fighting machine. *Where are you, you filthy blackguard?*

There!

He saw that the fighting machine was halfway between the river and Hyde Park and was, in fact, crossing the Mall between Buckingham Palace and Trafalgar Square. For a moment, he thought that it might attack the Palace, but it moved on without pausing. Cold knew that Victoria would not be there: she was at present in a much larger palace – one which would quite possibly become her mausoleum.

*

Sophia and de Chardin entered the hall devoted to the Martian exhibits, where the Queen was lingering while she listened to the head of the Exhibition Committee explain to her the origin and function of the various items on display. The contents of the hall were truly fabulous to behold. At its centre stood a one-hundred-foot-high statue of Yoh-Vombis, their greatest leader, which was carved in fantastic detail from a single block of rose-hued Martian quartz. The statue's arms were outstretched, as if in welcome to all who laid eyes upon him, and Sophia felt a near-uncontrollable urge to approach it and sit at its feet.

Elsewhere there was a fully functional recreation of the astrogation deck of an interplanetary cylinder, at the centre of which was a slowly rotating device, apparently the Martian equivalent of an orrery – although it was far more complex, and was constructed of thin, multicoloured shards of floating crystal. Several seats were ranged around the device, each of which possessed an instrument panel of mind-boggling complexity.

Further along the hall were examples of Martian architecture, painting, textiles, ground and air transportation, all of which, while clearly analogous to those of Earth, possessed characteristics of an aestheticism that was utterly, beautifully alien, and which held the human eye in a rapture that was all the more intense and seductive for the subtle trepidation it inspired. At the far end was perhaps the most astonishing sight of all: an enormous panel less than an inch thick, which the Martians called a 'hololith', and which displayed constantly changing scenes of life on Mars. The hololith would clearly become the sensation of the entire Exhibition, if the faces of those watching it were any indication.

From their vantage point, Sophia and de Chardin had a magnificent view of the strange device, and it quickly became apparent to them that the scenes it was displaying were not static pictures or photographs, but were actually moving. They could see the waters of the Martian canals glinting in the dim sunlight, while tiny figures moved along their banks and through the sinuously winding streets of their strange cities. In one particularly evocative scene, a flock of huge shantak birds, whose membranous wings were more like those of bats, wheeled through the pale pink sky above a vast shape on the horizon, which was clearly another representation of Yoh-Vombis, seen in profile.

'The Martian Parliament, I believe,' said de Chardin.

'How utterly marvellous,' whispered Sophia.

She was about to say something more, but was interrupted by the sight of a signal rocket rising into the air above the arched glass ceiling of the exhibition hall. Instantly, she clutched de Chardin's arm, and pointed. 'Look!'

'The lookouts,' he said. 'They've spotted it.'

A few moments later, the ugly cough of cannon fire reached them.

'It seems the waiting is over, Lady Sophia,' de Chardin said as he stepped forward to address the crowd. 'Ladies and gentlemen!' he shouted in a deep, commanding voice. 'May I please have your attention? I am Detective Gerhard de Chardin of New Scotland Temple. I must ask you to make your way out of the building by the first available exit.'

The crowd turned to him and regarded him with blank expressions, before returning their attention to the hololith. De Chardin repeated his entreaty more loudly.

At that moment another image appeared, but this one was not displayed upon the hololith, but hove into view directly above it. The walking machine could be seen through the huge panes of glass forming the far wall of the Martian exhibition hall, and at its appearance the audience gasped and burst into applause, for clearly they thought that this was another miraculous attribute of the singular viewing device.

'Good Lord!' said a man standing beside Sophia and de Chardin. 'How the dickens do they manage that? Quite extraordinary!'

Alerted by the signal rocket and cannon fire and by their commander's voice, the Templar Police began quickly to circulate through the crowd, ordering people towards the exits.

Her heart beating wildly in her chest, Sophia gazed up at the apparition through the windows. The cannons were hitting their mark, but the shells appeared to have no effect upon the fighting machine, exploding cacophonously against its armoured hull, but leaving barely a mark upon it. In response, the Heat Ray flashed out at varying angles, and Sophia assumed that it was aiming its fire at the gun emplacements.

Now aware that something quite obviously was not right, the crowd began to cry out and surged away from the hololith. Sophia heard the Templar Police shouting orders to remain calm and to follow them to the exits. A family nearby – husband, wife and three children – was caught in the rush; the woman stumbled and fell while her children began to cry in sudden terror. The man tried to bring his wife to her feet, but she appeared to have twisted her ankle and cried out in pain as the people buffeted her in their haste to get away.

Sophia sprang forward and joined the family, helping the man to get his wife up while simultaneously gathering the children to her.

'Lady Sophia!' shouted de Chardin.

'You must do your best to coordinate the evacuation, Detective,' she shot back. 'And you must find Her Majesty and get her away from the park. I'll do what I can here. Let's fall to it, sir!'

De Chardin nodded and, with a certain reluctance to be leaving Sophia, headed off in search of the Queen's entourage.

The fifty cannons which surrounded the New Crystal Palace roared again and again, and each time they were answered by the fearsome blast of the Heat Ray, and it seemed to Sophia, as she helped the family towards the nearest exit, that after each exchange, the number of cannon blasts diminished. *Oh dear God*, she thought. *They're losing the fight.*

Finally, they reached the exit. The man thanked her profusely for her help, then gathered up his wife in his arms and took her outside, followed closely by their panic-stricken children. Sophia glanced back into the hall and saw the same drama being played out as the one in which she had just taken part: people were stumbling and falling everywhere, their arms raised up pathetically in an attempt to shield themselves from the tide of running legs and stamping feet.

It would have been easy to flee through the exit, out of the palace and away from the violence and chaos, but the thought of ensuring her own safety did not even occur to her. Without hesitating, she forced her way through the fleeing tide of humanity, back into the hall, struggling to the fallen, dragging them to their feet and pushing them into the river of bodies that was surging towards the exit.

She didn't know how many times she did this; she only knew that she could not allow a single man, woman or child to fall and be trampled. But she was only one woman, and the constant buffeting and unintended blows she received eventually took their toll upon her. One final push sent Sophia sprawling to the floor, and so exhausted was she that she could no longer bring herself to stand.

Just as she thought she would be trampled to death, a man paused, reached down, dragged her to her feet and took her with him to the exit. She would have thanked him, but the man disappeared instantly into the throng that was spilling across the park, away from the New Crystal Palace.

Sophia looked up at the fighting machine that was rearing like a gigantic predatory insect above the building. The number of cannons firing at it had been reduced to a mere handful, and now the armoured hull swivelled around and tilted downwards towards the palace, and the Heat Ray flashed again, its beam ploughing through the roof of the exhibition hall, which erupted in an ear-shattering explosion of glass and steel.

The people still inside must have died instantly, seared into oblivion, and Sophia shut her eyes tightly against the thought and the horror and the carnage. The last of the cannons were still firing upon the marauding monster, but they might just as well have been firing rocks, for all the damage their explosive shells had done.

The fighting machine fired again, and more glass and twisted steel exploded into the air. Sophia sank to her knees, her body exhausted, he heart utterly lost. They had failed; the fighting machine would be triumphant. The New Crystal Palace lay defenceless beneath it, like an animal prepared for slaughter.

But then it appeared to hesitate, the Heat Ray momentarily extinguished, and as Sophia watched in breathless anguish, the armoured hull twisted around until it was directly facing her. Indrid Cold had seen and recognised her. She could dimly spy a figure in the observation blister, and the figure appeared to be staring back at her. On top of the hull, the dreadful weapon glowed red in preparation for firing.

I'm sorry, Thomas, Sophia thought, and closed her eyes.

CHAPTER SIX:
The Final Struggle

Blackwood was descending rapidly towards Hyde Park and the New Crystal Palace, and he saw that an entire section of the vast building had already been destroyed by the fighting machine. He noticed that the hull was at an odd angle and quickly realised that Indrid Cold's attention had been drawn to a solitary figure kneeling upon the grass. He looked into the telescope's eyepiece and cried out as he realised that it was Sophia.

The ruby-tipped Heat Ray projector was glowing a bright, livid red, and Blackwood knew that in the next few seconds, Sophia would be burned out of existence. He pushed forward on the joystick, pitching the Æther zeppelin into an even steeper dive and aiming the craft directly at the fighting machine. The armoured hull grew and grew until it filled the windows of the flight deck, and Blackwood, certain that he had arrived at his last moment of life, closed his eyes.

The collision was horrifying. With a tremendous, sickening crack and an ear-piercing shriek of metal against metal, the gondola smashed into the fighting machine's hull, knocking it off balance, so that Indrid Cold had to fight his own controls to keep it upright. The machine staggered away from Sophia, with the zeppelin, which had been carried forward by its momentum, still above it.

Blackwood was at once relieved and horrified to discover that he was still alive and gripping the joystick, which was the only thing preventing him from falling through the gaping hole that had been torn in the gondola's underside. All around him, the flight deck – or what was left of it – was a chaos of spitting electrical wiring and hissing gases erupting from broken conduits. The zeppelin was all but done for; the whine of the overheating Æther engines sounded loudly in Blackwood's ears, and he knew that in the next few seconds, the craft would veer uncontrollably away and bury itself in the ground. If he stayed onboard, his reprieve would be short-lived indeed, and the fighting machine, having now steadied itself, would finish the job it had come here to do.

Blackwood looked down and saw that he was directly above the fighting machine's dorsal surface. He judged the drop to be about twenty-five feet – a damnably long way to fall unprotected and with a shattered left forearm, but he knew he had no choice, and so, with a tremendous effort of will, he overrode his instinct for self-preservation and released his grip on the joystick.

He dropped through the hole in the gondola, and his fall seemed to stretch into an eternity whose illusory nature was brutally demonstrated when he struck the roof of the fighting machine's hull. He knew that if he struck it feet first, he would break both his legs and slide off to his death, so he flattened his body out, presenting as much surface area as possible to distribute the force of the impact.

When he smacked into the hull, he felt several ribs crack with the impact, and his left arm was plunged into more agony than he would have thought possible. For an instant, he blacked out, but he regained his wits just in time to grab the edge of a cooling vent and prevent himself from falling to the ground a hundred feet below.

Providence smiled on him at that moment, for his wildly flailing legs came upon a series of indentations: hand- and foot-holds designed for external maintenance of the vehicle, and he managed to steady himself and gain a firm purchase.

The hull was already swivelling around, preparing to fire again, and Blackwood watched in horror as the ruby-red Heat Ray projector disgorged its lethal beam. The air around the weapon's crystalline muzzle crackled with its awful power, and Blackwood felt the heat wash over him as another section of the palace burst apart.

Glancing to his right, he saw a large panel with a sign next to it, stencilled in English. Somewhere in the back of his mind, he wondered why a Martian vehicle would have English markings, and then remembered that this machine was the first in a shipment intended for Great Britain.

The sign read, EMERGENCY RESCUE.

The panel was an escape hatch.

Forcing himself to use his left arm as well as his right, and crying aloud with the resultant pain, Blackwood edged towards the hatch, supporting himself by means of the indentations set into the hull. Tears of agony streaming down his face, he located the release lever and pulled it.

Instantly, the escape hatch popped open, and Blackwood crawled inside, his cracked ribs grinding against each other, his left arm a miniature world of torture.

He found himself in the fighting machine's control room, a cramped space lined with flashing instruments and complex controls. Indrid Cold sat with his back to him before the observation blister, one hand gripping the vehicle's control wheel, the other hovering above a trigger mechanism which clearly activated the Heat Ray.

Blackwood drew himself to his feet and lunged at Cold, grabbing him around the neck and yanking him out of his seat. With no one at the controls, the vehicle immediately began to stagger back and forth, causing the floor to pitch crazily. Blackwood slammed Cold's head into a supporting brace, and the Venusian grunted loudly at the impact, a single crack appearing in the mask he wore. Nevertheless, his strength and reflexes allowed him to recover instantly, and he threw off his attacker with ease.

Even without his debilitating injuries, Blackwood would have found it difficult to best this creature, but now, he knew he stood no chance against him.

'Cold,' he panted. 'It's over. Give it up!'

'You're right, Blackwood. It *is* over… over for you, and the rest of humanity!'

He threw himself at Blackwood and floored him with a single blow. Blackwood felt blood filling his mouth as the floor of the control room continued to buck and heave beneath him. His broken ribs poured ceaseless waves of agony through his torso, and he drew his legs up to his chest in a convulsive movement.

Cold stepped forward and stood above him. 'I want you to look at the true face of your destroyer, Blackwood,' he said. 'I want you to see the true face of Earth's new owners.' He reached up and took off the mask, and Blackwood gazed with horror at the red eyes burning in a face that was a mass of writhing tendrils. At the centre of the mass, a hole opened up, a circular, lipless mouth. Cold leaned forward, and from his mouth, a gout of blue flame erupted, making Blackwood cough and choke and momentarily blinding him.

He opened his eyes and gazed blearily up at his nemesis… and at the open hatch in front of which he was standing.

With a sudden movement, Blackwood thrust out with his legs, aiming for Cold's knees. His feet struck their target, and he felt the crunch of breaking bone and snapping cartilage. Cold shrieked in pain and rage as Blackwood drew his legs back again, and again kicked out, this time at Cold's chest.

The Venusian tumbled backwards through the escape hatch. Blackwood doubted that the fall would kill him, even with two broken knees. He dragged himself across the heaving deck to the pilot's seat, crawled into it and took hold of the control wheel. He had no idea how to pilot the machine, but he didn't need to, for he didn't intend to pilot it anywhere.

He looked down through the observation blister and saw Cold hobbling away. How he could do so with the injuries he had sustained, Blackwood had no idea. His physical endurance was beyond belief.

Cold stopped, turned, and looked up at Blackwood with his burning, hate-filled eyes. He reached into a pocket and withdrew something that looked like a pistol: his energy weapon. He took careful aim at Blackwood, who doubted that the glass of the blister would be able to withstand the beam.

Taking a deep breath, Blackwood pushed forward on the control wheel, hoping that the action would have the desired effect. It did. The fighting machine pitched forward, the sudden manoeuvre making it finally lose its balance, and for the third time in the few minutes since he had returned to Earth, Blackwood stared death in the face. This time, however, he doubted that the Grim Reaper would back down.

The last thing he saw before his pain finally ceased was the figure of Indrid Cold, arm still outstretched, weapon still clutched in his hand, as the Martian fighting machine fell upon him, splashing him into eternity.

Epilogue

Blackwood opened his eyes and winced at the brightness. His first thought was one of surprise that he was still alive. His left arm was held immobile in a plaster cast, and he felt bandages upon his torso. He tensed his stomach muscles, felt a dull ache, and immediately relaxed them again. He was in bed in a hospital room, which, he supposed, was not surprising. What *was* surprising was the visitors who were standing at the foot of the bed.

Queen Victoria was there, as was Grandfather and Sophia. They were all looking at him, and when they saw that he had awoken, they all smiled.

'Your Majesty,' Blackwood said in a gravelly voice. 'Would you think it terribly remiss of me if I failed to stand in your presence?'

Victoria's smile grew broader as she replied, 'Indeed not, Mr Blackwood. But we wouldn't want you to make a habit of it.'

Blackwood gave a chuckle and winced as the ache in his torso momentarily flared into a sharp jab.

'Rest easy, old chap,' said Grandfather. 'You deserve it, for a dashed fine job.'

'What's the state of play?' Blackwood asked.

Grandfather stepped forward on his steam-driven legs. 'Indrid Cold is dead. Not much left of him, I'm afraid, not with a hundred tons of fighting machine on top of him. Lady Sophia pulled you from the contraption after you crashed it, and saw to it that you were brought here to be patched up. As for the New Crystal Palace, repair work has already begun, and the Greater Exhibition should be ready to reopen in a couple of weeks.'

'Lord Pannick is dead as well,' Blackwood said.

Grandfather nodded. 'I thought as much. Lady Sophia has filled us in on the details of what happened in Faerie and on your decision to go into space in pursuit of his Lordship.'

'Then war has been averted?'

'Indeed it has, Mr Blackwood,' said Victoria. 'We have sent a communication to the Martian Parliament, detailing everything that has happened, and they have replied that they are satisfied. The matter is closed.'

'But what about Venus?'

'The fate of that unfortunate world is not for us to decide,' the Queen replied. 'But I have asked the High Minister to consider offering the Venusians the hand of friendship once again, and to offer them aid in their plight.'

'A most noble gesture, Your Majesty,' said Blackwood.

'Well,' said Victoria. 'Grandfather is quite right: you should take some rest and allow your body to heal.'

'I shall see you to your carriage, Ma'am,' said Grandfather, as the Queen made ready to leave.

'Well done, Mr Blackwood,' said Victoria. 'Get well soon.'

'Thank you, Your Majesty. I'm sure I shall.'

When Victoria and Grandfather had left, Sophia walked around to the side of the bed and took Blackwood's hand in hers. 'How is the pain?' she asked.

'Barely noticeable. And how are you?'

'I'm very well.' She smiled as she reached down and smoothed away a stray lock of hair from Blackwood's brow. Her smile faded as she added, 'A lot of people died.'

'I know. But many more would have died had the Venusians succeeded in their plan.'

Sophia lowered her eyes and nodded.

'Where's Detective de Chardin?' asked Blackwood suddenly. 'Don't tell me he was one of the casualties.'

'Oh, no. I'm so sorry, Thomas, I forgot to mention that he sends his best wishes and apologises for being unable to visit.'

'What is he up to?'

'He already has his hands full with a new case. It seems there have been several disturbances on the London Underground, which New Scotland Temple have been charged with investigating.'

'Really? What kind of disturbances?'

'Well, apparently, there have been a number of encounters with ghosts and other strange beings. Some of the locomotive drivers and maintenance workers are refusing to go down there.'

Blackwood shook his head. 'Ghosts on the Underground... whatever next?'

Sophia's smile returned as she replied, 'I'm not sure, but I have a strong suspicion that Detective de Chardin will ask us to help him find out.'

FINIS

ACKNOWLEDGEMENTS

I'd like to thank Anna Lewis, Oliver Brooks and all of the lovely people at CompletelyNovel.com for their kind words and support over the last couple of years. Your enthusiasm for my stories has meant a great deal to me.

Much appreciation also to Anna Torborg for some wonderfully judicious editing (and for pointing out a couple of very silly mistakes!).

To all my friends at work: thank you for making it easier to drag myself away from the computer and go into the office each morning. Your friendship means more to me than I can say.

Finally, much gratitude to the late great Clark Ashton Smith (1893-1961), for countless spine-tingling weird tales, not least 'The Vaults of Yoh-Vombis', which is one of my favourite science fiction stories of Mars – so much so that I couldn't resist placing my Martian Parliament on the 'Plain of Yoh-Vombis'. Wherever you are now, Clark, I hope you don't mind!

A sneak peak from...

The
Feaster from the Stars

A BLACKWOOD & HARRINGTON MYSTERY

...coming soon from Snowbooks

CHAPTER 1:
The Kennington Loop

Alfie Morgan hated being in this part of the network.

He had been a train driver on the Central and South London Railway for nearly ten years and had grown used to the noise and darkness of the Underground, the heat and the cramped conditions and the sheer strangeness of ploughing through the miles of deep-level tunnels which wound beneath the bustling streets of London.

He had grown used to all that... but he had never grown used to being in the Kennington Loop, and he suspected that he never would.

The Loop was at the southern end of the Central and South London line and was exactly what its name suggested: a loop of tunnel which enabled southbound trains to turn around past Kennington Station before entering the northbound Charing Cross branch platform.

There were several things which annoyed Alfie about the Loop, things which made him uneasy and jittery, so that he always found himself counting the minutes until he was out of it and back in the main tunnels. For one thing, its diameter was such that the tunnel curved tightly around, causing the wheels of the trains screeched loudly, almost plaintively on the tracks; for another, there were frequent delays, during which trains were held in the tunnel for up to twenty minutes before being allowed to exit into Charing Cross.

At times like this, the drivers found themselves sitting alone in the subterranean darkness (for no train ever carried passengers into the Loop, and precious few inhabitants of the metropolis even knew of its existence), strangely mindful of the two hundred feet of London clay pressing down upon them, cutting them off from the light and air of the outside world.

It was nearly ten o'clock in the evening when Alfie pulled out of Kennington Station and headed into the Loop, leaving the subdued light of the station's gas lamps behind and plunging into a darkness only fitfully relieved by the lead carriage's electric headlights. The air was hot and close and carried upon it a strange taint: a combination of machine oil and the musty ancientness of the surrounding earth.

The train's wheels began their expected screeching and squealing as they turned upon the tightly curving track, and Alfie tried to ignore the eerie sound as he gripped the engine throttle. The tunnel curved away into the pitch-black distance, the ugly ribbing of its cast iron reinforcement segments catching the light and giving Alfie the unsettling impression that he and his train had been swallowed up by some ravenous denizen of the earth's depths.

Alfie wished that he were anywhere on the Tube but here, and he envied the construction crews and maintenance men who were at present working elsewhere on the network, replacing the electrified tracks with the new atmospheric railway system. They still had to work in the tunnels, of course, but at least there were lots of them around; at least they had company, and Alfie imagined the good-natured banter that would lighten all the hard work.

The atmospheric railway was a technological marvel of the modern age. Alfie had wanted to take his family to see the working model of it that had been on display at the Greater Exhibition in Hyde Park the previous month, but that madman from Venus had put paid to that idea when he attacked the New Crystal Palace with a stolen Martian fighting machine. What a mess that had been! They were still picking up the pieces and rebuilding the sections of the palace which had been destroyed by the maniac. Alfie had read about it in the illustrated papers; it had all been part of some plan to get Earth and Mars to go to war with each other, and it was only by the grace of God that the villain hadn't succeeded.

Bloody Venusians, thought Alfie as he recalled how the life of Her Majesty herself had been under threat during the attack. A load of bloody buggers, that's what they are! Why can't they keep to themselves without messing around in our affairs?

Alfie cursed aloud as a red signal light came into view, like a baleful eye in the darkness. He applied the brakes and brought his train to a halt. Must be clearing the platform at Charing Cross. Oh well, at least that damned screeching's stopped for a while.

As he sat in the darkness and the silence, Alfie thought again of the maintenance crews and how he'd have given anything to join them. As far as he understood it, the atmospheric railway system worked by means of a sealed metal tube running between the tracks, to which each railway carriage would be attached. The trains would be propelled by compressed air generated by the new Vansittart-Siddeley Ultra-compressors, which were being installed at pumping stations throughout the network. The idea had been tried once before back in the 1860s, in the early days of the Underground, but it had been abandoned because of the issue of keeping the metal tube properly sealed, so that the compressed air couldn't leak out.

That problem had now been solved, thanks to the use of Martian rubber of the same type that was used in the self-sealing neck rings of their breathing apparatus. It was amazing stuff, to be sure. Alfie had seen it being installed at Notting Hill Gate a couple of weeks ago. Strange stuff it was, completely sealing the pressure tube between the tracks, without even a seam visible – until a train passed over, whereupon it opened to admit the short pylon connecting the train with its drive cylinder. A clever bunch, those Martians, and no mistake!

A distant rumble sounded in the darkness, making the stationary train tremble very slightly, and Alfie cocked his head to one side, trying to gauge its direction and distance. Was that the train leaving the Charing Cross platform? Could he get going at last and take himself out of this infernal bloody tunnel?

The signal light remained on red, however, and so Alfie heaved a great sigh of nervous irritation and waited.

Presently, another sound disturbed the hot, heavy silence, and Alfie glanced over his shoulder in momentary confusion. It sounded like the clack of an interconnecting door shutting, back along the train. Alfie's experienced ear told him that the sound had come from one of the doors separating the last two carriages ... but that couldn't be true. He was alone on the train: the guard, old Vic Tandy, had got off at Kennington. He had waved to Alfie from the platform as the train headed for the tunnel leading to the Loop.

Alfie sat still and listened.

A few moments later, there was another clack – closer this time. The sound was coming from the interconnecting doors. Alfie frowned. Perhaps Vic had jumped back onboard before the train entered the tunnel – bloody stupid thing to do, if he had. Vic knew better than to do something like that: more than one passenger on the Tube had met an untimely – and very messy – end trying to jump onto a moving train via the interconnecting doors.

And why would he want to, anyway? Alfie wondered, as he gazed through the front window of the driver's cab, wishing that the red signal light would hurry up and change.

Another clack, a little louder still…

Alfie turned and peered through the window of the door between the driver's cab and the passenger compartment. The carriages curved away into the dark distance. Their gas lamps had been turned off; the only light came from the driver's cab, and it was barely enough to illuminate the lead carriage.

Clack.

Alfie stood up and leaned towards the door, pressing his face against the window. His hand trembled as he undid the latch and pulled the door open. 'Vic?' he called, his voice sounding flat and dull in the confined space of the carriage. 'Vic… is that you, mate?'

No answer came from the darkness.

It must be Vic, he thought. Who else could it be… who else?

Clack.

'Vic! Answer me, you old bastard!'

Why don't you answer, Vic?

Clack.

Alfie's mouth had gone dry, and his tongue felt like sandpaper as he licked his lips. His breathing sounded loud in his ears. The last sound had come from close by, between the second and third carriages, he reckoned. There was no doubt that whoever was on the train was making his way towards the front.

Alfie quickly closed the door again and glanced back through the front window at the signal. It was still on red. He thought of the stories he had recently heard, both at work and in his local pub afterwards… stories of things being seen in the tunnels – strange things, horrible things. He'd laughed at them and paid them no mind, but now…

Clack.

That was from the doors connecting the first and second carriages.

'Go away!' The words sprang suddenly to Alfie's lips, almost as if they had been said by someone else. 'You shouldn't be here, whoever you are. I'll have the police on you as soon as I…'

Alfie stopped, for he could see no one in the half-light of the carriage. And yet… the door leading to the second carriage had opened and closed. It had…

He glanced back once again at the signal light, and then at the throttle. It would be more than his job was worth to pass the light at red – but at least he'd be out of the tunnel. Suddenly, Alfie didn't care about his job. He'd get another one and never come into the bloody Tube Railway again.

I'll take it slow, he thought. I'll stop just before Charing Cross, and then I'll jump out and go the rest of the way on foot. That's what I'll do.

He was about to sit back down in the driver's seat and open the throttle when a sound from the carriage made him stop, a sound so strange that at first he was unsure that it was a sound. It was a grunt, a low moan, a sigh, a flapping of wings and a stirring of sheets, a movement in the air that was not quite movement and yet not quite stillness. Alfie stood there, frozen in place, not daring to move as he stared through the front window at the red signal light which shone dully like an ancient star in the blackness of space. He held his breath until it burned in his lungs, and then slowly let it out.

Oh God… oh God.

The sound came to his ears again; it was directly behind him, on the other side of the door leading to the passenger compartment.

Slowly, Alfie turned around. He didn't want to, and yet he couldn't help himself. He had to see what was making that sound. He leaned forward towards the window, and peered once again into the compartment.

And then Alfie Morgan began to scream.

Outside, the signal light turned from red to green, but the train remained where it was, in the Kennington Loop.